# LITERARY AND CULTURAL RELATIONS BETWEEN BRAZIL AND MEXICO

# LITERATURES OF THE AMERICAS

**About the Series**

This series seeks to bring forth contemporary critical interventions within a hemispheric perspective, with an emphasis on perspectives from Latin America. Books in the series will highlight work that explores concerns in literature in different cultural contexts across historical and geographical boundaries and will also include work on the specific Latina/o realities in the United States. Designed to explore key questions confronting contemporary issues of literary and cultural import, *Literatures of the Americas* will be rooted in traditional approaches to literary criticism but will seek to include cutting edge scholarship using theories from postcolonial, critical race, and ecofeminist approaches.

**Series Editor**

**Norma E. Cantú** is Professor of English and US Latino Studies at the University of Missouri, Kansas City, and Professor Emerita from the University of Texas at San Antonio. Her edited and coedited works include *Inside the Latin@ Experience* (2010, Palgrave Macmillan), *Telling to Live: Latina Feminist Testimonios* (2001, Duke University Press), *Chicana Traditions: Continuity and Change* (2000, The University of Illinois Press), and *Dancing Across Borders: Danzas y Bailes Mexicanos* (2003, The University of Illinois Press).

**Books in the Series:**

*Radical Chicana Poetics*
Ricardo F. Vivancos Pérez

*Rethinking Chicano/a Literature through Food: Postnational Appetites*
Edited by Nieves Pascual Soler and Meredith E. Abarca

*Literary and Cultural Relations between Brazil and Mexico: Deep Undercurrents*
Paulo Moreira

# Literary and Cultural Relations between Brazil and Mexico

## Deep Undercurrents

Paulo Moreira

First published in 2013 by
PALGRAVE MACMILLAN®
in the United States—a division of St. Martin's Press LLC,
175 Fifth Avenue, New York, NY 10010.

Where this book is distributed in the UK, Europe and the rest of the world,
this is by Palgrave Macmillan, a division of Macmillan Publishers Limited,
registered in England, company number 785998, of Houndmills,
Basingstoke, Hampshire RG21 6XS.

Palgrave Macmillan is the global academic imprint of the above companies
and has companies and representatives throughout the world.

Palgrave® and Macmillan® are registered trademarks in the United States,
the United Kingdom, Europe and other countries.

ISBN: 978–1–137–37986–3

Library of Congress Cataloging-in-Publication Data is available from the
Library of Congress.

A catalogue record of the book is available from the British Library.

Design by Newgen Knowledge Works (P) Ltd., Chennai, India.

First edition: December 2013

10 9 8 7 6 5 4 3 2 1

# Contents

# Introduction

The *Encyclopedia Britannica* tells us that Latin America is "generally understood to consist of" South America, Mexico, Central America, and the islands of the Caribbean, whose inhabitants speak a Romance language (Bushnell). Before being a geopolitical entity, the Latin America I am interested in is an idea, part of the geography of imagination that distinguishes "the worst architect from the best of bees" (Marx, 198) and has engaged Latin Americans' desire to know and their power to create, combining the sensible and the purely subjective in the process of confronting their existence. This idea of Latin America contrasts sharply with the one João Feres Jr. described as "the opposite of a self-glorifying image" (Feres, 10)[1] in his persuasive account of the negative connotations the term has "Latin America" has acquired in the United States. Feres Jr. goes so far as treating *América Latina* (in Spanish/Portuguese) and Latin America (in English) as two separate entities, but the *Britannica*'s emphasis on a rather vague "general understanding" is a revealing trace of the discrepancies in the meaning of the place, and in the use of the term moves beyond conflicting interpretations/interests in different cultures/languages. Latin America is one of "a hundred names" that overlap in attempting to describe what Miguel Rojas Mix calls *América*, "that thing which Columbus discovered."[2]

The whole "thing" to which Rojas Mix refers (The Indies, New World, *América*) was subdivided along the lines of the separate possessions established by the European nations that invented or colonized it and became pluralized: the *Américas*, split into Northern and Southern, Anglo-Saxon and Hispanic/Iberian/Latin, et cetera. The specific dichotomy that split the Americas in two and engendered Latin America has old roots in the opposition between Roman citizens and barbarian Germanic tribes in Tacitus's *Germania* and can be summarized in an oversimplified way as follows: On the lower part of the Americas, Catholicism, miscegenation, poverty, and underdevelopment; on upper part, Protestantism, segregation, affluence, and development. A closer look at the two Americas reveals blind spots in this simple dichotomy and much more complex and less dissimilar realities on both sides, but the harsh realities of imperialism and the Cold War seem to have deepened the divide between them. Globalization paradoxically brought these two Americas closer together as the currents of peoples and cultures intensified, and drew them further apart as anxiety over these flows currents have raised walls and reignited old prejudices.

A host of imaginative scholars, many of them based in the United States, has seized this current moment of ambiguity as an opportunity to shuffle and reshuffle the geography of imagination and look at the Americas with fresh eyes in a series of books. Among them are Earl Fitz's *Rediscovering the New World*, Kristin Pitt's *Body, Nation, and Narrative in the Americas*, Rudyard Alcocer's *Time Travel in the Latin American and Caribbean Imagination*, Idelber Avelar's *The Untimely Present: Postdictatorial Latin American Fiction and the Task of Mourning*, Julio Ramos's *Divergent Modernities*, Vickie Unruh's *Latin American Vanguards*, Leila Lehnen's *Citizenship and Crisis in Contemporary Brazilian Literature*, Fernando Rosenberg's *The Avant-Garde and Geopolitics in Latin America*, Robert Newcomb's *Nossa and Nuestra América: Inter-American Dialogues*, José Luiz Passos's *Machado de Assis, o romance com pessoas*, Pedro Meira Monteiro's *Um moralista nos trópicos: o visconde de Cairu e o duque de La Rochefoucauld*, Luis Fernando Valente's *Mundivivências*, Gonzalo Aguilar's *Other Worlds*, Raúl Antelo's *Maria con Marcel*, my own *Modernismo Localista nas Américas*, Charles Perrone's *Brazil, Lyric, and the Americas*, and Jorge Schwartz's *Fervor das Vanguardas*. These books build on the work of several other scholars who made an effort to look at the Americas beyond linguistic and national divides everywhere in the continent, from pioneers such as José Enrique Rodó, José Veríssimo, Manuel Bomfim, Pedro Henríquez Ureña, José Brito Broca, Alexandre Eulálio, Alfonso Reyes, Manuel Bandeira, Bella Josef, Ángel Rama, and Emir Rodríguez Monegal to translators and editors such as Rodolfo Mata, Valquiria Wey, Regina Crespo, Florencia Garramuño, Eric Nepomuceno, and Joca Reiners Terron.

One of the challenges many of these books have met is to cross-national and linguistic borders within and beyond Latin America, especially the dividing line that separates Spanish Latin America from Brazil, Mário de Andrade's "enormous stranger" (Schwartz, 185).[3] In a famous article in which he called for a renewal of multilingual Latin American studies, Jorge Schwartz alluded to the imaginary line separating them as the "Tordesillas Wall"—a clever image that blends the foundational (alluding to the treaty that split the New World between Spain and Portugal in 1494) and the hopeful, hinting at the Berlin Wall that had then just fallen.

Complaints about the mutual ignorance that pervades Latin American nations are as old as these nations themselves. Often they consist of rebukes for a lack of interest that ironically repeats the dismissive behavior from Western Europeans that Latin Americans resented. Here is one example, from José Veríssimo as he welcomes Rubén Darío in 1912:

> Sons of the same continent, almost the same land, coming from the same race, or at least from the same cultural formation, with great common interests, we Latin Americans live barely aware of or caring about each other and ignoring each other almost completely. (Schwartz, 185)[4]

A hundred years after Veríssimo, former president Fernando Henrique Cardoso was still coming up with variations for the theme, describing relations between the countries of Spanish Latin America and Brazil as those of Siamese twins joined at their backs.[5] The two halves of Latin America were, once again, intimately connected sides nevertheless unable to look at each other. The image is fatalistic: an organic, that is "natural" arrangement that irrevocably defines the relationship as a paradoxical existence of entities that can neither escape nor acknowledge each other. This fatalism is typical of many Latin Americans at the end of the twentieth century, when certain economical realities lumped under the label of globalization were supposed to be inescapable. This fatalism carried the message of conformity: all Latin Americans could do was cope with these realities the best they could.

Ironically Fernando Henrique Cardoso was a brilliant scholar who, in the 1960s, living as an exile, published the first version of his magnum opus *Dependency and Development in Latin America*, in Spanish, in Peru, under the auspices of a continental agency, the Comisión Económica para América Latina y el Caribe (CEPAL/EPAC), together with a Chilean sociologist, Enzo Faletto (1935–2003). Furthermore, that was a book determinedly opposed to fatalism or conformity with its promise to pay equal attention to "both aspects of social structures: the mechanisms of self-perpetuation and the possibilities for change" (xi). In that book, the bond between Latin American nations was defined by comparable trajectories leading to situations of dependency, producing similar structural conditions in the dialectic of alliances and clashes between external and internal interests. This "diversity within unity" (xvii) was attributed to similar colonial and postcolonial exchanges with Europe and the United States rather than direct interaction between Latin American nations.

Without denying the pivotal importance of these vertical relations with the cultural and economic metropolises of the Western world, *Deep Undercurrents* centers attention on the direct cultural dealings between Latin Americans, more specifically Brazilians and Mexicans, who generally see themselves as equals. Unveiling the context of these interactions and carefully looking at their products, I argue that the assumption of chronic mutual ignorance no longer holds true. When what are considered fragmentary, occasional exchanges and ephemeral efforts of a few exceptional, solitary figures are examined side by side, one realizes that the cultural relations between Brazil and Mexico are actually quite substantial. They have simply been kept outside the distribution of what is sensible, thus have been impossible to apprehend in more than fragmentary fashion.

Whereas the organization of the humanities in departments divided into national and linguistic fields makes it harder to study contacts across these spheres, Spanish and Portuguese have been together, for good and bad, in most literature departments in the Unites States. This book is in part the result of institutional opportunities I enjoyed at the comparative literature program at the University of California Santa Barbara and especially within the department of Spanish and Portuguese at Yale. Being a Brazilian scholar working in the United States has shaped my cultural, intellectual, and artistic interests to a certain extent. I have tried my best to take advantage of the opportunities and elude the limitations of this circumstance and this book is the result of my efforts to do that.

I have chosen to focus on two distinct national literary and cultural systems in order to avoid the risk of the superficiality that a broad, imprecise field such as Latin America can bring. It is essential for me to do more than get acquainted with a few canonical works from a dozen nations, relying on the strong US tradition of close reading without much contextualization. Literature only makes sense to me in the context of a network of historical and cultural references as well as literary and artistic traditions. From among all Latin American nations besides Brazil, I chose Mexico for two related reasons: during graduate school I read Juan Rulfo in classes taught by Sara Poot-Herrera, an excellent scholar who specialized in Mexico (and a wonderful human being whom I truly admire) with whom I shared many affinities. Because of them I fell in love with Mexico, and I hold true to Sergio Buarque de Holanda's admonition about Brazilians' oblivion to any form of coexistence that is not dictated by affection.

Mexico and Brazil are two cultural giants in Latin America, two of the most insular countries of the continent that have had the chance to build fully developed national literary systems based on a sense of cultural identity. All national cultural identities rely on some form of exceptionalism, that is, some claim to particular qualities that set them apart from all other nations and made them unique. There is, however, a vast repertoire of similarities and differences between Mexico and Brazil that is at the heart of this book, in the essays, poems, novels, and films that Brazilians and Mexicans made in cooperation with each other or inspired or provoked by each other.

The starting point for this project was the gathering of anecdotal statements and passing comments that indicated mutual interest between Brazilians and Mexicans. *Deep Undercurrents* is a systematic investigation of these encounters in an effort to go beyond the merely anecdotal and reflect on the implications of different modalities of cross-cultural interactions, different perspectives and practices of cultural border crossing. Although these contacts are not unsubstantial, they have been kept in near invisibility and are part of the deep undercurrents of Latin America to which my title refers. They have remained inconspicuous because of a gap in the formation of fully bilingual scholars interested in comparative work within the Americas beyond linguistic and national borders. Latin American studies in US academia have provided an interesting space for scholars with these qualifications to work and thrive. The comparative nature of *Deep Undercurrents*, across nations, languages, genres, and art forms within Latin America makes it relevant for scholars interested in comparative studies within Latin America and those concerned with transnational and/or multilingual approaches to literary studies in general. Individual works will arouse the interest of scholars focused on different aspects of Brazilian and Mexican cultures.

These contacts involve figures such as Antonio Vieira, Sor Juana, Machado de Assis, Alfonso Reyes, José Vasconcelos, Ronald de Carvalho, Carlos Pellicer, Manuel Bandeira, Cecília Meireles, David Alfaro Siqueiros, Érico Veríssimo, Juan Rulfo, João Guimarães Rosa, Rubem Fonseca, Nelson Pereira dos Santos, Paul Leduc, Beto Brant, Felipe Ehrenberg, and Gabriel Orozco. They wrote essays, novels, short stories, poetry, *crónicas*, travel books, and memoirs; they gave courses, lectures, and speeches; they edited and/or translated other people's work; they made art, filmed and photographed, performed and recorded music. In this corpus there is a strong comparative element based on a fundamental curiosity about an ambiguous, somehow familiar Other. It is also curiosity about oneself: an attitude of openness spurred by empathy as much as by self-absorption, by recognition and identification as much as by estrangement and otherness. These interactions across national frontiers are the basis for reconceiving Latin America, discussing how the idea of Latin America has evolved over the years and the multifaceted ambiguities of the concept.

Chapter 1 of *Literary and Cultural Relations Between Brazil and Mexico: Deep Undercurrents*, "First Undercurrents," briefly comments on the first literary manifestations of the flow between Brazilians and Mexicans, starting with Antonio Vieira and Sor Juana Inés de la Cruz and moving into the impact on Brazilian writers such as Machado de Assis of Mexico's troubles and strife in the nineteenth century. This chapter also tells the story of the Bernardellis, a family having Italian roots, who left a lasting mark on the performing arts, sculpture, and painting in Brazil and in Mexico. "Ronald de Carvalho (and Carlos Pellicer): Modern Poets of America" (chapter 2) focuses on two young avant-garde poets inspired by José Vasconcelos (another central figure in Mexican culture) to travel the continent and poetry resulting from their experience, taking advantage of the modernist aesthetics to represent a not entirely unfamiliar other to their readers. "Alfonso Reyes: Brazil and Mexico in a Nutshell" (chapter 3) centers attention on essays in which this central figure of Mexican culture attempts to summarize Mexico and Brazil for foreign eyes. Reyes's Brazilian experience is carefully contextualized as we delve into the potentials and limitations of his views on Latin American and national identities in the twentieth century. "When Mexican Poets Come to Rio de Janeiro" (chapter 4) examines several Mexican poets who wrote about Rio de Janeiro, transforming the city that has epitomized Brazilian wonders and worst nightmares into a feature of Mexican poetry and dramatizing the gaze into an almost familiar human and natural landscape that puzzles and fascinates. "Érico Veríssimo's Journey into Mexico" (chapter 5) is about a thoroughly researched travel essay written by one of the most popular writers in Brazil, a liberal deeply involved in the Pan American effort at the OAS. Veríssimo's famous understated style carefully calibrates opposing views of Mexico (incorporating interviews and profiles of figures such as Vasconcelos and David Alfaro Siqueiros) and his own experiences as a tourist to present to his readers a portrait of Mexico as a place of vitality and complexity. "João

Guimarães Rosa between Life and Death in His Own Páramo" (chapter 6) looks at Rosa's only mature story set outside Brazil, a novella suggestively named "Páramo." This posthumous piece is a foray into a world where the dead and the living coexist, with nods to Rosa's dear friend, the outstanding Juan Rulfo. "Páramo" also offers a window into the creative process that renders Rosa's eclectic influences into fiction. "Why and for What Purpose do Latin American Fiction Writers Travel? Silviano Santiago's *Viagem ao México* and The Roots and Labyrinths of Latin America" (chapter 7) follows Brazil's foremost literary critic and a gifted novelist in his most ambitious work, *Viagem ao México*, and in his daring comparative reading of essays on identity by Octavio Paz and Sérgio Buarque de Holanda. "Nelson Pereira dos Santos and the Mexican Golden Age of Cinema" (chapter 8) tells of how the legendary filmmaker faced the challenge of making a film about Latin American cinema as a whole to commemorate a hundred years of cinema. Nelson Pereira dos Santos adapted Sílvia Oroz's monograph on the melodrama of the Golden Age, but instead of a documentary he created a fictional story of unrequited love and Oedipal memories, with scenes from Mexican classics. Filmed in both Brazil and Mexico, *Cinema de Lágrimas* is a tribute to the filmmaker's childhood memories and a fresh look at a genre his generation despised and criticized for its alienation. "Leduc Reads Fonseca: The Globalization of Violence, or The Violence of Globalization" (chapter 9) takes a look at the adaptation of some of the most polemical of Fonseca's stories into *El Cobrador: In God We Trust*. This is a veritable film of the Americas, with locations in the United States, Mexico, Brazil, and Argentina and with a multinational cast. Giving a global scope to stories in which Fonseca announced modernity had arrived in Brazil on the wings of a brutal military regime and produced an urban nightmare, Leduc attempts to answer Tom Zé's provocative question, stated in the song that closes the film ("Who is planting dynamite in head of this century?") by pointing to the roots of the violence, social injustice, and desperation in the continent. "The Delicate Crime of Beto Brant and Felipe Ehrenberg" (chapter 10) brings into focus a productive partnership between a young Brazilian filmmaker and a veteran Mexican artist in a radical film project, an adaptation of Sérgio Sant'Anna's *Um Crime Delicado*. This film bravely flaunts frontiers between the arts (cinema, painting, performance, theater, criticism), between documentary and fiction, and, most important, between life and art. "Undercurrents, Still Flowing" (chapter 11) comments on the latest encounters between Brazilians and Mexicans as the Internet and globalization facilitate and intensify contacts unmediated by the centers of the Western world. These range from the influence of Brazilian neoconcrete artists on the contemporary Mexican artistic scene to *Fiat Lux*, Paula Abramo's wonderful book about the multinational roots of her family. The Abramos, another family of Italian origins, have left their mark in Brazil and are now poised to play a prominent role in Mexican literature in the twenty-first century as well. The conclusion is a journey through the different uses of the term Latin America in and outside the continent from the nineteenth-century European imperialism through the Third World struggles for emancipation during the Cold War until the acute crises having to do with the fall of the Berlin Wall and the encroachment of globalization. The goal is to propose the existence of another Latin America: a net of carefully woven currents of fragmentary knowledge of uncertain origins and unexpected appropriations. The steady stream across nations and languages forms the deep cultural undercurrents of Latin America.

*Deep Undercurrents* was conceived as a contribution to a wider project: to take a fresh look at Latin America not just by heeding Jorge Schwartz's call ("Down with the Tordesillas!") but by locating fragments and making evident and legible the mostly untold story of horizontal (south-south) contacts across a multilingual, multicultural continent. It is a story of encounters only briefly acknowledged by scholars trained not to heed them, much less to see them together with a simultaneous view on both sides of the linguistic divide. In this book I believe I was able to offer a glimpse of the vitality of these overlooked undercurrents and their relevance to a fuller understanding of the continent's culture.

I am grateful to many people who supported me in myriad ways: friends and colleagues, mentors such as David Jackson and Rolena Adorno. They supported my research and taught me more than they know. I am also grateful to those who preceded me in looking at Latin America beyond linguistic divides—they are many and I am afraid of failing to mention them all. I thank a host of scholars who graduated about the same time in the United States or came here to pursue an academic career. Their work exemplifies the limitations and possibilities of my own condition. They have inspired and challenged me to try my best.

# Chapter 1

# First Undercurrents

The relations between Brazilian and Mexican artists and intellectuals predate the establishment of these two paradigmatic giants of Latin America as independent nations. The first signs of contact involve no other than two outstanding figures of colonial literature: the Jesuit Antonio Vieira (1608–1697), who lived in Brazil from the age of 6 until 33, and *Sor* Juana Inés de la Cruz (1651–1695), born and raised in Nueva España. Sor Juana's *Carta Atenagórica,* published in 1690 by the bishop of Puebla, links the world-famous Jesuit preacher and the greatest poet of colonial Mexico. In this letter, Sor Juana offers a bold refutation of one of Vieira's *Sermões do Mandato* [Maundy Thursday Sermons] first heard in 1655 in the Igreja de Nossa Senhora da Misericórdia of Lisbon at the very height of Vieira's influence in the Portuguese court,[1] when Sor Juana was four years old.

A Maundy Thursday Sermon takes as theme the love of God for mankind. The title refers to the "new" commandment in John 13:34: "That ye love one another; as I have loved you, that ye also love one another." These sermons typically versed on the love of Christ, contrasting the perfect love emanating from God (*agape*) with the lesser one from human beings (*eros*), but in his sermon Vieira concentrates on two instances of divine love: God's love on the day of the incarnation of Christ and in the institution of the Eucharist. Vieira, with customary eloquence and wit, concludes that the latter is greater, since Christ gave us then his own flesh and blood through the sacrament and thus, in corporeal absence, He is incarnated in all of the faithful who commune with God in the Eucharist.

A fundamental element in Vieira's sermon and in Sor Juana's response is the notion of *fineza* (a powerful instance of *agudeza,* which means shrewdness or discernment), related in this sermon to the subtle power of Christ's "nonpresence" in the world as a powerful act of love devoid of earthly interests in reciprocity. Sor Juana parses each argument of Vieira's, proposing distinctions between different dimensions of *fineza*: its cost to the doer, its utility to the receiver, and its cause and effect. For the Mexican, *fineza* is a sort of performative act: "¿Es fineza, acaso, tener amor? No, por cierto, sino las demostraciones del amor: ésas se llaman finezas" (21). Sor Juana chastises Vieira for refuting three eminent church scholars (Augustine, Thomas Aquinas, and John Chrysostom) and then boldly refutes each of the main theses Vieira puts forward in his sermon. Her conclusion is a baroque rhetorical jewel in which she bids the reader to thank God for what He does *not* do:

> Let us appreciate the good God does to us in not doing to us all the benefits we wish from him, and also the good that His Majesty wants to do us but does not so He does not give us more to account for. Let us thank Him and ponder on the delicacy of the Divine Love in which to reward is a benefit, to punish is a benefit and to withdraw benefits is the greatest benefit; not doing a delicacy [fineza], the greatest delicacy. (27)[2]

Sor Juana's bold eloquence is couched in customary demonstrations of *humilitas*: the gracious opening declares her "admirable impact of the ingenuities" and her "secret empathy" to Vieira's "generous nation"[3] while the end contains an apology for her unpolished text, compared to a formless embryo. Nevertheless, there were repercussions for the daring nun, who was characterized by one of her critics as "una mujer introducida a theóloga y scripturista" (Poot Herrera, 77). Just as this *Carta Atenagórica* came out, three powerful men of the Church in México rallied against her: Antonio Núñez, sor Juana's Jesuit confessor and prefect of the Congregación de la Purísima Concepción de la Virgen María, Fernandez de Santa Cruz, the bishop of Puebla, who took the mantle of a fictitious Sor Philotea in order to include criticisms of Sor Juana's boldness in the very body of the publication of the *Carta Atenagórica*, and Francisco de Aguiar y Seixas, the archbishop of Mexico, who demanded a *profesión de fe* from the nun.

Ermilo Abreu Gómez describes a multicultural seventeenth-century Corte del Virrey, "mitad española y mitad portuguesa" (38):

> In that pseudo-court in the style of Felipe IV...filled with Portuguese and Jews, Juana Inés finished her language studies. Portuguese made it easier for her to read of the works of Father Antonio Vieira, whom she criticized in her *Carta Atenagórica*. In some of her *Villancicos*

[ballads], she introduced in popular form some less than pristine Portuguese expressions. (49)[4]

Furthermore, Abreu Gómez emphasizes Sor Juana's knowledge of Portuguese and its importance in her intellectual formation: "La limitación de su cultura por la escasez de los libros que podía leer en castellano, la instó a estudiar el latín y el portugués" (76), "que participaba tanto del lenguaje culto como del que arrastra el sentimiento de lo popular" (37).[5]

The discovery of a lovely group of *enigmas* written by Sor Juana Inés de la Cruz perhaps a few months before her death in 1695[6] confirms that not only did the nun continue to write after the affair of the *Carta Atenagórica*, but also that her relationship to the Portuguese world continued, since these enigmas were dedicated to a group of literate Portuguese nuns gathered around an *Asamblea de la Casa del Placer. Enigmas ofrecidos a la discreta inteligencia de la soberana Asamblea de la Casa del Placer por su más rendida y aficionada Soror Juana Inés de la Cruz, Décima Musa* (Martínez Lopez, 140–170) is a collection of riddles written in beautifully fluent *redondillas*. Martínez López assures that the answers to these riddles revolve around multiple definitions of love, proof that Sor Juana was still able to display her art, still preoccupied with the theme of Vieira's bold sermon, and still in close contact with Portuguese letters. Long before Brazil and Mexico became independent nations, deep undercurrents of Portuguese and Spanish exchange were rising closer to the surface, tracing a course that passed through Portugal and Spain, their colonial metropolises, which had been unified for almost 60 years.

The nineteenth century saw important Brazilian writers react to turbulent events in Mexico, with Maximillian's Mexican adventure capturing the imagination of Brazilians living under Pedro II's reign. In 1862 Joaquim Maria Machado de Assis wrote a poem called "Epitáfio do México" (*Chrysalidas*, 87–88), just as French troops brought Maximilian to power. The poem's epigraph alludes to the Grecian resistance against the Persians in the Thermopylae (grossly outnumbered, the Greeks lost but the Spartan hero Leonidas I resisted bravely until the end) and, while the poet laments "the lukewarm cadaver / of a vanquished people" (87), he prophesies the nation's rebirth "when the fateful voice / of holy freedom / comes in prosperous days" (88).[7] In 1865 Machado de Assis's column in *Diário do Rio de Janeiro* features lively exchanges with a reader who signs himself "O Amigo da Verdade" and writes in defense of Maximilian's regime

(*Correspondência* 89–105). Reacting to a speech by Maximilian's envoy about Brazilian and Mexican mutual interests and the two nations' "regime identity," Machado de Assis affirms unequivocally:

> In our opinion the empire in Mexico is the product of violence and a subsidiary of the French Empire. What reciprocity of interests can there be between this and Brazil's Empire, which is the result of the nation's will? ( ... ) Universal justice and the American spirit protest against the reciprocity of interests between the two empires. ( ... ) Brazil cannot share interests or concerns with Mexico, because our origin is legitimate and our spirit is, above all, America. (94–95)[8]

Benito Juárez's fight against Maximilian also had a great impact in Brazil. Still in 1865 the poet Fagundes Varella published his admired "Versos Soltos ao General Juárez" (*Poemas de Fagundes Varela* 79–81),[9] an exalted acclamation of the Mexican statesman whose name "It will be ( ... ) the magic word / The world will utter in remembrance of the glories / Of the Mexican race!"[10] Four years later Varela's last book, *Cantos do Ermo e da Cidade*, features another eulogy, "O general Juárez" (91–101), which calls the Mexican leader one of the few "among the children of these ungrateful times"[11] who deserves to be called a hero for fighting for the freedom and redemption that are the essence of the Americas:

> Nobody can erase
> The glory of a race from the vast book
> That belongs to future existence.
> Though slavery, wars, infamies
> May tarnish your brilliance,
> A nation cannot die, nor be disowned! (99)[12]

Firm in his belief that "the spirit of a People never dies" (97), Varela proclaims Juárez "more than a genius" (101),[13] a true Romantic hero, who finds a source of essential freedom in the depths of his own country:

> In America's bosom
> There is yet a new world to discover:
> Gentlemen from overseas,
> Would you care to know where it is?
> Do you want to know its name?
> Examine the heart of the American race,
> And in this endless sea,
> Yet warmed by the first sun,
> You'll see freedom! (95)[14]

About the same time, the conflict in Mexico reappears in Machado de Assis's *Phalenas*. Instead of glorifying the victorious Juárez, Machado de Assis, who always believed Maximilian to be well intentioned, centers attention on the dramatic story of Maximilian's wife, Carlota, who had been driven mad by her husband's debacle and death. "La Marchesa de Miramar" (21–26) focuses on tragic pathos, dramatizing the last moments of Maximilian's deranged wife and imagining that "a bloody dew falls in the Mexican night...." (24).[15]

In 1881 as the movement for the proclamation of the Republic gained momentum, the republican militant Quintino Bocaiúva turns the phrase *Olhemos para o México* [Let's Look to Mexico]—the title of his column in his newspaper, *O Globo*, into a *cri de coeur* against the monarchy and in favor of a closer relationship with Spanish America. The column had such profound impact that it would still be remembered in the 1930s, during the debates about oil exploration in Brazil.[16] One of the debaters, the author of *Petróleo para o Brasil*, was the 1930 revolutionary veteran Juarez Távora, his first name, still common in Brazil, a sign of Juárez's enduring popularity.[17]

While Bocaiúva sang praises to the progressivism of Porfirio Díaz's authoritarian republic in Mexico, at the other end of the political spectrum the monarchist Eduardo Prado criticized Mexico in *A ilusão Americana* (1893), accusing Bocaiúva of believing in *"estatísticas ultra-fantasistas"* (77) about Mexican development. Prado castigates republican regimes in Latin America as servile imitations of the United States, a form of government unsuited for the Latin peoples of the Americas, which "denied the traditions of their race and their history, sacrificed in the name of senseless principles of artificial political and legislative exoticism," (65) and calls Maximilian's regime "the most honest government Mexico has had since independence" (61).[18] For Prado, the Habsburg prince was the victim of the tragic fate that befalls the "chiefs of liberator states," but "in Mexico, the monarchic feeling is irresistible. It cannot restore the monarchy but it has thwarted the republic. Because in Mexico there is not, was not, and will not be a republic" (62).[19]

Mexico also interested Afonso Celso, a staunch right-wing monarchist and ultramontane Catholic known mostly for his treatise of uncritical patriotism *Porque me ufano do meu país* (inspiration for the neologism *ufanismo*, now firmly incorporated into the lexicon). A year before Joaquim Nabuco used the example of Chile to speak of a liberal republic of the enlightened—in his *Balmaceda*—Celso had presented Mexico the paradigm of the evils of Latin American republicanism in *Lupe*. This short novel describes the misfortunes of an attractive young woman who becomes destitute when her American father dies and is forced to move with her mother to Acapulco. In Mexico they suffer the bestial ignorance of a *pulque*-drinking "genuíno caboclo" (93) with all sorts of violence and humiliations during bloody *pronunciamentos*. The heroine of *Lupe* counts on nothing but her staunch Catholicism and strict moral code to console her.[20] Much later, in 1923, Celso would make a short speech at the Brazilian Academy of Letters, listing examples of "Brazil's appreciation for Mexico manifested in our letters" (*Revista da ABL*, 174) and defending Fray Juan Zumárraga (1468–1548), the first archbishop of Mexico City, against the accusation of having burned Aztec libraries, a libel made by those Celso called "anticlerical Mexican writers."[21]

This rebuke was a response to an essay also published in the same journal by Rodrigo Octavio (1866–1944), who would play an important role as arbiter in disputes with the United States during the Mexican Revolution. Octavio befriended president Álvaro Obregón, who took him on a tour of Chapultepec Palace and considered Mexico "the most interesting of the many countries I have visited" (*Minhas Memórias dos Outros*, 167), whose life "moves sometimes turbulently but always toward progress." The 1923 essay was titled "Na Terra da Virgem Índia" and described Mexico as the "seat of a new civilization" (166):

> In the domain of sociology as well as the arts, under the influence of its young statesmen as well as its painters, sculptors, and designers, also young, a brand-new world grows and gains clearer contours ( ... ) and surprises because it is not simply the product of Spanish civilization ( ... ) but of an adaptation of some of that civilization's principles to the indigenous character, temperament, aspirations, and ideals.[22]

Octavio's words echo ideas of José Vasconcelos but, while the Mexican saw Brazil as the seat of his triumphant *raza cósmica*, the Brazilian anticipates arguments about cultural blending that were to become commonplace in Brazil only in the 1930s under the auspices of Getúlio Vargas.

In 1935 Octavio's memoirs tell the tale of the Bernardellis, a family of accomplished dancers, musicians, painters, and sculptors, which played a distinguished role in the arts in Mexico and in Brazil in the nineteenth and twentieth centuries. An Italian dancer and violinist, Oscar Bernardelli (1835–1881),[23] returns to Paris from a tour in Moscow and falls in love with Celestine Thierry (18?–1908), a ballerina within the Scala di Milano[24] Conservatory, who had just performed at Covent Garden in London and Porte Saint Martin in Paris. In 1847 Oscar and Celestine toured Mexico together with the dance company and, in spite of her father's objections,[25] they got married in 1850. The young couple "remained for years as stars of the company at the Nacional with María Moctezuma" (*Teatro Musical y Danza en le México de la Belle Époque*, 41)[26] and had their first two children, Rodolfo (1852) and Francisca (1854) in Mexico. Their performances mixed fashionable European ballet with traditional Mexican dance: while Oscar starred in "Le violon du diable,"[27] a piece written in 1849, in which the male dancer performed and played the violin on stage, "la celestial Celestina" (337), was noted for being an expert performer of the popular *el jarabe* (60).

Forced to leave Mexico[28] shortly after Francisca's birth, Celestine and Oscar left their daughter with her godparents and embarked on an adventure down the Pacific coast to Chile, where they toured for four years in a troupe that included dancer Luis Corby and four other dancers and musicians. In Chile, Celestine Thierry "garnered people's applause with her performance of the *zamacueca*" (*Historia de la Musica en Argentina*, 94)[29] and the couple "made their name on the stage of the recently inaugurated Santiago Municipal Theater (1857)" (*Orígenes del Ballet en Chile*).[30] Their third son, Henrique, was born in 1857 in Valparaíso. In April of the next year the family moved to Santiago, and their last performance in the Teatro Municipal took place on January 16, 1859 (Milanca Guzmán). By August 1860, the same cast performed in Buenos Aires under the name "La Compañia Coreográfica Thierry" (Gesualdo 94) and Celestine was praised again for her extraordinary technique.[31] They also toured Rosario and Montevideo with "ever-growing acclaim" (*Enciclopedia dello Spettacolo*, 1291). After 1863 Oscar and Celestine performed under the name "*Companhia de Ballet Thierry*" (Sucena, 81) in Rio de Janeiro and elsewhere in Brazil. Their youngest son, Félix, was born in 1866 in Rio Grande do Sul and in 1878 Celestine starred in *Around the World in Eighty Days*, with a cast of 42 dancers (91). In 1881 the multitalented family moved to Rio de Janeiro to be mentors to the daughters of Pedro II and join the theatrical scene. Oscar played violin in the orchestra of the Imperial Chapel and taught dancing and violin classes. The three sons learned musical instruments (Rodolfo played the cello; Henrique and Félix the violin) and had careers as artists, having studied in the Imperial Academy of Fine Arts and completed their education during extended stays in Europe.

Oscar and Celestine's eldest son, Rodolfo, became the most respected sculptor in Brazil, director of the Escola Nacional de Belas Artes (ENBA) for 25 years, from 1890 to 1915. Besides a 60-piece collection housed in the Museu Histórico Nacional, Rodolfo Bernardelli's works are spread throughout Rio de Janeiro and define the urban landscape: his are the sculptures in the Teatro Municipal, the eagles that adorn the Palacio do Catete, and the statues of Pedro Álvares Cabral (Gloria), Dom João VI (Jardim Botânico), General Osorio (Praça XV), duque de Caxias (Praça Duque de Caxias), José de Alencar (Catete), and the visconde de Mauá (Praça Mauá).

The avant-gardists of the 1920s had less than kind words for artists such as Rodolfo – with typical verve Oswald de Andrade called the sculptor "the world's worst tiler" in 1922 (Boaventura, 74).[32] But the Bernardellis were not reactionaries. As teachers—Henrique left the ENBA in 1905 and Rodolfo in 1915—they were admired and considered modernizers, and when a group of painters rebelled against the strictures of the ENBA in 1931 they named their group Núcleo Bernardelli.[33]

This modernizing role is clearer in the case of Henrique, who went to Europe without a scholarship and remained in Italy for nine years. The landscapes of his first exhibition after his return to Brazil were hailed as models of modern painting "non-preoccupied with school conventionalism and strict academic prescriptions" (Dazzi, 165) and a few years later the symbolist Luiz Gonzaga Duque Estrada (1863–1911) went so far as to affirm, "no other modern painter will represent more accurately our natural landscape than Henrique Bernardelli" (166). Duque Estrada depicted Henrique as the quintessential heroic modern artist:

> Restless, nervous, hungry for impressions, an athletic build, with broad shoulders, strong chest, full muscles strengthened by healthy outdoor walks. In a corner in the room, one sees his likeness (sculpted by Rodolfo Bernardelli). It must be him. He is a strong man, small eyes, sure of himself, thick neck, full lips, a daring mustache with pointed tips, a close shaved beard, a large hat tilted to the side, giving his head the traditional arrogance of an old knight.
>
> He is his own work, whose expression is original, full of warmth and full of power.[34]

The youngest Bernardelli, Félix (1866–1905), also became a notable painter and musician. However, his father's death in 1881 and the discovery that his sister Francisca was alive took Félix and recently widowed Celestine back to Guadalajara in 1886. Rodrigo Octavio recalls the story in typical melodramatic fashion: after years of fruit-less inquiries, Rodolfo meets a *tapatío* [a native from Guadalajara] by chance in a restaurant in Italy. After they talk about "Fanny," who had been brought up in the Escorza family and married one of them, this unnamed Mexican man takes to his country a letter and photographs from Rodolfo. A few years later, Fanny's letter arrives in Rio de Janeiro and Celestine decides to go to Mexico to her long-lost daughter.

Félix accompanies his mother to Mexico and debuts as a violinist in 1887 at the Teatro Degollado de Guadalajara (*Teatro Musical y Danza en el México de la Belle Époque*, 337). He leaves shortly afterward to study in Europe for six years, as his brothers Rodolfo and Henrique had done before him. In 1892 Félix comes back to Guadalajara, where he opens a studio and provides training and mentorship to artists such as Jorge Enciso, Rafael Ponce de León, Gerardo Murillo (a.k.a Dr. Atl), and Roberto Montenegro, all of whom later played key roles in Mexico.

Félix Bernardelli was also an active member of Guadalajara's cultural scene in those years, having been one the founding members of the Ateneo Jaliscience (1903–1906), "an association of artists with the purpose of congregating the artistic and literary figures of Guadalajara" (Matute, 33).[35] His cultural influence was manifold: as a painter, a musician, and a Brazilian living in Mexico. On February 18, 1896 the 23-year-old Félix and the pianist Enrique Morelos arrived in New York, where Félix is said to have held an exhibit. On April 5 of the same year a note in the *New York Times* reports the two young men in Washington DC, where Félix shows his paintings and the duo plays at the Brazilian embassy. Among several musical events in Guadalajara, Félix staged Carlos Gómez's opera *Il Guarany* in the Teatro Degollado in 1904, and in 1907 was a founding member and on the faculty of a music academy with 104 students in the city (Matute, 33).

The importance of Félix as a teacher in Guadalajara is compared to the Catalan Antonio Fabrés, who arrived in Mexico a few years later and taught the latest painting techniques to Diego Rivera's brilliant generation. Many of Felix's students went on to study with Fabrés at the Academia San Carlos, bearing letters of recommendation from their master in Guadalajara and with a reputation for their technique and expertise. Luis-Martín Lozano compares Félix Bernardelli and Antonio Fabrés in the following terms:

> …in the quiet location of his studio he put to practice what he learned in Rome as well as Paris. He knew, furthermore, to perceive the climate

of stylistic innovations and open up to the reality of the Mexican context, an attitude that, for instance, the acclaimed Antonio Fabrés never
had. (Lozano, 66)[36]

Perhaps this openness to the reality of the Mexican context—expressed
in several paintings by Félix that depict the landscape and the people of Jalisco—came easier to him than to Fabrés simply because the
Brazilian had, after all, grown up in another Latin American country. Félix was certainly less prone to consider the local culture as not
worthy of attention and more attuned to the wish to develop local
artistic expressions that was so important in Latin America since
Independence.

In 1908 Félix spent a few days with his convalescent mother at
his brother-in-law's farm near Guadalajara, where he daily went out-
doors to make sketches of the local landscape. On May 18, back to
Guadalajara, Félix died of an Erysipelas, a streptococcal infection, at
the age of 46. Celestine died the same year.

Raised in Brazil by parents who were expert dancers of *el jarabe*
and the *Zamacueca*, and important members of the performing arts
scene in Imperial Brazil, the Bernardelli brothers were artists whose
lives traced comparable lines in Latin America at the turn of the
century. Whereas the Bernardelli born in Mexico became the most
influential sculptor at the turn of the century in Rio de Janeiro, the
Brazilian-born Bernardelli became the mentor of figures such as
Gerardo Murillo and Roberto Montenegro, and staged *Il Guarany*
in Guadalajara. These are the first deep undercurrents that bring
together Brazil and Mexico.

# Chapter 2

# Ronald de Carvalho (and Carlos Pellicer): Modern Poets of America

$M$ost people recognize the great importance, at least on a symbolic level, of the generation of writers, painters, architects, and philosophers that participated in the Ateneo de la Juventud,[1] a society for study and lecture founded after a cycle of conferences in 1907/1908 and active until 1914, after which its members continued to participate actively in the cultural, artistic, and political life in Mexico.[2] Their questioning of positivist tenets in the Escuela Nacional Preparatoria against the *científicos* (a group instituted as a government faction) and their defense of lay education against the interference of conservative Catholics gained symbolic momentum as these actions preceded the revolution that ended Porfirio Díaz's rule, which had lasted from 1884 to 1911. Because of that, the Ateneo de la Juventud has become a herald (to a great extent by its members' own account) of the new Mexico that came into being with the Revolution, even though their relationship with the old and new regimes was ambiguous.[3]

The two most influential *ateneístas*, José Vasconcelos and Alfonso Reyes, left their marks on Rio de Janeiro's urban landscape; and it is reasonable to say that Brazil left a mark on their intellectual life as well. Vasconcelos visited Brazil for the international fair in commemoration of the centenary of the independence in 1922. As the head of the largest international delegation, Vasconcelos brought a gift to the Brazilian capital: an imposing statue of the Aztec emperor Cuauhtémoc, a replica of the one that stands to this day in the Paseo de la Reforma in Mexico. Ironically, this statue was a relic from Porfirio Díaz's longtime relationship with the US company Tiffany & Co. and an example of *indigenista* art with which the anti-American and hispanist Vasconcelos was not confortable.[4] The Cuauhtémoc statue still cuts an imposing figure in a square of the same name in Aterro do Flamengo, surrounded by a cactus garden donated by Alfonso Reyes when he was ambassador in Rio de Janeiro in the 1930s. In "Las Estatuas y el Pueblo" (*Obras completas*, 61–64), Alfonso Reyes cites the Brazilian poet Murilo Mendes as his source to note approvingly that, by that time, *Cariocas* [inhabitants of Rio de Janeiro] had already adopted Cuauhtémoc as theirs, turning the emperor into an enormous amulet, a "mascot," an image propitiatory of good luck (64).[5]

Besides the festivities of the centennial in the capital, Vasconcelos visited Salvador, São Paulo, Campinas, Santos, Belo Horizonte, Ouro Preto, Barbacena, and Juiz de Fora, and insisted on traveling from Rio de Janeiro to Uruguay by train instead of by ship to "to see the country, not the waves, with their identical, innumerable multiplicity" (*La Raza Cósmica*, 131–132).[6] Vasconcelos's enthusiasm for Brazil's achievements and cultural vibrancy resembles at times what Brazilians humorously call *ufanismo*, but the account of this trip to Brazil is of no small importance in the works of the great *oaxaqueño*. This trip (and its continuation down to Uruguay and Argentina) makes the bulk of Vasconcelos's *La Raza Cósmica—Misión de la Raza Ibero-Americana*, whose prologue prophesied the coming of the "fifth race" (a mingling of white, black, yellow, and red) destined to found a "New Rome" in Latin America.[7]

José Vasconcelos's efforts to strengthen Mexico's cultural and dip-lomatic ties with South America went beyond his tour in 1922 and the subsequent publication of *Raza Cósmica* with its emphatic call to an Iberian-American cultural and political alliance in 1925. Vasconcelos invited writers such as Gabriela Mistral and Pedro Henriquez Ureña to come to Mexico to teach and see with their own eyes the achieve-ments of Álvaro Obregón's revolutionary government in educa-tion and the arts.[8] Among these visitors was a Brazilian diplomat, Ronald de Carvalho (1893–1935), who visited México in 1923 as a guest of honor and gave a series of lectures at the UNAM and in Guadalajara.[9]

At the age of 30 Ronald de Carvalho was already more than a promising figure. The acclaimed essayist of the highly esteemed *Pequena História da Literatura Brasileira* (1919)[10] was also the author of three appreciated volumes of poetry: *Luz Gloriosa* (1913), *Poemas e Sonetos* (1919), and *Epigramas Irônicos e Sentimentais* (1922). With the connections of a respectable family in the capital of the republic, the young graduate of a prestigious law school[11] received early sup-port from two eminent figures of the Academia Brasileira de Letras: the journalist, lawyer, and liberal politician Rui Barbosa (1949–1923) and the diplomat, novelist, and self-anointed spokesperson of the Brazilian avant-garde Graça Aranha (1868–1931). In spite of the early recognition by older generations and the connections with the political and literary status quo, Carvalho was also a pioneer of the avant-garde on both sides of the Atlantic. The young law graduate spent a few years in Europe and collaborated in Portuguese literary journals, most notably featuring as one of the editors in the first issue of Fernando Pessoa's *Orpheu* in 1915.[12] Back to Rio de Janeiro, Ronald de Carvalho hosted the first meeting between the *modernistas* from Rio and São Paulo and participated in the 1922 *Semana de Arte Moderna*, giving a lecture and reciting Manuel Bandeira's poem "Os Sapos" [The Frogs] to a jeering audience.[13]

This combination of prestige in the mainstream and in the avant-garde made Carvalho the leader together with Graça Aranha of one faction of *modernistas* (never a cohesive group, by late 1920s the *modernistas* were at each other's throats for political and aesthetic reasons).[14] Because of their access to the mainstream press, Carvalho and Graça Aranha were actually considered "the foremost elements of Modernism" whereas Mário de Andrade and Oswald de Andrade led what was then called the "small Futurist clique from São Paulo" (*Correspondência Mário de Andrade/Manuel Bandeira*, 198). Even among his rivals, Carvalho was considered "extremely intelligent and rarely reproachable from an intellectual point of view" (322), while in the eyes of admirers he "made all the others' prestige pale in comparison, exercising a literary dictatorship" ("Circulação de Idéias," 89).[15]

Carvalho was particularly interested in contacts with like-minded European and Latin American writers,[16] perhaps as an extension of his diplomatic career.[17] Besides collaborations with Portuguese *modernistas* and his Mexican contacts, Carvalho featured prominently at ceremonies with foreign dignitaries and literary figures in Rio de Janeiro and often published op-ed columns written from abroad— some of these pieces were collected in the book *Caderno de Imagens da Europa* in 1935. Thus Vasconcelos chose well, and his efforts paid handsome dividends, since Carvalho repeatedly expressed admiration and respect for Mexico. When the French *Journal des Débats*[18] complained about the admittance of Mexico to the League of Nations in the face of Mexican positions on the payment of its external debt,[19] Carvalho responded:

What the *Journal des Débats* said about Mexico is significant. Mexico's men of thought, the monuments of its ancient culture, its anthropologists, its poets, its moralists, its most refined writers, among

them honoring their tradition there is my dear friend, the ambassador
Alfonso Reyes, the sufferings of a race whose frequent heroism sur-
prises no one, all this represents nothing to Europeans. (*Caderno de
Imagens da Europa*, 79–80)[20]

At the heart of Carvalho's defense of Mexico is a familiar critique
of the ascendance of materialistic interests over humanistic values.
The idealist critique of capitalism as philistinism (and democracy as
the dictatorship of the uncultured masses) is clearly in tune with the
*Arielismo* of many familiar Spanish-speaking Latin American voices
such as José Enrique Rodó and Rubén Darío.[21] Furthermore, the
framing of the relations between Latin American nations and Europe
as a reinstatement of colonialist parasitic relationships echoes Manoel
Bomfim's *América Latina —Males de Origem* (1903).

In this same piece Carvalho warns his Brazilian readers that,
despite all protestations to the contrary, Brazil and the rest of Latin
America were viewed in Europe with the same condescending contempt since all had problems with the payment of staggering external
debts. He closes his article with an exhortation to a more confron-
tational stance: "Our arbiters are the defenders of the currency the
bankers have lent us to renew the miracle of multiplication of bread.
The wolves are drinking before us and it is our duty, perhaps our privilege to cut off their water."[22] This call for a combative Latin America
is distinctly Vasconcelian, an early articulation of the nationalism and
anti-imperialism that played a role in the discourses of left and right
throughout the twentieth century in Latin America.

Mexico took central stage in Carvalho's *Imagens do México*. The
book is based on notes of Carvalho's trip, which appeared as early
as 1923 in "México, Paíz de Belleza" in the magazine *América
Brasileira*[23] and form the bulk of a lecture at the Liga da Defesa
Nacional[24] sponsored by a Brazilian Centro Universitário Cuauhtémoc
in 1930.[25] *Imagens do México* (1929) and *Estudos Brasileiros —1a
Série* (1924) form a diptych in a manner similar to Reyes's "México
en una Nuez" and "Brasil en una Castaña," which will be looked into
in chapter 3. *Imagens do México* offers Brazilian readers an introduction to Mexico based on notes from the 1923 trip, while *Estudos
Brasileiros* is based on lectures to Mexican audiences about Brazil
during that trip. Both are efforts to introduce a relatively unknown
culture to a foreign audience.

Reyes described Brazil to Mexicans as an example of smooth political transitions and an unabashedly diplomatic disposition. For historical, cultural, and political reasons Carvalho presented Mexico to

Brazilians as an example as well. For him a nation is built upon the
cultivation of its cultural and historical roots, and Mexico's venerably
ancient pre-Columbian history and noble colonial traditions provided
a rich, solid cultural foundation. Mexico is also a political example:
for Carvalho, the Mexican revolution benefited immensely from the
emergence of a strong visionary leader capable of steering the nation
with indisputable authority into the path of a genuinely national culture truly faithful to its traditions. This leader is Álvaro Obregón,
whom Carvalho portrays as a veritable epic hero:

> Obregón came from the land and the land impressed on him the
> features of an exalted temperament. His youth was spontaneous and
> rebellious like that of all men who were born free. Riding sadleless
> horses, lassoing runaway bulls or competing against the finest horse-
> men from Sonora; with a cocked shotgun ready at hand, hidden in the
> low shrubs of the tranquil magueys or under the shade of thick forests,
> hunting for cranes ou for wild deer, Obregón lived the adolescence of
> a hero.
>
> Always close to the people, Obregon forged a fearless character in
> the freedom of nature. He did not search in universities for diplomas
> of graduate wisdom. He did not search in the galas of the powerful for
> the prestige of transitory favors. He never submerged the verities of the
> spirit in bookish sophisms. His one and only master was the diuturnal
> observation of the beings and things of this world. In a nutshell, his
> one and only master was life itself. (20–21)[26]

Carvalho's Obregón is the quintessential man of the Americas: a natural-born leader, unfettered by the mindless imitation of European
models, and thus able to guide Mexico to an encounter with its true
self, in this case, to fulfill the promise of a perfect fusion between the
descendants of the "voluptuous Castillians" (13) and of the Aztecs,
the "Romans of the Americas" (10) into "a sum of powerful factors"
(13).[27]

In *Imagens do México* and *Estudos Brasileiros 1a Série* Carvalho
fuses the Brazilian motif of a harmonic fusion of the races (European,
Indigenous, and African)[28] with Vasconcelos's conservative elitism
centered on a self-flattering cultivation of colonial cultural traditions and patriarchal noble roots of Brazil's "rural aristocracy" (43)
and Mexico's *criollo* elite. Although far from the pessimism of fellow *modernista* Paulo Prado, Carvalho compares the grand, imperial Mexican past favorably with the Brazilian "lowly" Indians and
Africans and its mostly rural, modest, colonial heritage. Mexico's
racial and cultural fusion involves a vibrant, sophisticated, urban

indigenous *and* colonial Mexico, superior to what he considers meager contributions of Brazilian Indians and Blacks in terms of culture and "temperament."[29]

Applied to Mexico, Carvalho's brand of conservatism fuses the *Hispanistas*' idealistic portrayals of Spanish colonizers as great humanists and conveyors of Western Christian civilization and values with the *Indigenistas*' equally idealistic portrayals of Aztecs and Incas as great noble empires founded on cultivated elites. The modern version of the strong-willed, authoritarian *caudillo* embodied in Obregón is not an undue remnant from the colonial past but a return to Latin American genuine national character in the pursuit of the continent's own brand of Western civilization, freed from the subservient imitation of exhausted European liberal models, understood as artificial and inadequate.[30] These conservative convictions do not oppose modernization and do not result from internal contradictions or a betrayal of past convictions. Neither belief in the cultural worth of indigenous peoples nor praise of miscegenation is indicative per se of a progressive standpoint. This became clear to me when Ruth Hill presented a lecture at Yale in 2007 called "White Skin, Black Masks: Aryanism from *Indigenismo* to Jim Crow" about the affinities between ideologues of US racial segregation such as James Denson Sayers and scholars of pre-Columbian civilizations such as Thomas Gann.[31] Likewise Vasconcelos (and Gilberto Freyre), paradigmatic figures in promoting miscegenation as a source of pride rather than shame for Latin America through theories of the "cosmic race" and the "racial democracy," were staunch defenders of the Spanish and Portuguese colonizers as well. These theories challenged the earlier conservatism that saw miscegenation and the presence of large indigenous and black populations simply as "the white man's burden," but preserved the idea of white minorities as "naturally" dominant. Vasconcelos, Freyre, and Carvalho saw Latin American racial relations in the context of an idealized view of colonization, an essential component of their conservatism. Their positions did not change but were merely exacerbated in the polarized cultural environment of the 1930s and 1940s in Mexico and Brazil.

*Estudos Brasileiros—1a Série*, originally addressed to a Mexican audience in the midst of a revolutionary process, and *Imagens do México*, published on the verge of the revolution that brought Getúlio Vargas and his *gaúchos* to the government, converge ideologically. Carvalho conflates racial and cultural discourses under an ideology of hierarchical order and religious discipline that views the colonial enterprise as the heroic endeavor of a few remarkable Catholic

Europeans of Iberian origins that generously allowed for the "contributions" of other races. Cultural influences and racial miscegenation become undistinguishable and the heterogeneous ethnic composition of Latin America results in a successful "humanistic" form of colonization, the sign of Iberian cultural superiority instead of a source of embarrassment. Miscegenation becomes the ultimate proof of a supposedly consensual, harmonic nature of Latin American ethnic relations, compared to the explosions of racial violence in the United States, to see in Latin America the cradle of a superior culture. Thus Carvalho celebrates widespread Brazilian miscegenation and yet maintains that "we pay tribute for the indigenous blood that still runs in our veins and we suffer exceedingly the terrible influx of the cosmic environment" (*Estudos Brasileiros*, 165) and, more bluntly, that "the peoples that have no discipline have no right to life" (*Estudos Brasileiros 3*, 170).[32] The first part of *Estudos Brasileiros—1a Série* (9–66) centers on secular and religious Portuguese colonizers, compared favorably to their Spanish counterparts for their capacity for enforcing the unity of an immense territory.[33] Sugar plantation masters were "admirable monsters, heroes" without whom "Brasil would not be a nation, but a collection of turbulent and irreconcilable countries" (26) and the Jesuits "embody above all the greatness of their order and their religion" (24).[34]

The ultimately conservative nationalism of several Brazilian *modernistas* in the first decades of the twentieth century seems to challenge but ultimately reaffirm nineteenth-century racial discourses in the face of new internal pressures caused by modernization, and new external pressures caused by the rise of the United States as an interventionist power. The abolition of slavery, industrialization, urbanization, immigration, and political upheaval created the need to accommodate somehow the new masses that threatened the hegemony of the white elite. Together with other key texts such as the pessimistic *Retrato do Brasil* and the triumphant *Marcha para o Oeste* by Cassiano Ricardo, Carvalho's essays and lectures exemplify the merits as well as the limitations of the Brazilian *modernistas* in the 1920s.[35] In this sense *Raza Cósmica* is an important companion to them. In José Joaquin Blanco's precise words, Vasconcelos "brought new life to social Darwinism and 'redeemed' it: instead of a doctrine that justified the purity of a dominant and separate race, Vasconcelos made it herald the abolition of all races through a great cultural miscegenation" (*Ulises Criollo*, 564).[36]

Vasconcelos and these Brazilian *modernistas* coincide in one more fundamental aspect: both argue for a literature and a political system that are genuine, effective expressions of national and/or Latin American cultures and realities, derived from a proud recuperation of the colonial past but at the same time fundamentally different from contemporary European culture and reality. For Vasconcelos and Carvalho, the renewal of Latin American culture, which both ardently advocate and compare in grandiose terms to the European Renaissance, can take place after a severe criticism of the liberal ideals epitomized by Juárez's 1857 constitution in Mexico and the 1889 proclamation of the Republic in Brazil. This liberal tradition is seen as artificial, an inadequate Anglophile or Francophile copy of alien culture and values. This cultural Hispanic Renaissance should redeem that which is supposedly most genuine: Latin America's Spanish/Portuguese, Catholic (and eminently authoritarian) roots.[37]

At the heart of this new view of Latin American racial, cultural, historical, and political problems is a particular reading of Nietzschean will to power and of Bergsonian vital force.[38] While Carvalho claims "there is an intimate, inner force that determines (the history of a people), an irresistible impulse that defines its characteristics, a throbbing flame that forever illuminates it: 'the spirit of the race'" (*Pequena História da Literatura Brasileira*, 40),[39] Vasconcelos chooses "por mi raza hablará el espiritu" as UNAM's motto. For both, the vital expression of this "spirit of the race" is eminently aesthetic. This will have particular implications in *Imagens do México*.

Ronald de Carvalho's essays are unique among the Brazilian *modernistas* because they explicitly bear the mark of the foreign (Mexican) gaze in the background. *Estudos Brasileiros—1a Série* is dedicated to "José Vasconcelos, constructor do México moderno" (5) and its Mexican imprint is so strong that Manuel Bandeira—who otherwise declares to have no objections to Carvalho's ideas about the national character expressed in the book—sarcastically comments in a letter to Mário de Andrade that the book should have been called "Conferências no México" (*Correspondência*, 139).

Compared to Reyes's essays on Mexico and Brazil, in Carvalho the presence of this foreign gaze has different repercussions. Carvalho is less prone to idealizations in *Imagens do México*, calling Mexico unique in Latin America because no sizable middle class was formed during the colonial period and the "melting" [*caldeamento*] of the indigenous and the European elements only took place *after* independence through a series of violent internal conflicts, invasions, and great institutional instability until Porfirio Díaz acted as "a reactive chemical [that] endows the amalgam with consistency."[40] Porfirio

Díaz, however, ruled over a country still without a middle class, with extraordinary land concentration and miserable peasants working for a pittance until social tensions explode and Obregón's revolution arrived (16–18). In none of Carvalho's essays about Brazil is one to find the same kind of honest assessment of social injustice.

Carvalho is most enthusiastic about Mexico in aesthetic terms, seeing there the "marvelous richness of the aesthetic instinct of a race that lives in a perpetual work of art through their clothing, their movements, even their everyday utensils" (*Imagens do México*, 24).[41] When speaking about art Carvalho is closest to Reyes's prose, writing as an elegant, ingenious essayist who is also a poet. That is the main reason why *Imagens do México*, condensed in a few evocations quickly sketched, aged much better than *Estudos Brasileiros—1a Série*, which was based on historical analysis but tended to the genteel, superficial commentary.

Writing about a national and continental spirit whose primary expression is aesthetic in *Imagens do México* Carvalho relies on poetic description rather than prosaic exposition and argumentation and structures the book around impressionistic poetic recollections from his trip. For instance, when he aims to describe to his Brazilian audience what he calls the "aesthetic instinct" of Mexico, he presents two "impressions" through which he wishes to convey most effectively to the Brazilian audience this quality of Mexican character. The two sketches in this case, "A Festa de Tonalá" and "Talavera de Puebla," do not come accompanied by any historical background or anthropological commentary.

I have seen every mystery of art in its most simple and direct expression in a *Talavera* workshop in Puebla.

Leaning over the primitive potter's wheel, the *alfaro* is a transformer. As in *Genesis*, the clay is alive at his command and order then reigns over matter. Through the soft, sticky, formless clay the wise fingers run. Under the drive from the nimble foot the wheel turns and the artist, buttressed by this initial movement, creates the Universe out of chaos. Cylinders, pyramids, and spheres come to being and then disappear behind the two scoops of his hands; lines curve or stretch, elongate, break, join and, in a flash of a moment, tall-bodied vases, candelabra, jugs, and cups of exquisite shape come to being.

There sang the esthete at the wheel and in the crackling fire; there sang too the earth, the same earth that had been dust rolling under the hooves of the animals outside and now had become a pitcher to fit the fresh, lascivious mouth of the Indian woman with a fertile womb. There sang the man because he had joined the earth and there sang the earth that had come back into the hands of her maker to become a monument to perfection.

And all around me there was joy, because that man was a god. (28, 29)[42]

The making of a work of art is a dialogue of gestures that connects human beings and the earth, and the poet's observation of this dialogue is another gesture of connection, an aesthetic experience in itself as well. First impressed on the poet's senses, the artist's transient gestures now affect the reader through a recollection written with a heightened poetic sense. Although ethnic stereotypes are still part of Carvalho's worldview and are perceptible in the "fresh, lascivious mouth of the Indian woman with her fertile womb," they play a minimal role in the main argument.

This kind of impression is an aesthetic rendering of transient, unsubstantial sensations, a poetically infused snapshot (or juxtaposition of snapshots) intended to build the text as a bridge between writer and audience and a bridge between art and life. In the context of modernist literature, Jesse Matz claims this kind of impression

> is by no means any merely sensuous, superficial, or insubstantial perception. ( ... ) [It] is nothing less than a name for the aesthetic moment itself, a new sign for the old bridge between art and life. Like aesthetic experience, it pitches consciousness between sense and reason. Hardly a threat to literature's intelligence, it gives the literary mind new links to life. (*Literary Impressionism and Modernist Aesthetics*, 13)

These passages of *Imagens do México* describe scenes following individual subjective experience, fusing thought and perception by imbedding the recollection of the latter with a reflection on artistic creation as an act of communion between humans and the world.

This concept of impression is fundamental to understanding Carvalho's two other works with a strong Mexican presence. One is "Jornal dos Planaltos," section of his most famous poetry collection, *Toda a América*, and the other is "Gravuras do México," third part of *Itinerário—Antilhas, Estados Unidos, México*, a posthumous travel book that is Carvalho's best prose work. "Jornal dos Planaltos" and "Gravuras do México" constitute another diptych, poetry and prose versions of the impact of the trip to Mexico under the influence of Vasconcelos. Several scenes that feature in short, epigrammatic poems in "Jornal dos Planaltos" become succinct sketches in a measured, elegant prose in "Gravuras do México."

The section that comes before "Imagens do México" describes the United States as the land of "the plenty, the thrift, the mediocre common sense of the bills paid on time, the tranquil philosophy of the books of reason" (50).[43] The narrator crosses the border and contemplates a strikingly different environment:

> Straight ahead unfolding in a tapestry of mica, in a sea of dry scintillations plucked by motionless, hard brilliance, there stands, in all directions, the primitive desert. Not a single human relief blotches the blank page of creation. Over the swaying of desolated aloes and the short palm trees that balance themselves in one-legged profiles, the frowning blue of the sky pours down. The warm wind that runs through the moving sands does not bring a drop of moisture to our thirsty palates. Not a single filament of water resists the suction from the earth, where grass withers like scorched thin threads. (50–51)[44]

The desert landscape is described as a dramatic feast to the senses, and in its "tragic solitude" it is inhospitable to birds of short-range flight. The only sign of animal life is a shadow, "tracing a long circle in the space," which belongs not to a cloud but to "the Aztec eagle, dominating the sky" (52). The meaning of this chapter's title, "The Desert's Lesson," becomes clear after the next one, called "The Desert and the Man," in which the narrator finds the human equivalent to the eagle: a humble shepherd wearing a "red, green, and blue sarape over his shoulders" (54), living in this barren landscape with "courage, resignation and spontaneous heroism" (54). The United States is a domesticated landscape, where the heroic human tragedy has been completely replaced by the tedious bourgeois drama. The northern neighbor is the foil to the Mexican desert, the place where an indomitable, formidable nature sets the monumental stage for the solitary human drama of survival.

Before we delve into the poems of "Jornal dos Planaltos," it is worth understanding the book it comes from by forming yet another diptych, this time juxtaposing *Toda a América* with another poetry collection, Carlos Pellicer's *Piedra de Sacrificios* (1924). *Toda a América* was published in 1926 in a lavishly illustrated edition with stylized Art-Noveau-esque pre-Columbian motifs.[45] This book's dedications in the Mexican section are evidence of Carvalho's Mexican contacts and proximity to Vasconcelos. Carvalho dedicates "Jornal dos Planaltos" to the poet Carlos Pellicer (1897–1977), Vasconcelos's secretary in 1921; "Querétaro" to Diego Rivera (1886–1957), who had left Paris to work on murals under the auspices of Vasconcelos;

"Guadalajara" to another muralist, Roberto Montenegro (1887–1968), a student of Henrique Bernardelli, who also worked closely with Vasconcelos in the remodeled old colonial Colegio Máximo de San Pedro y San Pablo;[46] "Tonalá" to Carlos Obregón Santacilia (1896–1961), an architect commissioned by Vasconcelos to design the Mexican pavilion at the international fair commemorating the centennial of Brazil's independence and the Escuela Primaria Benito Juárez (1923), neocolonial buildings that mark the early career of this pioneer of modernist architecture in Mexico.[47] All of them (except Rivera) had been to Brazil in 1922 and belonged to the circle of artists and intellectuals around Vasconcelos's Ministry of Education. *Toda a América* is part of the artistic output generated under the incentive and inspiration of Vasconcelos's Ibero-Americanism, a Brazilian counterpart to Pellicer's *Piedra de Sacrificios* (1924), whose prologue was written by Vasconcelos.[48] Speaking of a "new international family" that "needs proselytes to no longer be a sect, but a People" (1,2), Vasconcelos describes *Piedra de Sacrificios* as an ode to "the continental fatherland" (5) written by a "poet of beauty" (2).[49] Assessing *Toda a América* José Peregrino Júnior uses similar terms calling it a turning point in which the Carvalho wrote "his own lyric of the Americas" with the intention of "capturing the man of the Americas in his moral, spiritual, and ethnic totality" (18).[50]

Both *Toda a América* and *Piedra de Sacrificios* feature what Peregrino Júnior called "mural poetry, at once orchestral and architectonic." The reference to the mural, a wide-angled panorama composed of smaller, fragmentary, self-sufficient scenes is felicitous beyond its reference to Mexican painting. In both books the Americas are a monumental totality made up of fragments as the two poets cross over frontiers with joyful appreciation of the continental landscape as a common territory. Discussing the avant-garde in that period, Vicky Unruh sees Latin Americans in the 1920s "seized by a 'mania for totality'" (159) but also resistant to the idea of presenting this totality as one organic, unified whole, thus claiming their continent "as an all-encompassing" territory and, at the same time, thus writing books such as *Piedra de Sacrificios* and *Toda a América*, which Unruh cites as "an outstanding example of America's flea market of images in vanguardist works" (164). The tension between synthesis and fragmentation is typical of the modernism inflected by the vocabulary of the vanguards of the 1920s that informs both books.

One significant difference is that *Toda a América* ventures further into North America, for instance, in "Broadway," a poem dedicated to Mário de Andrade that celebrates the "ground that mixes all the different dust from the universe and where all the different human rhythms of feet mingle" (50).[51] The United States fits into Carvalho's American mosaic with the energetic industrial and urban dynamism fully in tune with the eulogies to machines and industrialization popularized by Marinetti's Futurism (the most influential European avant-garde in Brazil) but has no place in Pellicer's book under the auspices of Vasconcelos, who abhorred all things Anglo-Saxon.

The broad murals of *Toda a América* and *Piedra de Sacrificios* share another fundamental characteristic: a mix of long elegiac poems in free verse with shorter, condensed, and at times fragmentary poems based on modernist impressions. Comparing these two kinds of poems elucidates the possibilities explored and limitations imposed by their formats. Pellicer's book begins with a triumphant prophetic "Oda" [Ode] to "America, America of mine!" where "one common feeling, / will found the new Democracy." Two apostrophic elegies respectively glorify the Americas where "all in you is alive and fresh in your head and in your heart" and Ruben Darío, the prophet whom Pellicer thanks, among other things, for "the splendid news of Argentine progress, / wonderful messenger of our destinies." Pellicer follows Darío in prophesizing that "our spirit shall be your masterpiece / and thus you shall be the evoking soul of the New World."[52] Carvalho opens *Toda a América* with "Advertência" [Warning], a long apostrophe directed to a generic "European" inhabitant of a fully charted landscape "that fits all in the glass globe of your garden" (13). This European, "son of obedience, economy, and common sense" (13), the poet explains, cannot truly fathom the "joys of invention, discovery, and running" (14) of the American experience in a land above which "our rough, naïve spirit" (15) hovers.[53] Both opening poems maintain an exalted tone of exhortation, using apostrophes and an anaphoric free verse that builds on cumulative repetition and parallel structure and echoes biblical and/or Whitmanesque messianic tones. Under the influence of the avant-garde, both poems resort to heterogeneous lists that traverse with great speed enormous distances in the continent, assembling collagelike lists of more-or-less disparate cultural artifacts. Here is an excerpt of one such assemblage from Pellicer's "Oda":

America, my America!
from the cries of the savages
to the antennas of radio-telegraphy.
From the jungles without tracks and the shepherd's path over the hills,
to the locomotive and the hydroplane;

from the warlords to the Republic,
everything in you is alive and real in your head and in your heart. (2)[54]

And here is another one from Ronald de Carvalho's "Advertência":

> Europeans, sons of economy and common sense,
> you don't know what it is like to be American!
> Ah, the turmoil of our blood toned by leaps and charges over
>     the pampas,
> savannas, plains, deserts where the droves stampede, the hordes of
>     stomping feet and whirling horns
> ( ... )
> in this wave of formless masses where races and languages dissolve
> our surly, guileless spirit hovers over everything
> over all divinely rough things on which the wild light of the
> American day shines! (14, 15)[55]

*Toda a América* and *Piedra de Sacrificios* have been characterized as a whole by this kind of celebratory, messianic Americanism. This is true in the long poems of *Toda a América* such as "Advertência," "Brasil," and the five poems of the last section called "Toda a América" and in their counterparts in *Piedra de Sacrificios* ("Oda," "A Germán Arciniegas, en Bogotá," "Divagación del Puerto," and "Oda a Cuauhtémoc"). These poems are moved by grandiose ambitions to reinvent the Americas by celebrating its composite origins and to create a nonorganic, overarching synthesis of the whole continent. Their rhetoric soars to proclaim the glory of these reinvented Americas, but neither Carvalho nor Pellicer dare move into less secure realms, staying within the confines of optimistic certainty in a glorious future.

However, both *Toda a América* and *Piedra de Sacrificios* contain shorter poems that abandon this celebratory style and rely on these poets' remarkable powers of observation and expression. The best poems in *Piedra de Sacrificios* are about Rio de Janeiro, which we shall discuss in the next chapter in detail. The best ones in *Toda a América* are from "Jornal dos Planaltos," nine poems and impressions of Mexico, starting in the northern frontier with Río Grande and then moving through Xochimilco, Acolman, Cholula, Puebla, Querétaro, Mexico City, and Guadalajara. "Fronteira do Rio Grande" is the poetic equivalent to "Lição do Deserto," from *Itinerário*'s "Gravuras do México":

> Boiling sands,
> Thistles.

Thistles.
Magueys.
Rocks that rise and break through the horizon.
Scintillating floor.
Watchful silences.
Men behind every silence...
Goat bells.
Flaming sarapes.
Mexico![56]

Instead of the all-encompassing, symphonic portrait of an entire continent, Ronald de Carvalho tones down and concentrates on sharp, synthetic images that promote an attack on all the senses: the heat, the bright lights, the silence, the sound of goat bells, the color of the sarapes. The sense of excitement in the moment of entering a new, different territory is palpable and summarized in the simple one-word exclamatory verse. Here Ronald de Carvalho's impressions function poetically as an epigram,[57] a genre based on *brevitas et argutia* [brevity and ingenuity], a short commentary inscribed along with the memory of the traveler, treated as an eminently aesthetic experience.

Speaking about *Piedra de Sacrificios*, Gabriel Zaid says that

[Pellicer] has the creative confidence of a founder of cities, the Christian optimism of the *Ateneo* generation, the grand flights of fancy of Vasconcelos, and the artlessness of a citizen of the world. He has eyes to see the beauty of the concrete, happiness for being alive, and humility to be natural in nature, to accept limits as joyous forms (...) His oeuvre is above all a refreshing, heartfelt, reconciled homage to happiness.[58]

This optimism and joyous celebration of the world of the senses also appear in *Toda a América*, but Carvalho displays in his concise Mexican poems a voice of a less assertive nature. Several of them conclude with an apostrophic question aimed at the reader and/or the poet himself. These are not rhetorical questions masking assertions, but propositions to be considered. This happens in four of the nine poems of "Jornal do Planalto": in "Xochimilco ou o Epigrama da Índia Exilada" ("which waters will now be able to reflect me?"), in "San Agustín Acólman" (Bell of San Agustín, / is it a bird or the metal / that speaks through your mouth?), in "Puebla de los Angeles" ("This potter who draws the *talavera* / (...) / listening to the bells without looking at the sky / paints with his eyes or with his ears?"), and finally in "Querétaro" ("Querétaro, was it El Greco or Murillo who hung you in the Mexican landscape?").[59] These questions appeal to the senses, especially to vision and sound, evidence that these poems are less concerned with Mexico as an abstract idea than with Mexico as a concrete, aesthetic, individual experience. At the conclusion of "Visión de Anáhuac" Reyes speaks of an aesthetic experience that constitutes a common ground between all peoples and civilizations that have lived in the central valley where Mexico City stands nowadays:

> Whatever the historical faith to which one subscribes (and I am not of those who dream of an absurd perpetuation of the native traditions, nor do I even put too much faith in the survival of the Spanish), we are linked to the race of yesterday, without entering into the question of blood, by a common effort to master our wild, hostile natural setting, an effort that lies at the very root of history. We are also linked by the far deeper community of the daily emotions aroused by the same natural objects. The impact of the same world on the sensibility engernders a common soul. (*Vision of Anáhuac*, 29)[60]

The best moments of *Toda a América* are those in which the poet observes attentively and registers skillfully through these ingenuous but simple epigrams the common aesthetic experience "before the same natural object" to which Reyes refers. The relationships between the artist and his work and between his work and his audience are proposed through triangulations with the world experienced aesthetically. The limits to this approximation with the Other through triangulations with the experience of a common landscape lie in the poet's capacity for empathy and in the accuracy of his or her vision. In the case of Carvalho's poetic approximation with the Mexican experience, this becomes apparent when the conservative world view that is at the forefront of his essays on national identity surface, when Carvalho attempts to explain Mexican culture as character molded by race and environment. The focus on the aesthetic appreciation of the world of the senses and on a language that is more suggestive than assertive preserve the poems of "Jornal do Planalto" in *Toda a América* and the impressions in *Imagens do México* and "Gravuras do México" from these shortcomings, allowing them to be more than just evidence of the ideology of conservative modernists.

Ronald de Carvalho made quite an impression after his trip to Mexico, and the translation of *Toda a América* to Spanish in 1930 only reinforced his prestige. In a report to the Mexican diplomatic service in 1934 Alfonso Reyes mentions Ronald de Carvalho as a poet "muy conocido en México" (*Misión Diplomática*, 334). Three years before, Reyes had been chosen to speak at Carvalho's farewell dinner (the diplomat was going to the most coveted of all posts, Paris) and exclaimed: "The poet you now send to Paris is—with all honor and right—a continental messenger!"[61] Had it not been for his untimely death at the age of 42 in a car accident in 1935, when Carvalho was at the height of his political influence as senior advisor to President Getúlio Vargas[62] and as the *Príncipe dos Prosadores Brasileiros* [Prince of the Brazilian Prose Writers] according to a popular survey,[63] the author of *Toda a América* would have played a central role in cultural affairs during Vargas's *Estado Novo*, as did other conservative *Modernistas* such as Alceu Amoroso Lima and Cassiano Ricardo, who consolidated a modern, nationalistic, conservative discourse about national identity that still impacts Brazil.

But with the revolution and the rise of Fascism in Europe, the 1930s also sharpened and clarified differences between *modernistas* of the right and of the left. When Carvalho returned from Europe, he was, in the words of his friend Amoroso Lima, "the Integral Nationalist, the apologist of a Strong State, the defender of reactionary attitudes,"[64] and the voices of dissent on the other side of political/cultural spectrum could not be muffled anymore. When the magazine *Rumo*, directed by the young Carlos Lacerda, Evandro Lins e Silva, and Moacyr Werneck de Castro, wrote a piece about Waldo Frank's visit to Brasil, they did not fail to register with a hint of sarcasm a symptomatic scene: Carvalho offered Frank "a copy of *Toda a América*'s Italian translation with a preface by Mussolini,"[65] which the American author politely refused.

In *Itinerário de uma Falsa Vanguarda*, Antonio Arnoni Prado dismisses both *Itinerário de uma Viagem* and *Toda a América*, which he calls *ufanista* (261). I think this judgment reflects a fundamental misunderstanding about the meaning of modernism and the avant-garde that pervades this otherwise thoroughly researched and highly informative book: the idea that political conservatism and the literary vanguard are incompatible, and that those who jumped on the *modernista* bandwagon but sustained a conservative critical stance were "falsas vanguardas" [false avant-garde] (22). Neither the avant-garde nor other modernisms are necessarily progressive or conservative. In T. S. Eliot they were elitist and traditionalist; in Marinetti, iconoclastic and belligerently authoritarian; in Ezra Pound, fascist and normative; in Brecht, socialist and conceived as combative rhetoric; in Breton, a libertarian fusion of Freud and Marx; in Lorca, republican and full of passion for popular culture; in Borges, liberal and cosmopolitan. As André Botelho emphasizes at the conclusion of *O Brasil e os Dias,* the merits and shortcomings of Ronald de Carvalho are more typical than exceptional within Brazilian modernism as a whole.

This is not to say, of course, that the aesthetic and the ideological dimensions are not intimately related. The ideological dimension informs the final relationship between the text and the world it depicts or interprets, which is one of the three fundamental aspects of textual productions. As Pellicer,[66] Carvalho thrives in the vivid depiction of nature with exquisite formal economy, endowing what he observed and described with a sense of dramatic uniqueness. In these moments Carvalho's poetic voice gains depth and manages to go beyond the elegiac primitivism and conservative elitism that dominate most of his writings. *Imagens do México* and "Gravuras do México" are, in general, better than Carvalho's essays on Brazil because Carvalho benefits from the position of the traveler forced to focus on the sensorial surface of the world he sees. The Mexican poems in *Toda a América,* as well those moments in which he did not feel the need to be the interpreter of the national or continental spirit, are the best part of Carvalho's work.

# Chapter 3

# Alfonso Reyes: Brazil and Mexico in a Nutshell

Almost ten years after Vasconcelos, Alfonso Reyes arrived in Rio de Janeiro as the Mexican ambassador. Reyes lived in Rio until 1936 and participated intensely in the city's intellectual life. The diplomat cultivated the friendship of intellectuals of all kinds, from Alceu Amoroso Lima and Gilberto Freyre to Carlos Lacerda and Graça Aranha. Cândido Portinari illustrated for him, and Cecília Meireles counted on Reyes for material on Mexican education policies during the debates around the Escola Nova. Reyes was so integrated into the city's cultural life that he was the only foreigner at the celebration of Manuel Bandeira's 50th birthday[1] and one of Bandeira's best-known poems, "Rondó dos Cavalinhos,"[2] describes Reyes's farewell banquet at the Jockey Club: "Alfonso Reyes leaving, / And so many people staying..." (*Libertinagem*, 85).[3]

Alfonso Reyes was also quite prolific in Rio de Janeiro: he wrote 13 of the 14 issues of *Monterrey—Correo Literário*, his one-man literary journal;[4] some of his best short stories; an exquisite book of poems entirely dedicated to Rio de Janeiro (*Romances de Río de Enero*); a collection of short essays called *Historia Natural das Laranjeiras* (illustrated by Reyes himself); and several pieces for newspapers and magazines such as Augusto Frederico Schmidt's *Literatura*, later incorporated into *Obras Completas*.[5] Besides the cactus garden surrounding Vasconcelos's Cuauhtémoc in Flamengo, Reyes left his mark on the urban landscape of Rio de Janeiro in the form a more modest and personal gift to his beloved Jardim Botânico: a small statue of Xochipilli, the Aztec spring god of flowers.[6]

Beyond interesting anecdotes and their traces in Rio de Janeiro,[7] there remains the challenge of reading with contemporary eyes what these Mexican intellectuals wrote about or in Brazil and what these texts reveal about the particular gaze of a foreigner who is also a fellow Latin American. Here I focus on two essays written by Reyes: "México en una Nuez," written in Brazil in 1930, and "Brasil en una Castaña," published 12 years later, in 1942. The titles point to a relationship between the two essays that appeared together in Reyes's *Obras Completas* in 1959, but "México en una Nuez" and "Brasil en una Castaña" also share something less obvious. These two essays were conceived as bridges between different nationalities within Latin America: Reyes read "Mexico en una Nuez" in the Teatro Rivadavia in Buenos Aires during a festival for the Amigos de la República Española in 1937[8] and "Brasil en una Castaña" was first published in *El Nacional*, the Mexican government's quasi-official newspaper in 1942.[9]

"México en una Nuez" and "Brasil en una Castaña" are part of what Reyes called elsewhere the creation of a "Gramática comparada entre las naciones" ("Palabras sobre la Nación Argentina," 28), a project with two articulated aims: "we have just started to compare ourselves, one with the other and, ( ... ) from a similar comparison will be born a more precise knowledge of our own national being" (28).[10] To propose that people get to know each other in order to know themselves better was Reyes's way of defending cultural cosmopolitanism as a form of nationalism. Comparative texts with the national character in view, "México en una Nuez" and "Brasil en una Castaña" are thus also an interesting part of a greater corpus of texts written by Latin American intellectuals mainly in the first half of the twentieth century, their defining trait a consistent exploration of the national identity.

In *El ensayo mexicano moderno*, José Luis Martínez defines modern Mexican essayists by their focus on "their history, their culture, their economic and social problems, their literary and artistic creations, their past and their present" (Martínez, 17),[11] which is a common trait of Brazilian essays of the period as well. These texts are intellectual exercises at national reinvention through self-examination that helped forge renewed identities for these Latin American countries as they grew to become more modern, industrialized nations. This redefinition of national identity generally tries to distance itself from the ethnocentric pessimism of the previous generation, for whom "all that was worthwhile came from abroad and all the autochthonous, be it native or *criollo*, was supposed to be backward" (Brading, 9),[12] but otherwise vary greatly in terms of style, approach, and ideology.

In Brazil several writers, many somehow connected to the *modernistas* of 1922, published such essays. Among these there are some who, as their Mexican counterparts, are still influential because even though their approaches or ideas might have been at least partially contested, much of the current national imaginary and identity is still indebted to these books. Gilberto Freyre's *Casa-Grande e Senzala* (1933), Sérgio Buarque de Holanda's *Raízes do Brasil* (1936), and Caio Prado Jr.'s *Formação do Brasil Contemporáneo* (1942) are classics in this sense but also hallmarks of national historiography with foundations in scholarly research. In México the same could be said about Reyes's "Visión de Anáhuac" (1920), Vasconcelos's preface to *La raza cósmica* (1925), Samuel Ramos's *El perfil del hombre y de la cultura en México* (1934), and Octavio Paz's *El laberinto de la soledad* (1949).

Alfonso Reyes's exquisite style always couples verbal ingenuity with uncompromising clarity of expression. A relaxed, conversational tone infuses Reyes's erudition and formal inventiveness with unpretentious readability. This constant effort toward clarity has been described as Reyes's ideal of social commitment: a writer's unfailing disposition for dialogue with the reader as a foundation for literary democracy, a sort of "anti-authoritarianism in form" (Monsiváis, 49).[13] Another important aspect of Reyes's epistemology is that, although he draws from different fields of knowledge (history, geography, philosophy, anthropology, etc), his approach is in his own words *ultimately* literary: "each of us has our own window onto the world. Mine is literature" (*IX*, 29).[14] Accordingly, Reyes's arguments almost invariably center on images at once didactic and aesthetic,[15] from which the main ideas spring by parallel analogy as the images are at once interpreted and evoked. As Reyes himself explained,

> Historical synthesis is the greatest challenge to literary technique. One word alone substitutes for a digressive paragraph; the tinges of certitude (...) establish scientific probity; the artistic solution communicates by intuition what knowledge could only encompass through long circumlocutions. (*México*, 184)[16]

Reyes was a self-proclaimed classicist dedicated to a modern reinterpretation of classical culture, so these argumentative images are often derived from the Greeks or Romans.[17] The reliance on evocative and illuminating images is prominent in short pieces such as "Mexico en una Nuez" and "Brasil en una Castaña," which, as their names indicate, try to encapsulate in a few pages the essential features of national character.

Another important trait of Reyes is his determination not to take sides in prominent ideological debates of his time. This has been interpreted as a sign of Reyes's omission or simply a lack of interest in politics. In "Un hombre de Letras," Mario Vargas Llosa writes about Reyes with evident impatience for a public intellectual who seemed to be always in tune with the powers that be in Mexico, a man very much unlike Vargas Llosa himself, always combative and vocal in the defense of his beliefs. In his alignment with the government, the founder of El Colegio de México is far from being an exception in Mexico or in Latin America. Furthermore, Reyes did get engaged, albeit perhaps against his will, in a debate with nationalists such as Héctor Pérez Martínez, who questioned Reyes's "evidente desvinculación de México" in the 1930s. In that case Reyes does not question nationalism as an ideology, but claims that his cosmopolitanism is the best way to serve México as a nation—an argument that surfaces, as we have seen, in justifying inter-American studies.[18]

Alfonso Reyes was a classic liberal whose emphasis was never placed on the explicitly political. Described by some as the last *modernista*,[19] his beliefs include an idealistic notion of true knowledge. Free from flattering insincerity or rigid dogma as well as from strict subjection to political ends, such knowledge could dismantle all stereotypes and demagogic, melodramatic mystification. In practice this idealist view of knowledge as inherently neutral led Reyes to a sort of chronic intellectual equanimity, always attempting a strained synthesis between two opposing lines of thought: between cosmopolitanism and nationalism or between political engagement and the supremacy of the aesthetic.

The opening of "México en una Nuez" is exemplary of Reyes's reliance on the illuminating image: the encounter of American peoples and the Spaniards that marks the birth of Mexico is described as "the clash of the jug against the cauldron. The jug could be very fine and very beautiful, but it was also more brittle" (42)[20]. Ever the classicist and the diplomat, Reyes evokes the *Iliad* to interpret the Conquest simultaneously as a tragedy (for the indigenous population) and an epic (for Spain and the Church). The American peoples, endowed with an astonishing artistic sensibility, are doomed to defeat by their military frailty; the Spaniards, with an endless capacity for intrigue and deceit, are able to accomplish the extraordinary feat of conquering populations and territories several times larger than theirs. This tragic epic simultaneity enables Alfonso Reyes to refrain from embracing either of the opposing views of the conquest. Reyes sides neither with the *Hispanistas* who defended the Spanish colonial heritage as central to modern Mexico, nor with the *Nativistas* who defended the centrality of indigenous cultures in the establishment of a free, independent culture. Reyes repeats in "Mexico en una Nuez" a key maneuver from his most famous essay, "Visión de Anáhuac," evoking the shared experience of living on the high plains of Anáhuac, "crude basis of history,"[21] as that which unites indigenous and Spaniards' descendants in present-day Mexico. Affirming "I am not one of those who dream of absurd perpetuations of indigenous traditions and do not expect too much of the perpetuation of the Spanish ones" ("Visión de Anáhuac," 101),[22] Reyes defends the need to establish meaningful contemporary interpretations of national history that transcend such oppositions to build a national identity that accommodates both major strains.

Another evocative image, this time a humorous one, opens "Brasil en una Castaña": Reyes accounts for the magnitude of the country's natural landscape as the result of the work of a "demiurge or intermediary agent in charge of the works," a young artist who "used too much material and had the strength of inexperience" (187).[23] Again the image is derived from the classics (this time from Hesiod), but it is neither tragic nor epic. The underlying assumption here is the centrality of nature for the construction of an idealistic view of Brazil. That becomes clearer when Reyes claims that when such creative exuberance was applied to the making of the inhabitants of this country of superlatives, it originated "el diplomático nato, y el mejor negociador que ha conocido la historia humana" (188), enabling Brazilians to "desahacer, sin cortarlo, el Nudo Gordiano [untying without cutting the Gordian Knot]." Without quoting *La Raza Cósmica*, Reyes implies that Brazilians are indeed some kind of "Cosmic Race," albeit less grandiose and certainly less bellicose than Vasconcelos's messianic "new Romans."

A similar contrast between Mexico and Brazil appears when Reyes writes about the indigenous populations in the two essays. Whereas the pre-Columbian Aztecs are fierce oppressors of the other proud peoples of the central valley, the Brazilian Indians live in a perfect symbiosis with the luxuriant environment, inspiring Rousseau's "buenos salvajes" and having their poetry translated by Montaigne and Goethe.[24] Reyes implies that in Brazil the colonization shifted the land and its inhabitants from the realm of geography to that of history: the Portuguese disrupted this symbiosis between the Indians and their environment and, by accelerating changes in the ecology, turned Brazil into a subject matter for historians.

Contrasts between geography and history appear both in "Mexico en una nuez" and in "Brasil en una castaña" and center explicitly on the idea that "history is much faster than geography" (51)[25] and, implicitly, on the traditional view that culture is inherently Western and that the American peoples belong to the realm of the natural. But even after the arrival of the Portuguese and Independence, history in Brazil still moves with the "solid and slow pace of geological erosions" (188), in a stately *natural* rhythm that contrasts sharply with the "coleric and somehow improvised comings and goings that mark the transitions between phases in the other Latin American nations" (188).[26] For Reyes, the explanation for this comparative instability in Spanish Latin America is that the liberal republics implanted after Independence were artificial, that is, not natural regimes, which demanded political maturity from nations yet in their first infancy. For Reyes the gigantic dimensions of Brazil, its primary characteristic as established dramatically in the opening of "Brasil en una Castaña," *naturally* demand slow, smooth historical transitions from its people. The establishment of a monarchy after Independence is an example of one of the smooth transitions that supposedly gave Portuguese America time for political maturity before the arrival of the republic.

Again a vivid image clarifies Reyes's interpretation of Brazilian historical changes: "history is the stone that falls into the sleeping lake" (189).[27] The contrast is clear. In Mexico the cauldron and the fragile jar collide; in Brazil the stone plunges into the still lake: two striking images describe two types of encounters between Europeans and Americans in the New World. The first is an encounter between man-made artifacts, whereas the second involves natural elements. Both evoke the collision between something hard and something soft with inexorable outcomes, but the indigenous element in Mexico resists the shock and therefore breaks, whereas its Brazilian counterpart accepts it and thus incorporates the arriving Europeans. In Brazil "this intrusion [of the stone into the water, of the Portuguese into the continent] is not necessarily violent" (189)[28]: the water ultimately engulfs the stone and the scenery reacquires a stately calm.

Moving into the colonial period, geography and history continues to guide Reyes's parallels between Mexico and Brazil: the history of Brazil is primarily the history of man's struggle against a bountiful but indomitable nature, whereas in Mexico colonization takes place between "cruel realities" ("the distribution of land") and "bloody euphemisms" ("the entrusting of the indigenous souls") (44). Whereas Brazilian history is a succession of economic cycles related to the exploitation of natural sources (*Pau-Brasil*, sugarcane, gold, coffee, rubber, cotton, etc.), Mexican history is politics as a great tragedy of blood, from the conflicts between the Crown, the colonizers, the Church, and indigenous people during colonial times, to the bloody wars between *caudillos*, liberals, and conservatives, to

the long slumber of the Porfiriato peace, until the painful reawak-
ening of the Mexican Revolution. Commenting on the vicissitudes
of Mexican history, Reyes solemnly declares that "History's majesty
does not always accommodate easy solutions for great conflicts" (45),
and that this history of violent conflict gives Mexico its identity: "the
face of the new people is carved with knife strikes" (49).[29]

An eloquent defense of the Mexican Revolution closes "Mexico
en una Nuez"—an oratorical piece directed at an Argentine public suspicious of the radical changes and the instability in Mexico.
The Mexican Revolution put an end to years of self-denial in which
Mexico's Hispanic and indigenous heritages and cultures were a source
of embarrassment to the fantasy of a peaceful francophone republic
under Porfirio Díaz's iron fist; a moment of self-discovery, a chance
to realize the country's true potential and recover the treasures of its
past, Spanish and indigenous alike. Reyes's "México en una Nuez"
is a proud and reassuring defense of the Mexican Revolution, when
so-called excesses of the revolution, especially in terms of land reform
and laicization, were seen with suspicion by other governments in
Latin America:

> Some have pitied us with certain commiseration. The time has come
> for us to pity them. Woe to those who have yet to dare to discover
> themselves, for they still ignore the pains of this enlightenment! But
> know this—the scripture says—that only those willing to risk it all will
> save themselves. (56)[30]

Oratorical eloquence also closes "Brasil en una Castaña," but in
an enthusiastic panegyric to a nation of dazzling beauty and never-
ending generosity and happiness:

> And of all that results a beautiful and great nation that has never lost
> its smile nor its generosity amidst suffering, exemplary at once of
> courage and prudence, pride of the human race, promise of happiness
> in the sour days we live, fantastic spectacle of humanity and nature,
> whose contemplation obliges one to repeat after Achilles Tatius: "We
> are beaten, my eyes!" (195)[31]

Achilles Tatius is the author of the Greek "novel" *Leucippe and
Clitophon* in 2 A.D., and in the passage above Clitophon expresses
his wonder at the sight of Alexandria, a natural wonder as well as a
remarkable spectacle of the Hellenistic civilization.[32]

In a nutshell, for Reyes there are two European nuts within
American soil: the walnut (Mexico) is dry, wrinkled, hard, and bitter;

the sweet chestnut (Brazil) is moist, smooth, soft, and mild. In between the two essays, in a poem written in 1932 called "El Ruido y el Eco," nuts reappear in a contrast between the two nations:

> *While here coconuts from Alagoas*
> *Are embroidered in lace, there*
> *The nuts from San Juan de Ulúa*
> *Are carved with daggers.*[33]

The stanza shows the masterly use of a succinct and many-layered symbol, taking advantage of the multiple meanings of *labrar* (to carve but also to embroider) and *calar* (to pierce but also to hemstitch). The contrast here is between two different forms of craft with the same material, the coconut. From Brazil comes the delicate embroidery made with coconut fiber from the northeastern state of Alagoas—traditionally the domestic work of women. From Mexico come the elaborate carvings on the coconut turned into a cup or a coin bank—a work that demands great physical strength due to the hardness of the shell and was associated with the inmates of the notorious "Mexican Alcatraz" of San Juan de Ulúa, a fortress built by the Spaniards in 1528 in Veracruz, with a long and painful history.[34] For Reyes, Brazil and Mexico are examples of the Latin American capacity to rearticulate aesthetically European and non-European cultures, but Brazil is the country of the *en encaje*, the gentle face of a tropical, lush Latin America and Mexico, the country *con el puñal*, the somber face of our troubled, bloody history.

One could explain this idealization of Brazil with Reyes's biography. When he arrived in Rio de Janeiro, Reyes had been living abroad for 17 years. In 1913 his father, Bernardo Reyes (one of the most prominent generals of the Porfiriato) was gunned down in front of the Palacio Nacional in a failed attempt to overthrow the government. Soon afterward another general of the Porfiriato, Victoriano Huerta, succeeded at a counterrevolutionary coup d'état, but when Reyes refused an invitation to be the Huerta's secretary, he was advised not to stay in the country. Reyes left Mexico and entered the diplomatic service to escape the country's turmoil, but those were not tranquil years: he left Paris during World War I, went through financial hardship in Spain, and encountered a belligerent mindset in Argentina's intellectual circles and more political instability during Yrigoyen's second presidential term. Arriving in Brazil six months before the 1930 revolution, Reyes was deeply impressed by Getúlio Vargas's capacity for building a broad coalition out of left- and right-wing *tenentes*, the military, dissenting oligarchs, conservative Catholics, unions placed under the wing of the state bureaucracy, etc. Vargas's deft maneuvers from left to right, seducing former enemies and ostracizing old allies with a great sense of timing, were followed closely by the ambassador and contrasted sharply in his mind with years of violent instability of a revolution that, in Reyes's words, "took ten years looking for itself" (55).[35]

However, beyond Reyes's traumas and his admiration for Vargas and the apparently affable Brazilians, we should not underestimate how much "Brasil en una Castaña" reflects views that had wider acceptance in Brazilian intellectual circles at the time as well. Unlike José Vasconcelos, who, after a brief visit, fantasized about the Brazil of Epitácio Pessoa as a benevolent dynamo on its way to challenge Anglo-Saxon supremacy on the continent, Reyes was an avid reader and a thorough researcher who had great curiosity and cultivated relationships with important Brazilian intellectuals. An eloquent demonstration of Reyes's knowledge of Brazilian affairs at the time is the 600-plus pages of the second volume of *Misión Diplomática*, a recent compilation of diplomatic briefs from 1930 to 1936.

Such was the involvement with Brazilian intellectual circles that Reyes's *Monterrey—Correo Literario* contains the first reference to an idea discussed in Brazil to this day. The *Homem Cordial* appeared in a letter from the modernist Rui Ribeiro Couto entitled "El Hombre Cordial, Producto Americano" and published in the eighth issue of Reyes's journal. At the heart of Ribeiro Couto's argument is the idealization of a gentle colonization, an adventure in a welcoming, fertile land, an adventure "alimentada pelas redes nupciaes de indias bravias e pela sensualidade dócil de negras faceis":

> European selfishness, battered by religious persecution and economic catastrophe, changed by intolerance and hunger, crossed the seas and founded here, in the beds of primitive women and in all the vast generosity of the land, the Family of Cordial Men, who are set apart from the rest of humanity by two traits: the spirit of hospitality and the tendency to believe. In one term: the Cordial Man. (3)[36]

Ribeiro Couto claims this *Homem Cordial* as the symbolic middle ground between what he calls the primitivism of *indianismo* and the classicism of *hispanismo* in Latin America, a synthesis not unlike the one favored by Reyes himself. At the core of what is framed as a magnanimous synthesis between Western and non-Western aspects of Latin American culture lies an idealization of colonization as a romance (a presence in the imagination of the Brazilian elite since the *Caramuru* and José de Alencar's historical novels) with markedly patriarchal roles assigned to the colonizer (male) and its indigenous or slave counterpart (female) that functions as a double for the fertile native soil.[37] While Reyes assigns this narrative specifically to Brazil, Ribeiro Couto claims this *Civilização Cordial* was the greatest contribution of Latin America to the civilized world, then enveloped in the turmoil that would result in World War II. This new civilization is the result of a process that turned the European colonizer's selfishness and skepticism into the Latin American hospitality and the credulity of the *Homem Cordial*.

In accordance with Ribeiro Couto but restricting it to Brazil, Alfonso Reyes uses the term *cordialidade* in "Brasil en una Castaña" as a benign trace of Brazilian identity. The concept has had a myriad of uses but is known primarily as a key term in Sérgio Buarque de Holanda's 1936 classic *Raízes do Brasil*. Buarque de Holanda, who dutifully points to Ribeiro Couto's letter to Reyes as the source for the "expressão feliz" [fortunate expression] (146), offers a much less enthusiastic view of the colonization and, consequently, of the *Homem Cordial*. The negative aspects of the concept might not have been evident at first, but the author strives to be more explicit in a second edition of *Raízes do Brasil* in 1947 saying, "se eliminam aqui, deliberadamente, os juízos éticos e as intenções apologéticas" [one eliminates here, deliberately, ethical judgments and apologetic intentions].[38] A third edition of *Raízes do Brasil* in 1956 includes an essay by one of the main intellectual forces behind the dictatorship of the Estado Novo, the right-wing modernist Cassiano Ricardo,[39] the source of the "ethical judgments and apologetic intentions" to which Buarque de Holanda refers in the second edition. Ricardo exemplifies the discomfort of the right with Buarque de Holanda's use of *cordialidade* with such dissonant views of the history and character of Brazil: "Sérgio altered, he adulterated our cordial man" (293).[40] Sérgio Buarque de Holanda's curt reply restates his different view of the matter and proclaims: "I think we would never reach a perfect agreement about some of these aspects and I see no point in getting down to every detail in your response" (311).[41]

Here we see progressives and conservatives battling for a definition of *cordialidade*.[42] The status of *Raízes do Brasil* as a classic and the elimination of Cassiano Ricardo's letter in its following editions seem to attest to the victory of the progressives in this matter.[43] Nevertheless conservatives continued to use the term *cordialidade* to define Brazil's national character, drawing on the original appearance

of the term in *Monterrey* in order to complain against "foreign" ide-
ologies that "offended" Brazilians' inherent desire for a peaceful
social order. Ricardo's letter became an extended essay, "O Homem
Cordial" (Ricardo, 7–46) and the centerpiece of a 1959 collection
of articles. Reyes—together with Sérgio Buarque de Holanda—gets
cited in an influential newspaper column in support of a concurring
argument about the country's "social and political traditions" at an
important historical crossroads in Brazil:

> This cordiality, which Alfonso Reyes attributed to Latin America as a
> whole and Sérgio Buarque de Holanda considers typically Brazilian,
> does not seem to be the sign of a bad character. Or of lack of character.
> It is the sign of an eminently human character, lyrical, understanding,
> rational, which prefers alignments rather than oppositions as the rule
> in our native psychology and consequently our political history. To
> show that real blood runs in the veins of our people we have had our
> own crude fights and civil wars that lasted more than a decade, such as
> the Farrapos, bloody campaigns such as Canudos, violent repressions
> such as the ones during colonial times. But they are the exceptions
> that confirm the rule. If there is something we should cultivate in
> our national character and preserve in our history as typical of our
> Brazilian Humanism, it is precisely this inate tendency to search for
> peaceful solutions to our gravest political crises. Even with the tanks
> out in the streets...it is the landmark of our people, of our history of
> our civilization. Let us cultivate it with care. And March 30 has con-
> firmed this once again. (222)[44]

The newspaper was the *Jornal do Brasil* at its apex[45] and the author of
the passage above was Alceu Amoroso Lima, a.k.a. Tristão de Athayde,
"o grande crítico do modernismo" (Barbosa, 9). The text appeared a
few days after president João Goulart was overthrown and the military coup d'état, referred to in the passage above as "the March 30th"
is, for Amoroso Lima, a confirmation "with tanks on the streets" of
Brazil's inherent tendency to seek peaceful, conciliatory solutions.

The conservative credentials of Amoroso Lima were indisputable,[46] although he eventually transitioned from the rabid anticommunist conservatism of the 1930s[47] to one of the mainstream voices
denouncing the authoritarianism and brutality of the military regime
that remained in power for 20 years. This gradual change hinged on
Amoroso Lima's stance as a Catholic intellectual: a point of inflection in his opinions were the changes in the Catholic Church with
Pope John XXIII 1962 Second Vatican Council. When the military
regime hardened, the civil opposition prized Amoroso Lima's support

precisely because of his conservatism, which placed him above suspicion and immune to the accusation of spreading communist propaganda. In 1964, however, Amoroso Lima still agreed with Cassiano Ricardo, who claimed that "all revolutions in Brazil end up in an agreement, and the harshest punishment to our political crimes has never been more than temporary exile" (Ricardo, 41).[48]

In 1960 Alceu Amoroso Lima wrote an affectionate portrait of Reyes, "Homem de Proa," recalling their friendship in Rio de Janeiro since their first meeting in the midst of Vargas's ascension to power. Ironically it is Reyes who captivates the young Brazilian with his diplomatic tact and gentleness, offering asylum to figures of the First Republic and showing a vivid interest in Amoroso Lima's conversion to Catholicism.[49] For Amoroso Lima, Reyes was Latin America's greatest humanist who "know how to analize, penetratingly, the Latin American spirit when he for instance affirmed that we were the typical expression of the *homo cordialis*" (147).[50] In the early 1930s, the Mexican diplomat portrayed Alceu Amoroso Lima as "el maestro definidor de las derechas juveniles" (*Mission Diplomática*, 122). The compliments to Amoroso Lima's intelligence and articulation are tempered by someone who knows that the right-wing youth in Brazil "invariably tends toward a strict doctrine of Catholic authoritarian nationalism": "De trato insinuante y algo sinuoso, tiene el valor de quien se siente apoyado por las clases pudientes, por la Iglesia y por cierta sorda inercia nacional."

*    *    *

At the advent of the twentieth century, a growing number of Brazilians and Mexicans felt uneasy with the limitations, not only of the tenets of positivism and naturalism, but also (and perhaps most decisively) with classical liberalism in its Latin American mold. The epistemological, aesthetic, and political challenges to this status quo by intellectuals and artists gained decisive symbolic leverage with the occurrence of acute political crises in the two countries, but these crises are set ten years apart from each other and they differ in rhythm. In Mexico the crisis precipitates full-speed with the fall of Porfirio Díaz in 1911 and only acquires a certain stability in the 1930s. In Brazil the crisis flares up during the election campaign of Arthur Bernardes in 1922, but the cultural and political establishments manage somehow to contain the confrontation, which slowly builds up to explode with the end of the First Republic and the turbulent 1930s. The *Porfiriato* and the First Republic were identified at least symbolically with Positivism's cultural hegemony[51] and the debacle of these regimes changed the ideas and the careers of intellectuals and artists who would play a prominent role in Mexican and Brazilian cultures in the following decades.

This gap of about ten years between the two "centennial generations"—1911 in Mexico and 1922 in Brazil—explains, to a certain extent, the more prominent role of the avant-garde among Brazilian intellectuals and artists.[52] The *Ateneístas* Reyes and Vasconcelos played in Mexican letters the galvanizing role of younger *modernistas* such as Mário de Andrade, Lúcio Costa, and Gustavo Capanema in Brazil. Vasconcelos founded the UNAM and gave the university its motto ("por mi raza hablará el espiritu") but is ostracized from power in the 1930s, whereas in 1940 Reyes founded and presided over the El Colegio de México, a think-tank sponsored by the federal government, the Banco de México, Universidad Nacional Autónoma de México (UNAM), and the Fondo de Cultura Económica.[53] These are arguably still the main academic and cultural institutions in modern Mexico.

It should be no surprise then that Mexicans see the refutation of late-nineteenth-century aesthetics in Enrique González Martínez's "Tuércele el Cuello al Cisne"—a fairly conventional sonnet—whereas the same refutation in Brazil is identified with the *Semana de Arte Moderna*. Were Brazilians ironically compensating for "slow, gradual, and cautious" political change with fiery radical literary rhetoric? Was Mexico's legendary classicism, its attachment to the introspective "épica en surdina," a form of self-preservation during years of violent revolutionary turmoil? Instead of thinking of mutually exclusive exceptionalisms, we should take these historical accounts and their emphases either on continuities or ruptures with a grain of salt. We should think in broader terms, differentiating between "Modernismo," in Portuguese, with a capital "M" (a specific set of avant-garde movements from 1920s) and *modernism*, in English, with small "m" as something that includes but reaches beyond the avant-garde. The literary and cultural histories of Brazil and Mexico in the first half of the twentieth century can be seen then as two slightly diverging paths on the spread and development of modernism in Latin America, over a period from the end of the nineteenth century to the 1950s.

The uneasy feeling about positivism and naturalism and about Brazilian liberalism predated 1922, and writers such as Lima Barreto and Monteiro Lobato should not dwell in an indistinct limbo called *pré-Modernismo* as much as writers such as Graciliano Ramos and Guimarães Rosa, who felt a deep aversion to the aesthetics of the

*Modernismo* of the 1920s, should not be thought of as "second and third generation" *Modernistas*. In Mexico neither the *Generación del Centenario* represented such a radical rupture with prerevolutionary positivism and/or *modernismo* (the term here is used in its Hispanic meaning), nor the following generations in Mexican literary circles simply accepted the guidance and continued the work of the *Ateneístas*. Somewhere in between the excessive emphasis on the continuities between generations in México and the myth of 1922 as a complete rupture with an utterly obsolete past lies a more accurate view of the period, one that sees the history of the first half of the twentieth century in Mexico and in Brazil in its variety and complexity. Beyond differences and specificities, Mexico and Brazil have a lot in common.

Reyes cannot be placed upon the long line of conservative thinkers of Brazil or Latin America. Reyes, mostly uninvolved with politics, never expressed faith in authoritarian solutions such as the ones Amoroso Lima and Ricardo proposed over and over since the 1930s. Reyes's views of Brazil, as Stefan Zweig's in his *Brasil, País do Futuro*, are overly optimistic but unrealistic as were Vasconcelo's. "México en una nuez" and "Brasil en una castaña" are stylistic gems in which Reyes captures in a "nutshell" two aspects of Latin American identity. One Latin America is acutely aware, though not necessarily pessimistic, of the continent's violent history and difficult relationship with its European models. The other Latin America is proud and confident, perhaps overly so at times, in the future of a new, exciting culture, imagined as a felicitous synthesis of several racial and cultural strains in a fertile, tropical melting pot.

In Brazil, the process that started with the coup d'état in April 1964 and culminated with the AI-5 in December 1968 marked the end of illusions about the possibility of a peaceful resolution of the contradictions exacerbated by the modernization of Latin America, with rapid industrialization, urbanization, and the Cold War. In Mexico the massacre of civilians in Tlatelolco in October 1968 marked the end of the illusions about the perpetual continuation of the Mexican Revolution embodied by the Partido Revolucionario Institucional (PRI) as a progressive and constructive force guiding the modernization of Mexico with its nationalist rhetoric. In Brazil the following years, *Os Anos de Chumbo* [The Leaden Years in opposition to the Golden Age], would see the creation of a powerful modern repressive apparatus that included systematic torture and murder and bore no trace whatsoever of the *cordialidade* Amoroso Lima had hoped for the military regime. In Mexico the nationalist and progressive official rhetoric contrasted more and more with the encroachment of US interests and the repressive paramilitary apparatus of the *Halcones*— the title of a famous essay, "Atento Aviso: el que Haya Encontrado la Revolución Mexicana, Favor de Devolverla" [Serious Warning: if you found the Mexican revolution, please, give it back to us] (Aguilar Camin, 5), summarizes the spirit of disillusionment. In *La jaula de la melancolía*, Roger Bartra signals Tlatelolco (which almost coincides with the AI-5 in Brazil) as the end of a period, "for the obvious impossibility of explaining the tragic circumstances of 1968 through the myth of 'the Mexican'" (Bartra, 21).[54] There and then, both the myth of the gentle, natural-born diplomat in "Brasil en una Castaña" and that of the redeeming revolution that finally brought a country to confront and recognize itself in "Mexico en una Nuez" suddenly looked ancient and insufficient.[55]

# Chapter 4

# When Mexican Poets Come to Rio de Janeiro

The Brazilian poems of Carlos Pellicer and the Mexican poems of Ronald de Carvalho marked the beginning of a more sustained tradition of travel literature within Latin America. In these cases Latin Americans took advantage of an increase in contacts through the establishments of embassies and consulates and initiatives of cultural diplomacy to establish an important, if overlooked, line of contact between them. It only helped that several important Latin Americans worked in diplomacy and the consummate example of the multiple possibilities of such a situation is Alfonso Reyes's large literary output in Brazil, ranging from essays such as "Mexico en una nuez" to some of his best poems and short stories and even the detailed, shrewd political analyses in his diplomatic reports.[1] This production is considered eccentric only because it does not take place in Paris, the quintessential meeting place for Latin Americans in the knowledge or at least curious about cultures or languages relegated to the margins of the so-called World Republic of Letters.

There have been signs of increased contacts between the youngest generation of Brazilian and Spanish American poets,[2] but both sides still have much to learn and discover about the poetic traditions of the other. The main obstacle to a broader interchange beyond the contemporary production is that these traditions are only accessible to those willing to break the rules of what I call the international literary customs, a system of cultural flow based on an unacknowledged and pervasive surrender of the prerogative of choice concerning what gets to cross language and national boundaries. On both sides of the linguistic divide, translators, publishers, readers, and critics still translate, publish, read, and discuss little besides that which received the stamp of approval from the European and North American publishing and academic literary centers. This is true even with poetry, a literary form long ostracized in mainstream publishing. Latin American poetic circles only display openness to literatures other than those considered hegemonic to the extent that these literatures manage to secure approval in the cultural metropolises of the developed world. Their choices reproduce interests and affinities originating elsewhere. There is ample access to Fernando Pessoa and Pablo Neruda, but poets of the caliber of Ramón López Velarde, José Gorostiza, João da Cruz e Souza, and Carlos Drummond de Andrade are still largely ignored outside their native countries.

This chapter was originally conceived[3] as a modest but deliberate act of cultural smuggling: an introduction to Portuguese-speaking circles of important twentieth-century Mexican poets. Instead of an introductory canon of Mexican poetry with a survey full of vague definitions of phases and trends and dozens of names and dates, I chose to focus on eight different poets who happened to write interesting pieces whose setting was Rio de Janeiro. Alfonso Reyes (1889–1959), Carlos Pellicer (1899–1977), Luis Quintanilla (1900–1980), Jaime García Terrés (1924–1996), Gabriel Zaid (1934–), Hugo Gutiérrez Vega (1934–), Francisco Cervantes (1938–2005), and José Emilio Pacheco (1939–) are representative of twentieth-century Mexican poetry. Some lived in Rio de Janeiro, others stayed but for a few days, but all faced a similar challenge. Poets from the Latin American country that has been the most frequent object of attention from foreign artists and intellectuals now dealt with the pitfalls of the foreign gaze, the temptations of exoticism and its celebratory or derogatory mystifications. Together these texts—presented here in their chronological order of publication —lay out a genealogy of a Mexican approach to that challenge.

Pellicer was born in Tabasco and moved to Mexico City in 1908 to continue his studies. When he visited Rio in 1922, Pellicer was far from becoming the acclaimed poet who had a place in the *Rotonda de los Hombres Ilustres* in 1975. The student activist had impressed Vasconcelos with a speech against Juan Vicente Gómez in front of the Venezuelan embassy[4] and the minister of education decided to hire him as his personal secretary. In this capacity, Pellicer joined the Mexican delegation to Brazil's international fair in 1922. Later Pellicer contributed to *Falange* (1922–23), *Ulises* (1927–28), and *Contemporáneos* (1928–31), important journals that established avant-garde modernism in Mexico. When Vasconcelos clashed with the government leadership and lost the elections in 1929, Pellicer was arrested and ostracized, and made a living as a high school teacher for 20 years until he got a professorship in modern poetry at the UNAM and entered the Academia Mexicana de Letras in 1953.[5]

In 1922, while Vasconcelos gave speeches, made diplomacy, and took notes that would become *La Raza Cósmica*, Pellicer flew over Rio de Janeiro with the Mexican aerobatics squad[6] and wrote the seven Brazilian poems included in *Piedra de Sacrifícios*. Four of them appear as "Suite Brasilera—Poemas Aéreos." They are among the best in that book, bearing testimony to Pellicer's enthusiasm for aviation and his keen eye for the natural world. During the inauguration of the Cuauhtémoc in Flamengo, Pellicer was the copilot and only companion to Francisco Espejel in a risky maneuver: a daring loop at very low altitude with bad weather. Pellicer threw flowers from the plane over the statue and the crowd was frightened, an adventure that seems to have annoyed Vasconcelos greatly; Espejel was punished with detention.[7] Probably out of this adventure came "Primera Vez" [First Time], dedicated to Espejel and Juan Navas Salinas (both pilots died in accidents following the Brazilian tour). In this remarkable poem, Rio de Janeiro's vital physical and human landscapes, lighted by the midday sun, are rendered in Cubist fashion, juxtaposing fragmented and shuffled plains and perspectives as Adolfo Best Maugard's[8] drawing—the only illustration in Pellicer's book—emphasizes.

In "Primera Vez" the fragmentary landscape is not the result of an act of introspection centered on the fragmented subject but of a particular point view, from the cockpit of a small plane: a world shaped by the aerobatics pilot as he maneuvers in the sky. The poem follows the pilot's aesthetic experience: it feels as if the *world* rather than the airplane is moving, tossing and turning with every loop and somersault. This Rio is populated not by human beings but by objects visible from the distance in the airplane: the islets, the automobiles, the Sugarloaf turned into a proud scarecrow, and the "naked" palm trees shopping on the main thoroughfare of the city. The gaze from the outside world is absent and instead of existential angst, Pellicer offers a breathtaking ride that feels like "300 carats of diamonds / jammed into a good heart;" drinking to the brim from this bright midday landscape, the poet ends up with "the eyes blue / and salt water inside the heart."

The exuberance of "Primera Vez" is followed by "Segunda Vez," which contrasts the exhilarating freedom in the cockpit with the disappointing world the pilot-poet has left down below. Up in the air the poet is freed from the limits of his own limbs to be "a naked bit of sun" and to "Be, solely / be and nothing more;" there he "can ponder on the glory / of joining flags and sing songs." Down below a world of dispiriting and unpleasant realities awaits: "there are the widows and the lawmakers, / the Scott's Emulsion[9] and the big debtors." Furthermore, the world down below threatens to erase the aesthetic bliss that these poems wish to emulate and extend: "Below, in the bottom of the world / the ink of the poem has started to fade."[10]

Elsewhere Pellicer explained the similarities between pilot and poet: "the pilot is first of all an artist. (...) the act of flying is an act of beauty ("Dos textos inéditos," 19). This "act of beauty" bridges the gap between art and life and engenders a world of incessant movement and intense aesthetic bliss: "when the pilot is skilled in aerobatics, one has the impression that it is not the plane but the world that moves." Since most pilots are unaware of flying as an act of beauty, they are for Pellicer "great artists for their savage and spontaneous art"—a modernist trope that makes these pilots equivalent to the artisans that impressed Ronald de Carvalho in Puebla and Tonalá. Furthermore, for Pellicer "flying is an art that contains all other arts and saves us from the disagreeable task of externalizing them." It is up to the pilot-poet to perform the troublesome task of communicating through writing the wonders of this world spontaneously infused with poetic energy to an audience that inhabits the world down below, characterized in the poem as "a poor thing / full of Yankee tastes and considerations."[11]

Being a pilot and a poet allowed Pellicer to take maximum poetic advantage of airplane flying, a paradigmatic symbol of radical modernity that galvanized the imagination of so many other poets and artists in the period.[12] Instead of the familiar futurist-like exalted elegies to speed and machines, Pellicer throws a keen poetic gaze at the concrete physical landscape that the experience of aerobatic flying opens up: the tropical sun cut up in slices, the sea of automobiles of the modern city turned into the sky as the plane flies upside down, the boundless horizon that stretches all the way to the South Pole. Distances are pulverized and contrasting scenes juxtaposed in a Rio de Janeiro that seems to orchestrate a modernist ballet of mountains, islands, water, and skies. The poetic realization of this experience depends on what was then the fresh repertoire of the modernist vanguard,[13] which allows, for example, for the use of disconcerting perspectivism to condense palm trees, scarcely clad bathers, and a bustling downtown in a single dizzying image. In these poems such practices move beyond mannerisms to incorporate an intense sensual joy in experiencing the world.

Pellicer is often associated with the *Contemporáneos*, a heterogeneous assembly of poets known as "el grupo sin grupo," identified
with a host of tendencies from the reformist *postmodernismo* of Enrique
González Martínez[14] to various European avant-gardes. Named after
the literary journal that featured them prominently between 1928
and 1931, the *Contemporáneos* became a reference to following generations in Mexico not only because of the extraordinary quality of
the poetry of Pellicer, Xavier Villaurrutia, and José Gorostiza but also
because of the paradigmatic, heated polemics between its members
and nationalist intellectuals who accused them of elitism, senseless
fascination with foreign tendencies, and even "feminization."[15] These
two poems feature the qualities that set Pellicer apart from his fellow *Contemporáneos*: the keen eye to the physical world as a source
of wonder and aesthetic pleasure coupled with a verbal inventiveness
that does not sacrifice verse clarity and fluency, qualities particularly
helpful to reflect on the experience in a foreign land relishing details
and specificities without resorting to exoticism.

Things become more problematic when Rio is presented as a sum
of the Ibero-American continent: "Your sea and your mountains, /
(...) as synthesis of the beloved Continent"[16] in "Suite Brasilera—
Otros Poemas" (dedicated to Ronald de Carvalho). Placing these
poems after "Suite Brasilera—Poemas Aéreos" highlights the contrast between a careful attention to the particularities of the powerful
imaginary landscape of a bustling city worth describing in itself and a
generic, allegorical reading of Rio de Janeiro's landscape as an Ibero-
American synthesis.

In the most felicitous moments of "Suite Brasilera—Otros
Poemas," the focus is on paradigmatic natural elements from different perspectives. The sea appears in three distinctive moments. Up
close the sea washes between the poet's arms as its waves feed from
the poet's hands. In the afternoon the poet observes a swift bather
in Copacabana and notices her "almost blue" arms and "diamond
ankles." At night, from a balcony in Hotel Gloria, the "modern and
resounding" sea takes part in the symphony of Rio and slowly turns
the wheels of its old machinery. The ubiquitous "Páo de Assucar"
[*sic*] also features in different moments and perspectives. From the
airplane in flight, the Sugarloaf is a "superb scarecrow, made of logic
and fantasy." From the sea the poet sees it moving the city into the
Atlantic in a "grand chess move." Finally at night the poet observes
the Sugarloaf from the hotel and imagines a stately obelisk celebrating the "torrid mutinies of the Atlantic that break away at its feet."
The few passages that present Rio de Janeiro as a symbolic accessory

to argue for a common Latin American identity and continental solidarity are weak in comparison with those in which Pellicer throws
a loving gaze at the city and describes it as an endless source of aesthetic pleasure: "And this marvelous city / ( ...) shall be / the eternal
curve of my pleasure / which I shall stretch over the world" ("Suite
Brasilera—Otros Poemas, I").[17]

A few years later another Mexican poet was brought to Rio de
Janeiro in a diplomatic mission. Luís Quintanilla[18] (1900–1980),
a.k.a Kyn Taniya, was born in Paris into a wealthy family of Mexican
diplomats[19] and went to Mexico the first time at the age of 18. He
renounced his French nationality and entered the diplomatic service in 1921, serving in Rio de Janeiro from 1927 to 1929 as secretary to the ambassador Ortiz Rubio,[20] for whom he substituted for
a brief period between 1927 and 1928.[21] In the 1920s and 1930s
Quintanilla participated as a poet and public intellectual in Mexican
cultural life, especially with activities surrounding the avant-garde.
Quintanilla knew the Parisian avant-garde firsthand and sympathized
with the *Estridentistas*, who launched their manifesto in 1921. Being
abroad most of the time, Quintanilla was never a full member of the
group, tightly centered around the figure of Manuel Maples Arce and
based in the state of Veracruz under the sympathetic governorship of
Heriberto Jara, a revolutionary general with presidential ambitions.[22]
Nevertheless, his poetry is in tune with *Estridentismo* in the emphatic
use of free verse in exalted tones, in the enthusiasm for dazzling
images of electricity, speed, machines, and modern life in the metrop-
olis, and in its iconoclastic irreverence. Quintanilla published *Avión*
in this period (1923, under the pen name Kin Taniya), with a cover
by Dr. Atl, and *Radio* (1924) with a cover by Roberto Montenegro.
Two subsequent volumes were prepared in the 1930s (*Ward Line* and
*Estación K.T.*), but remained unpublished until 1986; Quintanilla
remained active afterward as a diplomat, essayist, and teacher, but
not as a poet.

At a farewell dinner the writer Álvaro Moreyra (1888–1964) said,
"You did more than the usual in the career you chose. You soon
became Brazilian. The person who leaves us tomorrow is a Brazilian"
(Moreyra, 90).[23] But only when previously unpublished poems were
gathered in *Obra Poética*, those written during his diplomatic appoint-
ment in Brazil surfaced. One of them, "¡Amazonia!" (Quintanilla,
60–62), is an emotional apostrophe to the "Henry Ford's bride[24] /
Macunaima's fatherland / sex of the world" (62).[25] Instead of Rio
de Janeiro this other iconic Brazilian region becomes the center of
the Americas: "¡Abre tus brazos en cruz / de norte a sur sobre las

dos Américas!" The allusion to Mário de Andrade's great modernist novel, *Macunaíma*,[26] at the time fresh off the press, is evidence of Quintanilla's involvement with Brazillian culture at the time.

Rio de Janeiro appears in "Ya no volará el mayor Carlo del Prete" (57–58), which again centers on flying and airplanes.[27] It is an eulogy to Carlo del Prete, the Italian pioneer of long- distance flying, who died in an accident during a demonstration flight in Rio in 1928. The tragic irony is that del Prete died while he and his companion Arturo Ferrarin were celebrating the new world nonstop straight-line distance record for flying from Rome to Natal—a feat that was the subject of Quintanilla's "Canto Lírico del Avión Trasatlántico" (95–99). Quintanilla's del Prete is an artist with an airplane of "alas plateadas," singing a transatlantic epic with a "poderosa voz ronca," and he is a national myth with "alas italianas," stretching over the ocean an "arcoiris sonoro verde, blanco y colorado." The mournful poet finally asks that

> For a moment put out the light
> of the Guanabara Bay
> the liquid light of the sky
> the liquid light of the sea! (58)[28]

This may be an allusion to Pellicer's "Suite Brasilera," conflating water and light in the sky and in the ocean of the Guanabara bay. The poet asks for that glorious light to turn itself off to mourn the death of del Prete, a modernist artist/hero, "de cuerpo horizontal mutilado por / la gloria" [his horizontal body mutilated by / the glory].

Alfonso Reyes was the ambassador in Rio from 1930 to 1936, in close contact with important Brazilian figures as we discussed. In Rio, Reyes wrote *Romances del Río de Enero*, one of his best poetry books, published in 1933:[29] tightly woven poems about the city, ranging from the hilly neighborhood of Santa Tereza to the red light district of the Mangue, the Botanic Gardens, the beach, and the mountains of Corcovado and the Pão de Açúcar.

Reyes was a classicist who rarely strayed from traditional fixed forms, and *Romances del Río de Enero* has a clear structural frame that endows the poems with a strong sense of mutual cohesion beyond the thematic unit: 11 poems composed of 11 four-verse stanzas of octosyllabic verses, with the second and fourth verse of each stanza always bearing the same assonant rhyme throughout. It is a modern *Romance*, poetic form that, in this case, is not derived from the local-ism that infuses Lorca's poetry, but from the need to respond to the

increasingly popular free verse, indirectly criticized in Reyes's notes at
the end of the book, when he suggests that poets "turn our backs on
the fateful freedoms—which are no more than abandonment" (40).[30]
More than evoking a glorious Iberian poetic tradition, the *romance*
"let into the voice a certain colloquial tone, a certain prosaic quality
that has caught on in our times, as evidence indicates" (40).[31]

Reyes's diplomatic temperament moderates his formal conservatism to offer a compromise between twentieth-century modernist
aesthetics and the classicism he always valued and wished to preserve.
The *romance* helps Reyes's elegant expression and clear diction in
exploring orality in Spanish and Portuguese. Portuguese elements—
Reyes uses the term *lusismos*—are discreet but consistent throughout
the book *"para dar sazón al caldo"* (40) [to season the broth]. The
two languages are mutually enriched in a game of recognition and
estrangement that Reyes calls *"contaminaciones."* These lusitanisms
are evident to the Spanish speakers, but might not be noticed at all
by Portuguese-speaking readers of *Romances del Río de Enero*.[32] The
opening stanza of the first poem, "Río de Olvido," is exemplary:

> Rio de Janeiro, Rio de Janeiro
> you used to be river and now you're sea,
> ever so gently you return
> the impetus you receive. (5)[33]

The use of *devagar* instead of the Spanish *despacio* is one such *lusismo*.
It is Portuguese, but sounds Spanish-like to Portuguese speakers who
customarily assume certain terms and expressions of Portuguese are
perfectly comprehensible in Spanish, when in fact they are not. On the
other side of the linguistic divide, a hypothetical "de vagar" sounds
close to Spanish, evoking a complement to the verb "return" that
means "in a lazily roaming, meandering way." This opening stanza
is also exemplary of the way the poems in *Romances del Río de Enero*
revolve around opposing and complementary terms such as river and
sea, receive and return, impetus and indolence, contrasted in a pendulum movement that governs form and content of each part and its
whole. It is a "common principle" derived from what Reyes calls his
*"experiências poéticas de Ríojaneiro"*:

> Something like a law of the pendulum, an oscillation, a bifurcation
> of emotions. The idea—always—starts and returns and then moves
> the opposite direction and cancels itself. When it was possible, I high-
> lighted this movement in the pendular movement of each stanza of
> every romance; make it in the swing of each sentence. (40–41)[34]

Such oscillation holds true as far as the emotional states of the poetic voice are concerned. The poet alludes to melancholy memories of acute crises passed, contrasted with a new state of mind that, if not peaceful, at least denotes a certain measure of serenity for which the poet is grateful to the city that has welcomed him with its soft gentleness, and also relieved. "Saudade" (16), for example, lists a series of *desterros* that marked Reyes's actual trajectory up to his arrival in Rio and announces the loss of his identity in a wordplay with verbs such as to lose and to find:

> Here a man has been lost:
> say it, those who find him.
> Among men he wandered,
> nobody identifies him. (19)[35]

More lighthearted moments—poems such as "Castidad," "Morena," "Desequilibrio," and "Berenguedén"—speak of an erotic innuendo with a *morena carioca*, but also rely on this pendular approach, contrasting chastity and temptation and worries and joy.

Whereas Reyes's essays revealed the extension and limits of his knowledge of Brazilian history and culture, his poetry about Brazil rests on his ability to observe the natural and human landscape of the city. Of all the places that inspired Reyes in Rio de Janeiro, the Botanical Gardens, which still display Reyes's Xochipilli deserved one of his best poems, "El Botánico." Anyone who knows the Botanical Gardens in Rio recognizes the scenes described in Reyes's poem as a faithful description, if only completely devoid of human presence. In the imagination of the poet the empty gardens become a crowded, agitated place with personified beings dressed as characters (Moses in Egypt, Don Quixote and Dulcinea, Quevedo and Góngora debating in *La Culta Latiniparla*), a Baroque literary stage peopled by a multitude of vegetal and animal beings in a carnavalesque parade of exhuberant colors acting out silent imaginary dramas. All plants, from the "noble" bamboo to the "democratic" cacti[36] pay homage to the exuberant *Palmeira imperial* [palm trees brought from the Caribbean by the emperor Dom João VI], who plays the queen at the center of the stage defined by the aisles lined with sedges acting as guards bearing long spears. Meanwhile smaller scenes unfold on the sides: among them the aromatic camphor and rue[37] play lofty, upright Don Quixote and the sweaty Dulcinea and the water timidly covers its nudity with water lilies while the *Victoria amazonica* in bloom plays Moses lying in his crib, floating over the water. A glorious spectacle of noble and plebeian, real and false identities in constant sensual inter-course unfolds until the night, "*señora desde su altura*," surges from the top of the mountain that rises at the back of the park, looming over every being and slowly dissolving everything in indistinct dark-ness, prevailing over the belittled actors on that stage now reduced to "*latiniparlas*" and announcing the closing of the gates and the end of the day at the Jardim Botânico.

Pellicer and Reyes present different approaches to poems that likewise foreground Rio's landscape and contrast the joy and free-dom of aesthetic experiences in an unpopulated world with the past sorrows or disappointments to come that the human world offers. While Pellicer attempts to represent the city's landscape by manipulating disjointed metaphors, short-circuiting senses in single images and phrases in "Poemas Aéreos," Reyes prefers personify-ing natural elements and then imagining them involved in dramatic reenactment of scenes from Western literary tradition in "Jardim Botánico." While aesthetic pleasure is a measure of an experience in the sheer physical world in Pellicer's poem, in Reyes' poem this pleasure depends on a natural world that is also pregnant with liter-ary allusions.

Reyes had the highest regard for these poems and expressed disap-pointment with their reception in Brazil in a letter dated March 6, 1952, to his friend Ribeiro Couto. Reyes comments on

> "this hiatus that divides our cultures," whose sad manifestation in my case was the complete silence in Brazil with regards to my little poetry book *Romances de Río de Enero*, all dedicated to Rio and written with heart and mind. Perhaps I'll re-edit it one of these days, because the first edition of 300 copies, printed in Maastricht by Stols, soon was out of print and didn't reach the public.[38]

This silence was conspicuous when Carlos Drummond de Andrade e Manuel Bandeira organized *Rio de Janeiro em Prosa e Verso* to cel-ebrate the 400th anniversary of Rio in 1965: among all sorts of liter-ary curiosities, there was no mention made of *Romances del Río de Enero*. It is an odd omission when we consider that Bandeira, Reyes's longtime friend and correspondent,[39] once called these *romances* "the most beautiful verses our Rio has ever inspired in any poet" (*Libro Jubilar de Alfonso Reyes*, 75).[40]

The poet, editor, journalist, translator, and diplomat Jaime García Terrés (1924–1996) played a prominent role in Mexican culture in the second half of the twentieth century in the Instituto Nacional de

Bellas Artes (INBA), UNAM, Revista de la Universidad de México, and the Fondo de Cultura Económica.[41] He translated John Donne, W. B. Yeats, Hölderlin, Blake, Ezra Pound, T. S. Eliot and (after living in Greece from 1965 to 1968) Greek poets such as Konstantínos Kaváfis, Ángelos Sikelianós, Giórgos Seféris, and Andréas Embiríkos. Born in 1924 in México City, García Terrés published his first essay at the age of 17 under the auspices of Reyes, but his poetic oeuvre is relatively small, although recognized for its outstanding quality.

García Terrés wrote two poems on Rio, published first in *Las Províncias del Aire* (1956) and later reprinted in the anthology *Poesía en Movimiento* (1966).[42] They are based on García Terrés's brief stay in Rio during the Carnival of 1951, registered in prose in his "Más Gloria que Poder: Graham Greene" (*El Teatro de los Acontecimientos*, 723–728):

> In Rio de Janeiro, besides a magnificent landscape, I would encounter days of carnival madness, scorching hot mornings at the beach (a few steps from my place in the so-called *Jardim de Alá* [The Garden of Allah] I had the beaches of Leblon and Ipanema) and a bunch of affable people. (725)[43]

The two months in Rio allowed García Terrés to get to know Machado de Assis, "that prolific, remote precursor of Borges" (726), to learn to dance *samba* and *baião*, and sing Dorival Caymi's songs. García Terrés also wrote two melancholy evocations: "Una invocación: (Guanabara)" (*Las manchas del sol*, 47–48) and "Ipanema" (49). In "Ipanema" the echoes of Carnival are faint and quickly fade away; they only linger in elliptic references to "ill-bred echoes" and "rude mockery." What clearly remains is the rainy afternoon, the striking image of rows of houses tearing themselves away, evoking fleeting memories that fade away as much as the slow process of decomposition that inexorably affects everything around us. "Ipanema" is poetry as evocation of memory in the way of Wordsworth's ideal of "emotion recollected in tranquility."[44] Years interposed between the poem and the urban scenery and its memory draw an impressionistic landscape where the human presence is a faint suggestion. García Terrés's Ipanema is dominated by the sea and a light curiously described as "copos de sol" [sun flakes]. In prose the poet described his stay in Rio as "two months of idleness, a stay with no clear purpose (which) involved a few solitary stretches, so much the harder by contrast with the moments of pleasure" (*El teatro de los acontecimentos*, 725); "Ipanema" is a poetic rendering of those "solitary stretches."

García Terrés avoids the clichés of Brazilian Carnival in "Ipanema" as a Mexican aware of the exoticism promoted by foreigners and the colorful celebratory nationalism that idealized a folkloric world. It is a recurring strategy for a poet who also wrote about Athens, Dublin, Lisbon, and Bath. Unlike Pellicer, this traveling poet favors subjective landscapes, emphasized in "Ipanema" in phrases such as *"a traves de los años"* [through the years] and "contra mis pupilas" [against my pupils].

In "Una invocación: (Guanabara)" García Terrés uses an apostrophe to address the stunning physical maritime landscape that captivated Pellicer, Quintanilla, and Reyes as well. A sensual relationship with the landscape appears again but the point of contact is not the eye but the mouth. The poet asks that Guanabara "cast a spell of soft truces in my mouth" [*hechice blandas treguas en mi boca*], "shower my throat with light" [*bañe de luz mi garganta*], and "kiss, rip open my lips" [*besa, rompe mis labios*]. While Pellicer's Rio was the personification of an idealized America, García Terrés's Guanabara is the teeth of an enigmatic figure called "El Sur" (The South). The beauty of the bay is charged with the implacable energy of this mysterious entity that "smells like lashings of poppy flowers" [*huele a latigazos de amapola*]. Born in the seas, the South dances drunkenly in the salt till it comes to the harbor, where it is welcomed by black men who hurl insults, calling the mysterious entity "coward" [*cobarde*] and "murderer" [*asesino*].

Gabriel Zaid (1934) is an important poet and essayist in Mexico, who won the Xavier Villaurrutia prize in 1972 and is a member of the Academia Mexicana de la Lengua and the Colegio de Mexico. Zaid started publishing in 1958 with *Fábula de Narciso y Ariadna* and also featured poems in *Poesía en Movimiento*. A member of Octavio Paz's circle, he was on the editorial council of the magazine *Vuelta* from 1976 to 1992 and is a poet and essayist like Reyes and García Terrés, having published books of essays such as *Demasiados Libros* and *De los Libros al Poder*.[45] Zaid's "Ipanema" was first published in Plural in 1975, when the quiet, beautiful beach suburb of the early 1950s had become a crowded neighborhood of 65,000 inhabitants. In a *crónica* published in *Vuelta* in 1986, Zaid comments on details of writing his "Ipanema," discussing successive versions of the poem up to its final form.[46] Expecting something akin to the neighborhood made famous by Vinícius de Moraes and Tom Jobim's "The Girl from Ipanema," Zaid is astonished by the prosaic urban landscape of Rio's Zona Sul and compares his experience to the discovery that the author of texts "that are liberated and tropical, in which nature saunters around naked, is a bespectacled gentleman dressed as a civil servant and carrying a briefcase." This disappointment becomes irony in Zaid's "Ipanema, " in which a "sea of automobiles" takes the poet to a bar at the seaside, where he scribbles the first version of the poem in the "playas blancas" of *Jornal do Brasil*—a reference to the newspaper's famous graphic design under the direction of the neoconcretist painter and printer Amílcar de Castro in the 1950s. This first version concludes with a verse in which "una mulata majestuosa y descalza como un automóvil" comes out of the waters, which he immediately discards for being "touristic." Substituting Venus for the touristic *mulata*, Zaid finds something analogous to a surrealist *objet trouvé* not in the surroundings but in Western classical tradition: "descubrí que el poema inesperado no era turístico sino botticelliano." Later Zaid eliminates the explicit mention to Venus, who stands not for the idealized *Garota de Ipanema* of the Bossa Nova of the 1950s but for another mythic entity, made of steel, in tune with the times of the capitalist prosperity under the military dictatorship in which even the sidewalks of Ipanema were taken over by cars.

"Ipanema" is Zaid at his best: maximum conciseness and simplicity in a short poem based on a brief insight, a sudden sparkle that sets the poem in motion and endows it with self-sufficient coherence. This "lean, idiomatic succinctness" (Tapscott, 322) means Zaid's short poems function less as fragmentary pieces than as self-contained short narratives or aphorisms in which the title is indispensable as the only reference to Rio. Instead of working by adding images in fast, consecutives cuts as Pellicer or Quintanilla or suggesting a baroque festival of colors with a rapid succession of erudite citations as Reyes, or working by elliptical allusions as García Terrés, Zaid's aesthetic is minimalist, manipulating a small set of elements with careful simplicity and straightforward language to amount to more than wit.

José Emilio Pacheco (1939) appeared in *Poesía en Movimiento* as did García Terrés and Zaid and has become the most important Mexican poet of the second half of the twentieth century.[47] The author of novels and short stories and translator of important authors such as Beckett, Pacheco is also a scholar specialized in Spanish American late-nineteenth- century modernism; he has been a member of El Colegio Nacional since 1986 and has taught at the UNAM and several universities in the United States, Canada, and England. In his poetry Pacheco revisits tradition with critical skepticism and suspicion toward the official history and the poetics of transcendence, with an acute sense of the isolation of the poet amidst what he calls "market Stalinism." This critical rereading, to which the worn-out label postmodernism could be applied, refutes the revolutionary rhetoric of the avant-garde as well as aesthetic conservatism, claiming in a poem significantly called "Manifesto" that "Todos somos 'poetas de transición': / La poesía jamás se queda inmóvil."

Two poems from *Irás y No Volverás* (1973) are called "Antipostal de Río de Janeiro" (137–138) and "La Lluvia en Copacabana" (143). Pacheco's "Anti-postcard" combines two important strains of Pacheco's poetry: his "postcards," poems based often on foreign landscapes or everyday scenes, and his animal poems, in which Pacheco often displays his talents as an ingenious miniaturist. Besides the moths of the poem above, *Irás y No Volverás* features owls, toads, elephant seals, deer, lions, fish, mice, pigeons, and cats.

The moths in *Corcovado* helplessly die in the heat under the scorching sun and to them the beautiful landscape of Rio means only hunger, horror, and pain. The poet witnesses and describes their sacrifice and his guilt is evident: the enormous moths eye him with "grandes ojos dolientes." Nature in Pacheco's animal poems is frequently ruthless and stern indignation is blended with a terrible sense of helplessness because there is no room for a meaningful intervention that does not incur peddling false hope to assuage the poet's and the reader's conscience. These moths join pigs, turtles, pigeons, mosquitos, and wolves, as stoic victims in Pacheco's poems. On the other side of the spectrum, the poet's bestiary displays owls, sea elephants, lions, and seagulls that act as agents of the cruelty that rules the universe. Nature, allegorizing human and animal universes, is idyllic on the surface but soon reveals its cruelty as in "Los mares del sur" (374–375): "what others call natural selection, balance between species // For me is the world's horror" (375).[48]

These poems present a structure analogous to the fable, with anthropomorphic animals suggesting allegorical readings flexible enough to allow for more than one interpretation, although they usually suggest a negative view of human existence. Pacheco alludes to historical references with enough indeterminacy to allow for two concomitant, nonexclusive readings, one closely related to a specific context and a more general one. The moths the poet sees in *Corcovado*, menaces to private property and enemies of the establishment, point simultaneously to the "subversive" groups then active in several places in Latin America (including Mexico and Brazil) in an unequal fight against brutal repressive apparatuses of authoritarian regimes and to any opposition annihilated by a powerful status quo anywhere. The heat of the rough stones at the statue of Christ the Redeemer in Corcovado kills the moths ruthlessly and reminds us of the "the world's horror," but also of the brutality of the *anos de chumbo*.

In Mexico the violent repression of the student movement asking for democratic reforms in Tlatelolco in 1968 triggered a pattern of illegal imprisonments and torture. In Brazil the anticommunist military coup d'état in 1964 encroached into a ruthless repressive apparatus in 1968 as well. The year 1968 signaled the end of illusions about the regime based on the Mexican Revolution and about Brazil's supposed capacity for peaceful, diplomatic, political solutions just as the two countries experienced a growth spurt that worsened the already scandalous gap in income distribution. These ruptures impacted intellectuals and artists of both countries.

In "Antipostal de Rio de Janeiro," the poet attentively observes the landscape, as in the poems by Pellicer, Quintanilla, Reyes, García Terrés, and Zaid. Pacheco crystalizes a gradual change in this approach: beyond the attention to the surface of things in an unknown environment, the poet converts the world he observes in an eminently allegorical reality, flexible in its multiple possible interpretations. In the case of Pacheco, multiple interpretations point to a world in which we live as a place of suffering (hunger, horror, torture) in a hard end of the century that "does not believe in happiness or in victory" ("Reloj de Arena," 27).[49] Pacheco's pessimism sees history as a succession of catastrophes caused by nature and/or human beings. In the cycles of suffering and in the transient nature of existence, Pacheco sees the defining traits of human experience through the centuries, but he refuses to see these cycles as natural processes. On the contrary, present and past catastrophes are related, historically contextualized, and thus gain new meaning.[50] In these catastrophes the poet finds the source of his poetry, denouncing and reflecting about it with forbearing discipline and concentration.

Catastrophe is a misleading term because the tragedies about which Pacheco writes can be small, apparently unimportant moments, in which the poet willfully projects a particular meaning into the landscape and/or the scenes he witnesses. Pacheco's second poem in Rio, "Lluvia en Copacabana," offers a good example:

> As the rain falls on the sea,
> to the ceaseless rhythm it collapses,
> that's how we flow into death. (143)[51]

Hugo Gutiérrez Vega was born in Guadalajara in 1934 and worked as an actor and founder of theatrical companies until he joined the diplomatic service (as Reyes, Quintanilla and García Terrés did before him). Besides having a notable career as a poet, Gutiérrez Vega is a distinguished journalist, writing a weekly column, *Bazar de Asombros* (later collected in a book of the same name), and working as the director of *La Jornada Semanal*, the weekly cultural magazine of that newspaper. He has also taught at the Universidad Autónoma de Querétaro and the UNAM [Universidad Autónoma de México]. In 33 years as a diplomat, Gutiérrez Vega lived in several countries (most notably Italy, England, Spain, the United States, Brazil, and Greece) and much of his prolific output concern his experiences abroad. As the poet explained in a 2007 interview:

> Each City where I lived has its book. There is a book written in Washington, another in Rio de Janeiro, one in London, another in Puerto Rico. (...) All are present in the poetry, especially the travels, this moving around like a snail with the house on the back.[52]

From 1986 to 1988 Gutiérrez Vega was the cultural attaché in the Mexican General Consulate in Rio, where he was a close friend of Manuel Puig and a regular in Puig's famous cine club. Suzanne Jill Levine recalls that "the cine club, which met on Monday, Wednesday, and Friday evenings, was especially meaningful for Silvia Oroz (...) who swallowed up every bit of history Manuel imparted during these video viewings" (354). Oroz appears in this book as the author of *Cinema de Lágrimas*, adapted to the screen by Nelson Pereira dos Santos.

Gutiérrez Vega's *Andar en Brasil* (1987) is his Brazilian book, with a prose companion as in the case of García Terrés and Zaid. *Bazar de Asombros*, with essays originally published in *La Jornada*, also features "Andar en Brasil." *Andar en Brasil* includes poems dedicated to Salvador and the old colonial towns of Minas Gerais, among other sections, but the book has poems set in iconic places such as Ipanema, Leblon, and Botafogo. The most interesting of these poems is "Carnaval" (dedicated to the poets Affonso Romano de Sant'anna and Vinícius de Moraes). The theme is recurrent in Brazilian intellectual circles: the ambiguity between authenticity and artificiality when Carnival becomes a spectacle for tourists. Instead of a Brazilian intellectual watching the street party from a distance, "Carnaval" features a cultured tourist, always ready to exercise his critical skills and willing to smell superficiality and falsity. The following lines in this one-stanza poem seem to corroborate the opinion of this suspicious tourist as two rather sinister figures, the shopkeepers and the bankers, take the stage:

> The retailers sell
> their happiness in cans
> and beneath the shouting

vampire bankers
sharpen their fangs.[53]

The happiness that seems to fill the streets during Carnival is seen as a commodity, artificially packaged and commercialized by greedy exploiters. Popular commotion turned commodity becomes a tool to further alienation and reinforce social exploitation: the deafening dim merely serves as a distraction from the sharpened teeth of the bankers—symbol of capitalist oppression, more so in the context of economic crises worsened by the International Monetary Fund (IMF) and foreign debtors in the 1980s and 1990s. However, the next line, strategically situated in the middle of the poem, points to a different direction:

> Nevertheless the bodies,
> the dancing and the glances,
> the enormous laughter,
> the costumes in tatters,
> bear the old rites
> in most lively rags.[54]

The ironic voice of the "cultured tourist" offers more than affirmation of the existence of an opportunistic commercial exploitation of Carnival and of the fact that Carnival's brief and intense joy may help perpetuate class alienation. The poem becomes an affirmation that, in the moving visible bodies and the sounds of laughter, something powerful and profound, uncontrollable and uncontainable survives, albeit in fragments in the festivities as they are celebrated nowadays. The "olfateador de enganos" is replaced by a hopeful voice. In a stark contrast with Pacheco's pessimism, Gutiérrez Vega is in tune with the measured optimism of the first years after the return of democracy to Brazil and prophesies the coming victory of "the people" against their exploiters here even more derisively called "rats." *Andar en Brasil* was written in the late 1980s when the perspective of a utopic democratic socialist regime in Brazil was on the horizon with the steady growth of the Worker's Party, but also when the last remnants of the long military dictatorship still stubbornly clung to power amidst economic chaos and international pressure for the implementation of neoliberal reforms. Gutiérrez Vega sounds this final, cautiously optimistic note, affirming the subversive power and the deep spirit of anarchic rebellion of the festivity that mobilizes crowds and takes over streets all over Brazil to celebrate the flesh before Lent.

Francisco Cervantes (1938–2005) had a deeper relationship, not just with Brazil but with Portuguese literary traditions. He translated Machado de Assis, Fernando Pessoa, and other important lusophone writers, and his collection of essays *Travesías Brasileño-Lusitanas* showcases his intimate knowledge of Brazilian culture and literature.[55] In one of these essays, "Mi Encuentro con lo Luso Brasileño" (9–21), Cervantes outlines a curious circuit of elective affections from his youthful enthusiasm for Carmen Miranda and Walt Disney's Zé Carioca till his acquaintance with Manuel Bandeira's *Panorama de la Poesía Brasileña* published in México in 1954. Some find in Cervantes' "interminable y viva lusofilia" (Orizaga, xl) a typical Mexican gesture of distancing from nationalistic self-absorption, but the marginal position of Cervantes in Mexico also reflects the ignorance of his critics about lusophone letters beyond Fernando Pessoa. Cervantes's peculiar language—mixing Portuguese, Gallego, Spanish, and their medieval antecedents—made Zaid claim once that "I can't quite figure out whether Cervantes writes in Portuguese, Galician, Galician-Portuguese, or a Macaronic of his own" (*Ensayos sobre Poesía,* 243).[56] Furthermore, the singularity of Cervantes is not the result of some deliberate stylistic mannerism, but of an existential devotion. Cervantes's "Brasil y Portugal," recited when Cervantes received the *Ordem do Rio Branco*[57] in 1986 and published in *El Canto del Abismo* (1987), sumarizes his profound commitment: "I know that I'll only have lived / in two countries I've loved (…) they are the same / in their language and in this illusion of mine" (*Cantado para Nadie,* 300).[58]

One remarkable expression of this profound commitment involves Rio. Cervantes wrote a few short stories collected in *Relatorio Sentimental* (1986) and *Ustedes Recordarán* (1997) and one of them, "Garota de Botafogo" (*Ustedes Recordarán* 99–108), takes place in the city. Unlike Cervantes's other stories, "Garota de Botafogo" abounds with specific references to its setting. A stranger—called "nuestro hombre"—approaches the narrator at the Café Lamas, a restaurant that has been the meeting place of the city's intelligentsia for 135 years, located since 1974 on Marquês de Abrantes Street, not far from the *Cuauhtémoc* Vasconcelos gave the city in 1922. *"Nuestro hombre"* tells the narrator an adventure in which he has but a few *cruzados novos*—this short-lived currency (it existed only from January 1989 to March 1990) also provides specific time coordinates.

In this very lively human urban landscape, Cervantes sets his two protagonists: the first person narrator, characterized as *"el hombre del sotaque portugués"* (105), and the man he calls *"nuestro hombre."* The two solitary men share strange tales involving a woman they meet once by chance and then seem to see in every woman's face in the city ever since. Their related ghostly tales set in the nightmarish decadence of the 1980s suggest they might be haunted by the fleeting image of the same woman, but there are so many uncanny resemblances between them that they can be taken as doubles instead.

Cervantes's story highlights an important part of Rio that had been neglected by his Mexican peers: an axis that links the less fashionable parts of the Centro with its *sebos* (second-hand bookstores), seedy restaurants, and more disreputable bars around Tiradentes Square to Flamengo, where the Cuauhtémoc stands. It runs a straight line through downtown to Lapa and Catete streets, where the Largo do Machado displayed Rodolfo Bernardelli's equestrian statue of the duque de Caxias until the 1950s. The area housed the Portuguese nobility in the early nineteenth century, but is now a middle-class neighborhood with several medium-size hotels and small shops in its main streets, where drug addicts and the homeless roam at night. Furthermore, at the end of the story Cervantes mentions "the musician Carlos Lyra, with his wife *Katy*" (108). Lyra is one of the most important figures of the *Bossa Nova*, who lived in Mexico from 1966 to 1971 and worked with Cervantes in the translation of his songs into Spanish, playing a central role in a massive migration of Brazilian musicians to Mexico in that period.[59] With this effortless demonstration of intimacy with Rio in "Garota de Botafogo," Cervantes made good on his assertion that he had only lived in Brazil and Portugal all his life.

Pellicer, Quintanilla, Reyes, García Terrés, Zaid, Pacheco, Gutiérrez Vega, and Cervantes dealt with an interesting challenge by no means new in Latin America and increasingly apparent to artists and intellectuals all over the world in this new century: how to approach experience from a foreign perspective, avoiding the repetition of common pitfalls in the relationship between self and other. None of these Mexican poets relied on the stock scripts[60] of the exoticism of the tropics in its two complementary faces, idealization and demonization. These poems also tell the story of the transformation of a mythical city in the eyes of Latin American foreigners who at first marveled at its natural beauty and then increasingly pondered on an urban landscape that presented itself as a not altogether unfamiliar puzzle.

# Chapter 5

# Érico Veríssimo's Journey into Mexico

Érico Veríssimo (1905–1975) is one the most popular Brazilian novelists of the twentieth century. His trilogy *O Tempo e o Vento*[1] fixed the image of his native state, Rio Grande do Sul, in the national imagination and Veríssimo became known as one of the few Brazilians authors who could make a living out of his work in mid-twentieth century.[2] He attained more critical acclaim than Jorge Amado, who also wrote a series of bestsellers, but either the sheer extent of his popularity or the large uneven corpus of novels he wrote has at times prevented Veríssimo from receiving his due as a major novelist in Brazil of that time.

A significant part of Veríssimo's extensive output comprises books about his life abroad, including three extended stays in the United States—something uncommon among Brazilian intellectuals born in the first half of the twentieth century.[3] Veríssimo was invited by the US State Department for a series of conferences over three months in 1941 and recounted his experience in *Gato Preto em Campo de Neve* (1941), aptly described on its cover as the "novel of a trip."[4] After problems with the Catholic Church and conservative groups during the dictatorship of the Estado Novo,[5] Veríssimo left again for the United States, where he taught Brazilian literature from 1943 to 1945, first [at the University of California], Berkeley, and then at Mills College in Oakland, California. As a result of this stay on the West Coast, his Berkeley lectures were collected in *Brazilian Literature: An Outline* (1945)[6] and he wrote another volume of memoirs whose name, *A Volta do Gato Preto* (1947), whose title relates it to the 1941 volume.[7] From 1953 to 1956 Veríssimo substituted for Alceu Amoroso Lima as the director of the cultural affairs department of the Pan-American Union (soon to become the Organization of American States) in Washington. This time, however, Veríssimo did not write about the United States, but about Mexico, where he went with his wife on an extended vacation in the spring of 1955. *México—História duma Viagem* (1957) became his most ambitious volume about a foreign country,[8] translated in the United States in 1960.[9]

Veríssimo's Mexican book deserves much more attention than it has received since its publication. Ledo Ivo wrote admiringly in a review that in *México—História duma Viagem* Veríssimo "offers a greater stylistic density than most of his novels, comparable to the text in the two volumes of *O Tempo e o Vento*" (Ivo, 3).[10] Such density is not accidental; despite all modest protestations of improvisation, Veríssimo prepared himself thoroughly for this trip and this book, probably with the help of Mexican friends such as the historian Ermilo Abreu Gómez and perhaps even the poet Luis Quintanilla, who also worked at the Pan-American Union at the time. Veríssimo spoke admiringly about the Mexicans, whom he considered to be, in the "intellectual sphere," "the bravest fighters, the most obstinate debaters, and the ones who resisted the most to accept defeat" (*México*, 266).[11]

Before the 1955 visit, Veríssimo had been to Mexico for a single night in 1941 and for about a week in 1954 on business with the Pan-American Union. However, Veríssimo read extensively before his third trip and did it with *México—História duma Viagem* in mind. A bibliography of more than 30 titles, placed at the end of the book as a suggestion to readers interested in learning more about Mexico, is an indication of Érico Veríssimo's extensive readings, including the latest books on Mexico in the 1950s such as Jorge Carrión's *Mito y Magia del Mexicano* (1952) and Ramón Xirau's *Tres Poetas de la Soledad* (1955). Most of these books briefly appear in Veríssimo's travel narrative: Werner Weisbach turns up in the descriptions of the Mexican Baroque; the Colombian architect José Moreno Villa is quoted to help describe the church of San Francisco de Acatepec (137); Graham Greene's (141) helps to understand the pathos of Church penitents; Paul Westheim's *La Calavera* is evoked to comment on the predilection for bloody images of Christ; and George Clapp.[12] Georges Clapp Vaillant's *Aztecs of Mexico* helps Veríssimo evoke pre-Columbian Tenochtitlán in Chapter 4, "Aspects of the Aztec World." When it comes to the colonial period, Veríssimo brings to his text Ramón Iglesia's then-recent book on Hernán Cortés's *Las Cartas de Relación*,[13] the chronicles of Bernal Díaz del Castillo, Bernardino de Sahagún's *Florentine Codex*, William H. Prescott, Francisco Clavijero, and Fernando Benítez. Frank Tenenbaum—dismissed by Vasconcelos as "a Jewish writer apologist of callismo" (204)[14]—counters Vasconcelos's view of the Mexican Revolution as a disaster. Other notable Mexican authors such as Justo

Sierra, Alfonso Reyes, José Vasconcelos, Samuel Ramos, and Octavio Paz are cited as Veríssimo presents the history, the culture, the literature, and the arts of Mexico. *México—História duma Viagem* is more than a travel memoir: the trip Veríssimo and his wife took through Mexico is a narrative frame for an interpretation of Mexican identity and national character not unlike the "*ensaios caracteriológicos*" [essays on (national) character] that were still in vogue in Brazil and Mexico at the time. Actually in its resistance to any grandiose assertion or unequivocal answer about Mexico's national character and its dilemmas, *México—História de uma Viagem* might be more interesting than most of those books.

Several important characters introduce, illustrate, and explain the main themes of *México—Historia duma Viagem*. More than a matter of offering a varied cast of characters beyond the historic figures such as Cuauhtémoc or Benito Juárez, these characters contribute multiple voices and points of view that turn this book into more than Veríssimo's personal interpretation of Mexico. These characters can be divided into three categories: informed foreigners, notable Mexican artists and intellectuals, and everyday people the author met during the trip, who get affectionate portraits, especially the children who offer their services as local guides in the couple's unaccompanied travels to the Mexican provinces, such as José and Alberto in Cholula and Juanito in Oaxaca. I want to have a closer look at some of these characters in order to clarify the delicate balance between allowing other voices to speak and ultimately controlling the narrative that animates this book.

Foreigners living in Mexico at the time function as guide figures, taking the Veríssimos to places in the capital and its environs, introducing them to locals, telling anecdotes, and sharing their own thoughts about the country. Among them are notable intellectuals such as the philologist Aurélio Buarque de Holanda[15] (lecturing for the Cátedra de Estudios Brasileños at the UNAM from June 1954 to December 1955), with whom the couple visits the *mariachis* at the Plaza Garibaldi, the traditional *cantina* called Tenampa, and Taxco. Two of these figures deserve special attention for what they reveal about the structure of *México—Historia duma Viagem* as well. One is the Argentine later naturalized Mexican Luis Guillermo "Tito" Piazza,[16] a colleague of Veríssimo at the OEA (Organization of American States, OAS in English), and the other is the essayist Clodomir Vianna Moog,[17] a fellow *Gaúcho* who lived in Mexico for ten years also working for the OAS.

Tito Piazza takes the Veríssimos to places such as San Angel and Xochimilco, but there are three instances when his role in

*México—História duma Viagem* becomes particularly prominent. When Tito Piazza and his wife take the Veríssimos to dinner twice, first at the famous five-star hotel Geneve at the Zona Rosa and then in their elegant apartment, the Argentine introduces three Mexican characters: Pancho, a handsome young Mexican man who entertains a rich Californian widow (56–57); Macaria, an old servant from Oaxaca (59); and Ermelindo, a messenger boy at the OAS (60). Pancho, Macaria, and Ermelindo are Mexicans who live in close contact with modern environments dominated by foreigners, respectively the rich widow in Acapulco, the Piazzas at their own home, and Tito at the OAS office. They seem to adapt to the circumstances, but signal with acts of stubborn resistance: Pancho sports an earring as a promise to the Virgen de Guadalupe; Macaria dismisses the new ways of serving the table as *supersticiones*; and Ermelindo refuses to call the speaking clock to know the time, calling his friend whose office stands by a church clock instead. None of these parallels are explicitly drawn in the text, and the three anecdotes told by Piazza are related as simple, interesting, and even picturesque notes on Mexican characters. Veríssimo, the novelist, mostly refrains from explicit essayistic interpretation. This reticence as the natural posture of the storyteller is declared elsewhere when the narrator mocks his own attempts at interpretation. Veríssimo meets another of his guides, Vianna Moog, a fellow *Gaúcho* with political affinities in his opposition to Getúlio Vargas's dictatorship. Moog is "pregnant with theories about Mexico" and Veríssimo even considers a joint book in which the roles of novelist and essayist are sharply divided: Moog would take care of the "interpretations" and Veríssimo of the "images." "probably a monstrosity" (71),[18] dismisses Moog; "quién sabe!" Veríssimo responds in Spanish, emulating what he sees as Mexican reticence. Moog will not offer Veríssimo anecdotes such as Piazza's but somehow sententious interpretations, often the target of Veríssimo's irony. For instance, as the two *Gaúchos* pass by two famous sights of Mexico City, the statue of Carlos VI on the Paseo de la Reforma and the monument to Juárez on the Alameda, Moog affirms Mexicans' general aversion to the *conquistadores* and gringos and then "delivers a dissertation on the great Mexican dichotomy: Indianism and Hispanism. And, absentminded, he turns the wrong way into a one-way street" (73).[19] Gentle sarcasm characterizes the encounters between Veríssimo and Moog: Moog takes Veríssimo to Teotihuacán and Toluca complaining that he is tired of taking every Brazilian friend to the ruins. Veríssimo retorts that Moog looks like Pedro Alvarado, a villainous captain of Cortés's army. In Toluca, Moog downplays Veríssimo's excessive enthusiasm for the local crafts, citing Samuel Ramos's assertion that the current-day indigenous artisan is not an artist because he merely repeats traditional patterns. Art or mere repetition, Veríssimo retorts, again in Spanish, "Viva México!" (237).

In addition to these fellow foreigners living in Mexico, Mexican intellectuals such as Ermilo Abreu Gómez,[20] characterized as Veríssimo's *cuate* at the Pan-American Union in Washington, offer their views on their own country. Abreu Gómez, who has been cited in this book about Sor Juana's closeness to Portuguese, talks about the unique character of his native Yucatán in México. Two of these Mexican characters become privileged interlocutors who appear in long interviews with Veríssimo that take up sizable chunks of the book: José Vasconcelos and David Alfaro Siqueiros, two major Mexican intellectual figures who had visited Brazil, respectively in 1922 and in 1933, and left a striking impression. The passages where Vasconcelos and Siqueiros appear are also revealing because Veríssimo, a liberal with a critical view of the Catholic Church and a friendly stance toward the United States, had clear political differences with both of them.

Chapter 8 is titled "Colloquies with José Vasconcelos," based on seven interviews with Vasconcelos that cover Mexico's history since the conquest until Vasconcelos's failed attempt to become president in 1929. Veríssimo introduces Vasconcelos as a prophet (contrasted with Reyes, the poet) and as leader of the *hispanistas* with evident empathy for "a rare man, of extraordinary vigor and lucidity, of an infectious enthusiasm—gay, restless, frank, the best of companions" (178).[21] Vasconcelos's voice seems to dominate—various passages are actually taken *ipsis literis* from Vasconcelos's *Breve Historia do México*[22]—and Veríssimo acts as a provocateur, for instance characterizing Cortés as paranoid. At this juncture Vasconcelos retorts that Veríssimo must have been reading Prescott and "American historians, indirect agents of Protestantism that wish to erase all traces from Spaniards in America"[23] (172) and insists on his view of Cortés as a great humanist. In spite of protestations of modesty such as "it was my hope that the professor would take the ball and hang on to it for the rest of the game" (179), Veríssimo follows these *colóquios* with two fragments ("A Colônia" and "O Grito") that seem to be advancing chronologically in the history of Mexico but are actually laying out Veríssimo's position: a diplomatic middle ground between admitting the atrocities of the Spanish colonization and claiming that in history there are no villains but only complex human beings. Refraining from showing disapproval toward Vasconcelos's questionable views,[24] Veríssimo resorts to subtle tactics, inserting brief comments that include authoritative sources in disagreement with Vasconcelos such as Samuel Ramos and Frank Tennenbaum. The chapter ends not with the late Vasconcelos's caustic view of his country under the hegemony of a party of brutal atheists, but with Veríssimo's enthusiastic elegy to Lázaro Cárdenas, compared to Getúlio Vargas as the "Pai Grande" (208) of the Mexican people. Among the problems faced by Cárdenas during his presidency, Veríssimo alludes to a "falangist movement of clear fascist tendencies" (208) but refrains to mention Vasconcelos's involvement with the Mexican *sinarquismo* and his Nazi sympathies in the 1940s; whether this omission is due to Veríssimo's ignorance (by the 1950s Vasconcelos's infatuation with Fascism received little mention in Mexico) or to his intent to safeguard the image of the old master, it is hard to tell.

After Vasconcelos, David Alfaro Siqueiros dominates Chapter 9, which is mostly dedicated to the muralists. The prestige of Siqueiros among Brazilians dates from his electrifying four-hour lecture at the Clube dos Artistas Modernos [CAM] in São Paulo. Years later Flávio de Carvalho recalled that memorable meeting thus:

> [he] was (...) a great orator who spoke for hours in a vigorous and imaginative improvisation that did not tire his audience...Siqueiros thrilled the audience, forming a veritable magnetic field in the room and keeping this magnetic field as powerful for hours, never missing a beat (...) he did not speak to explain but to complete something he had started visually. (...) His political ideas affected the color and form of his arguments only a few times—something unusual in people with radical ideas. (48)[25]

Just as with Vasconcelos, Veríssimo empathizes with Siqueiros, whom he considers the most endowed with a "sculptural sense of the monumental" (221) that is the soul of Mexican *muralismo* and a fascinating man "capable of every sort of violence and every kind of gentlemanliness," "mixture of Renaissance man, caudillo, political agitator, and prophet."[26] Over a dish of quesadillas stuffed with the exquisite *huitlacoche* truffles, which Veríssimo greatly appreciates, Siqueiros quickly summarizes his biography. Then the two men take a tour to different sites downtown where Siqueiros shows his murals and expounds on the ideological function of the artist in the modern world. Again Veríssimo functions as the provocateur, asking for Siqueiros's opinion of two rivals, Rivera and Tamayo, and Siqueiros obliges, saying that "if Rivera in his painting speaks a *Frenchfied* Náhuatl, Tamayo expresses himself in a French of bad construction and worse pronunciation"

(240).[27] Again the author of *México—História duma Viagem* inserts his own views carefully, choosing three strategic moments to offer counterpoints without seeming to undermine Siqueiros's opinion. First, Veríssimo comments on Siqueiros's *Retrato da Burguesia*, a mural at the headquarters of the electricians' union, as the one he "likes the least,"

> because of the excess of allegorical figures and because of the circum-stantial character of many of these symbols. It seems to me that the Aztec symbols and myths offer fewer risks, because I don't think that time can alter their meaning. (225)[28]

Veríssimo is bothered by the allusions that lump together Fascism and liberal democracy—storm troopers march into a burning neoclassi-cal building bearing the words *Liberté, Egalité, Fraternité*—in this famous 1939 mural that denounces the abandonment of the Spanish Republic,[29] a detail Veríssimo significantly omits. Siqueiros's political engagement does not bother Veríssimo, who in 1971 wrote *Incidente em Antares*, one of the most mordant denunciations of the Brazilian dictatorship. But he defends the artist's right not to choose explicitly political themes, as he makes clear when he defends Tamayo saying that "I don't believe an artist *must* practice politically engaged art; I think he *may*, if he wishes so, make this choice" (226).[30] It is the specific political message in *Retrato de la Burguesía* that displeases Veríssimo. Later, as the Mexican painter and the Brazilian novelist take a taxi, Veríssimo addresses this irritation indirectly as he notes that the car they ride in is

> a Plymouth, manufactured in a country where Siqueiros could only with difficulty find a dramatic subject in the factories where every workman owns a car as good as this one and earns a wage that permits him a standard of living better than that of the Mexican middle class. (241)[31]

The argument again reinforces Veríssimo's image of the United States as a well-managed place devoid of drama—the same image of the United States as Mexico's foil used by Ronald de Carvalho in *Imagens do México*.

Allowing characters to speak with strategic editorial insertions that discreetly frame their voices disguises Veríssimo's essay on Mexico as the unpretentious memoirs of middle-class vacation travels. Veríssimo's novels follow a similar strategy; they are generally considered highly readable because of a plain and accessible style that ostensibly performs its artlessness, but of course there is subtle artifice behind this deceptive sense of plainness in his prose. Moreover, Veríssimo's narrators constantly looked for a sense of closeness with the reader. In his essays Veríssimo deploys these textual strategies to seduce the reader into accepting his arguments as simple common sense and his stories as the plain truth. These subtle strategies inform Veríssimo's arguments about Mexico and about the two other countries that loom in the background of his book, Brazil and the United States.

The first-person narrator introduces himself as an unimportant office worker, "tired of bureaucracy and the world around him" (2).[32] He professes to love the United States, but Washington is for him a stifling urban space in its unerring symmetry, "which works like an electronic machine selecting cards" (3),[33] where this man is forced by the nature of his work to deal with an assortment of gentle, neat, and unerringly uninformed and pragmatic Americans obsessed with statistics or, worse still, with plain idiots such as the Latin American military attaché who sits next to him and berates Bach—his favorite composer—for the whole duration of a boring official dinner, only to say the exact opposite as the author timidly declares his admiration for the German composer. This is a balancing act that ensures his criticisms do not sound arrogant or offensive, presenting the reader the image of an affable, tolerant, unpretentious narrator.

Fond as this man who works in an inter-American diplomatic mission is of the United States, what Veríssimo takes to be the excessively logical Anglo-Saxon world exasperates him.[34] The main reason for such exasperation is that, while living in the United States, Veríssimo claims to have suffered from writer's block, a problem he attributes to a perfectly functioning environment that resembles "a colored postcard, lustrous, charming, yes, but lacking a third dimension" (3),[35] a landscape that tires him and a life that dulls his senses.[36] Veríssimo here seems to discuss difficulties he is indeed said to have experienced when writing the third volume of his *O Tempo e o Vento* trilogy, but not just while living abroad. *México—História duma Viagem* was written in 1957 in *Brazil* precisely in an interval after another failed attempt to write what was to become *O Arquipélago* in 1962.[37] Anyway, for the narrator of this prologue, living in this smooth, perfectly functioning world lacks, as he mentioned when riding in the taxi with Siqueiros, *drama*, something essential for him because it produces *friction*. To fire up the imagination, the Latin American writer (or at least this particular writer) needed the imperfection and the incoherence, the constant chaos that is for him a staple of the world from which he comes, from a Latin America where "the clock is merely a decorative element and time a subject for poetry" (4).[38] Veríssimo compares the writer to an oyster, "the repellent creature" (4): both can be made to produce beauty (novels and pearls) when "a certain special kind of irritation"[39] is produced. The Anglo-Saxon world produces irritation, but a sterile sort that "only leads to yawns" and melancholy boredom. This kind of literature simply does not do justice to life, which is too interesting and too short. That is how Veríssimo explains his longing for Mexico, enticed by his brief previous short visits. Mexico and Brazil here are parts of one whole Latin America and going to Mexico amounts to going home for this melancholy Latin American suffering from writer's block. Living in the United States makes Veríssimo Latin American, and he longs to find in Mexico "the Latin American disorder; the images, sounds, and smells of our little world" (4).[40] All this personal drama is light-heartedly exposed in a prologue humorously framed as a soliloquy to Shakespeare by a man who claims to have none of the grandeur of the Bard's tragedies. Veríssimo ends it with a typical apology to the reader for these flights of fancy: "Heavens! Can I be turning metaphysical? Positively, William Shakespeare, I urgently need a vacation" (4).[41] In *México—História duma Viagem* there are several other lyrical, emotionally charged passages. They are invariably followed by some humorous disclaimer or apology that reinforces the reader's expectations about the plain, modest persona of this narrator who is always guided by simple common sense.

The travelogue that follows this prologue sustains the same tone and the same rhetorical strategies. Veríssimo's unfailing modesty is not just a pose—he really distrusts the grand rhetorical gestures that propose broad generalizations about the national character. His vision of Mexico moves beyond the simplistic view of a perfect opposite of the United States. The contradictions and sharp contrasts in Mexico turn it into a country that resists easy classifications:

> I feel some sort of amiable irritation before this indomitable city that resists classification, one that repels every adjective I offer it, presenting itself to us sometimes as modern and other times as antique; now charming and then later on sinister; here beautiful and a few steps ahead ugly...After all, where are we? We aren't. It is better to walk on, to drink Mexico, to absorb Mexico through the eyes, the pores, the air we breathe, the voices we hear, the smells that enter our nostrils – burnt gasoline, dust from the asphalt, tortilla, fritters, the fragrances of flowers and herbs...(15)[42]

Veríssimo returns in the passage above to the idea of a place that produces irritation and friction, which is needed to entice a writer's imagination and make him produce. Irritation and friction defy an easy
characterization of Mexico. This list of contrasts, which Veríssimo
sarcastically reminds us is the bulk of every clichéd description of a
foreign place, does not mean much in itself. Veríssimo's Mexico City
is a city like no other because it was "erected upon the corpse of the
Tenochtitlán murdered by Cortés and his soldiers" (34); this is what
gives the capital "the aura of drama that envelops it" ( . . . ) "that dark,
ominous tone that gives the sensation that something tragic is about
to occur."[43]

In order to measure the bearings of this corpse over which Mexico
was founded, Veríssimo goes beyond absorbing attentively every sign,
sound, smell, and taste offered by the living capital. Veríssimo obviously researched extensively the history and geography of Mexico
and that research particularly informs the chapter dedicated to an
imaginative re-creation of life in Tenochtitlán before Cortés's arrival.
Veríssimo cites Bernal Díaz de Castillo, Cortés, and Diego Rivera's
murals as sources for his "fanciful" narrative, and it is obvious that
Reyes's *Visión de Anahuac* and George C. Vaillant's *The Aztecs of
Mexico* were also useful.

Mexico stands in Veríssimo's book as the symbol of a Latin
American world of poetical imagination, but also unpredictable disaster and brutal violence. This unruly world is constantly contrasted
with its foil, the United States, as the symbol of another America, a
world of logic and prosaic utilitarianism, predictable order, and gentle comfort. Veríssimo has learned to appreciate both. But to be an
artist and to be himself, the protagonist of *México—Historia duma
Viagem* needs Latin America, the world he identifies as truly his. But
the liberal intellectual who admires the United States also longs for
the peace and harmony of that prosaic and predictable way of living.
Hope and fear of change are constantly playing in this double consciousness and Veríssimo recognizes this at the end of his book:

> I knew the epilogue of this book couldn't be happy! I am probably
> condemned to oscillate the rest of my life between those two loves,
> without knowing exactly which I want more, the magical world or the
> logical. Only one hope of salvation is left for me. It is that, between
> the American thesis and the Mexican antithesis, Brazil may some day
> come to be the desired synthesis.
>
> *Y, quién sabe?* (326)[44]

The argument is flawed because countries are not logical or magical as this simplistic formula suggests. But the idea of a synthesis between logic and magic is a form of resistance to Weber's view of modernization as a disenchantment of the world. It is yet another reenactment of the dichotomy between barbarism and civilization that has animated Latin American letters, again infused with hopes and fears of modernization. The hope that this desired synthesis take place in Brazil is a sign that for Veríssimo the burden of the past and the internal tensions in Brazil were somewhat less complicated than in Mexico—an echo of Reyes's arguments about the two countries. Even with the final Mexican disclaimer (*Quién sabe?*), Veríssimo's dream is in tune with the Brazilian intellectual climate of the 1950s, when the country built a futuristic capital in its heartland in the firm belief that it could turn its back on the past.

The events that shook Latin America in the 1960s, when the continent found itself all of a sudden at the center of the Cold War, laid bare the limitations of the dichotomy between barbarism and civilization and also disproved completely the illusions of Brazil's "exceptionalism" within the continent. The idea of a sharp dichotomy between logical and magical societies in Latin America became increasingly problematic as modern and so-called archaic worlds were seen as two sides of the same coin, not juxtaposed but fully integrated in symbiotic interdependence. Veríssimo, a brave writer always willing to respond to his time and its dilemmas, had to rethink his liberal convictions with a much sharper view of the relations between Latin America and the United States and of his own country's history. And he did so in three politically charged novels: *O Senhor Embaixador* (1965), *O Prisioneiro* (1967), and *Incidente em Antares* (1971).

*Mexico—História duma Viagem* is full of empathy and affection for México and its people and marks the beginning of a shift from a more strictly US-informed idea of Pan-Americanism toward a view of the continent that privileges Spanish Latin America. This empathy, considering the hardships of Mexican-US relations, is largely absent from Veríssimo's previous travel narratives. In *Gato Preto em Campo de Neve*, Veríssimo barely mentions the Mexican presence in California: he briefly describes San Francisco's "barrio latino" and notes that Mexicans there were taking advantage of the fact that the United States seemed to be "tomada por uma febre pan-americanista" [taken by a pan-americanist fever] (316–317). Later in the same book he interviews Aldous Huxley, who expresses surprise at the Indian presence in Mexico and his amazement at the nation's extraordinary archeological treasures (382). In *A Volta do Gato Preto*, Veríssimo even expresses a disapproving view of a group of Mexican teachers he met at Oakland's Mills College. Besides a student called *Don* Remedios Mirando Sarazate, "of melancholy air and voice like an oboe" (93),[45] Veríssimo criticizes the behavior of Mexicans who take part in a summer course at the college. Subjected, we do not know whether willingly or not, to English-language classes with a phonetics specialist and philologist, these Mexicans, in Veríssimo's opinion, "displaying an aggressive frown and an attitude of open hostility towards their surroundings" (139).[46]

At the end of his travel memoirs Veríssimo returns to the United States and his house "has suddenly become mexicanized" (325). Far from understanding Mexico, Veríssimo claims to have fallen in love with it: "How many years will I need to digest Mexico? How many lifetimes should I live to comprehend it? But one consolation is left and it suffices me. I need not even a minute more to learn to love it" (324).[47] The text on the back cover reinforces the idea of a relationship that precludes a fully articulated understanding:

> One life is not enough to comprehend Mexico, not even enough to touch the heart of its mystery. I am not writing about this country because I have figured it out, but because I love it and I want to understand it, or at least sense it deeply. I don't believe anyone will have the last word about the Mexican...[48]

In the 1970s Veríssimo published two volumes of his life memoirs and returned to his relationship with Mexico:

> Be as it may, I feel an identification with that land and its people. Well, identified perhaps is not the right word. It would be better to say that I did not know Mexico but I loved it. Isn't it the same thing? But of course it is! Love, as art, is one of the most legitimate forms of knowledge. (*Solo de Clarineta—Segundo Volume* 7)[49]

Veríssimo started his book project fully equipped with the tools of ethnography, but reached a conclusion that perhaps only someone deeply committed to fictional narrative could find: in the attempt to grasp culture, love is a form of knowledge that preconditions not just an articulate understanding of the Other, but any true form of identification.

# Chapter 6

# João Guimarães Rosa between
# Life and Death in His Own Páramo

João Guimarães Rosa (1908–1967) was a narrative writer whose temperament and instincts were practically the opposite of prosaic, plainspoken Érico Veríssimo's.[1] However, Guimarães Rosa agreed with the centrality of affection in the search for any kind of meaningful knowledge, he being imbued with a deep love for language and its power, and for nature and its beauty. Guimarães Rosa believed affection somehow protected his fiction against what he saw as the excesses of rationalism, something he once famously called "the Cartesian bête noire" ("a megera cartesiana") (Bizarri, 90). The same could be said for religious faith, natural religion in the Hegelian sense. Guimarães Rosa was a man of faith, but quite heterodox; I would even dare say that he was typically Brazilian in his decision to believe pragmatically or, at least in principle, to be interested in all religious beliefs. In this sense, Guimarães Rosa had a lot in common with his most famous character, Riobaldo, who says in *Grande Sertão: Veredas*: "Here, I do not miss an opportunity for religion. I take advantage of all of them. I drink from all rivers... Just one, for me, is not much, perhaps it may not suffice."[2] His interest in mystery included superstitions. For example, although unanimously elected to the Real Academia Brasileira de Letras (Brazilian Academy of Letters) in 1963, Guimarães Rosa delayed the official inaugural ceremony for four years—the maximum length of time that his diplomatic ability afforded him. The reason behind this seemed to be a foreboding feeling or something that someone might have told him about what would happen next. The fact is that on Sunday, November 19, 1967, precisely three days after his induction ceremony at the Academy, Guimarães Rosa died at age 59, in his home.

Among his papers, a tentative table of contents was found for a book that would be titled *Estas Estórias* and would be published posthumously in 1969. This table of contents listed eight stories and the interview with Mariano the cowhand (previously published in three parts in the newspaper *Correio da Manhã* in 1947–1948 and in a special edition book in 1952). Four of these stories had already been published before; among them "Meu Tio o Iauaretê" (translated as "The Jaguar" by David Treece) is considered to be Guimarães Rosa's best story by some and, fortunately, available to Mexican readers in the anthology compiled by Valquiria Wey for the publishing house Fondo de Cultura Económica. Among the other four unpublished stories—already typed, but still without "a last revision by the author" according to the editor Paulo Rónai[3]—there was one sui generis story in all of Guimarães Rosa's work. This story is the only one (apart from first three that the young author sent to the magazine *Cruzeiro* in 1929 and which he never published) that does not take place in the mythical *Sertão Mineiro*, a northern region of the state of Minas Gerais where Guimarães Rosa was born. That story from *Estas Estórias* does not even transpire in Brazil and, additionally, its name evokes unmistakable resonances for Mexican and Latin American ears: it is called "Páramo" (177–198).

Despite its location abroad, we can consider this "Páramo" as part of a particular class of stories that Guimarães Rosa cultivated in his work since "São Marcos," "the best-crafted piece"[4] from his first book, *Sagarana*. They are complex stories, often times misunderstood by impatient critics due to the intricateness of the plot and a prose that seems to advance very slowly, filled with erudite or pseudoerudite interruptions by loquacious and arrogant first-person narrators who oscillate between the pathetic and the comic while their egocentrism makes them talk about humiliations, be they real or imaginary. Those stories by Guimarães Rosa are not only presented as real narrative labyrinths full of enigmatic references and symbols where one can easily lose oneself, but also as fascinating challenges for the curious reader.[5]

As I have stated before, Guimarães Rosa was a man of faith; however, in his works, the importance of faith was not as a religious profession, but instead as one more of his many literary artifices. The significance of religion in "Páramo" is apparent from its dramatic opening, where the nameless narrator addresses his "brothers" with a sermon-like tone. What religion is it? It's Spiritism, which arrived in Brazil in 1865 and today has 2.25 million believers—the religious group with the highest level in education in the country according to the 2000 census.[6] Created in France in the nineteenth century following the publication of *The Spirits' Book* by Allan Kardec (pseudonym for the French educator Hippolyte Rivail), eclectically incorporating elements of Christianity and other religions, Spiritists differ from the Catholics primarily because of their belief in the reincarnation of the soul and in mediumship.[7] The narrator/protagonist of "Páramo" begins his sermon by emphatically reaffirming the dogma of reincarnation, but announces that he wants to talk about another experience: living death.

Just like other narrator-protagonists in similar types of stories by Guimarães Rosa, the narrator in "Páramo" is loaded down with ambiguities—his pathetic story is mixed with pseudoerudition and mysticism in the service of what could be hypochondria and excessive egocentrism.[8] Besides, in the beginning, he doubts whether or not to identify himself as the protagonist of a story that exposes him to public disgrace. So he starts off by saying, "A man, still young, in the middle of a trip that had been imposed upon him [ ... ] finally saw himself in exile in a foreign city,"[9] and then all of a sudden assumes the first-person narration with an enigmatic phrase: "There, I received myself"[10] (178).

And where exactly is that "there" from the story located? The *páramo* to which the title refers is in Colombia, near Bogota, where Guimarães Rosa lived from 1942 to 1944 after five difficult years of diplomatic duty in Nazi Germany. In Bogota, Guimarães Rosa was left without Aracy Moebius de Carvalho, his life partner, whom he had met in Germany at the Hamburg consulate. Living at an altitude of 2,660 meters, Guimarães Rosa would complain about his difficulty in adapting to the altitude, mentioning the terrible "*soroche* (...) o mal-das-alturas" [*soroche*, the altitude sickness] (181).[11]

As is common in Guimarães Rosa's work, the story's location is significant, but it is presented indirectly—the narrator does not expressly mention Bogota a single time, although he does mention the Andes and describes the geography, the streets, and the buildings of the old center as well as the surrounding areas of Bogota.[12] It is not my intention to attempt to establish a supposed accuracy between the fiction and the author's biographical information or the characteristics of that particular location, since I believe that in literature biographical and contextual data are actually attached to the fiction, and not the other way around. Besides, Guimarães Rosa's fiction is not constructed with the idea of representation of reality as imitation, but, instead, as an imaginative interpretation, which means that, as the narrator of the story "*A Hora e a Vez de Augusto Matraga*" says, "there is no lie at all because this is a made up story and it isn't an actual case that occurred"(*Sagarana*, 343)[13] or, as Juan Rulfo also said in an interview, "literature is a lie that tells the truth" ("Una conversación con Ernesto González Bermejo," 6).[14]

The geographical space of fiction in "Páramo" is split into three places symbolically distinguished by their altitude. The middle space, "*en la cárcel de los Andes*" ("Páramo" 179), is Bogota, "Old, colonial, of an ancient era, perhaps the saddest of all" (178): "I will be imprisoned within her, for a long time, under the almost unreal rocks and the clouds that form ephemeral sculptures" (179).[15] Above the city are the *páramos* of the title and below another place name with clear Rulfian evocations, the llanos. Those three locations are defined, as is customary in Guimarães Rosa's works, as much by his meticulous care as an observer with the acumen of an ethnographer and a naturalist as they are by his prodigious verbal imagination, all of which endow those places with mythical power.

Those wastelands at the top of the Andes acquire that mythical consistency—I would say "luvinesque" or "luvinical"—when the narrator describes them in the following terms:

> And there are, elevated and invisible, the wastelands —that are elevated peaks of the mountain range, snow-capped and subject to blizzards, through which the mountain passes must cross, which bring them here ice-wintered! The wastelands, from whence the winds cross. There, it is a den of winds, great whirs, and lugubrious howlings. The humid cold that reaches those people, those streets, and those houses descends from there. From there, from that wasteland and desolation, death would come to me. Not the final death—equestrian, reaping, bony, so boisterous. But, the other, *that one.* (179)[16]

If the wasteland from whence comes a terrible chill of death that infects the entire city is further up, the plains remain below. That third location appears in the narrative when the protagonist speaks with a medical doctor, a Jewish man who lives with his family in the country, "clandestine and foreign" [clandestino e estrangeiro] (182), fleeing from the war in Europe.

> "Here, at least people eat, people wait, in any case. It's not like in the Llanos..." At first, he tried to live life in a small town lost in the torrid plains, in painful consolation, they ate yucca and plantains almost exclusively. There, they cried. Far away, in their homeland, was the war. Blond men like himself were destroying one another, killing each other in cold blood. There, in the Llanos, dark-eyed Indians watched him, for such a long time, so deeply, so mysteriously –it was as if suffering itself could see us. (182)[17]

During this progression in which the narrator-protagonist grows closer to the doctor character little by little, from the first part in quotation marks until the end where the Indians are not only looking at the doctor, but at both of them, the Llanos appear in contrast not only to the city, but also to the doctor's own country. Presumably, he is referring to Germany, from where Guimarães Rosa helped many Jews escape to Brazil—an undertaking for which the Israeli government presented his wife, Aracy, a medal. Guimarães Rosa, a writer who did not give more than six interviews in his entire life and who never spoke publicly about those deeds, once said to a surprised Brazilian poet that he had come face to face with the devil in Nazi Germany. Far from the stupid war and persecution where "blond men like himself were destroying one another," the doctor and his family find another form of grief: the desperation that comes with poverty and hunger. So, in Guimarães Rosa's torrid Llanos, sadness also prevails and the doctor views the indigenous people that he finds there as a silent presence in whose watchful gaze the image of grief is reflected.

In addition to the explicit references made to the *páramo* and the Llanos, these textual examples reveal a Rulfian walking of the line between a lapidary poetic language of mythical tones and an attentive observation of the harsh reality of an exhausting struggle against natural misery and human misery. One of the fundamental points that appear in the work of both Guimarães Rosa and Rulfo is the conscientious linguistic labor, although with different results, since the Rosa text gives the impression of being the result of a slow process of accumulation while Rulfo text gives the opposite impression, that of resulting from a process of subtraction in which only the essential is left. The other fundamental point of contact that is evident in these brief examples is the sharp attention, without condescension or sentimentality, to the existence and the subjectivity of the modest people of peripheral regions—issues considered by others to be incapable of leading to universal themes or to a complex analysis.

Beyond this important characteristic shared by both of these geniuses of modern narrative, it is specifically in "Páramo" that Guimarães Rosa more closely approaches Rulfo's literary territory, precisely by dealing with that curious topos of living death, in which the limits between life and death are erased, as indicated in the epigraph to the story in which Plato's Socrates asks himself: "Who knows if life be not death, and death life?" In the sermon that serves as a prologue to the story, the narrator explains:

> However, at times, it happens that we die, in some way, another type of death, imperfect and temporary, in the very course of this life. We die,

one dies, there is no other word that can define such a state, that crucial station. It is an obscure passing of oneself, continuous, a crossing
over that does not terminate our existence naturally, but one in which
the field of a profound and ruinous operation is felt, of an intimate
transmutation preceded by a certain standstill, always with a previous
destruction, an aching addiction; then, we miss ourselves. (177)[18]

Therefore, it is about the possibility of existing without existing, of
living without corporeality, "with neither weight nor sex" (182),[19] of
disappearing from oneself in life. From there, then, emerges a new
existence tormented by panic and anguish that tends to erupt in convulsive sobbing at any moment, an existence marked by a profound
feeling of loneliness and distance. The protagonist feels this loneliness in the middle of the crowded city, since "Not even an edge of
our souls come into contact" (183).[20] With living death, Guimarães
Rosa conceives a representation of the feeling of alienation in its most
extreme expression: not even one's own body escapes estrangement.

However, Guimarães Rosa—who practiced medicine before entering into diplomatic service—presents us with a phenomenon that is
not necessarily paranormal or in the realm of fantastic literature. In
a physiological sense, all of the things that the protagonist says he
feels—the suffocation, the insomnia, the convulsive sobbing— are
symptoms of *soroche* (mountain/altitude sickness) promptly diag-
nosed by the doctor. And still beyond the physiological, the express
conviction that the narrator died in life while he was in Bogota has
another clinical explanation. In 1880, Doctor Jules Cotard described
for the first time a clinical state considered to be a type of "agitated
melancholy" that he coined *"délire de negations."* He was referring
to what is now called Cotard's syndrome among psychiatric circles,
an illness that consists of delusions that range from the belief that an
organ has been lost to the certainty that one is dead or has lost one's
soul.[21] It is also important to note that Cotard's syndrome generally
affects people with acute depression, a disease spiritists have at times
referred to as a sort of "living death."[22]

Thus, the events in "Páramo" have physiological, psychiatric, psychological, and mystical/religious explanations. An attentive reading
of "Páramo" does not allow us to select just one of these to the detriment of the others, which is a common strategy in Guiramães Rosa's
fiction. It is a textual strategy that we could more aptly call Machadian
(I am referring to Machado de Assis): resistance to a univocal reading,
maintaining a fundamental ambiguity until the very end. Two brief,
but paradigmatic examples are: in Machado de Assis, the eternal discussion among readers of *Dom Casmurro* regarding the adultery of

Capitu, and, in Guimarães Rosa, the multiple oblique motivations of Diadorim and of Riobaldo in *Grande Sertão: Veredas*.[23]

In the case of Guimarães Rosa's "Páramo," we can interpret the acts narrated by the narrator-protagonist in mystical-religious terms and we can also establish an ironic distance from the narration, reading the account of someone who suffers psychic disturbances, and in both cases, the *soroche*—a problem of natural physiology—remains as a trigger for the deeds. The labyrinth, assembled in this way by Guimarães Rosa, offers us living death as a comprehensive experience, as a metaphor for alienation, and as an hallucination. An unresolved dilemma faces the reader who chooses one living death for the protagonist of "Páramo," and a more terrible hypothesis surfaces: this narrator-protagonist may have died in life three times simultaneously.

While he struggles against insomnia and the sensation of suffocation that persists throughout the night, the protagonist sees himself transported to an even worse nocturnal inferno, "a world of hatred" (186)[24] still more horrible than his diurnal melancholy existence. At night, the past and the present and all the places are confused as if "My spirit would know itself to be in diverse worlds all at once, equally interweaving itself through levels that were as far apart as possible" (186).[25]

In this world without time or space, the protagonist faces another infernal day's journey through the city, now inhabited by specters from the colonial past. They are terrifying figures, like that of an old indigenous woman who tirelessly shouts inside a tram, her mouth transformed into "a channel through which more hatred was brought into this world" (187)[26]; or another woman who had imprisoned an innocent young girl, gradually mutilating her and giving her disgusting pieces of food and water only so that she would continue suffering; or the grotesque figure of an obese father who always uses enormous clothes and utensils, evoking demons and reciting the list of the notorious medieval *Goetia* while he leads a row of other sinister figures.[27]

These figures from a past of hatred that are confounded with the present return the reader to the colonial past of the Americas (including the Anglo-Saxon one), full of injustice, hate, destruction, torture, and death—the past that makes Mexico City special to Érico Veríssimo. A past, therefore, that is not substantially different than the one from which the Jewish doctor is fleeing. Why does the protagonist —and we, alongside him—have to relive those deaths in life? Would it be a return to the consciousness of something that we always attempt to suppress, the consciousness of what a poem by José Emilio Pacheco declares to us: "The dust / that stains our face / is the vestige / of an incessant crime" (*Tarde o Temprano* 86)?[28]

In the same way that the physiological, the psychological, the metaphorical, and the mystical are nonexclusive in "Páramo," the ghosts of the past coexist with ghosts of an individual facing his tormented identity within his own body. At the end of this part, the most chilling in all of "Páramo," Guimarães Rosa takes up the image of the mirror again:

> Being dead is terrible, the way I know I sometimes am—in another way. With that lack of a soul. I breathe poorly; the cold undoes me. It's like the prison of a mirror. In a mirror into which my eyes fade. The mirror, so *cislucid*, only. A mirror below zero. (188)[29]

The mirror as a literary motif used for reflection on the process of alienation in the problematic relationship between the interior and exterior worlds of an individual in the constitution of his identity is a recurring motif in Brazilian literature since the story *"O Espelho"* by Machado de Assis from 1882, and is at the center of a story in which Guimarães Rosa responds to the master, a narrative that is also called *"O Espelho"* from the book *Primeiras Estórias* (1962).[30]

Guimarães Rosa adds the image of the double with a morbid appearance to that of the mirror's prison as deep self-alienation. The outsider in a foreign city feels alienated from all the people, but in all of them, he emphasizes a strange figure, a mysterious *doppelgänger* that pursues him day and night.[31] This double appears no less than nine times in the story, successively called by different variations of his first epithet, the *"homem com semelhança de cadáver"* [man who resembles a corpse]: with the appearance of a corpse, with the mien of a corpse, cold as a corpse, with something cadaverlike about him, et cetera. He is a phantasmal figure who represents the most dead among all the city's dead to the protagonist, but he is also a man "of his race," who looks like the protagonist, a presence that provokes terror and revulsion, with the Freudian *unheimlich*'s typical combination of identification and horror.

However, not even that morbid and haunting double escapes Guimarães Rosa's ambiguities, and he changes his appearance a bit in a particularly hermetic section of the story where temptations that are represented by three women he desires appear: a French widow, an imposing Russian woman, and a Spanish woman who is someone else's girlfriend, an evanescent figure whom he calls Doña Clara at first and then later "Evanira." At this moment, the *"homem que é um cadáver"* is transformed into a seducer and invites the narrator-protagonist to go down to the *tierra templada* (temperate land), something that the doctor had advised against. At this time, the narrator describes his *doppelgänger* as "straightforward and friendly" [correto e amigo] (190).

The mirror's prison, the profound isolation in a foreign city and a hostile environment, the supreme distancing of oneself within a living death, and the double with the appearance of a corpse who pursues and tempts him: the narrator-protagonist of "Páramo" lives the existence of a Kafkiaesque character of multiple and relentless alienation, what he calls "Job's blow." However, he is not a passive character or one who is fundamentally incapable of facing the obstacles that are placed in his path. The protagonist-narrator strives against his predicament: he walks every morning as the doctor advised, he searches for peace in a church (empty except for the repulsive presence of his double), he looks for help in a convent (where a nun does not understand his *"chirriado"* (184) and offers him sweets wrapped in a newspaper that displays sensual feminine figures), and he tries to force himself to no longer think about the *homem com o todo de cadáver* that pursues him buying a mysterious book to help him do that.

Besides the juxtaposition of suggested readings and the accumulation of ambiguities, "Páramo" has an intricate web of textual references that form pairs placed at strategic points of the text as in a game of mirrors. Only three examples: the fine irony of Plato's Socrates and the pathos of Psalm 51 *Miserere*; the ironic Catalonian poet Joaquin Bartrina contrasting chance and fatality and an English folk ballad about the forbidden love between an Englishman and a Spanish woman; two paintings by the Swiss symbolist Arnold Böcklin from his turn-of-the- nineteenth-century eclecticism and the hair-raising grotesqueness of Goya's *Caprichos*; the Greek letter that appears under the title of the narrative and which can symbolize either the end or death, and the hangman from a Tarot deck —the one that resigns from life in the name of enlightenment, "the killing and purging of the false self which precedes the creation of the true, inner self" (Cavendish 103).

Amidst that hodgepodge of quotes is that mysterious purchased book, "perhaps of poetry," that is called the Book (with a capital B). The protagonist always takes it with him on his walks so that his double does not see it nor read it without his permission, but he does not open it because he believes that he will definitely die if he does so. The revelation of that enigmatic Book is going to have a central role at the end of the story, in something that we can call the resurrection of the protagonist of "Páramo," or the end of his living death.

The catalyst for the change in the narrator-protagonist's state of living death is precisely one of the most uncomfortable aspects of the protagonist's condition: his convulsive sobbing in public, which causes him profound embarrassment and makes him hide among the farthest and darkest streets of the city. One day the sobbing arrives too quickly, "on a central public street" and "the scandal" is such that when the protagonist sees a funeral cortège that reminds him of a "Capricho de Goya" (196) he decides to join the entourage to conceal himself. The procession of modest people who possibly follow the body of a child (the casket is small) moves on slowly and the narrator accompanies them "from as far back as possible, behind all. Like a dog" (195).[32]

The book and the protagonist's foreign appearance make him self-conscious when they approach the cemetery. At the entrance, the protagonist realizes he is no longer sobbing and decides to hide in the labyrinth of the "city of tombs and statues" finding a far-off corner "between tombstones and cypresses, almost a nest" (194).[33] After offering his public tears to an unknown dead, outside the city of the dead-living in the city of the dead-dead, among ancient tombs where the names have already faded, the protagonist finally finds peace, "a refuge in the sacred, a relief, of nirvana, was coming to me, a taste of the end" (194).[34] Now the narrator confirms he is the protagonist of his story saying, "after, I came to there" (197) and feels he can finally open and read the Book, but his fear suddenly returns and he decides to leave the book in the cemetery "in a discreet corner, in the shade of a cypress and slab of slate."[35]

But irony is the trademark of Guimarães Rosa's fiction. Not just verbal irony, but situational irony: characters achieve what they desire when they no longer want it or when they stop trying, destiny constantly denies them and then surprises them offering their "hora e vez" [time and turn]. When the protagonist is about to leave the cemetery, he runs into a man who was searching for him; this man had accompanied the funeral procession and he hands the protagonist the Book he thinks the protagonist "has lost" (197). This poor, humbly dressed man is young and saddened but has absolutely no resemblance to the dreadful cadaver-man who torments the protagonist. He strikes up a short conversation with the protagonist, tells the name of the deceased whom the narrator now calls "our dead man," and offers timid consoling words. For the first time since his arrival in Colombia, the protagonist's soul and that of another man's touch, although only briefly.[36]

Now the protagonist decides to open the Book he has in his hands once again and...what book is it? We will probably never know. In the typed version of the story used by Paulo Rónai, there is nothing more than "a space, for a quote, that the narrator never got around to filling" (198). I consider Guimarães Rosa's "Páramo" as an homage—unfortunately unfinished—to the greatest Mexican author, Juan Rulfo. It is typical of Guimarães Rosa: a tribute with citations full of the typical ironic inversions that comprise all of the referencing in Guimarães Rosa's work, tiny gems encrusted in intricate murals in the shape of a labyrinth.

\* \* \*

The notion that Brazilian and Latin American literature follows paths that are completely independent of one another is still popular today. There is even an author-character created by Rubem Fonseca who sarcastically affirms that Latin American literature only exists "in Mr. Knopf's head" (*Contos Reunidos*, 468).[37] It's ironic to think that in 2003 Fonseca would win (rightfully so) the *Premio Juan Rulfo*. Rulfo was a serious connoisseur of Brazilian literature—the preface that Rulfo wrote for the Spanish edition of Machado de Assis's *Memorias Póstumas de Blas Cubas* is proof positive of Rulfo's knowledge and appreciation for Brazilian literature. Rulfo had a key role in the circulation of Brazilian literature in Mexico, especially in the case of Daniel Sada, whom Rulfo taught at the Centro Mexicano de Escritores' literary workshop. In a private conversation with Sada, he told me that it was precisely Rulfo who introduced him to Brazilian literature and to Guimarães Rosa in particular, a significant fact since Sada is an exceptional writer, perhaps the best of his generation, whom critics often liken to Guimarães Rosa.

Brazilian literature was not completely ignored during the Latin American literary phenomenon known by its not-very-pleasant name, *boom*, which the Brazilian poet Augusto de Campos sarcastically defined as "Latin American literature common market / (where only the Brazilians don't sell anything)" (Campos 161).[38] Guimarães Rosa was precisely the only Brazilian who made the most out of the *boom* in order to shine internationally. In that way, like Juan Rulfo, and in contrast to Jorge Luis Borges, Guimarães Rosa would not immediately achieve the resounding international success that the youngest authors, notably García Márquez, Vargas Llosa, Fuentes, and Cortázar did. Nevertheless, Guimarães Rosa, just like Rulfo, actively participated in the Latin American authors' organizations that stimulated the exchange among these countries at that time[39] and, more important, if we consider literary quality over publishing success in Europe and the United States, João Guimarães Rosa and Juan Rulfo are at the center and at the height of twentieth-century Latin American literature.

João Guimarães Rosa and Juan Rulfo knew each other since at least 1965, and a private and much less known event concretely indicates the particular relationship that existed between the two. In 1967, they both went to Guadalajara to participate in the Primer Congreso de la Comunidad Latinoamericana de Escritores (First Conference of the Latin American Community of Writers) with many other renowned authors, such as Miguel Ángel Asturias, Alejo Carpentier, and Ángel Rama. At the request of Guimarães Rosa, he and Rulfo returned to Mexico City alone by bus. That long ride, which has been the object of colorful stories, was confirmed to me by people who knew Rulfo and Guimarães Rosa and reiterated their mutual appreciation, on both personal and literary levels.[40] In 2008, I went to Guimarães Rosa's archives at the Instituto de Estudos Brasileiros (Institute of Brazilian Studies, IEB) in search of notes about this trip in his famous little notebooks, where he would take notes on all kinds of things for his work as a writer. At the IEB, I found just one annotation about the peculiar way in which Mexicans pronounced his name—"yoao"— and a label for a pumpkin sweet. It's not a rare case: A careful examination of the archives shows that various notebooks and booklets have disappeared or were perhaps destroyed by the very author, who in this way erased the tracks of his creative process.

"Páramo" as we know is an incomplete draft, but it is the proof that, if Guimarães Rosa had succeeded in delaying his ill-fated inauguration to the Brazilian Academy of Letters just a little bit longer, his friendship with Rulfo would engender more than anecdotes about supposedly eccentric writers. The way it was left, Guimarães Rosa's text is a lesson in how a great author can pay tribute to a brilliant colleague without superficial imitations or trivial quotes—this "Páramo" is not a mere accumulation of Rulfian borrowings, but a text that is wholly Rosian. The mystery associated with the citation from "the Book" that should appear at the end of "Páramo" remains without a solution. I like to imagine that in that blank space of the typed page there could be a quote from *Pedro Páramo* or "Luvina," such as, "Death is not distributed as if it were a benefit" or "So, what are you waiting for in order to die? / Death, Susana./ If that's all, then it will come. Don't worry" (*Pedro Páramo* 164), or even. "But if we leave, who will take care of our dead? They live here and we can't leave them alone" (*El Llano en llamas,* 108)[41]. But all we have is that blank space on the page, ready for the citation from a book that we still do not know.

# Chapter 7

## Why and for What Purpose Do Latin American Fiction Writers Travel? Silviano Santiago's *Viagem ao México* and *The Roots and Labyrinths of Latin America*

As fiction, "Páramo" was light-years ahead of the two dreadful novels written by Brazilians and set in Mexico, which we briefly mentioned in "First Undercurrents" (Affonso Celso's *Lupe*) and in the chapter dedicated to Érico Veríssimo's *México—História duma Viagem* (Vianna Moog's *Tóia*).[1] But it is typical of Guimarães Rosa's intricate baroque games of mirrors that his homage to Juan Rulfo was a short story set in Colombia, not in Mexico. The great Mexican novel in Brazilian literature was to be written in 1995 by Silviano Santiago, a fellow *mineiro* (born in the the state of Minas Gerais as was Guimarães Rosa).

*Viagem ao México* is part of a tradition of internationalization that is, in a way, typical of Latin America. There is a long list of Brazilian major literary works set outside Brazil in its entirety, or at least, in part: Tomás Antônio Gonzaga's *Cartas Chilenas* [written between 1783 and 1788 and published in 1845], Antônio Gonçalves Dias's *Leonor de Mendonça* [1847], Álvares de Azevedo's *Noites na Taverna* [1855], Sousândrade's *O Guesa Errante* [1871], Machado de Assis's superb short story "As Academias de Sião" [1884], Monteiro Lobato's novel *O Presidente Negro* [1926], Oswald de Andrade's *Serafim Ponte Grande* [1933], Érico Veríssimo's travel memoirs *Gato Preto em Campo de Neve* [1942], Vinícius de Moraes's *Nossa Senhora de Los Angeles* [1959], Guimarães Rosa's short story "Páramo" [1969], and Clarice Lispector's "Miss Algrave" [1974]. More recently, one could mention, among many examples, Silviano Santiago's *Stella Manhattan* [1985], João Cabral de Melo Neto's *Sevilha Andando* [1990], João Gilverto Noll's *Berkeley em Bellagio* [2002] and *Lorde* [2004], Nélida Piñon's *Vozes do Deserto* [2004], Bernardo Carvalho's *Mongólia* [2005], and Adriana Lisboa's *Rakushisha* [2007].

Even if there is a tradition of internationalized literature in Brazil, it is clear that the contemporary examples are more numerous; the quantity, if not the quality, of these works shows some sort of migration of the Brazilian literary imagination to foreign places. This internationalization is in tune with the rest of Latin American literature and with several trends increasingly prevalent since the last quarter of the twentieth century: the crisis of nationalist modernization projects and consequently of the role of the artist as a definer or promoter of national identity; the further opening of domestic economies to foreign players; the rapid increase in global human migration;[2] and the growing participation of the country in the international arena.

Two years ago, in 2007, there was a concrete, institutional example of the thrust in the direction of a greater internationalization of contemporary Brazilian literature. In March of that year the film producer Rodrigo Teixeira announced in the newspaper *Folha de São Paulo* his project *Amores Expressos*, clearly modeled after Mondadori's *Colección Año Zero*.[3] Teixeira invited 17 writers[4] to stay for a month in different cities around the world, from Shanghai to Mexico City. These authors would then write "love stories" [*sic*], which would be considered for publication by the most prestigious Brazilian publisher, the Companhia das Letras, and, perhaps later adapted to film. Voices of opposition to the project almost immediately made harsh accusations public in the main newspapers and magazines, mainly because of the possible use of the Lei Rouanet.[5] Defenders of and participants in *Amores Expressos* contested the accusations of cronyism and the lack of cultural relevance of the initiative with equally strong words, and eventually Rodrigo Teixeira's company and the Companhia das Letras decided to split all the costs of the project. The first novel of the series was published in 2008.[6]

Silviano Santiago was a pioneer in this internationalization, publishing novels and essays that reflect precisely this thrust toward internationalization and, at the same time, the permanence of certain paradigmatic preoccupations that have long marked Latin American culture. This native of Minas Gerais may recall Leyla Perrone-Moysés's *escritor-crítico* [writer-critic] but, unlike the figures studied in *Altas Literaturas*,[7] Santiago has built such a solid academic career that the brilliance of his critical work threatens to overshadow his equally distinguished literary accomplishments.

A graduate of Universidade Federal de Minas Gerais (UFMG), with a PhD from the Sorbonne and ten years' experience in US academia before returning to Brazil, Santiago wrote landmark essays such as "Eça, Author of *Madame Bovary*" and "Latin American Discourse: The Space In-Between." In the 1970s these essays were at once harbingers of poststructuralism and reaffirmations of an old Latin American obsession with the relationship between Europe and the New World and between Anglo-Saxon and Latin Americas.[8] Already well known in academic circles when he published his first major work of fiction, Silviano Santiago wrote at least two novels (*Em Liberdade* in 1981 and *Stella Manhattan* in 1985) that are among the best in the last quarter of the twentieth century in Brazil.

One should look *both* at Santiago's novels and his scholarly work in order to measure more fully his accomplishment and the two facets of Santiago's intellectual activity, which are by no means unrelated. However, when considering his fiction works, there has always been the temptation to use Santiago's criticism as a hermeneutical tool. This attitude creates a hierarchy between the two aspects of Santiago's intellectual labor, turning the criticism into a litmus test for perfect internal coherence between them. We should avoid reading Santiago's fiction as mere "applications" of his critical work as much as we should avoid placing the fiction as the raison d'etre for the criticism. These precautions are not measures out of prudish devotion to unperturbed close reading, but out of the pragmatic realization that Santiago's fiction needs to be taken on its own merits.

*Em Liberdade*, perhaps Silviano Santiago's best-known novel, is unique in its exquisite rendering of a confessional first-person narrative in the voice of the renowned Brazilian novelist Graciliano Ramos—to this date some readers still wonder whether Santiago really found a manuscript written after Ramos was released from prison by the Getúlio Vargas dictatorship, the missing final chapter of his *Memórias do Cárcere*. Thus, some reviewers rushed to link the carefully counterfeited memoirs of *Em Liberdade* to the narrative structure of *Viagem ao México*. That is because both feature protagonists who are renowned writers—Ramos and Antonin Artaud—and because of the legend of a 200-page manuscript titled *Voyage au Mexique*, written by Artaud and lost in Ireland in 1937 (Schneider 80–81).

Nevertheless, *Em Liberdade* and *Viagem ao México* are actually birds of an entirely different feather. The first-person narrator of *Viagem ao México* is another evidence of Santiago's daring literary skills and imagination, but far from the careful simulation of someone else's voice in *Em Liberdade*. *Viagem ao México*'s narrator is an unnamed writer very much like Silviano Santiago himself, born in the Minas Gerais countryside in 1936 and living in Rio de Janeiro in 1992, who reinvents himself in the persona of a gigantic sea monster modeled after Camões's Adamastor from the *Lusíadas,* in order to write the story of Artaud's trip to Mexico. This monster is described as an octopuslike behemoth that spreads itself across the oceans:

> Only one head and several tentacles, several leglike tentacles that settle in many different lands and many different seas, absorbing whatever these have to offer and offering the product of it all to the one-eyed Cyclopsesque head, assembled on a gigantic trunk from where extend arms from where extend hands braving new paths on the computer keyboard. The head is torn apart inside by the tentacles that travel farther away in search for new props. Each new prop, if it's not a caravel, is a new land; if it's not a new land, it's a caravel. If it's not a caravel and not a new land, it's a computer screen that has to be filled out.
>
> I am the mirror of that which frees me and imprisons me. I have a body made of mountains, the mountains where a haughty head reigns, whose mouth proclaims that, after a long arduous walk, the horizon is accessible and the breathing is less heavy. From up there I find out another horizon, other mountains, other horizons, vaster and wider and less accessible to walking feet, rolling wheels, and buzzing propellers. (20)[9]

This enigmatic, spectral figure travels freely in time and space; from Marseille 1922 to Paris 1935; from Cuba 1993 to Cuba 1936; and from Rio 1992 to Mexico 1936. In one of the chapters, Artaud simply disappears and we have an account of this narrator's own trip—apparently in less monstrous guise—to Havana in 1993. The narrator explains: "in 1993 Artaud looks at Havana through my Latin American eyes. In 1936 I look at Havana through his European eyes" (191).[10] The following chapter in the book brings us to Artaud's brief but significant stay in Havana in 1936. In Canto X (the book has one *Exórdio* [Preamble], thirteen "Cantos" and one "Epilogue"), Santiago's Artaud suddenly appears next to the narrator on a prosaic walk on Ipanema beach. This dynamic relationship between protagonist and narrator is far from stable: sometimes Artaud and the monster talk openly to each other; sometimes Artaud completely ignores the specter that follows him; and sometimes the narrator is literally left outside the door and resorts to third-party testimony to reconstruct events.

This relationship between protagonist and narrator is a frequent subject of commentary in *Viagem ao México.* The narrator explains: "the rules of construction of this fictional game are different from other fictional games; different and very explicit" (191).[11] Explicit but not clear, for these changes in the dynamic between narrator and protagonist take place with no predictable pattern. In any case, this spectral narrator is always willing to offer editorial comment and frequently addresses the reader, discussing his feelings about the narrative and his relationship with his protagonist.

*Viagem ao México* was not the first time Artaud appeared in Silviano Santiago's works. The reach beyond national borders of Latin American literature and criticism has always been implicit in one of the recurrent themes in Santiago's critical work: the relations between Europe and the New World and/or Anglo-Saxon and Latin Americas. Artaud figures prominently in one of the most important of these essays, "Why and For What Purpose Does the European Travel? (*The Space In-between*, 9–24) where Santiago claims to continue one of the lines of inquiry of his first essay collection, *Uma Literatura nos Trópicos*, namely the European presence in the Americas. This piece is an extended review of Umberto Eco's account of his travel to the United States, included in a collection of newspaper pieces, *Travels in Hyperreality*, originally less subtly titled in English *Faith in Fakes*.[12]

But before talking about Eco's book, Santiago takes us on a survey of fictional and actual journeys into the New World since Vasco da Gama's journey to India and Camões's account of it in the epic *Lusíadas*. In the course of this survey an important point of inflection lies in the passage from colonial to postcolonial relations between the two continents. After the independence of American nations, Santiago says, the traveling European is still an important figure in the continuing process of modernization and Westernization of the New World:

> The European's travel has a predominantly didactic and modernizing function. The European travels, then, as the member of a cultural mission, and often at the request of the country visited. He or she brings a diploma in his suitcase, preferably of a university degree. (197–198)[13]

Santiago divides this new traveling European into two basic types: one, epitomized by the anthropologist Claude Lévi-Strauss of *Tristes Tropiques*, mourns the demise of the non-Western Other in the name of an ethnocentric conquest he somehow has helped perpetuate; the other type is exemplified by Artaud:

> Contemporary of the Anthropologist but moving the opposite direction (...) Tired of the growing sclerosis that afflicted the European

bourgeois stage, Artaud leaves in search of "theatrical" expressions whose foundations of scenic experience had not been stifled by the process of commercialization and specialization of modern times. It is in this sense that, as a new Montaigne, Artaud inveighs against the dying European theater (and advocates in its favor by bringing a rejuvenating force) with the force of the sacred and the violent, the myth and the ritual, which faded away from Western stages due to scenic good behavior, the one and only uncompromising demand of bourgeois, naturalist theater.[14]

Artaud is here compared to the Montaigne in "Of Cannibals"—a well-known piece in the country of the "Manifesto Antropófago" and the centerpiece of Santiago's "The Latin American Discourse: The Space In-between" (*The Space In-Between*, 25–38)—in his genuine curiosity about the non-Western Other from the Americas and in his firm belief that Europeans have something to learn in the New World. This twentieth-century "new Montaigne" is a renegade surrealist who defected after the movement's adherence to the Communist Party, a man of the theater who comes to the New World once again looking for the magical aura lost in industrial modernity, a poet searching for a place where, in Santiago's Artaud's words, "the spiritual power of words had to be the same as the physical necessity of thirst and hunger" (36).[15] When he traveled to the New World, Artaud was not searching for the truth of mystic revelation in the depths of the unconscious nor in the chance encounter with the marvelous, but in the myths and rituals of non-Western indigenous culture in Mexico. For Santiago, Eco's problem is his self-sufficiency, his firm belief that he knows better than Americans about the true meaning of their culture. This self-sufficiency does not allow Eco to take into account, for example, the pervasive influence of the United States in European culture as a whole. In order to do so,

> Eco would have to have the true intellectual curiosity of Montaigne, Tocqueville, Artaud, and, instead of embarking on a tourist journey to the obvious in America, travel through his own Europe with a different worldview, perhaps less self-sufficient, certainly less naïve and possibly less authoritarian. Necessarily original and, because of that, perfectly indispensable. (203)[16]

Santiago admires Artaud for his "true intellectual curiosity," that which enables the traveler—from Europe or from the Americas—to skip the obvious, the confirmation of his or her prejudices, and to start the journey anew, now in his own home place, daring to look

at it with the eyes of a foreigner. This curiosity is, for Santiago, commonplace in the Americas. After all,

> New World intellectuals (noblesse oblige!) always had the courage to
> see the European that there exists in them. ( ... )
>     Aren't we now addressing a new question? Why and what for do the
> inhabitants of the New World travel? (203)[17]

Every comparatist is an intellectual traveler, and we can say that our
colonial and postcolonial past and present has always made Latin
Americans natural-born comparatists, bound to cross national and
linguistic borders. But our stance as international travelers in this
sense is far from unproblematic. What could be seen as a natural
thrust outward beyond national borders has often been muffled by
xenophobic nationalism and/or provincialism, two sides of an inferiority complex that has also plagued Latin Americans who imagined
themselves, as Sérgio Buarque de Holanda once described, as "exiles
in our own land" (*Raízes do Brasil,* 31). The history of Latin America
abounds with different examples of uncritical devotion to Europe
as well as paranoid rejection of all things European in the name of
unpolluted Nativism. Latin American literature has also offered some
of the most incisive criticism of these complementary sides of inferiority. The perception of what is Western and non-Western, the feelings
of recognition of the same and estrangement toward the other, and
the unstable notions of identity and alterity are inescapable aspects of
the relationship between Europe and the Americas or between the
developed and underdeveloped within the two continents. In "Why
and For What Purpose Does the European Travel?" Silviano Santiago
has pondered these aspects, but in *Viagem ao México* the novelist
moves one step beyond by juxtaposing two characters, the traveling
European (Artaud) and the traveling Latin American (the monstrous
narrator) to bring into relief several aspects of this relationship.

In the novel, the ethnocentric Europeans' rejection of the non-
Western in the Americas denounced by Santiago in his essay become
only one side of this troubled relationship. *Viagem ao México* also
highlights other Europeans' rejection of the Western same in the
Americas as a grotesque or obsolete copy of the original. That is the
case with Santiago's Artaud, whose irritation with Latin American
intellectuals because of their reverence for European culture and
because of their hopes for modernization is particularly visible in
two specific instances. The first one is when the French surrealist
meets with Jaime Torres Bodet, then the actual cultural attaché in the

Mexican embassy in Paris, to discuss preparations for his trip. After explaining his reasons for going to Mexico, Artaud engages in a tense discussion with Torres Bodet (Vasconcelos's former secretary and now the dutiful civil servant of Lázaro Cárdenas). The French writer is an enthusiast of pre-Hispanic culture, and is acquainted with the Sorbonne professor Robert Ricard's account of indigenous resistance to Christianity. Torres Bodet's angry rebuke mixes Vasconcelos's virulent defense of Spanish colonization and Cárdenas's nationalist drive toward the modernization of Mexico. In the name of the success of his trip as an official French cultural envoy to México, Santiago's Artaud silences his disagreements and quietly listens. Toward the end of this imagined reenactment of an actual meeting of which there seems to be no written record from either of the two participants, Artaud takes his notebook and scribbles some sentences in which "he takes note of the paradox of a national education whose cultural base is borrowed from elsewhere" (121).[18]

The second meeting between Artaud and a Latin American intellectual takes place in Cuba, when the French surrealist identifies himself as the author of an article featured in one of the issues of the *Nouvelle Revue Française* displayed in a bookstore in Havana. The storeowner greets him and takes Artaud to meet a writer identified only as "Aleixo" (which is the Portuguese for Alejo and thus obliquely refers to Alejo Carpentier). Back from the conversation with the Cuban, "his fellow writer," Artaud describes Aleixo as "a Torres Bodet with literary genius"[19] and then complains sarcastically:

> No sooner than they open their mouths there comes the same old song. These Latin Americans are all a bunch of miserable exiles, thrilled by the wonders of the industrialization they know nothing of and by a Western culture they know like nobody else. They believe factory chimneys are going to level the field in the world of letters and reveal the various hidden forms of capitalist oppression. They don't know what is in store for them the day they are no longer these deformed copies, more similar to the originals than the originals they envy so much. (231)[20]

It is noticeable that the narrator frames these two encounters differently. Whereas Torres Bodet is unmistakably identified full name and his meeting with Artaud is witnessed by the spectral narrator, the Cuban intellectual is ambiguously presented only as "Aleixo"— the actual Alejo Carpentier seems to have met Artaud but earlier, in Paris—and the narrator is left outside the bookstore talking to an insufferable "Pablito Conejo"[21] and forced to question Artaud about the meeting afterward. Furthermore, after the meeting between Artaud and Torres Bodet the monstrous narrator explains in detail what was invented and what was historically documented in it, while he gives us no such editorial explanations about the boundaries between reinvention and reconstruction in the meeting in the Cuban bookstore other than the following enigmatic statements:

> As I write this narrative I get more and more used to this triangulated conversation. Our triangle is scalene. If Artaud's words take up the longest side, mine fill the shortest. To the interlocutor there remains what there is to remain, squeezed in between the blatant asymmetry between the two antagonistic sides of the triangle. (230)[22]

The Greek root of word "scalene" is indicative of the less than candid attitude of this unusual narrator; besides a triangle with three unequal sides, *skalénós* also refers to "limping, crippled" and "crooked, oblique." The oblique relationship between narrator, protagonist, and other characters has three different sizes (quantities) and angles (perspectives), but there is a deceptive hierarchy of length. The interlocutor's role is "squeezed in between" the other sides, but is larger than the narrator's. Besides, the spectral narrator, a fully developed, quite talkative character—as similar as he may be to the actual Santiago— the protagonist—as close to the actual Artaud as he could possibly be—and everyone else in *Viagem ao México* have been drawn by the same hand, the author's. The rules of this crooked narrative game are far from explicit or clear.

Instead of an editorial account of what has been imagined and what has been reconstructed, what follows after the meeting in Havana is an enactment of that triangle: Artaud's reluctant recollection prompted by the narrator in an increasingly ironic and tense exchange. For instance, the narrator abruptly interrupts Artaud to make sure the Frenchman understands he is now talking to a Latin American intellectual:

> At any cost they want to imprison their artistic invention—
> Our artistic invention, you mean. Anch'io—
> —in the prison-house of history where they will be waiting for
>     recognition to come from the skies. (232)[23]

As they continue to discuss Artaud's and Aleixo's different readings of Havana's architecture, it is Artaud's turn to interrupt and ask abruptly the narrator two pointed questions. "Artaud stops talking. He asks me—I take note of what he says—if in fact I think the same way as

Aleixo. Wouldn't it be easier if you invented this passage in the novel?" (234).[24] The questions come in sequence, each framed differently, first in indirect speech, then in free indirect discourse without quotation marks, testing one way and then another the blurred boundaries between the voice of the narrator and that of the protagonist. To both questions the narrator enigmatically responds with a smile.

Santiago's Artaud is a man immersed in the solitude of profound incomprehension both in Europe and in Latin America. André Gide, Breton, Torres Bodet, Aleixo, Elías Nandino, José Gorostiza, Xavier Villaurrutia, José Ferell, the government's primary-school teachers called *rurales*, the audience of his conferences French or Mexican: nobody really grasps what Artaud says, and his uncompromising vision of magical redemption through mysticism only alienates him further. Even the Guatemalan Luiz Cardoza y Aragón,[25] the one Latin American in *Viagem ao México* who seems to understand Artaud's predicaments as a fellow foreigner living in Mexico City, is incisive when Artaud speaks about teaching Latin Americans to "unlearn what Europe has taught you for so many years." Cardoza y Aragón retorts "teaching to unlearn in a country like Mexico, isn't that not very constructive?" (315).[26] The actual Cardoza y Aragón edited a collection of Artaud's writings in México and wrote a beautiful prologue in which he describes the French poet as "the sinister one, whose only star is dead and whose starry lute bears the black sun of melancholy" (*México*, 7).[27] But in the same prologue Cardoza y Aragón also affirms that "because of his desperation Artaud mistook the New Continent for a New content. There is some of it here, but it wasn't enough for his absolute need. Much of Europe died in us as well." (12).[28] In *Viagem ao México* Cardoza y Aragón sympathizes with Artaud but is also implacable with the ambitions and illusions of the French surrealist:

> When the European brain is tired, he likes to go for a ride through the old civilizations that are not part of his tradition, as if, during these auspicious vacations, the grey matter, exposed to the emanations of the heat in the tropics, could rid itself from the burden that weighs on it in that historical moment. In the past, Europe traveled to invade; now, as it does not possess the economic and military power to do so, Europe travels to set fire to the sensitive minds of the youth, to develop in them a taste for furious abstractions. (316)[29]

Artaud's brand of surrealism was undoubtedly dissenting from Breton's orthodoxy and somehow influential in Latin America, especially in México. But Artaud's iconoclastic stance within Surrealism is recognizably a manifestation of a common exaltation among European modernists of what one critic has once called "the happy garden of organic society" (Eagleton, 34) from where we all have been expelled by industrial modernity. Artaud's conviction that mystical exaltation of "Mexico's Indian blood (that) kept an ancient secret of the race against all the "caricatures of life" (*Viaje al País de los Tarahumaras*, 35)[30] invented by European consciousness reminds me of a scathing critical statement made in another, though not completely unrelated, context:

> ( ... ) the simultaneous exaltation of aesthetic modernism and social premodernity are shown to be compatible: the priests of the modern art world, feeling that their autonomy and symbolic power are fragile because of the advance of state powers, the industrialization of creativity, and the massification of audiences, see an alternative in sheltering themselves in an idealized antiquity. (Canclini, 92)

Nestor García Canclini is in this case criticizing the idealization of revolutionary *Zapatismo* by Octavio Paz, which is a case of very late reenactment of this exaltation of "organic society" against industrial sterile rationalism, one that sounds almost as an involuntary parody in the 1970s of the avant-garde discourse of the 1920s. But the criticism could be aimed at Artaud as well—the exaltation of this brand of Nietzschean irrationalism was, at best, "a recipe for political inertia, and thus for submission" (Eagleton, 43) at the time Hitler was professing pacifism and consolidating his power and the Spanish Civil War broke out. From the ideological point of view, Artaud's stance is close to what another harsh critic of Paz called "the professionally vain point-of-view of a writer of the writer and the printed word ( ... ) as the center of the world" (Aguilar Camín, 281).[31]

Perhaps this kind of judgment is too harsh when applied to Artaud in the 1930s. After all, the French poet and dramatist experienced the encroachment of industrial modernity between the traumas of World Wars I and II, with the Great Depression, the rise of Fascism, the Nazis, and Stalin squeezed in between and, in any case, the printed word was very, very far from the center of Artaud's world. Nevertheless, what sense would it make for most Latin Americans—even those frankly sympathetic and curious about indigenous and black cultures—to sustain that one should "quemar las escuelas, las imprentas, cerrar los museos y devolverle la cultura su vitalidad dinámica" [burn the schools, the presses, close the museums and give back to the culture its dynamic vitality] (Artaud, 36)? Latin American intellectuals dedicated to cultural vitality were generally deeply committed to do exactly the opposite: to promote the cause of building schools, publishing books and newspapers, and establishing museums. Many Latin American intellectuals since the 1930s, even if limited by different degrees of ethnocentrism, defended the worth of oral culture and argued for a prominent place for the indigenous and Afro cultural strains in their nations, but it would be hard to find one of them seriously advocating at the same time the destruction of schools, printing presses, and museums in Latin America, or anywhere else for that matter.

Beyond the entrapments of irrationalism there is an even more problematic aspect to this kind of approach. Artaud's worldview starts from the premise that it is fairly easy to tell the Western from the non-Western. Even in Anglo-Saxon America, where there seems to be an obsession with precise ethnic labeling, the European and the non-European cultural strains are already fused so deep in the culture's roots that contemporary attempts to make rigid separations simply do not stand any examination beneath the most superficial appearances.

This issue leads us to a contemporary cultural trend where these rigid separations of the Western from the non-Western have served the idealization of pure and congealed cultural identities disguised as "liberating" or "empowering" discourse: the iconoclast of the twentieth century is replaced by the iconolater of the twenty-first—another recipe for political inertia and submission. In a recent interview Santiago explained his attraction to the 1930s by saying that "the 1930s is the most important decade in the twentieth century. It is all there, in miniature" ("Entrevista com Silviano Santiago," 166).[32] Books written about the past are also about the time they are written: two moments in which *Viagem ao México* veers into the 1990s make this case abundantly clear.

The first-person narrator lends a reticent smile when he is asked whether he agrees or not with Artaud's critique of Latin American intellectuals, but he seems quite—if not openly—sympathetic to the Frenchman's brand of primitivism. This comes to the surface in the two passages that take place in contemporary Latin America and feature not Artaud but a less monstrous narrator as the protagonist. These are "Cuba, January and February 1993" (the whole Canto VII) and "Rio de Janeiro 1994" (the first half of Canto X).

In 1993, the narrator visits Cuba in the *período especial*, when the collapse of the Soviet Union worsened the already devastating effects of the US embargo to such an extent that the Havana that once fired the imagination of every anti-imperialist Latin American in the 1960s reminds him of the postapocalyptic movie *Mad Max*. The European tourist resurfaces in this context, when the dollar "corrupts the human and working relations between foreigners and Cubans" (200).[33] This tourist is ironically characterized as "a useful and desired invader," an indiscriminate predator as a promoter of "an inelegant and anarchic space" "within the reigning socialist asepsis" (201).[34] After noticing the grim faces of three percussionists in a musical performance, the narrator wonders if music has turned into a "working-class rite" and somehow naively asks himself "if it wasn't the island's mass literacy programs that had turned Cubans critical and skeptical of the excesses of orality and confidence" (210).[35] This disingenuous commentary echoes Artaud's vehement opposition to what he sees as Cárdenas's teachers' use of Marxism to westernize Mexican Indians.

In 1994 Rio de Janeiro, *Viagem ao México* becomes a parody, in a manner that resembles the "Carta pras Icamiabas" in Mário de Andrade's *Macunaíma* and other writings from the Brazilian *modernistas*. Artaud and the narrator stroll on the beach and openly mock the provincial prudishness and the mindless worship of Western theatrical naturalist tradition represented by a gallery of aggressive grotesques: a couple, "Ah!otexto" and "Oh!otexto," and a sixteenth-century scholar named "Unicórnio Eunuco."

Santiago's interests fortunately go well beyond these specific aspects of the relationship between the Americas and Europe. In *Viagem ao México*, Santiago seems to be particularly interested in more than just Artaud's disposition to remain defiantly open to non-Western alterity in the face of the surrealists' adherence to communism and the Latin Americans' unwavering admiration of Western culture. This curious novel also focuses on something harder to find, a rare attitude on both sides of the Atlantic that depends as much on cognitive as on affective courage: a disposition to remain truly open, body and mind, to that precipitous moment in which firm values and established world views lose their cohesiveness and suddenly crumble. These moments of profound instability are also moments of sheer humanity and moments of true openness when only the really brave ones can seize the crisis as an opportunity for some kind of death and resurrection. Santiago's Artaud experiences such crisis twice, one in Cuba and one, at the end of the book, with the Tarahumara Indians during the peyote ritual. Here I quote from the first one:

Artaud's murdered body will be reborn. It will be reborn without the old personality that had led him to paths inauspicious to real fulfillment. From there he will come, freed from the bonds that tied him to old customs and desires. ( ... ) It is the *orixás* that celebrate in their party, which is the party of everyone.

> Through that moment, in peace and dancing, in music and ecstasy, in the voices and in friendship, Cuba, Africa, and Europe mingle. The ocean is abolished, slavery is erased, and all skins shine in one marvelous shade. (244)[36]

The ecstasy during the height of the Afro-Cuban ritual, entirely translated in Silviano's novel into the words of the Brazilian *Candomblé*, announce the rebirth of Artaud after the first-hand encounter with the non-Western ritual magic he longed for. In the second moment of crisis, climbing the Sierra Madre, Artaud leaves everything he had brought behind him. His body hardens and he feels as if he sheds his flesh and turns into "puro osso" [sheer bones] and a skin that feels like "uma enorme gengiva irrascível" [an enormous irritable gum]. The narrator, somehow melancholy, notes that Artaud "hasn't done it to enter a new world, but to escape a fake one" (382)[37] and ends the book mourning the premature death of the twentieth century. At the end of the book there is no resurrection, no rebirth anywhere in sight.

Santiago recognizes *Viagem ao México* is his most ambitious novel and he seems to agree with William Faulkner when the great Southern novelist said every novel of his generation should be rated as "a splendid failure to do the impossible" (Gourevitch, 44). In a recent interview he expressed both personal appreciation and disappointment: "*Viagem ao México* is an unreadable book. I call it my small *Grande Sertão: Veredas*. I had to write it, it was what I had to write. The sum of my labors" ("Entrevista com Silviano Santiago," 171).[38]

Santiago did not exhaust what he had to say about Artaud in *Viagem ao México*. In 2000 Artaud is again compared to Lévi-Strauss in "A Viagem de Lévi-Strauss aos Trópicos"[39] and Santiago announced this was "a version of the first part of a long essay on the concept of travel in Lévi-Strauss and Antonin Artaud." When the article was collected in *Ora (Direis) Puxar Conversa!* in 2006 (293–336), it still announced an unpublished piece about Artaud and Lévi-Strauss now to be named *A Viagem: o Etnógrafo e o Poeta*. This could also have been the title of *Viagem ao México*, the sum of the labors of a monstrous narrator and a mad poet, the sum of the labors of a brilliant scholar and a daring artist.

As ethnographers, as poets, as tourists in search of "love stories," as writers trying to write a bestseller that can be turned into a movie, or simply trying to get a good grant: what is the best stance for new Latin American writers as their fictional imagination moves them beyond their national borders? In other words, for what reasons and with what purposes are Latin American writers going to travel in the twenty-first century? The answers to these questions will shape the work of several contemporary Latin American writers in the years to come.

In 2006 Silviano Santiago would turn his attention to Mexico again, this time not with a novel, even though Santiago provocatively called his essay a "narrative." *As Raízes e o Labirinto da América Latina* is a comparative study focusing on two Latin American essays that hold primary importance among the many attempts at rearticulation of national identity in the face of industrial modernization in Latin America: Sérgio Buarque de Holanda's *Raízes do Brasil* (1936) and Octavio Paz's *Laberinto de la Soledad* (1950).[40]

*The Labyrinth of Solitude* is undoubtedly the most popular book about Mexico outside of the country. Its allure is unfortunately more due to its shortcomings than to its best qualities: Paz provides the foreigner, particularly the reader from developed countries, with a series of elegant sentiments about the Mexican (invariably a male in interaction with his symbolic mother-lover Malinche and his father-rival Cortéz) and about Mexico as the privileged site of the persistence of the resilient Other—be it the fascinating and/or horrifying savage or the tragic, defeated barbarian—that is a constant trope of the Western imagination. Paz's Mexican is an entity of mixed-race ethnic origins who is at once the site of affirmation of national uniqueness and of hopeless resistance to modernization, conceived as the ultimate absorption of Latin America into the West.

In his prose Octavio Paz operates rhetorically over and over the same trope: turning dualisms—tradition and rupture, I and the Other, etc.—into elegant but also potentially meaningless paradoxes. In Paz's prose the dichotomy turned oxymoron hides its own hierarchy that subjugates one term to the other. Paz neutralizes (without saying he does so) one of the sides of each proposed dualism: rupture dissolves into tradition, the Other dissolves into the construction of the ego. Then history seems simply to annul itself in an eternal pendulum movement from one side back to the next, a movement that renders place and time no longer capable of producing something specific, mere particular instances of the general principle that contains them both. In Paz's prose all opposition (and all conflict) melts into principles of a complementary relationship and eases into a simple and elegant figure of rhetoric. There is no contradiction between Paz's prose and his increasingly conservative political stances after 1968.

The influence of surrealism in Paz is subordinated to the determining influence of two eminent Mexican intellectuals: Alfonso

Reyes and Samuel Ramos. Reyes furnished Paz a powerful model of an elegant rhetoric driven by the conciliatory desire to dissolve the difference between opposites. In *El Perfil del Hombre y de la Cultura en México* (1934) Ramos defines Mexican national identity through a series of analogies that merge psychology and sociology by performing a psychoanalysis of a social type *pelado* (a member of the city lumpenproletariat that typically lives in slums and resorts to illegal or informal means of subsistence) in an attempt to understand Mexican identity. This procedure in Ramos's book is clearly the model for *Labyrinth of Solitude*. The aggressive class prejudice that lies on the surface of Ramos's contempt for the *pelado* is smoothed over in Paz's rendering of his *pachuco* by the elegant rhetoric of pacification he learned from Reyes.

*Roots of Brazil* is also a book about national identity and it also offers at times what seems to be an analysis of the psychology the Brazilians in general (again understood as essentially male). However, Buarque de Holanda follows a fundamentally different path in *Roots of Brazil*, especially after he reviews the 1936 version of the book in a defensive gesture against the conservative interpretation of his ideas by Cassiano Ricardo during the *Estado Novo* dictatorship. The second edition of *Roots of Brazil* tries to emphasize the negative aspects of the *cordialidade* as well and thus distances Buarque de Holanda's use of the term from its original, celebratory use in Ribeiro Couto's letter to Reyes published in *Monterrey*. In Ribeiro Couto, Latin American *cordialidade* is its greatest contribution to civilization because of a contrast any reader of Rodó can easily recognize: in opposition to the cold impersonality of the Anglo-Saxon businessman, the warm, friendly, aestheticizing Latin American offers an escape from the ugly realities of industrialized nations' ruthless materialism and vile nationalism. In its refusal of modern impersonality, the *cordialidade* in *Roots of Brazil* resists not only the negative aspects of modernization, but also true democracy and a more equitable justice. *Roots of Brazil* also differs fundamentally from *Labyrinth of Solitude* because the social type Buarque de Holanda analyses is a member of the traditional Brazilian elites, not some *caboclo* or *caipira* that could function as an analog of the *pelado* in Ramos or the *pachuco* in Paz. Thus, the sharp blade of Buarque de Holanda's critical voice is pointed primarily at the elite of the country.

In these two influential books, Buarque de Holanda and Paz play the part of the Latin American essayist on national character—occupied with what Samuel Ramos once called with characteristic aplomb *caracteriología* (12). Thus they are forced to face the primary hurdle in these efforts to rearticulate national identity: circumventing ethnic, class, and gender differentiations to deal with what Roger Bartra calls "the idea that there is a single subject of national history" (22).[41] Beyond the most obvious objection—the predictable choice of the male as the representation of the national subject in essence— all the essays on national character in Latin America display a subtle choreography of pronouns as the authors dance around their subject matter (be it the *homus mexicanus* or the *homus brasiliensis*).

As a result there is a series of shifts back and forth from "we" to "he" or "they" in both books. For instance, when Paz attributes to his quintessential Mexican an indifference toward death that is derived from an indifference toward life (48), he is obviously not talking about himself. Paz, as Ramos before him, is clearly borrowing from Lucien Lévy-Bruhl's idea of the savage and the barbarian's natural slowness and emotional richness as the Other of cold Western rationality. When Buarque de Holanda's *barão* rejects modern rationality he does so in the name of his attachment to the old colonial roots of a slave-based society—and this perversely *cordial* Brazilian is obviously not a former slave or a poor squatter living on the fringes of plantation and mining export economies.

One particular aspect of Santiago's *As Raízes e o Labirinto da América Latina* is that there is a great discrepancy between Santiago's readings of *Roots of Brazil and Labyrinth of Solitude*. A quick parallel between two consecutive chapters respectively called "Quadruple Divine Vacancy. The Poet as Prophet" (203–218) and "Geographer and Historian of Brazil" (219–237) is enough to illustrate this discrepancy.

Whereas Buarque de Holanda's text is read against a detailed understanding of the social and political context from where it came from, Paz's is read in a much more rarefied context, more attuned to specifically literary genealogies. Conversely, Buarque de Holanda is "a historian of such caliber (...) that [he] knows in the structure of Brazilian social fabric there is no loose thread" (226), while in Paz "the urban ethnographer (...) is placed in the wider context of the lettered hermeneut" (206). Buarque de Holanda's positions on education (231–234) or on the nature and role of government bureaucracy (234–236) in *Roots of Brazil* are analyzed not just in terms of the text itself but in the context of the oscillating attempts at a modernizing reform of public education and civil service in Brazil in the thirties. Paz's decision to place the poet (i.e., himself) at the place of high priest and prophet of the modern world (210–217) is understood vis-à-vis Paz's Romantic and surrealist affiliations, but little to nothing appears of Paz's entanglement in Mexican social and political context since the 1950s with the consolidation of the Partido Revolucionario Institucional (PRI) as a more institutional than revolutionary party.

But Santiago is always a subtle and interesting reader and even when you may disagree with him, there is always a lot to learn and reflect upon. Both chapters are not just somewhat shortsighted but also brilliant and they are so for quite different reasons. "The Poet as Prophet" climaxes with a doubly sacrilegious and highly entertaining parody of St. Paul's *Epistle to the Romans* (5, 12–21) in which "world" is replaced with "México" and "Jesus Christ" with "Octavio Paz" (212); "The Geographer and Historian of Brazil" reaffirms the torturous struggles between the old patriarchal order and the new modern one that battle in a tormented country and in the tormented text of Buarque de Holanda.

In a recent article about Silviano Santiago, critic Raúl Antelo sees *Viagem ao México* and *As Raízes e o Labirinto da América Latina*, among other less noticeable examples as instances in which the presence of Mexico plays a pivotal role in Silviano Santiago's work, something Antelo suggestively calls *dispositivo México*:

> In Silviano Santiago's oeuvre Mexico constitutes an almost secret but very efficient *apparatus [dispositif]* to leave literary studies and, at the same time, introduce the poetics machinery into cultural studies.[42]

The oscillations and discrepancies in the chapters on Buarque de Holanda and Paz demonstrate that such mutual interpenetration between the "poetics machinery" and "cultural studies" may be less neatly resolved than it seems. Antelo also sees *As Raízes e o Labirinto da América Latina* as Santiago's return through the lenses of post-structuralism to the issues already placed in *Viagem ao México*: "The roots and the labyrinth of Latin America find, in the exhausted contemporary literature, a form of emptying out the icons of the past." That may be truth but I also see *As Raízes e o Labirinto da América Latina* as an instigating restatement of *Viagem ao México*, a powerful illustration of several interesting reasons and purposes for Latin American writers to continue to travel beyond national and linguistic borders and yet within the continent.

Antelo's article points to a little-known piece Silviano Santiago wrote for the *Suplemento Literário Minas Gerais* in 1973 called in the original "Las Botas y el Anillo de Zapata" (1–2). It is not a text about Mexico but about Minas Gerais, Santiago's home state (and mine). The title translates into Spanish a famous verse originally sung in

Portuguese in a song called "Tudo que Você Podia Ser," which was written by the brothers Lô and Márcio Borges and opens the album *Clube da Esquina*, a landmark in Brazilian music in 1972. Written from a voluntary exile at a time when many left Brazil because of the brutal dictatorship that viewed with suspicion any artistic or cultural endeavor that implied an appreciation for freedom and social justice, Santiago's touching article is full of longing for Minas Gerais. Weaving together several references to the songs of that album and other artists from Minas Gerais, Santiago speaks of *Mineiros* as people being driven by a paradoxical urge for exile and a profound love of home. These people, torn between the love of home and love of everything beyond home, created this *Clube da Esquina* [Corner Club] as an imaginary place where their conflict is momentarily solved:

> The corner club is this club without doors and without windows, without outside, where musicians and audience are mixed, where all that matters is friendship, openness, acquiescence, and desire to cut loose and be free. Where, in the middle of the street, in the middle of the road, one dances and stages a spectacle. (2)[43]

The "only password and emblem" of this boundless club made up of voice, music, and poetry is none other than "las botas y el anillo de Zapata"; Santiago translates the verse into Spanish in the article.

Márcio Borges's lyrics feature a poetic voice that addresses the listener and reader as "you" and reminds this figure that he or she once dreamed of a better world, whether rain or shine, who dreamed of being "the great hero of the roads," of fearlessly being everything he should be. The voice then laments that the "you" he addresses no longer speaks of Zapata's boots and ring; that this once-defiant figure is now afraid and thinks of nothing but coming back. However, the song ends with an ambiguously optimistic tone of defiance saying:

> Ah, sun and rain on your road
> But it doesn't matter, there's no harm
> You still think, and this is better than nothing
> All you can get to be or nothing[44]

In the midst of the worst period of authoritarian rule in the history of Brazil, a small group of *Mineiros*—Silviano Santiago included—still dared to write and sing of dreams and of freedom. And their shibboleth was Zapata, a Mexican peasant hero. It had come to them through the deep undercurrents of Latin America and it was also an expression of the vivid interest of these *Mineiros* in a distant country on what used to be the northern extreme of Latin America. This was their reason for venturing outside the boundaries of their beloved Minas Gerais; this is what made them *Mineiros*.

# Chapter 8

# Nelson Pereira dos Santos and the Mexican Golden Age of Cinema

Nelson Pereira dos Santos (1928) is arguably the most influential Brazilian film director after Glauber Rocha (1939–1981), having been cited as a reference by a number of Brazilian filmmakers, from Rocha himself to Walter Salles.[1] Although Pereira dos Santos has often been identified with *Cinema Novo*, he actually belongs to an older generation. Since his debut, a few years before the Brazilian *Nouvelle Vague* of the 1960s, Pereira dos Santos pioneered themes, approaches, and aesthetic formats that were subsequently taken up by other Brazilian directors. To contain his 50-year-old career strictly within the scope of *Cinema Novo* is an oversimplification of the importance of his work for Brazilian cinema.

In 1995 Nelson Pereira dos Santos released *Cinema de Lágrimas* [Cinema of Tears], a film in which the classic Mexican cinema of the 1940s played a central part. In order to understand how this particular film fits into the filmography of Nelson Pereira dos Santos we shall quickly go through five films spread out through the course of his career. Not only do these films showcase Pereira dos Santos's will to experiment but also some preoccupations that have galvanized his long and distinguished career.

Pereira dos Santos's very first feature as a director, *Rio 40 Graus* [*Rio 100 Degrees F.*] (1955), was a turning point for Brazilian cinema for three reasons. The film was one of the first to adapt to Latin America ideas of Italian neorealism, such as the use of nonactors and real-life locations and the commitment to portray everyday people and their struggles on screen—something that had a profound impact on the next generation of Brazilian filmmakers.[2] *Rio 40 Graus* also provided a landmark for a long lineage of films set around the life of *favela* dwellers, one of the main themes of Brazilian cinema, including films such as *Favela dos Meus Amores* (1935) by Humberto Mauro, *Cinco Vezes Favela* (1962) by five directors,[3] and *City of God* (2002) by Fernando Meirelles and Kátia Lund. Finally, the cooperative production scheme that turned *Rio 40 Graus* into a viable project in the aftermath of the crisis that bankrupted all major Brazilian production studios at the time lighted the path for filmmakers in Latin America to circumvent the restrictions of a strictly market-oriented film industry dominated by the United States after the demise of the big, Latin American studios.

Pereira dos Santos's fourth feature, *Boca de Ouro* (1962), was his first commercial success and set the tone for more than 20 cinematic adaptations of the work of Nelson Rodrigues[4] well before the playwright was recognized as a master of a fruitful exploration of the traditional motifs of the melodrama, upsetting the conservative premises of the genre by exposing the dark side of the sexually repressed bourgeois values in an interesting, unorthodox Freudian reading of the limits of sublimation. Pereira dos Santos's pioneering adaptation of a play that had been staged for the first time a couple of years before in São Paulo and had been written by a playwright who "was considered taboo by the Left" (Sadlier 2003, 24) and he did this ten years before Arnaldo Jabor adapted Rodrigues's *Toda a Nudez Será Castigada* (1972) and *O Casamento* (1975).

*Vidas Secas* [*Barren Lives*] (1963), an adaptation of the 1938 novel by Graciliano Ramos, paved the way for the international recognition of the younger directors of the *Cinema Novo* with a notable participation at the Cannes Film Festival in 1964. This unsentimental portrayal of the dry backlands in the Northeast, filmed with a remarkable natural-light photography based on contrasts between sun-drenched exteriors and dark interiors, is considered by many one of the best films of Brazilian cinema. Still impressive, *Vidas Secas* bravely approached the gap between political and aesthetic relevance that raged in the 1960s and went well beyond the political engagement that had marked the cultural initiatives of the Centro Popular de Cultura (CPC).[5]

In spite of the international acclaim given to *Vidas Secas* because of its aesthetic rigor, Nelson Pereira dos Santos kept experimenting and innovating. In 1970 he wrote and directed *Como Era Gostoso o Meu Francês* [*How Tasty Was My Little Frenchman*] (1971), loosely based on the autobiographical book of the adventures of the German Hans Staden (1525–1579) in colonial Brazil in the mid-sixteenth century. Filmed in color on the lush tropical coast of Paraty, the film contrasts in every aspect with the barrenness of *Vidas Secas*. Furthermore,

*How Tasty Was My Little Frenchman* is a superb critical revision of Latin American *Indigenismo* infused by the revision of the 1920s *Modernismo* promoted by the *Tropicalismo* of the late 1960s, with practically all dialogue written in indigenous Tupi by the legendary pioneer filmmaker Humberto Mauro.

Ten years later Nelson Pereira dos Santos surprised audiences and critics again with *Na Estrada da Vida* (1981), a successful musical biography of the singer duo Milionário e José Rico. Darlene J. Sadlier links *Na Estrada da Vida* to "Manifesto por um Cinema Popular" [Manifesto for a Popular Cinema] (1975), in which the filmmaker defends "a cinema that will focus on the people, appeal to a large audience, and compete at the box office with the U.S. and other foreign imports" (Sadlier 2003, 95) by tapping into a positive projection of popular values. Although Pereira dos Santos pointed out in interviews that the so-called manifesto was nothing but a collection of interviews arranged by Marco Aurélio Marcondes with marketing purposes,[6] the text points to an idea that has actually long featured among the filmmaker's main concerns: the fundamental contradiction in the idea of a people's revolutionary cinema that nevertheless promote the alienation of large audiences from its projects. *Na Estrada da Vida* combined a great box office with almost unanimous critical rejection, an indication of the prevalence among critics of ideas concerning high- and low-brow cultures that the filmmaker wanted to challenge. *Na Estrada da Vida* clearly anticipates strategies that form the structure of Breno Silveira's biopic *2 Filhos de Francisco—A História de Zezé di Camargo and Luciano* (2005), one of the greatest box-office hits of all times in Brazil. However, Pereira dos Santos's film also points to the past of Brazilian cinema, indirectly referring to the many films of the popular comedian Amácio Mazzaropi (1912–1981), who started his career in 1952 and combined with remarkable consistency a popular acclaim and critical disdain until the end of his career in 1980.

This reconsideration of the harsh critical judgments about the mainstream of Latin American cinema in its most popular period, in the 1940s and 1950s features prominently in Nelson Pereira dos Santos's *Cinema de Lágrimas* (1995), an affectionate, revisionist look at the most fluent and influential articulation of a language of suffering and redemption for the masses in Latin America: the cinematic melodrama whose most prominent examples came from Mexico between the 1930s and the 1950s. Nelson Pereira dos Santos paid homage to the genre as a powerful syntax to tell stories and dreams of pain and happiness with an innovative project perfectly in tune with cinema in the 1990s during the so-called *Retomada*, which primarily reassessed the problem of the confinement of domestic production into a shrinking art circuit.

*Cinema de Lágrimas* is typical of the *Retomada* (and of Nelson Pereira dos Santos) in many different aspects. In it Pereira dos Santos displays an internationalist flavor perceptible in the film itself and in its unconventional production scheme. A large portion of the film takes place in a foreign setting (Mexico City) and is spoken in a language other than Portuguese, something many critics have pointed to in several other key films from the period.[7] Strong links with television and with foreign sources of financial support also place the film within the scope of the *Retomada* and with Pereira dos Santos's search for new ways to make Latin American film production viable. In an environment hostile toward domestic cinematic production in Brazil, *Cinema de Lágrimas* started with an invitation from the British Film Institute and ARTE (a French and German TV channel) to join a project for a series of films to commemorate 100 years of cinema. Several acclaimed directors from different parts of the world made films—most of them documentaries—that somehow cast a retrospective look at the cinema in different places.[8] These films were to be shown at the Cannes and Berlin festivals, but also on television, and companies such as Channel 4 and TV Asahi were coproducers of the projects that focused respectively on British and Japanese cinema.

As Nelson Pereira dos Santos wryly expressed in later interviews, he was at first dismayed that the organizers of the series decided to fit Latin America as a whole into a single film. The decision implied that the organizers of the project believed it would be impossible to contain in a single film a historical, coherent retrospective of cinema in countries as diverse as Argentina, Brazil, Cuba, Mexico, and Venezuela.[9] Faced with such a challenge but given much freedom to devise his own project, Pereira dos Santos decided that instead of a comprehensive documentary, he would film a fictional feature that focused on the so-called Golden Era of Latin American cinema and its most influential product: the melodrama. In this aspect the blend of critical acumen and affection that Pereira dos Santos displayed, for instance, in *How Tasty Was My Little Frenchman* was fundamental for *Cinema de Lágrimas.*

Placing the Mexican melodrama at the center of Latin American cinema, Nelson Pereira dos Santos signaled a willingness to counter two established prejudices against those films. These criticisms typically came from two groups that to a great extent overlapped. On the one hand, the younger postwar generation of filmmakers had harshly criticized the melodrama for its social and political alienation; on the other, the ascending Latin American elite of the 1950s equally despised the domestic production for being a poor copy of Hollywood, geared toward the unsophisticated masses. These revisions were highlighted in interviews at the time the film was released. Instead of seeing social irrelevance, political backwardness, and poorly crafted imitations in these melodramas, Nelson Pereira dos Santos pointed out that "the melodrama ( ... ) was the only moment in which there was a real cinema industry in Latin America" and that "these are exquisite films; the directors were great craftsmen."[10]

Such revision could have been expounded in a conventional documentary, but Pereira dos Santos's courage to flaunt conventions moved him to articulate these ideas into a hybrid fictional movie. How does Nelson Pereira dos Santos place the 1950s Mexican cinema at the center of a fiction film in the 1990s? More than half of this film is composed of very carefully chosen extracts from 17 classics of that era. They range from the first sound feature, *Santa* (1931), to Luis Buñuel's idiosyncratic incursion in the genre, *Abismos de la Pasión* (1953). Except for two Argentinian films—*Madreselva* and *Armiño Negro*—they are all Mexican films, but there is no attempt to furnish time and place coordinates to frame a history of Mexican or Latin American cinema in that period. The excerpts are not arranged chronologically and most of the time their names are discernible in opening credits of the films themselves. Narratively speaking, these fragments can generally stand on their own, including significant dialogue exchanges, complete action sequences, and five excerpts of singing numbers.[11]

In spite of the lack of historical and geographical markers, nothing is random in the way these excerpts are presented and their organization is clear to the viewer. They are explicitly clustered in *Cinema de Lágrimas* around four main themes: love, passion, incest, and the centrality of female figures in unstable conditions, rendered as mothers or home wreckers on the verge of social ostracism. This arrangement is easily understandable by one of the main characters in the film, a graduate student named Ives, who is engaged in a research project sponsored by a veteran actor-producer, Rodrigo (played by the superb Raul Cortez). Rodrigo hires Ives because he longs to see the films his mother and aunts loved so much when he was a child in order to help himself unearth painful old memories that he has long buried. Ives finds and selects the movies that Rodrigo sees and he also furnishes critical commentary. This commentary never refers directly to the specific films that appear on the screen but to the themes they are supposed to exemplify, and Ives functions either as a talking head who is shown reading from a notebook under a reading light at the back of the screening room, or as a voiceover that overlaps with the beginning or the end of the film extracts. The simplicity of the arrangement that takes at least half of the film's length is deceptive because the extracts do not serve as mere illustrations for the academic speech. These scenes retain their power to enthrall the viewer emotionally, in sharp contrast with the rational articulation of the academic discourse that lacks a deeper comprehension of the emotional power of these movies and of their intense relationship with its original audience.

The source for this thematic arrangement and for the commentary in Pereira dos Santos's film is a book that lends its title to the movie. *Melodrama—O Cinema de Lágrimas da América Latina* is Silvia Oroz's survey of the classic Latin American movies of the 1940s and 1950s, first published in Brazil in 1992. Pereira dos Santos's biographer Helena Salem[12] suggested Oroz to work with Pereira dos Santos for three reasons: Oroz "knew in great detail a large number of films, knew how to locate them in the various film archives in the continent, and had made a critical reflection about the melodrama" (Salem 359).[13] Oroz herself writes in her book that "the melodrama was essentially structured around four myths of Judeo-Christian culture: *Love, Passion, Incest,* and *Women*" (60).[14] It is worth remembering that three of Pereira dos Santos's four paradigmatic films (*Boca de Ouro, Vidas Secas,* and *How Tasty was My Little Frenchman*) were adaptations, as are other important films in his career such as *Jubiabá* and *Memórias do Cárcere*. It is indicative of Nelson Pereira dos Santos's creativity that he gives his film the title of Oroz's book and has her coauthor the screenplay with him. In an interview with Salem, Pereira dos Santos explains that for him "Adaptation is not a prison, it is a reference that leads to great discoveries" (Salem, 163). *Cinema de Lágrimas* is a loose (and fittingly melodramatic) adaptation of a scholarly book that is a critical survey of the Latin American cinematic melodrama that eventually encompasses more than Oroz's book, offers but never betrays the core of her arguments.

The fictional and nonfictional sides of *Cinema de Lágrimas* eventually intersect and become indissoluble. The selection of film extracts and critical commentaries by Ives and Oroz come together as they outline the circumstances surrounding undoubtedly melodramatic events of the life of Rodrigo, events that culminate with his mother's suicide after she arrives from the movies, the subject of a recurring nightmare that torments the protagonist. Whereas the voice of Ives denounces the reactionary mind frame that articulates the main themes of the Latin American melodrama and perhaps explains its remarkable success with the public, Rodrigo—seated right at the front row—sits back and revels in the aesthetic pleasure of the beautiful photography and the fascinating charisma of those stars, specially María Félix, who dominates the screen several times in films such as *Doña Diabla* and in three different sequences from *Camelia*, the adaptation of Alexandre Dumas's 1848 *La Dame aux Camélias* [*The Lady of the Camellias*].

Film clips and commentary also allude indirectly to Rodrigo's childhood as a time fraught with conflicted visions of his mother blurred by incestuous desires, fear of abandonment, and preoccupations with honor and social shame. Rodrigo's mother appears to have been cornered among the idealized figures of the virgin, the good wife, and mother, and the hated home wrecker and prostitute, and the torment of becoming a social outcast leads to her suicide as a last resort against her worries about her son's shame in the face of her "loose" life.

The clips also document one of the greatest accomplishments of Mexican melodrama, which was "long before the radio soap operas and the proliferation of *telenovelas* ( . . . ) reproducing and transfiguring the sentimentality rooted in the private sphere and giving it a friendly wink of solidarity" (Paranaguá, 4). To reinforce this clearly melodramatic story, the ambiguous relationship between a smitten Rodrigo and a mysterious and unpredictable Ives gradually also reveals melodramatic tones. Ives's seemingly impersonal, scholarly comments on the nature of the melodrama also refer cryptically to his own troubled condition, as the unfolding of the story again will make clear. For instance, after inexplicably shunning one of Rodrigo's advances, Ives speaks about the prevalence of deadly diseases in doomed love affairs in which passion battles against social conventions, and his speech is illustrated by María Félix playing the death of her cancer-ridden, blind character on stage in *Camelia*. Instead of cancer or tuberculosis, we will later find out that AIDS is the disease that spells doom for an impossible love affair between Rodrigo and Ives, who is additionally hounded by mysterious dealings with drug dealers and a botched attempt to immigrate illegally to the United States.

Writing about contemporary approaches to the melodrama as a fictional system in *The Melodramatic Imagination*, Peter Brooks argues "it is perhaps part of our postmodern sophistication that we don't quite take melodrama 'straight' anymore ( . . . ) but always with a certain ironic detachment" (ix). Although I take issue with any attempt to assign perspectival superiority to what Brooks calls "our postmodern sophistication," he is right when he speaks about ironic detachment, especially if we consider that there are many ways of detachment other than the obvious resort to parody. *Cinema de Lágrimas* is by no means an anachronistic reenactment of the cinematic melodrama of the 1940s, but the film also refuses simply to poke fun at the often overblown rhetoric of the melodrama. As far as ironic detachment is concerned, the stories of Rodrigo and his mother as well as that of Rodrigo and Ives constitute at the most a rather timid pastiche of cinematic melodrama. They feature a partial reenactment of specific motifs, such as the doomed love affair driven by passion but condemned by society, the tragedy of lost women and their fall from grace, and the dramatization of motherhood to the extremes of insinuations of incest. And the delivery of the two stories that bind together Rodrigo's childhood and his mature years is far from the heightened, sometimes strident, tone of the classic melodrama. Without the dramaturgy of hyperbole, excess and overstatement, excitement and acting out, the fictional portion of *Cinema de Lágrimas* turns into subdued drama. There is no attempt to echo the aesthetics of cinema from the 1940s and 1950s, which is by the way visible in all its vitality in the extracts from the 17 movies from that era that take up at least half of *Cinema de Lágrimas*'s running time. Pereira dos Santos's choices in terms of soundtrack, acting, or photography for the segments that depict Rodrigo's story are in fact subdued and clearly contemporary, without any hints of nostalgic referencing to black-and-white melodrama. The disjunction is such that one reviewer lamented, "the film clips and the contrived fictional plot don't quite mesh" (García Tsao). Although I think they in fact establish a relationship of sorts, it is a subdued one and there is the risk that one simply misses the melodrama in Rodrigo's story when it plays against the emphatic voice of its counterparts from the Golden Age of Mexican cinema.

Perhaps with the initial intentions of the project in mind, Pereira dos Santos manages to link *Cinema de Lágrimas* to the cinema of the 1960s and 1970s in Brazil and elsewhere in Latin America as well as the Mexican melodrama. Every day as Rodrigo and Ives go up the stairs of the Colegio San Idelfonso in downtown Mexico for a new film session, they pass by classrooms where Ivan Trujillo[15] and Silvia Oroz herself make brief appearances while giving lectures that mention Paul Leduc, Fernando Pino Solanas, Tomás Gutiérrez Alea, and Glauber Rocha. Rodrigo and Ives then walk by the door of the classroom where the camera shows billboards of Paul Leduc's *Reed, Mexico Insurgente*, Fernando Pino Solanas's *La Hora de los Hornos*, the *Twelfth Festival Internacional del Nuevo Cine Latinoamericano*, and a poster that reads "El Nuevo Cine Latino Americano" and brings a list of filmmakers that is a Who's Who in Latin American cinema in the 1960s and 1970s.[16] In these short scenes we also hear fragments of class discussions in which appear themes that were central to Latin American directors in the 1960s and 1970s: the struggle of newcomers against the congealed remnants of the cinematic industry in Mexico in the 1970s, the political and social meaning of the theory of the *cinéma du auteur* in Latin America, and the relationship between art and reality in a continent stricken extreme social injustice.

These are moments in which the fictional in *Cinema de Lágrimas* again incorporates into its narrative elements associated with the expository mode. A movement toward a hybrid form takes place not only in the film excerpts often accompanied by something akin to voiceover authoritative commentary, but also in the appearance of several other posters in the halls of Museum of Modern Art of Rio de Janeiro (MAM-RJ); these posters functioning as visual documents of important films from the 1960s and 1970s, pointing "in various ways to the archival coexistence of the two forms" (Sadlier 2009, 105), namely the melodrama and *Cinema Novo*. There is also the use of iconic Mexican locations such as the Zócalo (where Rodrigo passes by drum-and-dance performances by *concheros*) and the Colegio Idelfonso in Mexico City (where Pereira dos Santos sets the exhibition rooms of UNAM's famous *filmoteca*—the best in Latin America—which is actually located in the university's main campus many miles from downtown).

At the heart of Pereira dos Santos's defense of the Latin American cinema of the 1940s and 1950s there are three ideas that also form the critical backbone of Oroz's *Cinema de Lágrimas* as well. The first idea is a refutation of the melodrama as necessarily promoting alienation in the masses by claiming that classic Latin American melodrama should be interpreted in the light of Arnold Hauser's famous assertion that "artistic progressivism and political conservatism are perfectly compatible" and that "every honest artist who describes reality faithfully and sincerely has an enlightening and emancipating influence on his age" (Hauser, 29). The second one is again a refutation, this time of the Latin American melodrama's aesthetic frailty and its inherent conventional superficiality. Oroz again takes up Hauser when she presents tragic myths as the basic thematic structure of the melodrama, which becomes a form of "popularized, or, if one likes, corrupted" classical tragedy (*Rococo, Classicism, and Romanticism*, 187). The third critical stance is a vigorous rejection of a strict division between art produced by mass media and erudite art, which is embodied in Oroz's refutation of Dwight Macdonald's division of culture into low-, middle-, and high-brow, and his suggestion that the uncompromising option for the last one was a political antiauthoritarian gesture. Oroz affirms:

> The categories *highbrow* e *mass-cult* ( ... ) exclude and segregate in our culture and are therefore among the most conservative movements of contemporary aesthetics. The segregation of culture involves rigid schemes that do not take into account the enourmous development of mass culture and contemporary social dynamics. (41)[17]

To understand Oroz's critical stance it is interesting to look at the origins of her interest in the despised Latin American cinematic melodrama. In that respect it is no coincidence that the book by the Argentinian critic was first published in Brazil in 1992 and then in Mexico in 1995.[18] Oroz moved to Rio de Janeiro in 1979 and became close friends with a fellow countryman also living in Rio de Janeiro, the writer Manuel Puig, to whom Oroz dedicates the book as "the one who taught me not to fear the melodrama" (5). Puig was an ardent admirer of melodrama as well as of classic Hollywood films when such enthusiasm was not common at all among Latin American intellectuals, and he organized an informal cine-club in Rio de Janeiro with his friend, the Mexican cultural attaché Hugo Gutiérrez Vega (whose poetry on Brazil we briefly discussed in the chapter about Mexican poets in Rio de Janeiro). The group used to meet three times a week to watch films from Puig's large collection, and Oroz herself described elsewhere Puig's peculiar system of classification:

> He had classified our movies in three types: films, movies, flicks. The first were auteur productions—Fellini, Godard, et cetera.—we never watched those. The movies were good routine melodramas (Hollywood forties, et cetera.); and the flicks were unbridled melodramas like Ninón Sevilla's *Aventurera*, or Leticia Palma's *Hipócrita*. Our sessions, two or three per week, concentrated on Mexican and Spanish melodramas. We had another category for the masters, that is, Dreyer, Ozu, Mizoguchi, Ulmer—quirky, not mainstream, but eccentric geniuses of cinema. The works [called] *vista* (flick) and *cinta* (literally, tape, but meaning movie) were what the lower classes in Argentina in the forties and fifties called the movies. (Levine, 354–355)

The attention paid to the much-despised Latin American melodramas of the 1930s, 1940s, and 1950s was not a surprising choice coming

from Puig, one of the first Latin American authors willing to challenge the strict assertion from left-wing intellectuals that the melodrama was nothing but a form of promotion of people's alienation
and a grotesque copy of the Hollywood studio production of the
period. The use of working-class slang to differentiate between auteur
films and others was also indicative of Puig's peculiar understanding of the class prejudice unwittingly implicit in the prejudice against
melodramas—the class prejudice of which Oroz accuses Macdonald
and, indirectly, the intellectual establishment of Latin America in the
twentieth century.

In Manuel Puig we see a pioneer of a new wave of Latin American
artists, writers, and filmmakers who question more and more point-
edly the old truisms concerning mass culture, popular expression,
and political engagement. Simplifying this change of attitude in
terms of a conflict between generations does not help to understand
the phenomenon in all its complexity. If we followed generational
attachments to define individual instances about these issues, we
could never think of Nelson Pereira dos Santos as someone "new"
articulating a radical criticism of the previous generation. *Cinema de
Lágrimas* sees an undercurrent linking the melodrama and the cinema of his own generation and has no wish to discard either of them
but to look at both with critical but affectionate eyes.

In the preface to the 1992 edition of *Melodrama—O Cinema de
Lágrimas da América Latina*, Cristovam Buarque[19]—a man of the
same generation and similar political convictions as those of Oroz
and Pereira dos Santos—returns to the problem of reaching a wider
audience and to the classic melodrama as an example to be followed
in that concern:

> One of the paradoxes of the history of Brazilian culture is that people
> ceased to go to the movies since filmmakers took on analyzing realisti-
> cally the tragedy of Brazilian people. The Left put the people onto the
> screen and drove them out of the movie theater. But that is an explain-
> able paradox. The people were considered as a theme but ignored as a
> beneficiary. (Oroz, 12)[20]

Only when the string of brutally repressive military dictatorships that
had become the rule in Latin America during the 1970s finally came
to an end with the end of the Cold War, Nelson Pereira dos Santos,
his generation, and the younger ones as well were able to engage in a
revision of their critical stances toward the melodrama. The hostility
toward mass culture as unequivocal alienation and the mechanistic

relationship between political engagement and art in general that demanded that artists convey a clear political message, lost their hegemonic grip over Latin American cultures, especially in the South Cone. Nevertheless, Latin American cinema is still far from reclaiming its past popularity and combining it with renewed aesthetic and critical vigor.

At the end of the twentieth century, *Cinema de Lágrimas* proposed a new retrospective dialogue between the popular Latin American melodrama of the 1940s and 1950s that had constituted a veritable cinematic industry in Latin America but was crushed by external pressures and the daring avant-garde Latin American cinema of the 1960s, which dreamed of a cinematic revolution to help usher in a revolution that could change the continent. When these two tendencies, one in decline and the other on the rise, clashed in the 1960s, most of the filmmakers within the revolutionary *Cinema Novo* saw their predecessors as much enemies as Hollywood, establishing a sharp dichotomy between the uncompromising auters fighting alienation and the mass-media industry in its untiring promotion of conformism.

At the end of *Cinema de Lágrimas*, after finally unlocking the secret of his mother's death by watching Carlos Hugo Christensen's *Armiño Negro* on a VCR tape sent by Ives with a letter in which the graduate student explains his predicament, an emotional Rodrigo runs into a packed room where young people are watching Glauber Rocha's *Deus e o Diabo na Terra do Sol* [*Black God, White Devil*]. Rodrigo joins them and we cannot help but see that the scenes from Rocha's black-and-white classic indeed have a lot more in common with some of the best scenes we have seen from the Mexican classics by Emilio Fernández and Alejandro Galindo than we would have supposed. Darlene Sadlier compares them thus:

> Pereira dos Santos invites us to ask exactly how Rocha's shot of the couple's embrace or Corisco's death at the hands of Antônio das Mortes differs in kind from the close-ups of passionate lovers in *Camelia* or the dramatic death scene in Buñuel's *Abismos de la Pasión*, in which the lovesick and crazed Alejandro (Jorge Mistral) is shot in the eye as he leans against his beloved's open coffin. The couple's race away from the villainous Antônio das Mortes and across the *sertão* is as melodramatic as any escape scene from the older movies. The soundtrack that fuels the eroticism of the prolonged kiss in Rocha's film is as stirringly sensual as Richard Wagner's *Tristan und Isolde*, which in Buñuel's film accompanies Alejandro's kissing of his beloved's decomposed corpse. (Sadlier 2007, 107)

His faced lighted by the flickering light of Rocha's film, Rodrigo bursts into tears and then smiles at the iconic final scene in which the two protagonists race toward the sea. His response to *Deus e o Diabo na Terra do Sol* is not unlike his reaction to the films Ives selected for him. It is an expression of pleasure. Sadlier may be right when she claims that "ultimately *Cinema de Lágrimas* is about the pleasure of watching both types of film" (109) and that would suit the general intention of the BFI series to celebrate cinema at its hundredth anniversary.

Not only is *Cinema de Lágrimas* a vindication of the Latin American melodrama, but also a celebration of the emotional power of the *Cinema Novo*, here epitomized by Glauber Rocha's 1964 film. For Pereira dos Santos,

> Glauber Rocha represents all of us. He represents Latin America's cinema just as the Mexican melodrama and melodrama in general may represent it. And also this sudden appearance of Glauber [in Cinema de Lágrimas] is also the personal component of my movie: a remembrance of a comrade in arms in cinema, of all the comrade in arms in cinema that I've lost, but that linger on in my memory. (Pierre, 91)[21]

The emotional homage to Rocha in the interview and in *Cinema de Lágrimas* resembles something Carlos Diegues once said about the relationship between the younger filmmakers of his generation and a slightly older and more experienced Nelson Pereira dos Santos in the 1960s. Diegues tells Helena Salem that, "we had different favorite foreign filmmakers: Glauber loved Eisenstein, Paulo César Sarraceni loved Rossellini, Walter Lima Jr. loved John Ford. But our idol, truly, was Nelson" (Salem, 180).[22]

At the ending credits we listen to Caetano Veloso and Gilberto Gil's song "Cinema Novo." The song itself is a smooth combination between the lyrics of a boisterous *samba enredo* (the songs composed and performed especially for the *Carnaval*-thematic parade of the *escolas de samba*) and the soft-pulsing rhythms of the soothing guitars of *bossa nova* in an album that aimed to celebrate 25 years of the 1968 album *Tropicalia, ou Panis et Circenses*. This 1993 song is a passionate defense of the glories of Brazilian cinema at a time when it had just faced virtual extinction with the neoliberal reforms championed by the administration of Fernando Collor de Mello in 1990. The elegiac lyrics speak of a dialogue among music, poetry, and cinema, understood as three entities that mingle and morph into each other in their attempt to represent Brazil. It also cites dozens of names that comprise the story of cinema in Brazil since well before the *Cinema Novo* itself. In a particularly meaningful sequence of verses, the singers imagine that Cinema wishes to "come back to *Atlântida* and go beyond the eclipse / Kill the egg and see *Vera Cruz*."[23] The verses play with the proper meanings the mythical Atlantis and Vera Cruz (one of the first names given to Brazil) and the names of two studios (*Atlântida* and *Vera Cruz*) that produced the most successful films of the 1940s and 1950s in Brazil. The spirit of affectionate revision of this song and of *Cinema de Lágrimas* is very similar as is their final defiant reaffirmation of the pride in past tradition.

In spite of being an adaptation of a scholarly book that incorporates elements commonly identified with the expository mode, Pereira dos Santos's homage to the melodrama cannot be reduced to a film with a thesis. Pereira dos Santos otherwise defines *Cinema de Lágrimas*: "c'est un film d'amour, y compris envers la culture, et envers le livre. L'amour de la vie et l'amour de la culture se mélangent dans ce film" [This is a film about love, and it is also about the culture and also the book. The love for life and the love for culture blend in this film.] (Pierre, 91).

# Chapter 9

# Paul Leduc Reads Rubem Fonseca: The Globalization of Violence or The Violence of Globalization

The only contemporary Mexican filmmaker who features prominently in *Cinema de Lágrimas* is Paul Leduc (1942). In 2006 Leduc
would reciprocate Nelson Pereira dos Santos and make a "Brazilian"
movie: an adaptation of a series of short stories by Rubem Fonseca
called *El Cobrador—In God We Trust*. The appearance of the name
Leduc in *Cinema de Lágrimas* is not accidental nor a whimsical
choice on the part of Nelson Pereira dos Santos. The initial strategy
in this chapter is parallel to the one I used in the previous chapter:
we shall go through three important films by Leduc to understand
*El Cobrador* within the context of Leduc's works and particular interests. Paul Leduc is the director of three hallmarks of post–Golden Age
Mexican cinema: *Reed: Mexico Insurgente* (1971), *Frida, Naturaleza
Viva* (1984), and *¿Como Ves?* (1986).

Leduc's debut was *Reed: Mexico Insurgente*, an independent film
(made entirely outside the government-sponsored Mexican film
council) featured in the Cannes and Berlin festivals. Based on the
journalist John Reed's 1914 *Insurgent Mexico*, a firsthand account of
the events in Mexico that focused as much attention on the myth of
Pancho Villa as on the common soldiers of the Mexican Revolution
and the chaotic, unglamorous realities of battle, Leduc's film is the
first, major post-1968 film about the Mexican Revolution. *Reed:
Mexico Insurgente* is about the political awakening of John Reed in
his direct contact with the revolution, but it also "demystifies the
revolution, blending documentary and fictional elements in a manner
that is consistent with the aesthetic and political strategies" (Pick,

9) of the New Latin American Cinema in which Nelson Pereira dos Santos played a prominent role.

In 1984 Leduc released *Frida, Naturaleza Viva*, a remarkable biopic that coincided with the reemergence of the painter Frida Kahlo but went contrary to the tendency of this revival of stripping Kahlo from her active engagement in Mexico's social and political life. The film also searched for a language fully compatible with the artist it depicts, shunning a linear narrative and keeping dialogue to a minimum in a series of almost independent segments that rely much on Kahlo's own paintings and sensibility.[1] The film's whimsical iconography and sharp contrasts of monochromatic colors builds a mise-en-scène that anticipates Leduc's exploration of the baroque in his *Barroco* (1989).

In 1986 Leduc directed another, less known landmark: *¿Cómo Ves?*, an unadorned look at the underground culture that thrived on the outskirts of Mexico City and the city's punk-rock scene. Leduc and José Joaquín Blanco wrote the screenplay based on texts such as *crónicas* and newspaper pieces by writers such as José Agustín and José Revueltas that focused on the youth in Mexico City. Leduc provocatively dedicates *¿Cómo Ves?* to the IMF, and the film focuses on the desperation of Mexican youth as the country's poor suffered with recession and inflation amidst periodical financial crises and cuts in social services during the years Latin Americans would later call "the lost decade." As the twentieth century came to an end, the illusions about Latin American modernization were dissipated and the result was described in a review of *¿Cómo Ves?* as "a modernity that seems primitive: it is apocalyptic" (Ronquillo).[2]

In spite of a successful career that made many consider him the most prominent director of his generation, Paul Leduc announced his retirement from the cinema in 1993. In one of the interviews of that period Leduc said,

> Cinema, as we conceived of it and as we dreamed of it for the last hundred years, is over. What made me want to make movies was the chance to work as a team, where everyone shared and believed in the same ideas. ( ... ) Our films, produced outside Hollywood, circulate only in festivals and among friends. They have no public and they don't pay off anymore. (Caetano, 196)[3]

Leduc's pessimism about the viability of commercial Latin American cinema is the result of his own troubles with the financing and distribution of his films after years of acclaim in critical circles in Mexico and abroad, and is perfectly in tune with the difficult times Latin American cinema faced then. The 1990s saw the encroachment of an already dominant Hollywood practically all over the world, gaining further ground from embattled local industries. The mood at the time was not different in Brazil after the traumatic extinction of Embrafilme [Empresa Brasileira de Filmes] by Fernando Collor de Mello brought film production to a complete halt.[4]

However, just as, once again, Brazilian cinema rose from the ashes, Leduc changed his mind about quitting making movies; and he claimed to have done so because of Brazilian writer Rubem Fonseca. In 1999 Leduc bought the rights to Fonseca's short stories and embarked on an ambitious project that took him seven years to complete. *El Cobrador—In God We Trust* features locations, actors, and production crews from four different countries of the Americas (Argentina, Brazil, Mexico, and the United States) and a multinational network of sponsors and producers from both sides of the Atlantic—again something typical of twenty-first century Latin American cinema.

Leduc considered "odd and actually a bit depressing" (Portal)[5] that several interviewers began their conversations with him by asking about how he got to know Rubem Fonseca's work. The fact that Leduc became acquainted with Rubem Fonseca's work is not an expression of this Mexican director's interest in all things Brazilian, nor a felicitous accident. Practically all of Fonseca's works have been widely available in Mexico now for quite some time. The Mexican publisher Ediciones Cal y Arena[6] has translated no less than 18 of Fonseca's books since 1990,[7] most of them by Rodolfo Mata, professor at UNAM's prestigious Instituto de Investigaciones Filológicas, who has done an invaluable service in promoting Brazilian literature in Mexico.[8]

Furthermore, Rubem Fonseca's prominence in Mexico was consolidated when he won the prestigious Juan Rulfo Prize of Latin American and Caribbean Literature in 2003. The critic Julio Ortega at the time wrote a small presentation in which he compliments Fonseca for his capacity for powerful concision and calls him no less than "el Rulfo brasileño" (Ortega, 14). The publication celebrating Fonseca for the prize also publicized in Spanish words of praise, which Mario Vargas Llosa included in a review of Fonseca's novel *High Art* in *The New York Times Book Review*. In this review Vargas Llosa compares Fonseca to Umberto Eco and Manuel Puig claiming that the Brazilian writer "is one of those contemporary writers who have absconded from the library to create high-quality literature with materials and techniques stolen from mass culture" (Vargas Llosa).

But what was it in Fonseca's short stories that captured Leduc's interest and motivated him to work on a full-feature film? First of all, it is important to clarify my own view of the relationship between literature and cinema in film adaptations. Instead of framing film adaptations as intersemiotic translations, I would rather think of them as a peculiar form of interpretation. Film adaptations are not bound by the literary texts on which they are based in the same way translations are. As much as translations can be thought of as re-creations, they are not ordinarily granted nearly the same freedom as the average film adaptation. Furthermore, criticism based on notions such as source and derivative is bound to offer predictable results: comments on the "missing" parts from the original in the adaptation. Just as Nelson Pereira dos Santos interpreted Silvia Oroz's book in light of his own ideas about the Mexican melodrama, Leduc interpreted several short stories by Fonseca in *El Cobrador*.

This is how Paul Leduc explains the process of adapting Fonseca's stories:

> I offered Rubem Fonseca the chance to participate in the making of the script, but he preferred not to. He gave me total freedom to adapt his short stories. I gave the stories different political coordinates and national contexts because I didn't want to simply transpose the text into images, but rather voice my own concerns through them. I think there is no meaning in adapting a literary text if not in this way. However, this by no means implies that I was not faithful to Fonseca's work and I believe that is how he perceived it, too. I do not think that there is any meaning in working from a literary text just to betray what it had to say. (Portal)[9]

What are the specific "concerns" to which Leduc alludes in the passage above? In an interview for the newspaper *La Jornada* Leduc summarizes them as the need to understand the "the globalization of violence generated by the violence of globalization."[10] A perverse combination of the erosion of the achievements of a hundred years of labor movements and others forms of social protest, coupled with the worsening of already precarious living conditions and staggering social disparities with the expansion of global capitalism to the far reaches of the globe, produces what Leduc defines as the core of what Fonseca showcases in his stories: the existence of a "social resentment that has been roaming around the world, that finds no legitimate outlet and is channeled by violence" ("Exhiben Mexicanos sus Filmes en España").[11]

With these specific concerns in mind—concerns that he sees articulated in interesting and incisive ways in the literature of Rubem

Fonseca—Paul Leduc builds *El Cobrador—In God We Trust* by weaving together the following five short stories: "Night Drive 1 & 2" [Paseio Noturno 1 & 2] from *Feliz Ano Novo* (1975), "The Taker" [O Cobrador] from *O Cobrador* (1979), "Placebo" from *Buraco na Parede* (1994), and "City of God" [Cidade de Deus] from *Historias de Amor* (1997) (this being a story with no relation to Paulo Lins's novel nor to Fernando Meirelles's film). One could see this adaptation as the result of gathering together a small anthology of five pieces and shaping them into one whole—something we would call in literary terms a novel. It is worth going into the specifics of this process of creative interpretation to understand Leduc's film, Fonseca's stories, and their relation to each other a little better.

The title indicates the centrality of the nameless character I will call *el cobrador* (a wordless part played with great intensity by the Brazilian actor Lázaro Ramos) and his partner in love and in crime, Ana (played by the Argentinian Antonella Costa, the star in what is perhaps the best Argentinian film about the country's dictatorship, Mauro Bechis's *Garage Olimpo*). However, two other characters based on Fonseca's stories are equally prominent in the film: a man referred in the credits as Mr. X (played by the American actor Peter Fonda) and Zinho (played by the Brazilian actor Milton Gonçalves).

*El cobrador* travels to New York, Mexico City, and Brazil, exacting ruthless revenge against everyone who he feels owes him for his troubles in the world. He meets Ana, an Argentinian journalist living in Mexico, just as she is seen struggling with the fact that the man she thought was her father had killed her real parents and adopted her, taking advantage of the fact that he was a member of the large repressive apparatus of the military regime that terrorized Argentina since 1976, with its sinister *Proceso de Reorganización Nacional*. They start a torrid love affair and she joins him in his vigilante streak of murders to exact revenge against a powerful figure in Mexico who had caused the death of a militant friend during a protest. The couple then escapes Mexico and arrives in Brazil, where they perform their most spectacular act before returning to New York in search of the powerful Mr. X. This is more or less a reenactment of the short story "The Taker," one of the most brutal of Fonseca's notoriously violent stories, except for its internationalist flavor.

Fonda's Mr. X is a very wealthy businessman, based on two different character protagonists from "Night Drive 1" and "Night Drive 2" (stories that feature the same narrator-protagonist) and "Placebo." Mr. X is first seen in Miami, where he does pretty much what Fonseca's unnamed narrator does in "Night Drive": he relieves his frustration with work and his feeling of alienation from his own family by becoming an unpunished serial killer behind the wheel of his sleek car. In Fonseca's story, the unnamed narrator drives his powerful sports car around deserted streets of Rio de Janeiro every night until he finds a woman he runs over; in Leduc's film, Mr. X runs over Hispanic women he finds in the streets of Miami with a big, shiny SUV. But that is not all there is to Mr. X; he also suffers from a debilitating disease—as does the protagonist in "Placebo"—and that takes him, later in the film, to a trip to Buenos Aires. He is desperately in search of a cure and reluctantly follows the guidance of a sardonic gypsy played by the veteran Mexican indie star Isela Vega, who takes him to a dubious witch doctor with extremely unorthodox means. These are roughly the bare bones of Fonseca's "Placebo," which nevertheless takes place entirely in Brazil and features the CEO of a multinational.[12]

A third strand in the film focuses on Zinho, a ruthless drug lord of Cidade de Deus and the dweller of a fancy condo in Barra da Tijuca, who becomes the involuntary tool of his lover's horrific revenge against her true love in "City of God." Not only does Leduc move Zinho away from Rio de Janeiro but he also adds a completely new dimension to this character. Leduc's Zinho becomes a curious adaptation of an infamous real-life figure: Sebastião Rodrigues de Moura, a.k.a *Coronel Curió*, a member of the army forces sent to the central north of Brazil to hunt down guerilla fighters in Araguaia in the 1970s who later became the quasi-official ruler of the gold mines in *Serra Pelada*.[13] We eventually realize that *el cobrador* had worked in the mine under the ruthless supervision of Zinho, who led an implacable repression of a botched attempt at rebellion in which *el cobrador* participated.

This important addition to the character created by Fonseca highlights the focal point that makes all these three strands coalesce into one big mosaic of globalized violence and the globalization of violence in the Americas. *El Cobrador—In God We Trust* disperses the action of these stories throughout the Americas, originally revealing many different facets of the city of Rio de Janeiro. Rubem Fonseca takes us everywhere in Rio: from Avenida Atlântica and Vieira Souto to the projects at Cruzada de São Sebastião in Leblon, from Cidade de Deus in Zona Oeste to the nouveaux riches of Barra da Tijuca, from a bustling Cinelândia teeming with seedy types to a misleadingly tranquil Lagoa Rodrigo de Freitas, and so on. Paul Leduc's film moves deftly in consecutive sections—separated by black screens with indicative subtitles—set in the streets of large, paradigmatic cities of the Americas: New York City and Miami, Mexico City, Rio de Janeiro, and Buenos Aires (the film has a final section that takes us back to New York). But it is in Leduc's version of a *Serra Pelada*—actually filmed in one of the many open mine pits around Belo Horizonte—that we find the point of convergence of all the stories and their characters. Lázaro Ramos's el cobrador used to work at the mines, Milton Gonçalves's Zinho (as I mentioned before) ruled over them, and Peter Fonda's Mr. X owns them. Although images from the mine appear since the film's opening, all these aforementioned links are unveiled slowly as the film advances. For instance, it is only in the final third of the film that we see Mr. X barking orders over the phone to shut down the no longer profitable mines regardless of protests or complaints, because his investment group—that also has ties with Mexico—is not into gold anymore; they are now focused on oil and energy.

The film shifts back and forth from two distinct moments in the history of the mines. Representing the past, when the mine was working at full speed, there are several short scenes, alternating close and panoramic takes, which are strict cinematic renderings of the famous photographs by the Brazilian photographer Sebastião Salgado, showing swarms of men covered in dust and mud, carrying heavy sacks of gravel out of the pit up the steep walls. In some of them a taciturn Zinho appears clad in military uniform and surrounded by soldiers clutching assault rifles. In others *el cobrador* appears as one of the miners and a silent conspirator preparing an uprising, which Zinho stifles before it begins. Representing the present, when the mines have become an eerie, abandoned wasteland, there is an almost deserted bar where a few souls drink. There is also a series of aerial shots as a deranged helicopter pilot—played by the legendary director Ruy Guerra—describes the place as being 15 times the size of France and belonging to Americans who want everything turned into either dust or gold. This pilot is bringing Zinho back, now with an American police officer, involved in a hunt for *el cobrador* because of the murders he had committed in New York.

It took Leduc seven years to finish his adaptation, and he has suggested that his travails this time were not due only to the usual difficulties in financing independent Latin American films. Aggravating Leduc's troubles, this film became extremely polemical after 9/11. After all, even the protagonist of Fonseca's "O Cobrador" is already a kind of nihilistic terrorist, who, after a series of gruesome and fairly random murders, announces his future plans to blow up a Christmas party where all the jet set of Rio de Janeiro is supposed to meet.

Leduc turns him into an international terrorist who has a global reach and a target comfortably established in the United States.

Fonseca's short story that lends its title to the film—and, to a certain extent, the book that contains it—was a daring rebuke of the military dictatorship censors who had banned his former short-story collection, *Feliz Ano Novo*—which contained "Night Drive." The ban on *Feliz Ano Novo*, imposed 13 months after its publication in 1975, would last 13 years and involve a long legal battle. *Estado de São Paulo*'s columnist Sérgio Augusto recently retold the story to commemorate the 35th anniversary of the ban, which he called "the most talked-about literary-judicial scandal of the military regime."[14]

In their official statement, the censors declared that the book featured

> in almost its entirety characters who have complexes, vices, and perversions, with the aim of focusing on the dark side of society in the perpetration of bad behavior, bribes, assault and murder, without any sign of disapproval, utilizing very lowly language and where pornography is largely employed with quick derogative allusions to those responsible for the future of Brazil and the work of censors. (Augusto)[15]

The moralistic reproach to the book's foul language and pornography is typical of the hypocrisy of the military regime at times when the *pornochanchadas* [nonexplicit pornographic comedies] produced in São Paulo's *Boca do Lixo* thrived, but the censors point to an important aspect of those stories, an aspect that would in fact be further exacerbated by Fonseca in "O Cobrador": the lack of any hint of condemnation on the part of Fonseca's narrative voices of any of the gruesome acts perpetrated by his characters, even in stories where what we could call an editorial voice is clearly heard, such as "Intestino Grosso" [Large Intestine], which is an interview with an unnamed writer accused of more or less the same charges leveled against Fonseca by the censors.

Disturbing as it indeed is, I by no means want to voice a moralistic concern about Fonseca's literary violence. The stories selected by Leduc are interesting, among other things, precisely because they are disquieting in their unmediated violence, and the lack of rhetorical signs of condemnation of these acts is an important piece of Fonseca's strategy to enhance their impact. Fonseca's fictional violence ignores the conventions of self-ironizing postmodern horror and manages to go beyond the sadomasochistic play of "terror put into an accomplished enough artistic form," which "becomes enjoyable, and so self-contradictory" (Eagleton, 20).

These stories have also been considered somehow prophetical by highlighting urban violence long before this topic replaced inflation as the main concern of Brazilians in general. After a trip to Sarajevo, where a screening of the landmark documentary *Notícias de uma Guerra Particular*, which he directed with Kátia Lund, caused a deep impression in a young audience from a deeply scarred city in the aftermath of a brutal war, João Moreira Salles summarized the tragic situation of the urban centers in Brazil as thus:

> From April 1992 to November 1994, 11,600 people died in Sarajevo. In the same period 13,000 people died violent deaths in the city of Rio de Janeiro, almost 2,000 more than in a city in a state of war. (84)[16]

Besides the staggering number of deaths, a sad reality Mexico has had to face as well in its ill-fated war on the drug cartels or in the systematic murders of women in Ciudad Juárez, Walter Salles's brother emphasizes the challenge of facing "a solitary violence, encapsulated in itself ( . . . ) an individualized, decentralized violence devoid of utopias," the result perhaps of "the hegemony of the marketplace, where the nonmeasurable dimension of dreams loses importance" (Salles). Moreira Salles also highlights the invisibility of most of the victims of this violence, poor people born in the Zona Oeste, on the "wrong side" of the Rebouças tunnel, but still wonders about the roots of such violence:

> For all those reasons I suspect Brazil is facing a new phenomenon, yet to be explained. One understands the violence in Sarajevo, in Israel, in Colombia. Brazilian violence, whose exemplary manifestation takes place in the streets of Rio de Janeiro, is still something unknown. I don't think there is an adequate theoretical apparatus to understand this phenomenon.[17]

Fonseca's fiction is remarkable not only because it foretells this crisis, but because it looks for answers to the questions João Moreira Salles raises, the questions voiced in the song by Tom Zé and Gilberto Assis that opens and closes Leduc's film: "Quem é que tá botando dinamite na cabeça do século?" [Who's planting dynamite inside the head of the century?].[18] One only has to turn to a single passage of "Feliz Ano Novo" to understand what I mean. Hidden in *Cruzada de São Sebastião*—a housing project built in the 1950s under the inspiration of the Catholic Church with the aim of solving the housing crisis that originated and encroached the *favelas* of the city and the place where the protagonist of Fonseca's "O Cobrador" buys his Magnum and then executes a man driving a fancy car who honks at him—the escaped criminals Zequinha and Pereba explain:

> To tell the truth, time is running against me, too, said Zequinha. The cops are playing rough. See what they did to Home Boy? Sixteen bullets in his head. They grabbed Vevé and wrung his neck. And Minhoca, shit! Minhoca! We grew up together in Caxias and he couldn't see a thing more than ten feet away and he stuttered a little too—they grabbed him and threw him into the Guandu River, all busted up.
> It was worse what they did to Tripé. They burned him. He turned into pork rinds. The cops are not taking it easy, said Pereba.[19]

What we have in the passage above is a concise list of the methods of the infamous Death Squads that the military regime either tolerated or openly sponsored. If you add the stark contrast between the hungry, frustrated criminals in a decrepit flat and the opulence of the festivities of the end of the year in a São Conrado mansion you have, in a nutshell, without any trace of didacticism, the dynamite that was planted in the urban areas of Brazil in the 1960s and 1970s and exploded in the 1990s.

This sort of laconic critical acumen that Fonseca applies to the post-1968 Rio de Janeiro, Leduc transposes to the post-neoliberal and post-9/11 Americas with a multinational cast that speaks English, Portuguese, and Spanish in locations in Argentina, Brazil, Mexico, and the United States. Paul Leduc is in search of the dynamite that has been placed in the head of the twenty-first century—and it is significant that the film briefly shows the smoking towers of the World Trade Center in a small television screen at the bar in *Serra Pelada*. In *El Cobrador—In God We Trust* we catch a glimpse of that dynamite: the accumulation of staggering wealth and the simultaneous expansion of shocking destitution; the relentless drive toward environmental depredation and ethnic and cultural genocide all over the globe; and the pitfalls of an increasingly abusive state legitimized by a travesty of democracy, where the choice lies between two versions of the same politics. No wonder a last, spectacular explosion fills the screen till it turns blindingly white, closing Leduc's adaptation of Fonseca's literary world with Tom Zé's voice singing "Defeito 2: Curiosidade," with its relentless questions about "the head" of the twenty-first century:

> Who's planting dynamite ( ... )?
> Who's planting so much lice ( ... )?
> Who's planting so many bugs ( ... )?[20]

The last, more hopeful stanza in the song wonders "who can get a pillow" for the new century. "Defeito 2: Curiosidade" is part of a 1998 conceptual album by the legendary *Tropicalista* Tom Zé, who calls his own work *"imprensa cantada"* [singing press] (Dunn, 217). Since the late 1960s, Tom Zé has played a dissonant voice in Brazilian popular music, questioning the national truisms with a sharp satirical voice that doubted economic development as a panacea to the country's problems and a conservative notion of citizenship contained within private consumption. The album from which "Defeito 2: Curiosidade" comes from, which is called *Defeito de Fabricação/Manufacturing Defect* (1998), is a perfect musical companion to Leduc's remarkable reading of Rubem Fonseca. It contains two interesting texts in the liner notes, one of which is worth quoting at length:

> The Third World has a growing population. The large majority becomes a sort of "android," almost always illiterate and with little specialized working skills. ( . . . ) These androids are cheaper than the factory robots manufactured in Germany and Japan. But they show some innate "defects," such as creating, thinking, dancing, dreaming; these are dangerous defects to the bosses in the First World. In their eyes, when we practice such things we are manufacture-defective androids. Thinking will always be an offense. Having ideas, writing songs, for instance, is to be bold. On the threshold of History, the idea of gathering vegetal fibers and creating the art of weaving was a great audacity. Thinking will always be. (*Defeito de Fabricação*)[21]

One of such defects is exemplified in the song Leduc chose to open and close his adaptation of Fonseca's short stories. Curiosity is a form of audacity because it dares to ask for the ones responsible for a misery that is often attributed to an impersonal and sometimes inscrutable figure: the market.

The most probable source for Leduc was Alfaguara's *Los Mejores Relatos de Rubem Fonseca*, a 1998 book that contains the four stories that were chosen by Leduc for his return to the cinema. This anthology was translated and edited by Romeo Tello Garrido, who also translated Davi Arrigucci Jr.'s excellent book about Julio Cortázar, *O Escorpião Encalacrado*. Tello Garrido also wrote an interesting prologue, in which the UNAM professor stresses ambiguity as a form of expression that allows the Brazilian writer to approach the social and cultural issues from a perspective that is radically different from the Latin American left-wing tradition of social ventriloquism, in which artists and intellectuals believe they can and should speak on behalf of the people and the nation: "while they are not indifferent to the problems of individuals, they do not adopt a didactic posture when they expose them (...) willing to parody the reductionist and Manichean discourse that attempts to explain human and social phenomena in a progressive fashion" (Garrido, 15).[22]

In *El Cobrador—In God We Trust* Leduc dares again to do exactly what Fonseca and Tom Zé have done: to think creatively about violence from the perspective of Latin America as one of the world's wastelands. This perspective is based on a double negation. Faced with the choice between an apocalyptic and a utopian view of speaking from the margins of globalized capitalism, the film accepts neither of them. Instead Leduc proposes that we follow Frantz Fanon's proposition that "the Third World is not cut off from the rest. Quite the contrary, it is at the middle of the whirlpool" (*The Wretched of the Earth*, 76) and expose, as emphatically as possible, the scandalous contrast of opulence founded on the blood of modern-day slaves and on indiscriminate environmental destruction.

# Chapter 10

# The Delicate Crime of Beto Brant and Felipe Ehrenberg*

$B$eto Brant is one of the most talented of the generation of filmmakers who appeared in the 1990s during the so-called *Retomada*. Brant shares with other directors of his generation—not only in Brazil, but in Argentina and Mexico, the two other Latin American countries with strong cinematic traditions—some basic traits. Some experience with other forms of audiovisual production (TV advertising and music video clips); a certain reliance on the submittal of projects for foreign and/or government grants as sources of financing for self-produced movies; and the exploration of elements commonly associated with documentaries, such as relatively small, mobile crews, real locations, and nonactors. However, unlike most of his peers, Brant is willing to experiment beyond the conventional model of the well-made plot that has marked the Brazilian production, preoccupied with recovering the ground lost to Hollywood in the national box office.[1]

An example of Brant's creativity and skills is his most successful and critically acclaimed movie, *O Invasor* [*The Trespasser*] (2002), made after two promising exercises in the same genre, *Os Matadores* [*Belly Up*] (1997), and *Ação entre Amigos* [*Friendly Fire*] (1998). The originality of *The Trespasser* is in the aesthetic sophistication of a project specifically designed to win a special grant for low-budget productions.[2] Most of the cast—highly recognizable names in Brazil including the rock singer Paulo Miklos[3]—was enlisted as co-producers. The soundtrack featured new talent from the underground rap, and hardcore scenes from São Paulo selected with the help of the rapper Sabotage,[4] who also played a small part and helped write some of the dialogue. Filmed with inexpensive and highly portable 16 mm handheld cameras with no shots or countershots and no artificial lighting in "unprepared" real locations in São Paulo, the original footage was converted to HDTV and digitally retouched before being transferred to a more conventional 32 mm. Brant's long-time collaborator Marçal Aquino[5] wrote the screenplay and a novel at the same time and published both in a single book illustrated with stills from the movie.

*The Trespasser* won various awards, among them the Latin American Cinema Award at the Sundance Festival in 2002, and was considered by a pool of Brazilian critics one of the five most influential movies from the *Retomada*.[6] Often compared to Fernando Meirelles and Kátia Lund's *City of God* as an irascible, harsh denunciation of Brazil's chronic social problems, corruption, and violence, *The Trespasser* is more than a naturalist portrayal of social inequities and moral quandaries of contemporary Brazilian society; the film is an expressionist take on a man's nightmarish descent into guilt and hypocrisy.[7]

Brant's next film, *Crime Delicado* [*Delicate Crime*], is perhaps his most daring. Even more than *The Trespasser, Delicate Crime* is a project unconcerned with the recovery of lost ground in the national box office or the naturalist denunciation of violence and injustice in contemporary Brazil. Taking advantage of the inherently collective nature of cinema, Brant establishes fruitful partnerships with several professionals from other arts, allowing visual and performance artists to leave an indelible mark in *Delicate Crime*. Among these, perhaps the most notable is the Mexican artist and performer Felipe Ehrenberg.

This instigating encounter between film, drama, and the arts derives from the fact that the film is an adaptation of *Um Crime Delicado* [*A Delicate Crime*], an acclaimed 1997 short novel by Sérgio Sant'Anna[8] that explores literature, drama, and the arts. In the novel Antônio Martins, a stern theater critic, tells the story of a love triangle of sorts between himself, a mysterious foreign artist, and his model. As it happens with several successful film adaptations, Brant and his collaborators are not afraid of distancing themselves from the original in search of their own vision of the central issues of Sant'Anna's novel. This fruitful gap between the novel and the movie is an interesting point of entry to Brant's *Delicate Crime*, and I start with a small but telling detail: the name of the artist who is the nemesis of Martins.

In Sant'Anna's novel, the artist is called Vitório Brancatti, a man who, according to Martins, acts as some sort of theater producer-director, manipulating his model and the critic to have them perform parts in an elaborate piece of performance art. Accused of having raped Inês, Martins argues that Brancatti used Inês to lure the critic into a relationship and then convinced her to press charges against him. Thus, for Martins, Brancatti mocks criticism as Martins exercises it by staging a farcical piece of conceptual art, complete with a public scandal and a trial. This artist's name could be an allusion to the Italian novelist Vitaliano Brancati, a writer who satirized totalitarian male fantasies of seduction and sexual prowess,[9] to characterize an artist who exploits Martins's illusions of sexual and intellectual superiority with an elaborate game of mirrors in order to expose the critic publicly with the trial and an installation at the *Documenta* in Kassel, Germany.[10] In Sant'Anna's novel Brancatti is portrayed as a calculating artist, but only insofar as we trust Martins's questionable point of view, practically the only one available in the novel. The artist never speaks and is barely visible: Martins only sees him once from a distance at a collective art show and speculates endlessly (and perhaps unconvincingly) about Brancatti's artistic methods and his intentions toward Inês and Martins himself.

In the film Brant changes the artist's name to José Torres Campana, a possible counterallusion to yet another figure of twentieth-century Italian literature, the poet Dino Campana.[11] The author of *Canto Orfici*, persecuted most of his life for his erratic behavior with charges of insanity, is a *poète maudit*, a mostly self-taught Nietszchean who fashions himself as a radical iconoclast searching for the poetic absolute in a poetry of lyric frenzy and exalted hallucinations. Campana's name here indicates a shift: the painter, a full character in the movie, embodies himself a sort of antithesis of Martins's exacerbated rationality in his approach to art.

In the film Martins also accuses Torres Campana of being a perverted "fetishist" who turns his beloved and helpless Inês into "his porn actress" (45:50) and "takes advantage of [her] physical disability" (54:06).[12] But José Torres Campana is not a calculating manipulator and, most important, his central focus is not Martins but Inês and Torres Campana himself. Instead of a cerebral conceptualist staging an elaborate farce with Martins as his satiric target and Inês as his supposed instrument of seduction, Torres Campana is invested in experiencing the artistic process with Inês. Furthermore, Torres Campana, played with gusto by Felipe Ehrenberg, not only appears on the screen, but, eventually, dominates it completely.

Born in Tlacopac near Mexico City in 1943, Felipe Ehrenberg is "a reference in experimental and nonobjective art in this country" (*Manchuria*, 11).[13] Important on the Mexican art scene in the 1960s and especially the 1970s with the collective Proceso Pentágono,[14] the iconoclast Ehrenberg has maintained a reputation as an outsider and a *maudit* in Mexico, even if this may no longer be the case.[15] Beyond national boundaries, Ehrenberg can be said to be one of the unacknowledged pioneers of a distinctive Latin American performance and conceptual art together with the Brazilians Hélio Oiticica and Lygia Clark. Having relinquished for most of his career the traditional role of the artist as a producer of marketable objects, Ehrenberg defines himself as a *neólogo* [neologist], working, often simultaneously, as a journalist, a critic, a political agitator, a social organizer, a teacher, a craftsman, a writer, an editor, and an archivist.[16]

A prolific creator of self-mythologies, Ehrenberg has claimed contacts with Brazilian arts that precede his stay as a cultural attaché, connections parallel to Ehrenberg's view of himself as a bridge between the muralist tradition and the contemporary forms of politicized, nonobjective art in Mexico. Just as he claims his masters to be the Mexican self-taught muralist José Chávez Morado (1909–2002) and the constructivist pioneer Matthias Goeritz (1905–1990), Ehrenberg claims to have worked as an assistant to Emiliano di Cavalcanti (1897–1976) when the Brazilian *modernista* painted a mural in Mexico City[17] and Ehrenberg harbored a long friendship with the Brazilian *tropicalista* Rubens Gerchman (1942–2008).[18]

Speaking about his stay in Brazil, Ehrenberg emphasized his role as a promoter of Mexican art and culture:

> I believe my work has never fit into this complacent market. That's why I am interested in my internationalization through my travels and in this sense my work as cultural ambassador of Mexico in Brazil has made clear that my investment is in the promotion of Mexican culture and that my work, as an artist and as a promoter of Mexican art, should be seen as an invitation to look beyond our northern neighbor. (Cárdenas Pacheco, 1)[19]

Accordingly, Ehrenberg's partnership with Beto Brant renders Mexico a constant, if subtle presence in *Delicate Crime*. Inês recites a poem by the Mexican singer-poet Margarita Martínez Duarte.[20] When he visits José Torres Campana's studio, Antônio Martins picks up and eyes suspiciously a small *calavera* dressed as a *charro* placed on a table. Another, larger *papier- maché calavera* is visible on a shelf in the background as Torres Campana paints. Naturally, it is during the section in which Ehrenberg (Torres Campana) is interviewed that the Mexican presence is most salient: the artist recalls the aftermath of the 1985 earthquake as a macabre festival of sheer violence and death, discusses his view of life as a field traversed by the energies from destruction, and creation as an influence of Mayan and Aztec cosmologies, and describes the famous bone tattoos on his left hand as an homage to José Guadalupe Posada, who best represents "Mexico's fascination with death as a metaphor for life" (1:19:30).[21]

Ehrenberg points to a different and equally instigating direction for the artist character in Brant's film. José Torres Campana would be Ehrenberg's personal suggestion (*Manchuria*, 210)—an allusion to Jusep Torres Campalans, a fictional creation of Max Aub.[22] Aub wrote the novel *Jusep Torres Campalans* in 1958, simulating a monograph on a supposedly forgotten avant-garde pioneer artist. Aub's book includes an elaborate biography with photographs[23]; color reproductions of several paintings by the artist (painted by Aub himself); a "Cuaderno Verde" [green notebook] containing Torres Campalans's notes and aphorisms written from 1906 to 1914; and Aub's interviews with *don* Jusep in the outskirts of San Cristóbal de Las Casas. The fictional in this case purposively extrapolated the pages of the novel when Aub followed the publication of his novel with a retrospective of Jusep Torres Campalans's work in a respected art gallery in Mexico City.[24]

Ehrenberg's allusion to Aub is more than an expression of admiration. It is a declaration of affinity with forms of artistic creation that have a knack for the self-ironical hoax and deftly cross the boundaries between genres and media, defying easy classification. The exhibition catalogue *Manchuria—Visión Periférica* exemplifies this aspect of Ehrenberg's work. More than an illustrated summary of the exhibit, this book is an elaborate autobiography edited by the artist himself to supplement the retrospective at the Museo de Arte Moderno. *Manchuria—Visión Periférica* makes the same trajectory as Aub's *Jusep Torres Campalans,* only in reverse: from exhibit to book, the retrospective extends its existence into another medium.

The hypothetical allusions are by no means mutually exclusive. The fictional iconoclast Jusep Torres Campalans who claims that "art burns or is not" [el arte arde o no es] (*JTC*, 188) has a lot in common with Dino Campana, the real-life iconoclastic self-proclaimed "*poeta notturno*" (*Canti Orfici e Altre Poesie*, 42). Furthermore, the Orphic ideal of poetry, which, guided by instinct, comes closer to the mysteries unreachable by human rationality and the intuitive, visceral avant-gardism that refuses to accept the strict separation between life and art, have a lot to do with Ehrenberg, the self-proclaimed *neólogo* who claims that "la estética es una pasión compartida" [aesthetics is a shared passion] (*Manchuria Video*, 6:14).

Brant's film is deeply imbued with all these associations. *Crime Delicado* is willing to cross the line that divides fiction and nonfiction. It also explores the commitment to art as a shared passion and Dino Campana's nocturnal commitment—the night scenes are shot in vivid color whereas the few day scenes (all set in institutional places:

a tribunal, a newspaper's office, and a museum) are always in black-and-white. All these three figures (Dino Campana, Jusep Torres Campalans, and Felipe Ehrenberg) have attitudes that unequivocally reject Antônio Martins's stance as "an intellectual who measures his perception of life by reason" (Joaquim, 1)[25] or, in one character's blunt assertion, a man who "only functions from the head up" (33:02).[26] In a paradigmatic scene, the film director Cláudio Assis[27] finishes his small but striking participation in *Delicate Crime* by confronting Antônio Martins at a bar, shouting in a remarkable improvisation, "You sucker, now that's the question: I love; you love nothing! Who are you?" (40:15).[28]

Could these allusions be at odds with the novel's allusion to the down-to-earth *neorealista,* clear-eyed, critical attention to social mores and hypocrisy? In fact, the allusions to Dino Campana and/or José Torres Campalans and to Vitaliano Brancatti merely show that Brant's film and Sant'Anna's novel confront from different angles the same stifling and presumptuous intellectual attitude whose symbol is Antônio Martins; significantly, a character whose name does not change from the novel to the movie. In the novel, in one of the very few moments when his voice is silenced, Martins is described as

> a vivid, eloquent example of the pathological extremes that may be reached by a character remarkable for containing his feelings through an exacerbated rationality, which, suddenly, frees itself through a crime. (130)[29]

Martins sees the work of art as a calculated act of sensual and emotional seduction directed at the audience, a seduction the critic must first resist, then dismantle and possibly denounce. The violent, antagonistic undertones of this definition are underscored when Martins is cited as an example of "the critic as art's rapist" and finds the concept "most interesting" (130).[30] Martins appreciates artistic pathos, but wishes to remain immune to it by using criticism as a means to neutralize and control art's emotional power. Furthermore, his desire to contain and control all sensual and emotional drives extends beyond the critical activity to his private life. Under the guise of critical and emotional independence, Martins tries to maintain a dominating position in his relationship with art as well as with women. Art and sex are thus conceived as performances that may entice Martins's senses and intellect but should never truly interfere with his life. Both film and novel dramatize the encounter between this controlling man, an artist as his nemesis, and Inês, a figure that undermines his defenses and eventually destroys his capacity for domination. This close connection between Martins's critical stance and his personal life is one of the main themes of the novel and it remains so in the movie, and that is why Martins's critical activity is important in both. The plays Martins sees as well as the reviews he writes about them echo the drama that plays out in his life after his encounter with Inês and Brancatti (Torres Campana). Again the specific differences between novel and film are interesting to highlight the inventiveness of Brant's adaptation.

Sant'Anna's narrator discusses at length two reviews he writes while Inês becomes part of his life: one is of a fictitious play called *Folhas de Outono* [*Autumn Leaves*] (17–22) and the other for an imaginary staging of Nelson Rodrigues's classic *Vestido de Noiva* [*The Wedding Dress*] (66–67, 75–76).[31] The first review is written under the impact of Martins's first encounter with Inês and the second after a disastrous date with one of the actresses in *The Wedding Dress*, Maria Luísa—a failure he attributes to Inês's impact on him. Martins admits these encounters influenced his reviews and calls his failure to separate his emotions from his work a "fault" or "sin" (21)[32] that compromises his professional integrity. The two passages establish the peculiar connection between the fear of involvement and the desire to control that direct Martins both in his professional and his private life. In the first review Martins tries to counter the emotional reach of *Autumn Leaves* with the "antidote of cruel irony"[33] by character-izing this pathos as an unintended effect, but in the review of *The Wedding Dress* he helplessly feels "the great discomfort of watching his personal and professional lives escape his control" (76).[34]

Beto Brant worked closely with theater director and dramatist Maurício Paroni de Castro[35] to stage scenes of three plays especially for the film. These are Paroni de Castro's *Confraria Libertina*; *Woyzeck, o Brasileiro*, an adaptation of George Büchner's unfinished play, and the 1846 classic of Brazilian drama *Leonor de Mendonça*. Staged in a sadomasochism club in São Paulo, *Confraria Libertina*'s fragmen-tary sketches revolve around the struggles for sexual liberation and the emancipation of women. The scene chosen from this play for the film there is a clear parallel between the triangle among the doctor, his wife, and the dominatrix and the triangle among Martins, Torres Campana, and Inês,[36] and Martins berates the play and laments the use of Schubert's sublime Piano Trio No. 2 in E flat major, D. 929 (Op. 100) amidst so much "self-promotional hysteria" (3:45).[37] The scene from *Woyzeck, um Brasileiro*[38] shows the working-class protago-nist, tormented by jealousy and hatred, confronting his wife's infidel-ity, threatening her and finally claiming in desperation that "every

man is an abyss" (17:03).[39] This time Martins criticizes the decision
to interfere with Büchner's "unfinished and extraordinary grammar"
(18:57).[40] Finally, *Leonor de Mendonça* brings a confrontation between
the protagonist and her enraged husband, Dom Jaime, who, moved by
pride rather than love, falsely accuses Leonor de Mendonça of adultery
and threatens not just to kill but to humiliate her in public as well.[41]
The three scenes show different women facing overbearing, threatening male figures that try to assert their domination through different
degrees of violence and sexual intimidation. Dr. Kraft, Woyzeck, and
Dom Jaime fight—and ultimately fail—to preserve their control over
women in relationships where paranoid jealousy and wounded pride
are two sides of the same coin. Martins criticizes the first two plays,
complaining about their lack of ethical and/or textual integrity. In the
aftermath of the third play, Martins takes the actress Maria Luísa to
dinner and humiliates her, bluntly asserting that she had invited him
out to trade sex for a good review of her performance. However, later
in the apartment he fails to get aroused and imagines the actress naked
in bed on stage laughing together with a theater audience at the man
humiliated by his impotence.[42]

In Brant's *Delicate Crime*, the scenes from the plays present more
emphatically Martins's obsession with Inês, his clumsy attempt to
interfere with her relationship with José Torres Campana, and the
rape he denies vehemently. The scenes chosen by Brant and his collaborators in the screenplay[43] have a sharper edge not only because
they actually materialize on the screen and thus speak for themselves
but because they illustrate what the playwright Gonçalves Dias had
asserted in the introduction to his play in 1846: "if women were not
enslaved, as they in fact are, D. Jaime would not have killed his wife"
(*Leonor de Mendonça*, 5).[44] Furthermore, Martins's reactions to the
three plays exemplify both his fascination with emotional intensity
and his desire for control and clean-cut separations between categories, an ideological complex built around the idea of integrity through
purity and perfection, with all its contradictions and blind spots.
Brant's movie underlines a double emphasis on aesthetic and gender
kinds of violence and on the authoritarianism imbedded in the critical discourse, aspects already important in Sant'Anna's novel, but the
film adds clarity to the idea that the proclaimed separation between
the arts and life is not just a matter pertaining to the vitality of the
arts, but also the vitality of life itself.

Another crucial departure from Sant'Anna's novel, whose narrator
completely frames Brancatti and Inês, has to do with the opening of
the story to other perspectives. Although one could argue that such
a departure was to a certain extent inevitable, taking into the account

the essential differences between novelistic and cinematic languages, the choices made by the screenplay writers certainly make a difference and deserve attention for their organic connection to the movie as a whole. Brant's *Delicate Crime* exposes the spectator to a neutral point of view in scenes such as the trial (written by the writer/attorney Luis Francisco Carvalho Filho) and accurately described by Paroni de Castro as "objective reality settling scores with that bunch of mad people."[45] This neutral point of view is decisive in the rape scene, modifying the ambiguous nature of the original story; and it is a sign of the adaptors' shrewdness that *Delicate Crime* is enriched rather than impoverished by that choice. This change from a story completely immersed in first-person subjectivity to one that allows not only a neutral point of view, but also the subjective points of view of the artist and of the model is even more relevant to understanding the film, as Martins practically vanishes and José Torres Campana and Inês dominate the four sections that take up the last 24 minutes of Brant's film [58:00–1:22:22].

In three of these sections the construction of the fictional characters José Torres Campana and Inês Campana and the documentation of the work of the artist Felipe Ehrenberg and his partner Lilian Taulib unfold simultaneously. As Ehrenberg and Taulib play Torres Campana and Inês and at the same time play themselves, the traditional boundary between what is within and what is outside the fictional story collapses and the vitality of these two people's life and their artistic experience together is injected onto the screen.[46] In these sections, *Crime Delicado* becomes more than an art documentary because, more than registering different stages of the creative process, the film becomes a fundamental piece in a multidisciplinary conceptual work of art conceived with the essential help of Ehrenberg.

The first of these sections (58:00 to 1:09:27) is a long sequence of takes of Torres Campana (Ehrenberg) and Inês (Taulib) in a night's work at the studio. The beautiful cinematography created by Walter Carvalho[47] in this sequence is a fundamentally austere chiaroscuro with a small bedside lamp and a single light source off the screen illuminating the two naked bodies, their height and distance creating large portions of shadow on the screen. The shots from multiple points of view remain mostly close to the two bodies, therefore revealing them but never presenting the viewer full frontal nudity. The cameras also remain static but somehow pulsate, because Brant asked the cinematographer to keep the camera in his hands resting steadily on his lap instead of using tripods. This aesthetic results in an intense focus on the two actors in these scenes, reinforced by the fact that there is no music and practically no background noise and also no discernible props in the artist's studio besides a bed. Torres Campana (Ehrenberg) directs Inês (Taulib) to a certain position and then draws the two intertwined bodies: we see their heads and faces, their limbs and their torsos, and the pen moving on the paper as the sketches slowly materialize on the blank page. Although artist and model are naked and Torres Campana (Ehrenberg) draws them in various intimate positions, the atmosphere is not sexually charged in an aggressive way, but rather affectionate and, most important, completely absorbed in the work. Torres Campana (Ehrenberg) often pauses to show the sketches to Inês (Taulib) and the two actor-performers exchange a few impressions on the work, always connoting a sense of warm partnership.[48] This sketch session planned by Ehrenberg as well as the cinematic aesthetics designed by Brant and Carvalho attempt to avoid the customary relationship in which the artist uses the model as an object to be observed and then represented. The stern cinematographic aesthetic makes perfect sense in a context where Ehrenberg and Taulib are not just actors playing the roles of José Torres Campana and Inês Campana but human beings whose life experiences and bodies are traversed by destructive and creative forces and imprinted both on canvas and on film.

Next the artist appears alone and the camera documents the long, silent, and solitary process by which Torres Campana (Ehrenberg) slowly turns one of his sketches into a finished painting on the canvas. Layer upon layer of colors, textures, and details are added to the canvas and the artist pauses from time to time to ponder on what he did, looking at the painting from up close and then from a distance, either standing or lying exhausted on the floor. These scenes, which the ellipses suggest to be the summary of a many-hour process, are filmed with the same austere cinematography—all that one hears is the din of the traffic outside and the noise of the brushes or spatulas or Ehrenberg's hands stroking the canvas (1:04:06–1:09:27).[49] The result is one of the paintings that Antônio Martins has seen at the collective exhibit he attended twice, first on the opening night at the Inês's request and later on his own in the scenes that precede the studio section.

Later a third section in the studio returns to the relationship between artist and model, articulating verbally what had been wordlessly illustrated in the studio scenes as Torres Campana (Ehrenberg) simply faces the camera and speaks in the pidgin of Portuguese and Spanish (known as *portunhol*),[50] an unscripted and unrehearsed interview out of which the interviewers have been edited.[51] Speaking with fluency and a sense of purpose, Felipe Ehrenberg and José Torres Campana clearly fuse into a single entity[52] in this interview that may be divided in three parts separated by abrupt cuts. First, the artist expounds on one of Ehrenberg's obsessions and recurring themes: the chaos that followed the earthquake that struck Mexico City in 1985.[53] Right after that, Torres Campana (Ehrenberg) comments on the sketch section with Inês (Taulib), spelling out the rationale behind the productive process the audience has already seen:

> It is a moment so intimate that it neutralizes any possibility of violence. In this moment that demands softness, demands sweetness, that demands (pause) love possibly I don't know, in this moment there are *arkles*—I don't know arkles, how do you say it—lightning bolts. When the model is naked and the artist is naked, the relationship between power and vulnerability is over. Both are equally vulnerable or equally powerful. (1:17:23–1:18:12)[54]

Torres Campana (Ehrenberg) verbalizes his view of what we have seen before: a process tailored to suspend the traditional roles of subject and object in figurative painting in order to avoid the acutely uncomfortable sense of trespassing involved in the act of capturing somebody else's painful experience with physical disability. The film maintains an interesting rhetorical silence as it represents visually and verbally the same process and also shows the painting on the canvas, the concrete product of this process. It is entirely up to the viewer to decide to what extent Torres Campana's (Ehrenberg's) vision holds, true given that the film has shown us that the painting based on the sketch is the result of the painter's solitary work and that the painting seems to privilege the model's rather than the painter's body. In the third and last part of the interview, Torres Campana (Ehrenberg) draws on his view of artistic expressions of Pre-Columbian cultures to describe human existence as in a perpetual state of transformation: simultaneously charged with energies derived from destruction (death and pain) and from creation (sex and pleasure). This last part suggests the link between the account of the horrors in the aftermath of the earthquake and the artistic relationship with Inês (Taulib): the intimate relationship between destruction and creation in Torres Campana's (Ehrenberg's) life. The artist concludes by stating that the raison d'être of the artist is to share these life transformations with his audience, so that art and life, charged sometimes simultaneously with Eros and Thanatos, are natural extensions of each other.

Torres Campana's (Ehrenberg's) view of art and the artist's role is opposed to Martins's dry aestheticism expressed in the critic's reviews, which is intent on guarding the separation between life and artistic experience. In the novel Martins affirms that "to be a critic is to exercise reason before subverting emotion, or before an attempt at aesthetic involvement that we must decompose, not to say denounce, whenever possible, with elegance" (18–19),[55] echoing Ortega y Gasset, who once stated that "wanting the borders well defined is a symptom of mental cleanliness. Life is one thing; poetry is another" (*Deshumanización*, 42).[56] Ehrenberg's (Torres Campana's) Eros and Thanatos are energies Martins wishes to contain and control either in the name of fear or of power. As a result, by his own recognition in the film, Martins "always lived in the third person" (41:26),[57] and the tensions he wishes to control completely accumulate until this obsession with mental cleanliness explodes in a most unhealthy manner.

Martins's ultimate failure to control himself as he succumbs to his passion for Inês is at once his doom and his moment of passionate transcendence over his own fear and arrogance. Marco Ricca—another long-time partner of Brant's[58]—delivers a wonderful performance as he avoids all the clichés of the cerebral scholar, thus allowing his Antônio Martins to reach remarkable intensity when he confesses that before falling in love with Inês he "looked at the world with the pretense of those who think they have been inoculated" (41:50).[59] Movie and novel again differ significantly at this point: while the novel ends with Martins unchanged in his views, acquitted at the trial due to the proverbial lack of evidence, and reinstated as the powerful theater critic at a rival newspaper, the movie leaves the critic vulnerable and confused, no longer aseptically separated from the world, forced to leave his post at the newspaper, embroiled in the preliminary stages of the trial, and still utterly impacted by the force of his passion for Inês.

Novel and film again differ significantly in their treatment of the delicate but criminal act that the title refers to. In Sant'Anna's novel the rape of Inês remains an accusation denied by the narrator whose primary motivation is to prove that he has been set up. This first-person narrator retells his final encounter with Inês in imprecise and ambiguous terms and insists he could not possibly have raped a woman he loves so passionately. Furthermore, when Martins admits he finds the idea of the critic as a rapist of art interesting, he either half confesses or extends the meaning of the title to his critical stance or to Brancati's artistic work. In Brant's movie, however, the rape is not a mere supposition: it takes place on the screen, filmed with a Yasujiro-Ozu-esque low-angle camera in theatrical, full-bodied, steady shots from a distance and the same chiaroscuro aesthetic of the scenes with Torres Campana (Ehrenberg) and Inês (Taulib), only darker and more somber. Furthermore, after the sections that document the production of the painting, *Crime Delicado* abruptly leaves the artist's studio to show a somber Martins listening to Inês' testimony before the judge. Inês faces the camera and the viewer takes the point of view of the judge as the plaintiff dismisses the declarations of unconditional love from the critic as eccentricities from a man she barely knew and declares she is profoundly offended by Martins's dismissal of her work with Torres Campana as pornography, because that violates "what is most sacred in my life, my relationship with José Torres Camapana."[60] As much as we hear Martins's version of the events in court as well, the rape scene and Inês's testimony in the movie are unequivocal.

Brant's film removes Sant'Anna's story from the complete immersion in Martins's point of view[61] and relinquishes the ambiguity of the novel, but those changes do not imply a simplification because Brant opens the original story to multiple of points of view and makes *Delicate Crime*, in Brant's own words, "the most open to different interpretations"[62] of all his movies. This is corroborated in Brant's subtle change in the title: *Crime Delicado* drops the indefinite article of Sant'Anna's novel (*A Delicate Crime*) and adds no definite article, tending to a more general phrase perhaps best translated as "Delicate Crimes." Perhaps both offenses—to the artistic and the physical integrity of the woman Martins claims to love—complement each other and perhaps they are compounded by the violence inherent in Ehrenberg's (Torres Campana's) art process and in Brant's film as well.

To reach such precise balance between asserting a specific approach to art and life and leaving as much room as possible for the viewer to interpret the film in his or her own way, the peculiar plotting of *Delicate Crime* plays a central role. In his review of Brant's film Ruy Gardnier claims that,

> *Crime Delicado*'s most impressive characteristics are its concision and its laconism. Each scene serves less to affirm something than to raise questions. Brant's film raises questions from the narrative point of view (...), but, first and foremost, moral questioning: how much further can you go within a limit and what is the line of transgression?[63]

The "laconism" to which Gardnier refers is a rhetorical silence that characterizes Brant's film: the absence of devices that more or less subtly indicate to the spectator a moral center from which he or she is supposed to judge what appears on screen. These devices are described by Gonzalo Aguilar as traditional forms of political engagement in Latin American cinema:

> All of this is generally referred to as "preaching to the spectator" (*bajar la línea*, or, literally, "to lower the line"). The phrase is apt, as it refers

not only to the pedagogical action (at times implying an underestima-
tion of the spectator) but also to the fact that the line (*línea*) of the
film extends toward a space that, while working itself out in the script,
is actually outside of it. The ethical character does not speak from
within the story but has the privilege of being able to judge it from
without. (*Other Worlds*, 19)

The absence of judgment "from without" does not mean the absence of
political implications. In its rhetorical silence *Delicate Crime* is a radical
film that gives a valuable lesson to those who reflect on the dilemma
of the artist who recognizes the limitations of conventional political
engagement but also refuses to become the producer of culturally
irrelevant, entertaining aesthetic pleasures. The film indeed refrains
from giving the spectator easy answers and ready interpretations to
the story, but it is anything but laconic. *Delicate Crime* is based on a
system of repetitions with variations or verbal and visual reiterations
of previous scenes that mark the peculiar rhythm of Brant's film from
beginning to end. Each apparently fragmentary scene finds a place in
the movie as a whole as it repeats and/or reiterates motifs and themes
from previous scenes. A few examples suffice for the sake of illustration. The scenes from the plays are followed by Antônio Martins's
reviews of these same plays. A dream scene with Inês dancing on a
stage evokes the previous nightmare scene with Maria Luísa in bed,
mocking the impotent critic. The rape scene is later told and interpreted by Inês and Martins in their court depositions. Martins talks to
Inês in a restaurant and they go to her apartment; later Martins talks
to Maria Luísa also in a restaurant and then they go to his apartment.
The bar and restaurant scenes with Inês and Maria Luísa are reiterated
when Martins munches on a sandwich alone at a humble diner downtown and observes three disjointed conversations between strangers.
Antônio Martins looks at Torres Campana's painting in the crowded
opening night at an exhibit and again at the same exhibit at an abandoned building, this time all by himself. The painting we see in both
scenes is slowly brought to existence on the sketchbook and then on
the canvas in the artist's studio, and Inês looks at the same painting,
first by herself in the studio, then another day in a public space at the
end of the movie. These multiple reiterations indicate an affinity with
Ehrenberg's art, a mixture of obsessive themes and motifs stated in
multiple forms that cross over genres and forms of expression.

But no adaptation strategies, network of allusions, cinematography, or plotting suffice to describe the uniqueness of *Delicate
Crime*. Brant's movie develops its character through its openness to
unplanned interferences, to the unrehearsed, the unpredictable, the

unrepeatable, and the exposure to chance that are important aspects of performance art. These aspects, which the director calls "a series of illuminating strokes of chance,"[64] endow Brant's film with a vitality that is practically absent from mainstream contemporary cinema. Here the importance of Ehrenberg's presence beyond his role as promoter of Mexican art is reaffirmed. Commenting on the film, Ehrenberg sees *Delicate Crime* as a form of performance art as he explains:

> Beto agreed (on) [to] my idea of assuming a persona, a performative role ( ... ) so in the movie you see Felipe Ehrenberg playing José Torres Campana and working as Felipe. ( ... ) When the painting finally gets done no one knows if I played the role or if I played myself. This performance was shown in commercial cinemas ( ... ) No way I've stopped or exchanged anything for anything! On the contrary, it's all about developing other ways of operating as a performance artist ... beyond the usual forums ... " (*Manchuria*, 209)

The process of making, the documenting of this process, and their function as parts of this mosaiclike movie are the work of art in question as much as the painting on the canvas. Ehrenberg's participation in *Delicate Crime* is a coherent move in the career of a perceptive artist who, in 1976, announced his decision to quit traditional painting on canvas in the following terms: "Painting was an artifice that I had to use when I could only see. Now I see, feel, and have premonitions ... I quit painting when I saw that it only made us marvel, without changing anything" (*Manchuria*, 15).

Ehrenberg's decision to quit painting had to do with his view that art was not just about expression or formal experimentation but also about the mutual interference of experiences in art and in life. This attitude is a crucial tool with which Brant bravely faces the challenge of avoiding the exploitation of real-life pain and pleasure, the dreadful turn from the documentary to the pornography of which Martins accuses Torres Campana. It is undeniable that Lilian Taulib bravely exposes herself by adding to the film the intensity of her life experiences—the visceral pain caused by the visible, physical absence. This intensity is most palpable at the end of the sketch and painting scenes, when Inês (Taulib) comes back to the studio, lies down on the bed, and looks at the finished canvas in silence and in tears. But this movie, as Brant himself suggests in an interview, "is more interested in affection than in violence."[65] In the preservation of Taulib's individual and artistic dignity lies the key to the artistic integrity of Brant's *Delicate Crime* as much as the artistic integrity of Ehrenberg's (José Torres Campana's) work.

This integrity has to be different from that defended by Martins and cannot be based on aseptic purity or perfection. The poignant closing scene, which follows the interview with Torres Campana (Ehrenberg), is paradigmatic of this integrity. The scene features Inês (Taulib) alone again before Ehrenberg's painting, now in a public space, a Biennalesque exhibition in the Ibirapuera pavilion.[66] She looks at the painting, gets closer, takes her prosthesis off and places it on the floor, below the painting (Taulib lost her right leg to a cancer when she was 16 years old). As she leaves, a low-angle, distant shot fills the screen with the prosthetic leg on the floor and the painting on the wall. The image lingers for an instant and then Schubert's Trio, which opened the movie and was cited as an example of the artistic sublime by Martins, starts again, together with the closing credits.

This closing scene exemplifies the decision to leave the story's meaning open to the spectator without being merely laconic, the determination to embrace the vitality of a passionate connection between art and life that remains open to the unexpected and to the other, and, most important, the commitment to produce and experience art under a notion of aesthetic and ethical integrity that does not exclude imperfection and impurity and does not ignore pain and suffering. An attempt to assign a definite, unequivocal meaning to this last scene would be an act of interpretive (delicate) violence, but its openness also clearly invites the spectator (and the critic) to do it. This last scene was added to the story at Taulib's suggestion, and she describes what she does as a symbolic gesture to mark her decision to stop using a cosmetic prosthesis, whose function is only to hide or correct what is perceived by society as an imperfection. More than a way to come to terms with the perceived incompleteness of her own body, this is the culmination of a painful process triggered and documented by the movie and by her work with Ehrenberg. Paroni de Castro prepared Taulib, who had no previous acting experience, for the role and described this process as an attempt to articulate artistically "the suffering caused by absence."[67] Art, as Ehrenberg had expounded in the interview section, is a form of sharing with others the artist's pleasure and pain, the destructive and creative forces that traverse his or her life. But pleasure and pain have to be somehow articulated in order to communicate happiness and suffering. As Paroni de Castro explains, "you can't be happy without a syntax to tell the story of your own happiness and you pay a visit to hell when you can't tell the story of your own suffering."[68]

# Chapter 11

# Undercurrents, Still Flowing

In 1991 the Mexican artist Gabriel Orozco (1962) bought his first camera—an instrument that was to become a key element of his work—and spend some time in Brazil while his wife worked on a research grant. In several interviews Orozco highlighted the importance of this stay in Brazil in his artistic development:

> I was very impressed when I discovered the Brazilian landscape as well as Brazilian sculptural and musical traditions from the 1950s on. Those months were influential in my life and on my work; for the first time my travel and my work became complementary techniques and disciplines. (*October Files*, 85–86)

During that stay in Brazil Orozco produced one of his first major works, *Turista Maluco* [*Crazy Tourist*]. This piece consists, as it was to become a habit in Orozco's work, of a photograph that registered the artist's lonely intervention in the after-hours of a street market in Cachoeira, a small colonial town on the margins of the Paraguaçu river in the state of Bahia. Its name (originally in Portuguese) came from "two or three drunk guys" who amused themselves by shouting out loud "turista maluco!" while Orozco arranged a few unsalable oranges over the stalls of the deserted market and started snapping photos (*To Make an Inner Time*, 189).

The oranges in *Turista Maluco* are small, precise, vivid yellow dots suggesting a careful if subdued composition in stark contrast with the abandoned, worn-out stalls, which are arranged in more or less crooked lines and display signs of various, improvised repairs. Each of the stalls is adorned with a pair of sustaining structures for plastic roofs no longer in place at the time of the picture. Together these structures resemble an eerie procession of crosses. Deep blues of painted walls and boxes and dark greens of the vegetation loom in the background in carefully balanced composition with the lighter and darker shades of the wood with rotten stains, cracked crevices, and pieces of twine.

Writing about *Turista Maluco* Miwon Kwon affirms, "what becomes highlighted in a gesture that seems at first to be random and nonsensical, turns out to be a precise articulation of what has been, that which is no longer, a residue of what is missing, and evidence of what we miss" ("The Fullness of Empty Containers," 56). In *Turista Maluco* Orozco combines with great simplicity two different dimensions that were to reappear in different configurations in his work since: the human one (a ghostly presence in the empty market) and the natural one (the fruits on the verge of becoming rotten, discarded matter). In both dimensions mortal transience is a faint presence in what is less a spectacle than a realized, unexpected event. *Turista Maluco* is the visual register of a simple, quiet gesture that points to a world teeming with meaningful physicality, a world in which art dissolves into life.

Orozco mentioned in the quote above that his stay in Brazil was also important as it allowed him to get to know the work of Brazilian artists with whom he found common ground. In another interview the artist elaborates on what these artists would be and why they interested him:

> I got very interested in Brazilian art of the 1950s, like Oiticica and Lygia Clark. Before that I didn't know them. And I also got to know the work of contemporary Brazilian artists like Tunga and Cildo Meireles. I found I was in tune with other artists even though I was doing rather different things. I was not so close to Mexican artists then, even earlier conceptual artists. I was interested in sculpture, and in Mexico we don't have a very strong tradition in sculpture since colonial times. ("Crazy About Saturn: Interview," 159)

It was in the *Neoconcretistas* such as Oiticica and Clark and in the artists that followed them from the 1970s on that Gabriel Orozco, the son of Mario Orozco Rivera (art teacher and close collaborator of the muralist David Alfaro Siqueiros), raised literally within the *muralista* tradition that still held sway over mainstream art in Mexico way after its heyday, found another Latin American tradition with which he felt comfortable. In a context of radical contestation of the truisms of the regime installed after the Mexican Revolution and of the PRI's subsequent swerve into neoliberalism, it is understandable that Orozco did not feel comfortable in that artistic tradition—even though one might find traces of a Mexican countertradition that has only recently found institutionalized spaces to increase its visibility.

Traveling abroad offered Orozco the chance to find other traditions and, in the case of Brazil, the chance to retain his sense of belonging to his own culture by coming across another Latin America that spoke more keenly to his own interests and affinities. The Brazilian tradition of *Neoconcretismo*, with its initial questioning of the strictures of concrete geometric abstractionism and subsequent delving into performance, conceptualism, and new forms of political engagement, was epitomized by the work and critical reflection of Lygia Clark and Hélio Oiticica. Their work also preserved a strong attachment to the idea of a strong Third-World identity that remained nevertheless open to freely absorb foreign influences when these served their purposes. This is visible, for example, when Orozco discusses the relationship between the artist and the art market:

> The market is an arena where the individual evolves according to his or her ideology, interests, and values. The market is not to blame. Many in Mexico still speak of the art market as if it were the devil: this is like blaming the sea for drowning. The market is actually another space for art, just as the museum, the street, or the living room; another space where art circulates publicly. The market has an impact on the public life and that's how we should understand it, as the other institutions in general. The auctions and the speculation attract the most attention; it is the market's show, but the market is more than that. Above all there is an aspect of the market that has not been analyzed by art theoreticians, which is the way we produce works of art. And that is crucial in my work. How much money you spend, what material you use, how you work: a specific attitude is built from these aspects. Part of my explorations as an artist have to do with this, with the awareness of the economic system of production of the artistic object, something that will influence not only the aesthetic result (if it is made of gold or cardboard, if it is big or small, if it is fragile or sturdy, if it is waterproof or not, etcetera), but also that will impose rules of distribution and consumption in the cultural and financial market of the work of art. The political, economic, and ideological attitude of an artist begins to define itself in the moment he or she decides how to execute a work of art. And that has consequences also in the piece's destination, where it will end up: in a museum, in a house, in a public institution, or in trash can. ("Interview with María Minera")[1]

It is only within the context of this discussion that makes use of a Marxist vocabulary with a misleading accommodating tone that may be construed as an accommodation to the impositions of the market, one understands the full implications of Orozco's gesture in *Turista Maluco*. By turning the street into a workshop, every ordinary material at hand is imbued with an impure human dimension and every simple gesture realizes an accident and perhaps invites an equivalent from the viewer on his or her way back home. Sculpture for Orozco becomes a way of experiencing reality, involving experience, gesture, and image.

Gabriel Orozco also represents a new possibility (and a new challenge) for the career of Latin American artists. Having lived many years away from his home country and consolidated his name first in the monetary centers of the world art system, Orozco nevertheless managed to keep contact with the Mexican scene and refused to become fully attached to some other national artistic scene. In fact Orozco maintained an acute awareness of his status as a Latin American, that is, peripheral artist:

> The idea of a specific place, of a specific intervention, of a contact with a culture and its signifiers that I was interested in exploring and developing, obviously went hand in hand in a very natural way with my own identity, my way of being a Mexican travelling around the world. (*Gabriel Orozco*, 2005, 134)

Away from Mexico for much of the 1990s, Orozco did not sever ties with a certain circle of Mexican artists. Furthermore, a great retrospective of his work in the prestigious Museo Rufino Tamayo in 2000 marked his triumphant comeback by drawing large crowds and proportionally furious criticism from the Mexican critical circles.[2]

The most articulate criticism came from the curator-critic Cuauhtémoc Medina, who wrote about Orozco at the time of his retrospective in his biweekly column:[3]

> Orozco represented the last hope of critics and curators of the artistic centers. He became a Third World artist whose reluctance, level of abstraction, and proximity to the postminimalist and Conceptual traditions were most easily assimilated to the metropolitan culture. They idolized the Latin American whose proximity to Cage's methodology and Borges's spirit could dissipate the baroque and outrageus Latin American "bad taste." Just as this operation benefited Orozco it also harmed his objects and photographs with an inclination for a quite prudent, institutional good taste that suggests a melancholic state of grace and seduces the eye with fleeting moments of passivity.[4]

There is no doubt that the subdued elegance of much of Orozco's work may be one of the reasons for his acceptance in the metropolitan centers, but that does not mean Orozco's work is necessarily less Mexican or Latin American. In addition, what Medina identifies as Cage's methodology is what Orozco found in the work Hélio Oiticica and Lygia Clark. Oiticica, Clark, and Orozco, of course, are legitimate expressions of a diverse Latin American art and culture that cannot be completely contained in the baroque or neobaroque, nor in expressions that challenge notions of "good taste." Certainly the extraordinary penetration of Borges in the canonical centers has to do with how easily Borges could fit into the interests and preoccupations of these centers. However, the fact that some form of institutional or subdued good taste seems to be in tune with some of Borges's or Orozco's aesthetic choices is neither to the advantage nor to the detriment of their own work per se.

Orozco's influence in Mexican contemporary art extends beyond the impact of the exhibit of his own work. For a period of more than five years starting in 1987 Orozco met with a group of slightly younger artists (Damián Ortega, Gabriel Kuri, Abraham Cruzvillegas, and Jerónimo López Ramírez, a.k.a. Dr. Lakra), who formed what was to be called "Taller de los Viernes" [Friday Workshop] in Orozco's house every Friday. Elements of this group have since had an influential role in Mexican culture through the gallery Kurimanzutto, which they opened in 1999, and through the independent publisher, Alias. Kurimanzutto featured the work of these artists and organized, for instance, "A Propósito," said to be the first exhibit featuring installations in Mexico. The same gallery also started the nonprofit editorial project Alias that showcased important artists in books such as *Conversando con Marcel Duchamp* (2007), *Hélio Oiticica* (2009), and *Cildo Meirelles* (2009). More than simply translating or republishing unavailable titles that it deems important for Mexican contemporary artists to know, Alias produces a range of books published in other countries by reconditioning these larger and more expensive books to fit into a more affordable format.

Responsible for Alias is Damián Ortega (1967), who also had a distinguished career as a graphic illustrator and cartoonist for the newspaper *La Jornada*. Ortega has a more established relationship with Brazil than Orozco, having shown his work there a few times, most notably between 2003 and 2006, with a solo show at the important gallery Fortes Villaça and a notable participation at the entrance of the Twenty-seventh Bienal de São Paulo. Ortega has also made several other pieces in Brazil, including *Matéria em Repouso* (2003), *Futebol Neoconcreto* (merging Lygia Clark's paintings and soccer game panels), and *Ordem, Réplica, Acaso* (2004) a site-specific installation, which Ortega recently showed in the United States as *Projeto Belo Horizonte*.

Before editing for Alias books about Hélio Oiticica (1937–1980) and Cildo Meireles (1948), Ortega cited Oiticica in an interesting graphic piece, a hybrid essay somehow inspired by the cartoons of Ad Reinhardt in defense of abstract art. This 12-page piece was created by Ortega for the catalogue of Orozco's exhibition in 2000 and was called "The Bird: for Beginners" (*Gabriel Orozco 2000*, 105–119)—Orozco's nickname among friends being "el pájaro." A section of "The Bird: For Beginners" discusses Oiticica's ideas (117–118) and that discussion serves to understand the reading contemporary Mexican artists such as Orozco and Ortega have made of Oiticica.

Ortega describes Oiticica's work as "a work that has to be read in its specific cultural site and that through its individuality attains the status of inventor of a new identity in a reality that constantly energizes and transforms itself" (118),[5] the result of a series of a reflections on the relationship between experimental art and underdevelopment, between poverty and exoticism, and between foreign and local experience and ideas. When artists such as Orozco and Ortega reflect on the ideas and the works of Oiticica, they establish—as did Oiticica himself, who lived years of self-imposed exile in New York during the military dictatorship—another kind of international dialogue. This new dialogue does not lose sight of the relationship between center and periphery but refrains from falling into a relationship marked by the mixture of proud refusal and subservient copy that constitutes the Latin American inferiority complex, and it also actively searches for contacts within Latin America toward a relationship based more on identity than on estrangement.

Orozco and Ortega did not get to know Oiticica, Clark, Meireles, and Tunga through New York or London, but more directly, through the contacts Orozco made during his first trip to Brazil. This kind of direct, unmediated interchange is becoming increasingly common, and online social media have intensified and facilitated such encounters. The deep undercurrents of Latin America are thickening and slowly becoming more visible at the surface, although they are still far from being noticed in the increasingly fragmented cultural mainstream of the two countries, Mexico and Brazil. Some of the most interesting contemporary writers, intellectuals, and artists in Brazil and Mexico have taken advantage of this less visible by-product of globalization. On the margins of the encroachment of the cultural hegemony of US mass culture, the fruits of these direct interactions are many.

In the prologue to *La Edad de Oro* (2012), an anthology of contemporary Mexican poetry, Luis Felipe Fabre mentions a "compulsive and generalized interest" (Fabre, 8) in what was going on elsewhere in the continent among the new Mexican poets as part of their questioning with regard to the mainstream of twentieth-century Mexican poetry. Whereas that tradition had conceived the poem "as a suspended, illuminated moment, outside history and the calendar, already inscribed in eternity" (Fabre, 14), these new poets were willing to do the opposite and search for:

> ...the incorporation of the context of the poem into the poem itself, which assumes not understanding poetry anymore as something outside—something above—the world, in order to (once again) see poetry as a language in relation with the moment and the place where it is produced. (Fabre, 13)

This renovated interest of Mexican poets in poetry beyond the national frontiers also crosses the linguistic divide and reaches out to Brazil. In January 2008, for instance, the Brazilian poets Sérgio Cohn (1974)[6] and Angélica Freitas (1973)[7] went to Mexico to participate in Tránsitos y Geografías—Encuentro de Poesía Brasil-México, a series of events organized by the small press El Billar de Lucrecia, the Centro de Estudios Brasileños, and the Brazilian embassy. The event served to promote the publication of a bilingual anthology, *Caos Portátil: Poesía Contemporánea del Brasil* (2007). Cohn, Freitas, and other other Brazilian poets that were featured in *Caos Portátil* appeared again in another anthology, *Sin Red ni Salvavidas—Poesía Contemporánea de la América Latina* (2009).[8]

This trip to Mexico was particularly fruitful for Angélica Freitas. It provided the starting point for her to subsequent publications: the graphic novel *Guadalupe* (2012), in which she collaborated with the Brazillian illustrator Odyr Bernardi. *Guadalupe*, whose story is set in contemporary Mexico City and Oaxaca, and Freitas's celebrated book of poems, *Um útero é do tamanho de um punho* [*A Uterus Is the Size of a Fist*], which was chosen by the critics at the *Folha de São Paulo* as one of the best books of 2012 (*Folha de São Paulo*, December 31, 2012).

Freitas was invited to a funeral with live music accompaniment, which is the trigger for a road trip in *Guadalupe*, whose protagonist's grandmother's last wish was to be buried with music in Oaxaca.

Freitas never attended that funeral because she accompanied another friend on a visit to an abortion clinic in Mexico City. The hostility outside the clinic, where protesters confronted patients and clinic workers left an impression on Freitas, who started at the time writing *Um útero é do tamanho de um punho* [*A Uterus Is the Size of a Fist*].

*Guadalupe* is the creative processing of a not-altogether-unfamiliar world that often involves these encounters between Brazilians and Mexicans. The illustrator Odyr Bernardi described in the following words his creative effort to invent Mexico for the story:

> I could create a personal Mexico, half researched and half invented and traversed by stuff I have seen along the years. And I was lucky to have Mexican friends who patiently helped from a distance, answering my questions, sending me photos, films, internet links. (*Diário de Guadalupe*, III)[9]

The facilitated flow of information in the age of the Internet is evident, but Bernardi "experienced" Mexico long-distance, also mediated through the advice of Mexican friends—the filmmakers Ivan Ávila Dueñas, Ivonne Fuentes Mendoza, and Elena Pardo. More important, citing the advice of the master of graphic novels Alex Toth, Odyr emphasizes the need for distancing to allow the research to be fully absorbed by the artist:

> Researching for visual references is good to learn details, the kind of thing you don't know or don't remember, but the ideal situation is that later you draw the page far from them, so that your frame becomes an organic whole. The image stored in your mind will suffer transformations in contact with other visual imagery and ideally you will come up with a version of your own of it. (*Diário de Guadalupe*, III)[10]

Featuring a *muxe* who owns a bookstore and turns herself into an improbable *Muxe Maravilha* [*Wonder Muxe*] invoking the powers of the discotheque cult-band Village People, *Guadalupe* is a good-humored mixture of the conventions of the comic-book genre with contemporary life in Mexico (and Brazil) and made-up myths such as the gods XYZótlan and Popolancomelatle.[11]

The contrast of *Guadalupe* with the stiffness, for instance, of Affonso Celso's unimaginative summaries of facts about Mexico handed to him second-hand and then placed in the mouth of his heroine Lupe Hedges a century earlier is stark. So much has changed

and not only in the mores and in the availability of unmediated information: one hundred years of what we could call, at the risk of oversimplification, decolonization has had a remarkable impact on Latin
American artists and intellectuals in the twenty-first century.

Another remarkable recent book is Brenda Ríos's *Del Amor y Otras
Cosas que se Gastan por el Uso. Ironía y Silencio en la Narrativa de
Clarice Lispector*, a sensitive exploration into Lispector's fictional
world articulated by an original and rigorous blend of literary theory
and personal essay. Ríos, herself a gifted writer, describes in the following terms her encounter with Clarice Lispector:

> Fear. A subtle and strange fear. A mixture of fascination, surprise, and
> disbelief overwhelmed me when I first met Clarice Lispector's writing.
> ( ... ) Besides, why such fear of a writer who writes in a language that
> does not belong to me? (9)[12]

Part of the answer may lie in the fact that that "language that does
not belong to." A Spanish speaker is so close to it as to provoke a sense
of an uncanny feeling of seeing a familiar face in a complete stranger.
Ríos calls this subtle fear she felt "the face of literary spell" (10)[13]
and understands it as a symptom when one reads Clarice Lispector to
remember the importance of feeling in a world split between noble
ideals and brutal practices.

The most impressive product of the deep undercurrents that keep
binding Mexico and Brazil in the twenty-first century comes from the
Mexican-Brazilian poet Paula Abramo (1980). Born in Mexico, she
is the daughter of the Brazilian Marcelo Abramo Lauff, an anthropologist who went to Mexico when escaping persecution from the
military regime that took over Brazil in 1964 and stayed after the
end of the dictatorship in 1984. The Abramo family is famous for
many talented figures who left a mark on Brazilian culture: the artist
(later naturalized Paraguayan) Lívio Abramo (1903–1992), the critic
and theater director Athos Abramo (1905–1968), the actress Lélia
Abramo (1911–2004), the activist Fúlvio Abramo (1909–1993), and
the journalist Cláudio Abramo (1923–1987). They are brothers, children of two Italian immigrants, Vincenzo Abramo (1869–1949) and
Afra Yole Scarmagnan (1882–1966), raised between their father's
sophisticated library and humanistic culture and their mother's anarchist roots; Yole's father was Bortolo Scarmagnan (1848–1932), an
expert Italian baker specialized in the production of panettones and
amaretti and also a veteran of the Soviet Red Army.[14]

Paula is the granddaughter of Fúlvio, a pioneer Trotskyite militant who led the Frente Única Antifascista (FUA) in an epic battle in the Praça da Sé against 6,000 *integralistas*, militants of the Brazilian Fascist movement. Fúlvio was arrested in 1935 because of a botched revolution attempt by the Communist Party with which he had no relation to and, when he left prison 18 months later to await for his trial, Fúlvio decided leave for Bolivia, where he spend the next ten years teaching at the School of Agriculture and Veterinary of Santa Cruz de la Sierra.

All these stories of the Abramos, including her father's flight to Mexico, compose the bulk of the poetry collection *Fiat Lux*, which Paula published in Mexico in 2012. There are multiple prose sources for the family's story: Lélia Abramo's memoirs, *Vida e Arte* (1997) and the testimony given by Fulvio Abramo to *Teoria e Debate*, the magazine of the Partido dos Trabalhadores (Workers' Party, known as PT) and collected in *Rememória—Entrevistas sobre o Brasil do Século XX* in 1997 (11–27).[15] *Fiat Lux* turns their story into a remarkable literary achievement. Paula Abramo's book was considered one of the best in Mexico in 2012 by the art magazine *La Tempestad*: "*Fiat Lux* confirms the good news: Mexican poetry is open to new courses after years of stagnation"[16] and the book subsequently won the first Premio Joaquín Xirau Icaza in 2013. In the ceremony at which Abramo received the prize, Elsa Cross described *Fiat Lux* as

> one of the best collections by young authors in recent years, whose consistency comes from the extremely polished poetry in which the author approaches the most concrete things but refrains from becoming prosaic, connecting classical references and the most contemporary poetics, showing erudition and effortlessly displaying an enormous range of expressive resources. (*Milenio*, March 21, 2013)[17]

*Fiat Lux* is not a series of poems linked by vague references, but a tightly woven collection in which the order plays an important role and gives the book a narrative quality. It is an exploration into the past of the Abramos, a family of Italian origins that, like the Bernardellis in the nineteenth century, left their mark on Brazilian and Mexican cultures. The Bernardellis and the Abramos came from Italy to the Americas in the nineteenth century and traveled for decades, often in precarious situations, throughout the continent, moved as much by desire as by necessity caused by civil wars and political repression.

*Fiat Lux* is intensely personal but stops short of the author's own life at the moment of her father's exile in Mexico. In this manner *Fiat*

*Lux* follows the calculated wayward manner of Lawrence Sterne's *Life and Opinions of Tristram Shandy*: the poetic voice revolves around the life of her ancestors instead of her own, following her grandfather's advice repeated several times in this book: "No mires hacia dentro" [Do not look inward]. In this manner *Fiat Lux* is a deeply personal book that nevertheless circumvents the tendency of lyricism to excessive self-centeredness in the twentieth century and confessional exhibitionism in the twenty-first. Paula Abramo's book's emotional strength comes from the figures that rise up and come back to life on its pages: the anarchist Bôrtolo Scarmagnan, the veteran of the Red Army Rudolf Josip Lauff, the match factory worker Anna Stefania Lauff and her husband the anti-Fascist militant Fúlvio. These figures are not heroic in the grandiloquent manner of an epic. Born out of Abramo's verses, they are extraordinary figures in their vitality and will to live and dream of a better life. Their sheer existence is more important than their triumphs and defeats in their struggles. They existed in real life and exist in *Fiat Lux,* and that is what counts.

The strength and vitality of these characters and their stories are the result of a poetic text of high quality in its attention to meaningful detail and in an original voice that explores lyricism but avoids the "elevated" tone and diction often associated with it. The poetic voice is unafraid of being objective and of looking toward the surface of things and also of reasoning by images in the best tradition of João Cabral de Melo Neto, a poet Paula Abramo has translated into Spanish. It is also unafraid of "difficult" words that come up without a trace of pretentious erudition. This is a host of felicitous choices that allow Paula Abramo to get the best out of her own temperament as a poet, something remarkable in a first book.

*Fiat Lux* also retains an unusual sense of urgency. Its revival of the dead is not the result of nostalgia or melancholia. It is about bringing back to our lives extraordinary characters built out of the material of Abramo's living memory with a purpose of emphasizing the will to live and fight of Bôrtolo, Rudof, Fulvio, Anna Stefânia, Marcelo, and Angelina, the notable character who opens and closes *Fiat Lux.*

Angelina is the only character with no family name, an indication that she may be closer to the fictional than the other characters. She is also given a less-defined context in place and time, but that does not deprive her of the vital presence that abounds in *Fiat Lux.* Angelina brings about the book's first *fiat lux*, the lighting of the match that becomes a remarkably consistent motif throughout the book. Angelina does it after a command in the imperative, this "poor mode" whose *"essential lack"* is its relative impersonality—she is a housemaid whose boss tells her to light the stove to fry some shrimp in a kitchen "almost a corridor" (11).[18] Similar to the poet in *Fiat Lux* Angelina carries the burden of history within her, in this case the past of a humble *nordestina* [migrant from the poor Brazilian Northeast region], of forced migration, of hunger and drought: "her grandmother's hunger" (11). Angelina appears in this book of lively ghosts to assert the continuation into the present time of hunger, "this marionette of bad taste" (75), and of "an enormous and badly distributed wealth / of crustaceans in the world, and of books and of time / to read them" (75).[19] Furthermore, Angelina reaffirms the possibility of disobedience "in the minute frontier that mediates / between the order and the act of following it" (76),[20] taking possession of the *fiat lux* that was at first an imposition, and eating "three out of every four" fried shrimps. Angelina is "brief and fictitious" (75), an indelible presence with which Paula Abramo opens and closes her book, reaffirming the greatest passion of Fúlvio and many others in the Abramo family: the right to choose "between compliance and noncompliance" (76)[21] and to take possession of the fruit of one's own labor.

The title of the book and the series of reflections about it empha-size the rich texture of Paula's verses, steeped in the classics, her major at the UNAM. The *Fiat Lux* of the title embodies this interesting combination of urgent vitality, history, personal memory, and erudi-tion. *Fiat Lux* is, simultaneously, the biblical command that set the history of the world in motion in the Latin version of Genesis and the sentence printed on the label of every box of matches in Brazil, the matches that appear and reappear in each of the poems in this book, passing through the hands of these two unforgettable women, Anna Stefania Lauff, who works in the match factory and Angelina, who lights the stove with them in the kitchen where she works.

Paula teaches Brazilian literature at UNAM and has translated an already impressive series of literary works by Brazilian authors such as Ferreira Gullar, João Cabral de Melo Neto, and Raul Pompéia. Angélica Freitas, Brenda Ríos, and Paulo Abramo belong to a new generation of writers less willing to follow the mapped routes that bind each Latin American country first and foremost to the United States, the former colonizers, and Western Europe. For the first time since Alfonso Reyes's *Poemas de Río de Enero*, one of the best poetry collections of Brazilian literature in a year is written in Spanish. With books like hers (and Brenda Ríos's and Freitas's) the deep undercur-rents of Latin America are little bit closer to the visible surface, a little bit harder to ignore.

# Conclusion

Marred by postcolonial inferiority complexes, political hypocrisies, and opportunistic commercial purposes, and permeated by an obsession with Western Europe and the United States as an idealized construct, the idea of Latin America that emerges via several examples in this book remains interesting because of its potential as a form of subtle antagonism. Latin Americanism becomes a latent shadow-identity that avoids the absolute predominance of the nation-state by disturbing the exceptionalism at the foundation of all national (and also ethnic and regional) identities and evades the dualism obsessed with the separation from and the comparison and contrast with an idealized West. It also becomes a countertradition that quietly refuses the idea of Latin America as a future task by focusing on performing empathy rather than promoting future solidarity. Fugitive and vague when approached as a homogeneous, stable identity, this idea of Latin America hovers tenuously against the background of stronger ethnic, national, and linguistic allegiances and dubious conventions of geopolitics, disrupting the cultural and linguistic divides that set Brazil apart from Spanish-speaking Latin America and both apart from the United States. It unsettles both the cosmopolitanism that sees nothing but continuities between Europe and the Americas and the national particularity based on essentialisms.

At the heart of the idea of Latin America as antagonism, there is an uncanny awareness caused by estrangement as much as by recognition. The realization of Latin American identity originates in the realization that what one previously thought was unique to one's culture might actually have come from somewhere else or at least has also been long adopted as their own legitimate cultural heritage by people he or she considers foreigners. In these moments, the exceptionalism at the foundation of sharply defined national identities, naturalized by consistent and pervasive institutional promotion in every level of culture in every modern nation, reveals itself as a cultural construct forced to share space with this other, less palpable presence.

I do not wish to dispute or even relativize colonial and postcolonial commonalities, much less to discard the history of the myriad uses of the idea of Latin America as obsolete. But there are more than just the parallel routes in the chains of cause and (effect) established by colonial and imperial conditions. Latin America is shaped as well by what I call deep cultural undercurrents, which have always silently floated across national and linguistic borders, which cannot be magically abolished, only silently bypassed. I came across the phrase *"profundas corrientes invisibles"* in an unpretentious note by Emir Rodríguez Monegal published in 1968. At the height of the Latin American *Boom*, Monegal uses the expression as a tentative explanation for inexplicable but remarkable similarities he sees between João Guimarães Rosa's *Grande Sertão: Veredas* (1956) and Mario Vargas Llosa's *Casa Verde* (1966):

> That Vargas Llosa has written his splendid book without prior knowledge of Guimarães Rosa's masterpiece (Brazil is more disconnected from the rest of Latin America than from Europe or the United States) shows that there are deep, invisible undercurrents that link the epic style of courtly romance and of the narratives of today's Latin American writers. The medieval world of the Peruvian jungle and of the deserts of Minas Gerais somehow match the medieval world of those European late middle-age *novelas andariegas*.[1]

I do not particularly care for Monegal's explanation for the striking similarities between Vargas Llosa and Guimarães Rosa. It is only a brief aside, a disclaimer after noting striking similarities between these two paradigmatic Latin American novels across the linguistic/cultural divide. Monegal echoes the common strategy of associating certain traces of Latin American culture with archaic, that is, premodern or even medieval Iberia, which is in my opinion a misconception complicated by an equally superficial and mechanistic understanding of the relationship between European and non-European threads in Latin American culture. I do not think it is impossible to establish such clear-cut breaks between the medieval and the modern Iberian world before and after the colonization of Latin America, nor do I think it is productive to think of those cultural traces as "archaic" when they are expressions of earlier forms of modernity. What attracts me in Monegal's phrase is the image of cultural currents flowing underneath the smooth surface of grammatical colonial and postcolonial narratives of Latin America, underneath the cohesive history and literature framed across neat geopolitical and linguistic barriers, silently ignoring simplistic binaries, exhaustive categorizations, and neat hierarchies in subtle and unexpected ways.

In 1952, discussing the puzzling prevalence of the rabbit story cycle among blacks in the South of the United States in contrast with the predominance of the tortoise story cycle among blacks in Brazil, the Brazilian folklorist Câmara Cascudo called attention to the difficulty in establishing unequivocal origins for narrative motifs in oral literature:

> For a long time there was a simplistic process to place the origin of influences. You found a story in Brazil and another similar one in Africa? African origin. Couldn't it be that Portugal took these motifs to Africa and Brazil? Is it not true that stories that feature in "Kalila and Dimna" are heard in the north and south of Africa? Could it be that the black Africa, in the sixth century, influenced India, from where the physician Borzoyeh brought those stories? Finding stories long established in Africa in Central and East Europe, in Lapland, in Finland, in Lithuania, or in the farthest Oceania, disturbed this method. The ethnographic maps can only outline the diagrams of trajectories but not an undisputed starting point. (Câmara Cascudo, 149).[2]

Câmara Cascudo warns against simplistic cultural assumptions that assign clear routes for the flow of culture, but he also outlines the convoluted geographies of the imagination, the deep undercurrents that allow for Brazilian and Mexican cultures to seep into each other unknowingly. A contemporary Brazilian or Mexican unsuspecting reader of anyone between the Bernardellis and the Abramos may be receiving foreign influences in fragments these figures brought with them from foreign lands.

These undercurrents are made up of fragments, more often than not of uncertain provenance: narrative bits, anecdotes, motifs, isolated words, turns of phrase, gestures, accents, foods, spices, songs, voice inflexions, musical riffs, etc; fragments that do not flow necessarily against but certainly underneath the cultural mainstream, the prevailing academic paradigms, the flashy forefront of mass culture, and the now-decadent cultural supplements of Latin American newspapers. Carrying no utilitarian motive and thus essentially ambivalent, these fragments are not necessarily subversive or conservative and neither support nor undermine any ideology until they are incorporated one way or another by those who, wittingly or not, make use of them to articulate their own discourse.

If these are undercurrents, what is then flowing above them? Roger Bartra—in a book that is another landmark in the late-twentieth-century crisis of the national-development state in Mexico—called it "the logic of the game, which superimposes itself over the particular and individual expressions as well as over the circumstances" (*La*

*Jaula de la Melancolía*, 22).[3] The "logic of the game" is the ingredi-
ents and the recipes with which we have "cooked" our national identities and the tools for Bartra to articulate an overarching framework
that pervades texts otherwise very different in style and content: the
promotion of the consolidation of the modern Western national state
as our ultimate destiny, or at least as our desired future.

  Bartra's book is a response to the situation he had laid out in "La
Crisis del Nacionalismo en México," a sharp assessment of the meaning of the crisis in the 1980s and its deep implications for the ideology of the so-called revolutionary nationalism, "ideological and,
above all, cultural cement of the system" (214),[4] which had supported
the hegemony of the PRI in Mexico since the 1930s. In the face of
the void of political ideas and national projects, the myth of a revolutionary fusion between the state and the people under the banner
of nationalism was no longer capable of sustaining the framework of
political power.

  Bartra's book is close to Fernando Henrique Cardoso's discourse
cited at the introduction of this book or to Canclini's *Latinoamericanos
Buscando Lugar en Este Siglo* [Latin Americans Looking For Room
in This Century] (2002), whose title implied that all Latin Americans
could do was to carve out a little space for them in a hostile new
world order. Theirs is an eminently conformist stance, and still
centered on the idea of Latin America as a task, which they deem
more or less impossible to achieve in present circumstances. Bartra
aimed to dismantle the dividing line between dominant and popular cultures, but only briefly acknowledged the blurred boundaries between national and foreign. Câmara Cascudo's unpretentious
commentary, however, reveals a more complicated situation: the frequent presence of that which has been so thoroughly absorbed that
it cannot be so easily identified as foreign or national anymore.

  There is a flow of fragments from Brazil to Mexico and from
Mexico to Brazil that have been barely traced on ethnographic
maps. I hope my book has demonstrated that fragments from
Brazilian culture may very well have percolated inadvertently into
the subjectivities of a young Mexican writer who knows nothing
about Brazil but the names of some soccer players, but read José
Vasconcelos, Alfonso Reyes, Julio Torri, Salvador Novo, Carlos
Pellicer, Luis Quintanilla, Jaime García Terrés, Juan Rulfo, Gabriel
Zaid, José Emilio Pacheco, and Daniel Sada, and saw films star-
ring the *rumbera* Ninon Sevilla or directed by Paul Leduc, and art
by Gabriel Orozco and Damián Ortega. Likewise, fragments from
Mexican culture may very well have percolated inadvertently into

the subjectivities of a young Brazilian writer who knows nothing about Mexico but the name of Zapata and Pancho Villa, but who read Machado de Assis, Fagundes Varella, Affonso Celso, Manoel Bomfim, Ronald de Carvalho, Manuel Bandeira, Cecília Meireles, Érico Veríssimo, João Guimarães Rosa, Rubem Fonseca, Silviano Santiago; who saw films by Nelson Pereira dos Santos and Beto Brant; and who listened to João Gilberto's and Carlos Lyra's recordings made in Mexico.

Notwithstanding the particularities of twentieth-century Mexican nationalism, its symbiotic relationship with popular culture is not the result of the revolutionary process or of its consolidation under the hegemony of a single party. Similar symbiosis developed elsewhere in Latin America. Brazil and Argentina, which underwent political processes in which no political party like the PRI ever appeared, nonetheless constructed strong adaptive national identities based on the incorporation of popular culture as well. Perhaps the conclusion of *La Jaula de la Melancholia* moves in that direction as Bartra looks at this phenomenon as a particular manifestation of something long present in Western culture. However, Bartra comes up with yet another duality: an archetypal pair, melancholia–metamorphosis, whose myriad Latin American manifestations are barbarism–civilization, country–city, feudalism–capitalism, sertão–litoral, Ariel–Calibán, etc. In an unconvincing poststructuralist restatement of the theory of dependency, these dualities are in Bartra's view nothing but "a powerful solvent of social contradiction" or "the thousand faces of class struggle" (234).[5]

These deep undercurrents of ambivalent fragments of indefinable origin across Latin America are profoundly upsetting because in their lack of semantic precision and clarity they do not offer a counter-task to replace the rules of a game, not even Bartra's undertaking of clearing of the field. Since 1968, the rules of the game of national developmentalism seemed increasingly like a cynical farce or, at best, an unintended parody and the grotesque repetition of worn-out rhetorical formulas, and seemed less a matter of choice than an increasingly desperate repetition of old routines vis-à-vis realities that offered bleak prospects for Latin America in the global economy.

In terms of Portuguese and Spanish, these deep undercurrents are particularly repressed and therefore even more surreptitious. Decades before the crisis at the end of the twentieth century brought Latin American nationalisms to an untenable position, Mário de Andrade intuited the potential upsetting effect of a greater proximity between Portuguese and Spanish Americas when he commented on what he saw as the dangers of the peculiarly close relationship between the two languages:

> It is funny: there are cultures whose influence is dangerous whereas others are not. For example, I think Spanish culture is very dangerous to us, because it garbles the most subtly intimate traces of the national language. Every cultural influence fills a language with loan words; there is no doubt about it. But it is curious how loan words from French, English, or German do not disturb the psychological sensibility of our syntax. Maybe that is because they come from languages that are too distant from our national one. But the much more subtle and less "visible" influence from Italian and especially Spanish has the frightening gift to garble the intimate essences of our language. (17)[6]

Mário was above all a subtle, critical reader, which makes even what I consider to be his misunderstandings illuminating and thus productive. The reasons for his uneasy feelings about the proximity between Spanish and Portuguese lay in the potential to interfere with "the most intimate characters of the language" and "the psychological sensibility of syntax" and the "intimate essence" of the other. This treacherous proximity, which indeed can touch the intimate essences of my native language, is for me a source of attraction rather than fearful repulsion. Comparing and contrasting these deceptively close languages reveals a linguistic minefield: a dense forest of inhabited by cognates, quasi-cognates, and false cognates that invite and confound the native speaker of either of the two languages. At least for a speaker of Portuguese like me, navigating between the two languages constantly bring the uncanny realization that words and turns of phrase that sound at first so familiar are actually completely foreign and that seemingly foreign constructions are actually novel, uncanny usages of my own native tongue. This bilingual field is pregnant with possibilities that include productive misunderstandings: new, interesting resemantizations given to decontextualized or miscontextualized bits, which might appear even nonsensical when compared to their use in their original context. Each borrowed word, melody, narrative bit, mannerism, etc., is pregnant with unprecedented meaning to the culture that has appropriated them.

It is thus not a matter of getting or not getting it "right" when confronting the Other, which is by definition someone we are basically ignorant about. What happens when instead of fear and suspicion the Portuguese and Spanish sides of Latin America inspire curiosity and openness to each other? The best moments of this trajectory of encounters between Mexicans and Brazilians are the result of such attitude, in spite of occasional misunderstandings. Silviano Santiago defines this question with most propriety in "Why and For What Purpose Does the European Travel" (*The Space In-Between* 9–24). With precision and refined irony, Santiago points to a delicate balance between motivations and prejudices that determine European views of the colonized Other and contrasts these with the true openness of Michel de Montaigne, ironically a European who never set foot outside his own country. In "Of Cannibals," Montaigne discusses the uses and customs of the Brazilian Indians and also the limits of the European notion of barbarism based on a man who had lived "ten or twelve years in the New World" (91) in the Antarctic France in Rio de Janeiro. This unnamed man, ironically described by Montaigne as "a plain, ignorant fellow, and therefore the more likely to tell the truth" (93), behaves exactly the opposite of those men Valery complained about, those who search only for something they already found.[7]

Therefore, misunderstanding nonproductively the Other is not just a matter of ignorance but of surrendering to the asymmetries that define the dialogue between cultures in global capitalism. The conjunction of ignorance and what could be called inferiority or superiority complex depending on the case results in a lack of true openness and a tendency to gloss over anything that can truly upsets one's own self-congratulatory view, which bases itself on giving "the title of barbarism to everything that is not in use in his country" (93). The relationship between Latin Americans in a space understood as a multicultural and eminently multilingual one is a privileged site for the study of what happens when one opens up to what is at first foreign and of cultural ambivalence as a form of subtle antagonism, a vital presence underneath the smooth, linguistically homogenous, grammatical order of culture. The amount of energy generated in these encounters depends on the openness and the creative spirit of those involved to make the most out of these feelings of identification and otherness, which by no means indicates that Latin American culture has been freed from its ghosts: the Latin American obsession with Western Europe and the United States, these fatherly-otherly figures, looming in the background, giving this dialogue a triangular perspective.

The usefulness of the idea of these deep undercurrents in Latin American cultural life goes beyond explaining affinities between writers who did not know each other's work. My first book, *Modernismo Localista das Américas*, has plenty of examples of how these undercurrents played a significant role in the works of fundamental Latin American writers such as Rulfo and Guimarães Rosa, but they play a no less significant role in cultural experience in its broadest sense.

The realization of the actuality of these undercurrents came to me as an epiphany about the existence of a significant cultural blind spot in my own frame of reference. For instance, they became perceptible when I realized that, when I knew little about Mexico or Argentina, I heard the Portuguese version of the Mexican standard *Cielito Lindo* chanted by a crowd of soccer fans celebrating the approaching end of a victorious match in the stadium, and impressed relatives coming from out of state with copious servings of *dulce de leche* or *pasta de guayaba* with Minas cheese. To hear that same song performed in Spanish as a national Mexican treasure by *mariachis* in Plaza Garibaldi or to taste sort of the same sweet as a traditional delicacy in Palermo, in Buenos Aires (or in Puerto Rico), aroused in me the uncanny feeling I mentioned before: the sudden realization that certain rituals of Brazilian everyday life had long been as familiar to people who lived far away and spoke a foreign language. This is the source of my curiosity about Latin America: this instability and uncertainty about what belongs to others and what I call mine, the strange sensation of sharing an intimate family secret with what seems to be complete strangers.

Finding in a foreign land those cultural traits that were thought to be unique is uncanny because it pierces through what Marilena Chauí called a *semióforo*: "that which never stops finding new manners of expression, new languages, new values and ideas, so much that the more it seems to be something else the more it is a repetition of itself" (*Brasil—Mito Fundador e Sociedade Autoritária*, 5).[8] According to Chauí, *semióforo* is the core of a foundational myth, as in Hegel's account of Romulus and Remus and the constitution of Rome, "something conceived as perennial (almost eternal) that traverses and sustains the temporal course and endows it with meaning," something that "purports to place itself beyond time, outside of history, in a never-ending present under multiple forms and aspects" (5).[9]

In view of this uncanny pleasure, my approach in *Deep Undercurrents* may have seemed counterintuitive: focus on national cultures (Brazil and Mexico) rather than on Latin America as a whole regardless of nationality. But if you deny the *semióforos* their power, the importance of piercing through them is also gone. Anyway, whatever claim to a movement toward the erasure of national boundaries by means of a scholarly book is an act either of naïveté or hypocrisy that any Latin American who has been through the immigration and customs offices to enter Europe or the United States is well aware of. Rather than a limitation of scope, this strategy has allowed me to delve deeper than I would be able to had I chosen the continent as a whole.

I do not wish to affect the position of a scholar detached from his subject of study, approaching his work with suprapolitical objectivity. The circumstances of my life and my beliefs bear a decisive place in the course of my enquiry. I was born and raised in Brazil and I have developed my professional life so far in the United States. In that position I am constantly exposed to the gap between the perceptions of equivalent events in the two cultures. Then I had the privilege to define from scratch my PhD's fields of study rather than getting a set of fixed choices. Studying Latin America in depth as a whole, taking culture in its broadest sense as well as literature into consideration, seemed to me an impossible task. I feared that I would have a very sketchy, superficial knowledge base consisting of a few main authors and books of each national canon. Juan Rulfo (and Sara Poot-Herrera, of my dearest mentors) made me want to focus on twentieth-century Mexico and immerse myself in Mexico's literary tradition, reading major as well minor literary works and learning everything I could about the country's history, geography, politics, music, cinema, the arts, etc.

I embarked on this project with the ambition to alter the distribution of the sensible by giving visibility to cultural contacts between Mexicans and Brazilians as an example of contacts within Latin America. Calling these contacts deep undercurrents of Latin American culture goes beyond giving a name to what was mostly invisible and inaudible; it is about creating a space for a field of knowledge to come into existence. I dislike an excessive emphasis on the idea of the binary marginal versus central in comparative studies. Not because it does not make sense to see the world unfairly divided into rich and poor nations, and not because I downplay the importance of the asymmetry in the power relations between these two unequal sides. I dislike such emphasis simply because, as I mentioned in Chapter 9, I believe in what Frantz Fanon once wisely said: "the Third World [ ... ] is at the middle of the whirlpool" (*The Wretched of the Earth*, 76). Centrality in this sense does not depend on whether Latin America plays a key or a minor role in the decisions of international relations or in the large economic movements that make or break whole nations in a matter of months.

What is the potential meaning of Latin America beyond the constraints and limitations of thought strictly based on a binary opposition between the continent and Western Europe and United States? What is the meaning of Latin America beyond the grandiose discourses about continental identity and solidarity and the dysphoria produced by the unstable blend of arrogance and insecurity of its elites? The answers to these questions were the ultimate motivation behind this comparative labor. In the absence of what Edward Said called "flexible *positional* superiority" (Said, 7), the relationship between Mexicans and Brazilians demands genuine openness and curiosity. This peculiar spirit of inquiry is articulated in myriad ways in the cultural and aesthetic objects collected in this book. They are articulations born out of the need to move into relatively uncharted territory with a tense oscillation between identification and estrangement. That need and that oscillation are also mine.

# Notes

### Introduction

1. In the original in Portuguese, "o oposto de uma imagem auto-glorificada."
2. In the original in Spanish, "eso que descubrió Colón."
3. In the original in Portuguese, "um estrangeiro enorme."
4. In the original in Portuguese, "filhos do mesmo continente, quase da mesma terra, oriundos de povos, em suma da mesma raça, ou pelo mesmo da mesma formação cultural, com grandes interesses comuns, vivemos nós, Latino-Americanos, pouco mais que alheios e indiferentes uns aos outros e nos ignorando quase que por completo."
5. I have found no written register of the former president's speaking in these terms, but I rely in this case on my friend and colleague Rex Nielson, who told me about one of Fernando Henrique Cardoso's lectures at Brown in 2007. The image of the Siamese twins is one Cardoso has used in other contexts as well.

### 1 First Undercurrents

1. Vieira's prestige was at its highest in the Portuguese Empire from 1641, the date of his arrival in the Portuguese court from Brazil, to 1656, when King Dom João IV died. The *Sermões do Mandato* were delivered annually on Maundy Thursday, in conjunction with the feet-washing ceremony. Vieira delivered a total of six such sermons, identified by their year (1643, 1645, 1650, 1655 manhã, 1655 tarde, and 1670). The two sermons in 1655 are named respectively "Sermão do Mandato de 1655, manhã" [morning] and "Sermão do Mandato de 1655, tarde" [evening] or "Sermão Segundo do Mandato."
2. In the original in Spanish, "Estimemos el beneficio que Dios nos hace en no hacernos todos los beneficios que queremos, y los que también Su Majestad quiere hacernos y suspende por no darnos mayor cargo. Agradezcamos y ponderemos este primor del Divino Amor en quien el premiar es beneficio, el castigar es beneficio y el suspender los beneficios es el mayor beneficio, y el no hacer finezas la mayor fineza."

3. The term *nation* here means something different from our modern understanding of the word: it is not a juridical-political concept (such as *povo* and *patria*), but a biological one, referring to a group of common ancestry and used for foreigners as well as pagans to contrast with Christians.

4. In the original in Spanish, "En aquella semicorte al estilo de Felipe IV...poblada de portugueses y judíos, Juana Inés completó su cultura idiomática. El portugués le facilitó la lectura de las obras del P. Antonio Vieyra, a quien había de criticar en su *Carta Atenagórica*. En algunos de sus *Villancicos* introdujo, en forma popular, expresiones no siempre castizas de la lengua lusitana. (49)

5. The same scholar discovered in Portugal an interesting volume of poetic riddles sor Juana wrote expressly for Portuguese nuns at La Casa del Placer, "un lugar físico–un locutorio, un definitorio, una academia–de reuniones literarias o una asociación cultural, y literaria también, a la que pertenecerían desde sus respectivos conventos las monjas cultas de Portugal" (Poot Herrera 13).

6. The text was published posthumously in 1716, but the censors date their reviews January 1695. Sor Juana Inés de la Cruz died in April of that year.

7. In the original in Portuguese, "o cadaver tépido / de um povo aniquilado" and "quando a voz fatídica / da santa liberdade / vier em dias prósperos."

8. In the original in Portuguese, "Em nossa opinião o império do México é um filho da força e uma sucursal do império francês. Que reciprocidade de interesses podia haver entre ele e o império do Brasil, que é o resultado exclusivo da vontade nacional? ( ... ) A justica universal e o espírito americano protestam contra a reciprocidade desses interesses entre os dois impérios. ( ... ) o Brasil não pode ter comunhão de interesses nem de perigos, com o México, porque a sua origem é legítima, e o seu espírito é, antes de tudo, americano" (94–95).

9. José Veríssimo, who otherwise has a stern judgment of Varella as a poet, affirms that Varella's "belos versos a Juarez" (*Estudos de Literatura Brasileira*, 144) are one of his best among the few in which his potential shone through his limitations. Alfredo Bosi castigates Varela for contributing very little besides what the great Romantic poets (Gonçalves Dias, Álvares de Azevedo, and Casimiro de Abreu) had already written, but sees in Varela the first voice of nationalist liberalism in nineteenth century Brazilian poetry (Bosi 118–119).

10. In the original in Portuguese, "Será ( ... ) a mágica palavra / Que o mundo falará lembrando as glórias / Da raça mexicana!"

11. In the original in Portuguese, "entre os filhos d'este ingrato tempo."

12. In the original in Portuguese, "A gloria de uma raça / Ninguém pôde apagar no vasto livro / Que pertence ao porvir. / Embora a

escravidão, guerras, flagícios / O brilho lhe escureção, / Não morre uma nação, nem se aliena!" (99)

13. In the original in Portuguese, "o espírito de um povo nunca morre" (97) and "mais do que um gênio" (101).

14. In the original in Portuguese, "Há no seio da America / Um mundo novo a descobrir-se ainda: / Senhores de além-mar, / Quereis saber onde esse mundo existe? / Quereis saber seu nome? / Sondai o peito à raça americana, / E n'esse mar sem fundo, / Inda aquecido pelo sol primeiro, / Vereis a liberdade! (95)

15. In the original in Portuguese, "orvalha sangue a noite mexicana..."

16. Porfirio Díaz's achievements with his administration of *científicos* was "widely circulated and praised by a tireless publicity effort" and their slogan "Let's Look to Mexico" was "contagious" (*Historia Geral*, 338). Many years later, when complaining about the absence of Brazilian journalists in Russia in the early twenties in his own newspaper articles in *A manhã*, Monteiro Lobato would refer to Quintino Bocaiuva's gesture in this manner: "Outr'ora a senha de Quintino Bocaiúva era—Olhemos para o México. Hoje no mundo inteiro a senha é:—Olhemos para a Rússia. O dia de amanhã ferve lá, como o dia de hoje já ferveu em Paris, na Convenção. Mas nós só vemos a Rússia com os óculos pretos que o francês nos dá" (*Na Antevéspera: Reações Mentais de um Ingênuo*, 70).

17. Among the many Juarezes in Brazil, there are the sociologist Juarez Brandão Lopes (1925–2011), the soccer player Juarez "The Tank" Teixeira (1928), the Bossa Nova musician Juarez Araújo (1930), the artist Juarez Machado (1941), the sports commentator Juarez Soares (1941), and singer/priest Father Juarez de Castro (1969).

18. In the original in Portuguese, "renegaram as tradições da sua raça e da sua história, sacrificando ao princípio insensato do artificialismo político e do exotismo legislativo" and "o governo mais honesto que o México tem tido desde a independência."

19. In the original in Portuguese, "chefes de estados libertadores" and "no México, o sentimento monárquico é irresistível. Não pode restaurar a monarquia mas tem tornado impossível a república. Porque no México não há, não houve, nem há de haver república" (62).

20. *Lupe* marks the beginning of a fortunately not very long lineage of ghastly Brazilian novels featuring beautiful, tragic Mexican heroines in love with self-satisfied male Brazilian narrators. The tradition culminates 50 years later with Vianna Moog's *Tóia*, less prudish but certainly as shortsighted.

21. In the original, "apreço do Brasil pelo Mexico, manifestado, assim, nas letras pátrias" and "escritores mexicanos anticlericais."

22. In the original in Portuguese, respectively "o país mais interessante dos muitos que tenho visitado" "se agita turbulento, por vezes, mas progressista sempre," "assento de uma civilização nova," and "No domínio da sociologia como no da arte, sob a influencia de seus

jovens homens de estado, como de seus pintores, escultores e deco-
radores, jovens também, se fermenta e esboça a perspectiva de um
mundo novíssimo ( ...) e supreendente, porque não é ele simplesmente o produto da civilização espanhola ( ...) mas o da adaptação
de alguns principios dessa civilização à índole, ao temperamento, às
aspirações e aos ideais indígenas" (166).

23. While Eduardo Sucena writes that Oscar died in 1886, in his
1825 *Storia della musica nel Brasile* Vicenzo Cernicchiaro claims
Celestina's husband died in 1881. Because it seems less unlikely that
Félix and his mother could move to Guadalajara on such short notice,
I prefer 1881 as the year of Oscar's death.

24. Celestina Thierry studied with famous Italian choreographer Carlo
Blasis, teacher at La Scala Theatre Ballet School from 1838 and
1853, brother of Virginie Blasis (first singer at the Royal Italian
Theatre in Paris), and author in 1820 of one the first books on ballet
techniques, *Traité Elémentaire, Théorique et Pratique de l'Art de la
Danse* and in 1830 of *The Code of Terpsichore—The Art of Dancing,
comprising its theory and Practice and a history of its rise and progress
from the earliest times: intended as well for the instruction of amateurs
as the use of professional persons*, which, according to the *Brittanica*,
"still forms the basis of classic dance training." In 1838 Celestine
Thierry's father, Eugenio Thierry, sculpted a bust of Blasis (*La
Sténocoreographie*, 100).

25. Her father, the sculptor Eugenio Thierry, also traveled to Mexico,
where he exhibited his work in 1851 at the fourth exhibit of the
Academia Nacional de San Carlos de México (*Espectador de México,*
44–45). It is said that Eugenio decided to "enclaustrar en su misma
casa a su hija Celestina" (Matute, 48) to keep her from marrying
Oscar Bernerdelli.

26. In the original in Spanish, "permanecieron durante dos años encabe-
zando la compañia del Nacional con María Moctezuma."

27. "Le Violon du Diable" was a ballet in two acts with choreography
and libretto by Arthur Saint-Léon (1821–1870), music by Cesare
Pugni, sets by Despléchin and Thierry, and costumes by Lormier.
It premiered Jan.19, 1849 at the Paris Opera, with Saint-Léon (who
played the violin on stage) and his partner Cerrito in the leading
roles. *The Oxford Dictionary of Dance* states, "In the ballet, a retell-
ing of the Faustian legend, the young violinist Urbain is in love with
Hélène and allows the sinister Doctor Matheus (Satan in disguise)
to bewitch his violin so that its beautiful sound will win over the
reluctant Hélène. When Matheus comes to claim the violinist's soul,
Urbain refuses. The ballet ends happily when Urbain is delivered
from evil and the lovers are united."

28. There are two conflicting versions for the decision to leave Francisca
Bernardelli behind. While Laura González Matute cites "azares del
destino" (22) as the reason Thierry and Bernardelli left Francisca

behind in Guadalajara—the young couple thought they would be able to return to Guadalajara after their tour in South America—, Rodrigo Octavio mentions upheavals in Mexico and the young age of Francisca as the reasons. In 1854 Mexico was confronted with a filibustering attempt to occupy the northern state of Sonora and break away from the republic. Then came the beginning of the armed revolt against the dictatorship of General Santa Anna in Guerrero, on the southern Pacific Coast, which later involved the country as a whole and ended with Santa Anna's exile. Octavio's version, probably from Rodolfo Bernardelli, seems reasonable enough, although he claims Augustine Thierry had come to Mexico to work on a monument to Juárez, an extremely unlikely reason since Celestine's father got to Mexico in 1850.

29. In the original in Spanish, "arrancaba las aclamaciones del pueblo, con su interpretación de la zamacueca."

30. In the original in Spanish, "marcarán época sobre las tablas del recién inaugurado Teatro Municipal de Santiago (1857)."

31. The *Enciclopedia dello Spettacolo* describes the couple as thus "agile ballerina che eseguiva I più difficili passi sulle punte; ballava anche la polka sulle punte, usando aggraziati movimenti della bracchia, della testa e del busto; suo marito, Oscar Bernardelli, ballerino di notevole eleganza" (1290–1291).

32. In the orginal in Portuguese, "o pior marmorista do mundo."

33. The group remained active until 1941. For the story of this group, see the entry at the *Enciclopédia Itaú Cultural de Artes Visuais* at http://www.itaucultural.org.br/aplicexternas/enciclopedia_ic/index.cfm?fuseaction=marcos_texto&cd_verbete=3765&lst_palavras=&cd_idioma=28555&cd_item=10

34. In the original Portuguese, "Irrequieto, nervoso, sôfrego de impressões, uma dessas organizações athleticas, munidas de espáduas largas, forte peito, músculos desenvolvidos e reforçados pelo hygienico exercício das caminhadas ao ar livre. Em um canto da sala vê-se-lhe o retrato [esculpido por R.B.]. Deve ser aquelle o artista. É um forte, o olhar miúdo, porem seguro, o pescoço rigidamente modelado, os lábios carnudos, o bigode atrevido, arrebitado nas pontas, a barba rente ao rosto, o grande chapeo desabado posto à banda, dando-lhe à bela cabeça a tradicional arrogância de um cavalheiro antigo. / Ele é a sua obra, cuja expressão é original, cheia de calor e cheia de força."

35. In the original in Spanish, "la sociedad de artistas cuyo propósito era congregar a los elementos artísticos y literarios de Guadalajara."

36. In the original in Spanish, "…en la callada localidad de su estudio puso en practica lo aprendido aquí y allá, lo mismo en Roma que en París. Supo ademas percibir el clima de las innovaciones estilísticas y abrirse a la realidad del contexto mexicano, actitud que, por ejemplo, el laureado Antonio Fabres nunca consiguió."

## 2   Ronald de Carvalho (and Carlos Pellicer): Modern Poets of America

1. The group was renamed *Ateneo de México* in 1912. That influential generation has also been called "La generación del centenario" because of the festivities of the centennial of Mexican independence in 1910.

2. In addition to José Vasconcelos (1882–1959) and Alfonso Reyes (1889–1959) it is worth mentioning Pedro Henríquez Ureña (1884–1946), Antonio Caso (1883–1946), Julio Torri (1889–1970), Martín Luis Guzmán (1887–1977), Enrique González Martínez (1871–1952), Jésus T. Acevedo (1882–1918), Manuel M. Ponce (1882–1948), and Diego Rivera (1886–1957).

3. Justo Sierra, Porfirio Díaz's minister of education, was a strong influence on the *ateneístas* and supported their efforts to curb the influence of positivists and fight attempts to undermine laic education by Catholic groups. Don Porfírio himself was invited to one of their acts. In this sense it is interesting to contrast Carlos Monsiváis's "Prologue" (32–42) and Alfonso Reyes's own account of that time in "Pasado Inmediato (fragmento)" (133–174) in the anthology *México—Alfonso Reyes.* In "Notas sobre la Cultura Mexicana en el Siglo XX," Monsiváis even questions the actual relevance, novelty, and depth of the famed conferences in which Antonio Caso refuted positivism (*Historia General de México,* 968–976).

4. For an interesting account of this trip and its particular significance for Vasconcelos, see Mauricio Tenorio's "A Tropical Cuauhtemoc—Celebrating the Cosmic Race at Guanabara Bay."

5. In the original in Spanish, "un inmenso amuleto, una 'mascota', una imagen propiciatoria de la Buena suerte."

6. In the original in Spanish, "ver el país, no las olas, que son iguales en su multiplicidad inumerable."

7. A proof of the endurance of Vasconcelos's terminology can be seen in unlikely places, such as the work of Darcy Ribeiro, a left-wing nationalist and an anthropologist famous for his passionate defense of indigenous cultures and indefatigable fight for better public education for all in Brazil. Ribeiro's *O Povo Brasileiro,* a late addition to the tradition of essays about the national identity in Latin America intended to be his intellectual testament and an instant bestseller in Brazil in 1995, highlights the term "New Rome" in its last chapter, "O Destino Nacional" (441–449), again relating the mingling of races and a glorious future for the Brazilian nation.

8. General Álvaro Obregón (1880–1928) raised to arms to defend Francisco Madero in 1912 and served as president from 1920 to 1924. He handpicked his successor, Plutarco Elías Calles, and won a nonconsecutive second term in 1928, but was killed by the Catholic militant José de León Toral in San Ángel before he could be sworn in.

9. In March 1923 a note in *América Brasileira* announced the invitation of Ronald de Carvalho as vice-president of the newly founded

Instituto Varnhagen. The head of the Mexican embassy, which had been opened the previous year, Álvaro Torres Díaz presented José Vasconcelos's official invitation in the name of the Mexican government. Ronald de Carvalho went to Mexico with a group of Brazilians that included Rodrigo Octávio, a fellow diplomat and member of the Academia Brasileira de Letras. Octávio's account of the trip appears in a speech at the ABL in November, 1923, together with seven photographs taken during visits to places such Teotihuacán and Mexico City (*Revista da Academia Brasileira de Letras*, 145–170).

10. In the first preface of his *Formação da Literatura Brasileira*, Antonio Candido acknowledges Carvalho's literary history's historical importance: "li também muito a *Pequena História*, de Ronald de Carvalho, pelos tempos de ginásio, reproduzindo-a abundantemente em provas e exames, de tal modo estava impregnado das suas páginas" (Candido, 11). The book was translated to Italian by Ferruccio Rubbia in 1936 with a preface by Roberto Cantalupo and to Spanish by Jaime E. Payró in Argentina in 1943 for the tenth volume of the series *Biblioteca de Autores Brasileños Traducidos al Castellano*.

11. The "Faculdade Livre de Ciências Jurídicas e Sociais" was founded by Fernando Mendes de Almeida and began classes in Almeida's law firm right after the proclamation of the Republic, which permitted the creation of such institutions in Brazil. Among the 1914 graduates were Ronald de Carvalho, Alceu Amoroso Lima, and Rodrigo Octávio Filho. In 1920 this law school merged with a similar institution (the "Faculdade de Direito Livre") and became "Faculdade Nacional de Direito," basis for the Universidade do Brasil with the School of Medicine.

12. The magazine featured prominently Fernando Pessoa and Mário de Sá-Carneiro and became a landmark of Portuguese modernism. Ricardo Daunt's "A Passagem de Ronald de Carvalho por Portugal" briefly summarizes the participation of the Brazilian author in literary journals in Portugal.

13. On May 25, 1923, in a letter to Mário de Andrade found at the IEB archives in São Paulo, Ronald de Carvalho links their *Modernismo* to his incoming trip to Mexico writing, "I am going to face another battle confident that my hard work will reflect somehow positively on our Modernist cause. Your name will sound on the golden and silver walls of the Aztec palaces."

14. Regardless of their later differences, in 1922, the year of the *Semana de Arte Moderna*, Oswald de Andrade declared that "Graça Aranha enontrou a reação estética brasileira e pondo-se a frente dela mostrou ser o indiscutível chefe do seu tempo e o glorioso condutor do espírito de seu povo" (Boaventura, 22). In a note, also from 1922, Mário de Andrade simply called the *Semana* "bela idéia de Graça Aranha" (137).

15. The first three quotes from a letter from Manuel Bandeira to Mário de Andrade in the original are respectively: "Ronald é inteligentíssimo e muito raramente deixa brecha sob o ponto de vista intelectual"; "grupinho futurista de São Paulo" (a quote from *Rio-Jornal*); and "elementos primaciais do modernismo." As the differences in temperament and aesthetic/political sympathies deepened, Manuel Bandeira and some younger modernists from Rio such as Sérgio Buarque de Holanda and Prudente de Morais Filho resented the self-procclaimed leadership of Graça Aranha and Ronald de Carvalho. In São Paulo, Mário de Andrade agrees with Bandeira but refrains from a public rupture while Oswald de Andrade openly criticizes Graça Aranha and De Carvalho, who retain the sympathy of the Catholic and other conservative *modernistas*. In this letter Bandeira expresses concern about Sérgio Buarque de Holanda's boldness in openly criticizing De Carvalho, Graça Aranha and Renato Almeida in his literary journal *Estética*. The last quote in this sequence is taken from Tasso da Silveira's testimony on the occasion of the 50th anniversary of *Modernismo*. In the original, "também longamente fez empalidecer em torno a nomeada e o prestígio dos demais', exercendo uma verdadeira 'ditadura literária' no Rio de Janeiro dos anos 20."

16. Two other *modernistas* should be mentioned in this aspect: Mário de Andrade and Manuel Bandeira. The former worked tirelessly as a cultural agent in Brazil but also in Argentina, while the latter was the first to translate Borges and taught Hispanic literature to Bella Jósef, arguably the greatest Spanish American scholar in Brazil, and published a manual *Literatura Hispano-Americana* in 1960. Bandeira's friendship with Alfonso Reyes will be discussed in the chapter dedicated to Reyes.

17. Ronald de Carvalho joined the *Itamaraty* [the Brazilian diplomatic service] in 1914 and climbed hierarchical positions until acting as Deputy Secretary of State in the government formed after the 1930 revolution that brought an end to the First Republic For an interesting analysis of Ronald de Carvalho's career within the diplomatic service, see André Botelho's "Circulação de Idéias e Construção Nacional: Ronald de Carvalho no Itamaraty."

18. Published since 1789, the Parisian paper was then past its prime, which had been in the first half of the nineteenth century, when it belonged to the Bertin family and published Chateaubriand, Renan and Taine. The commentary to which Carvalho responds appears on page 6 on September 10, 1931, following the announcement of Mexico's acceptance to the invitation to the League of Nations on the first page. "La Bourse," column dedicated to economic news, criticizes revolutionary Mexico ("depuis vingt ans") as "partie de la phalange des Etats qui n'ont pas tenu leurs engagements" and recalls a note from the previous year, which complained about the Mexican focus on the internal debt and the adoption of the silver monetary

standard as "un non-sens." All issues of *Journal des Débats* are available at http://gallica.bnf.fr.

19. The revolutionary government defaulted on the external debt in 1914, 1924, and 1927. Tense negotiations with bankers represented by Thomas Lamont continued through the 1930s and 1940s until World War II, when not only Mexico but also Brazil gained leverage with the United States and negotiated more favorable agreements. Ronald de Carvalho probably knew about Mexico's international disputes. Rodrigo Octavio traveled to Mexico with Carvalho to work as the presiding commissioner that negotiated the Treaty of Bucareli between the United States and Mexico during Obregon's administration. Octavio was appointed to similar commissions established to arbitrate between Mexico and Germany and Mexico and France. The Special Claims Convention between the United States and Mexico presided by Octavio dealt with US claims for compensation due to "losses or damages either to persons of property of American citizens" during the armed struggles between 1910 and 1920. See "United States and of America v. The United Mexican States" in *The American Journal of International Law,* vol. 26, no. 1 (Jan., 1932), pp. 172–183.

20. In the original, "O que o 'Journal des Débats' disse do México é significativo. Seus homens de pensamento, os monumentos da sua antiga cultura, seus anthropologos, seus poetas, seus moralistas, seus escriptores finissimos, dos quaes o meu querido embaixador Alfonso Reyes honra as tradições, no Rio de Janeiro, os soffrimentos de sua raça, onde o heroísmo já não causa espanto, tudo isso nada representa."

21. One of the most enthusiastic promoters of Rubén Darío in Brazil was Carvalho's friend Elysio de Carvalho, owner and editor of *América Brasileira* (see note 23). The culturalist stance of Darío and Rodó (hence the name "Arielismo") denounces philistine capitalistic culture (represented by the United States) in order to protect humanistic values of a Latin American culture based on Western cultural traditions; a version of the rebuttal of middle-class Philistinism common since the nineteenth century in France and England.

22. In the original, "Nossos juízes são os defensores das moedas que os banqueiros nos emprestam, para renovar o milagre dos pães. Os lobos estão bebendo diante de nós. Cabe-nos porem, o privilegio de toldar-lhes a agua" (*Caderno de Imagens da Europa,* 80).

23. Ronald de Carvalho's "México, Paíz de Belleza" appeared in October 1923 in *América Brasileira.* Elysio de Carvalho's magazine lasted from 1922 to 1924 and cultivated relations with French, Spanish, and Portuguese venues. Besides Rubén Darío and Ronald de Carvalho, *América Brasileira* featured important authors such as Rufino Blanco-Fombona, Mário de Andrade, and Graça Aranha. Maria de Fátima Fontes Piazza's "Tal Brasil, Qual América? América

Brasileira e a Cultura Ibero-Americana" contains an overview of this periodical.

24. Founded by Olavo Bilac, Pedro Lessa, and Miguel Calmon in 1916, the League displayed a mixture of nativism and elitism. It sought to educate figures described as the "moral patrimony of the land" about the importance of nationalism as well as it led a successful campaign to establish mandatory military draft as a form of inculcating discipline and patriotism in the masses. In the 1940s the League was revived to defend Brazil's participation in World War II.

25. In 1930 there appears in *Bandera de Provincias*, a note titled "Amigos Brasileros" that announced the creation of the "Centro Universitario Cuautémoc" in Rio de Janeiro to promote the contact between Latin American countries ("Voces Cruzadas" 804). In his memoirs Alejandro Gómez Arias remembers being designated by the UNAM to welcome of a "misión especial de simpatía del Brasil" from the "Centro Universitario Cuautémoc" for the inauguration of Pascual Ortiz Rubio, who had been the Mexican ambassador in Brasil from 1926 to 1929 and ironically had just defeated José Vasconcelos in a highly contested election (*De Viva Voz*, 401). I have not been able to find any other mention of the Centro Universitario Cuautémoc anywhere.

26. In the original, "Obregon veio da terra e a terra imprimiu-lhe o feitio dos temperamentos exaltados. Sua mocidade foi espontânea e rebelde, como a de todos os homens que nasceram sem compromissos. Já montado no lombo nu dos cavalos, laçando o touro tresmalhado ou competindo com os mais adestrados ginetes de Sonora, já, de espingarda pronta, escondido entre a vegetação humilde e rasteira dos magueis tranquilos ou à sombra dos bosques espessos, para derribar as garças ou os gamos selvagens, ele viveu a adolescência de um herói. Sempre em contato com o povo, Obregon apurou o caráter destemeroso nas livres trajetórias da natureza. Não foi pedir às Universidades os diplomas da Sapiência graduada. Não foi buscar, nos salões oficiais, o prestígio dos favoritismos transitórios. Não mergulhou no sofisma livresco as claridades do espírito. Sua mestra exclusiva foi a observação diuturna dos seres e das coisas. Foi a vida, em suma."

27. Respectively in the original, "castelhano voluptuoso," "romanos da América," and "uma soma de fatores poderosos."

28. Carl Friedrich Philipp von Martius's suggestive motif of a Brazilian national character derived from the contributions of "the three races" has had a tremendous impact in Brazil. Von Martius wrote "Como se deve escrever a história do Brasil" [How to Write the History of Brazil] in response to a request from the *Instituto Histórico Geográfico Brasileiro* claiming that "the Brazilian man" was the result "do encontro, da mescla, das relações mútuas e mudanças" [of the encounter, the mingling, the mutual relationships and changes]

of these "três raças, a saber: a de cor de cobre ou americana, a branca ou caucasiana, e enfim a preta ou etiópica" [three races, which are: the bronze color or American, the white or Caucasian, and finally the black or Ethiopian] (442). Brazilian history is, for Von Martius, the result of the *"lei particular"* [particular law] that governs the *"movimento histórico"* [historical movement] of the three races, which implies the subjection of the two other races to the "sangue português (...) poderoso rio que deverá absorver pequenos confluentes das raças india e etiópica" [Portuguese blood (...) powerful river that shall absorb the small tributaries of the Indian and Ethiopian races] (443).

29. The term temperament here indicates a conflation of the cultural and historical and the racial and biological that may elude a contemporary reader as it apparently downplays the biological and avoids the terms of the racism inflected by social Darwininsm, only to redeem both of them as cultural categories. A paradigmatic Brazilian example is Affonso Celso (1860–1938), who, besides *Lupe* (see chapter 1), wrote the chauvinistic *Porque Me Ufano do Meu País* in 1901. This popular book full of exaggerated and simplistic praise of all things Brazilian, which inspired the satirical term *ufanismo* (something like jingoism), lists the contributions of blacks to the "national character" as their affable disposition, "their affection," and their "stoic resignation."

30. In Brazil the contrast between genuine and artificial national identities has an important antecedent in João Capistrano de Abreu's influential *Os Caminhos Antigos e o Povoamento do Brazil*, which derided urban areas on the coast as mere extensions of Europe and contrasted them with the backlands where the true Brazil was to be found.

31. They all shared a belief in diffusionism, a theory at the beginning of the twentieth century that pointed to a common civilized origin for all races but explained the existence of supposedly uncivilized peoples to the fact that those had "degenerated." Based on this theory, segregationists blamed the decline of Maya, Aztec, and Inca empires not on the Spaniards' deliberate, systematic depredation but on these peoples' avowal of miscegenation and predicted the same tragic outcome to the Anglo-Saxon culture in the event that segregation did not prevail.

32. In the original, respectively, "pagamos o tributo do sangue indígena que ainda circula em nossas veias, e sofremos por demais o influxo terrível do ambiente cósmico" and "os povos sem disciplina não têm direito a vida".

33. This argument has been traditionally used by monarchists to justify the violent repression of several local revolts that shook Brazil in the first twenty years of its history.

34. In the original, respectively, "monstros admiráveis, heróis" and "o Brasil não seria uma pátria, mas uma coletânea de países turbulentos

e irreconciliáveis" and "encarnam soberanamente toda a grandeza da sua ordem e da sua religião."

35. In *Meninos, Poetas, e Heróis*, Luiza Moreira has studied the poetry, the essays and the journalism of Cassiano Ricardo and thus outlined with precision the guidelines of this form of right-wing nationalist modernism that had a prominent role in the political and cultural life of Brazil and a defining role for a considerable part of the twentieth century during the Vargas dictatorship and the military regime installed after 1964.

36. In the original, it became "revivió el darwinismo social y lo 'redimió': en vez de que esta doctrina justificara la pureza de una raza cerrada y dominante, la hizo proclamar la abolición de las razas por medio de un gran mestizaje cultural."

37. There is a change in Vasconcelos's thought from the man who, in a conference in 1916, claimed "al mezclarse con el indio, el español se separa de su tronco y el indio abandona el suyo. Querer volver a uno u outro temperamento es renegar de los hechos y asustarse con la vida. Porque no tenemos pasado, nuestra patria y nuestro imperio es el porvenir."

38. Ronald de Carvalho and José Vasconcelos select aspects of the German philologist's thought. They are attracted to Nietzsche's antiliberal elitism, which fit their own conservative views. In their portraits of Obregón, for instance, one identifies Nietzsche's idea of the geniuses of the race as messianic "explosives in which a tremendous force is stored up" (*Twilight of the Idols*, 547), untamed and thus capable of tapping into the "kind of will, instinct, or imperative, which is antiliberal to the point of malice: the will to tradition, to authority, to responsibility, for centuries to come, to the solidarity of chains of generations, forward and backward *ad infinitum*" (543). Obviously other aspects, such as Nietzsche's iconoclastic, virulent anti-Christian views do not seem to hold much appeal for Carvalho and Vasconcelos.

39. In the original, "há uma força íntima e superior que a determina, um impulso irresistível que lhe define as características, uma chama palpitante que a ilumina perenemente: a alma da raça."

40. In the original, "um reactivo que desse consistencia ao amálgama."

41. In the original, "maravilhosa riqueza o instinto estético de uma raça que, das suas roupagens dos seus movimentos e até aos seus utensílios domésticos, vive numa perpétua obra de arte."

42. In the original, "Vi todo o mistério da arte, em sua expressão mais simples e direta, numa fábrica de Talavera de Puebla. Acurvado sobre o torno primitivo, o "alfarero" é um transfigurador. Como no Gênese, ao seu comando anima-se a argamassa e a ordem domina a matéria. Na argila macia, pegajosa e informe, correm-lhe os dedos sábios. Ao impulso do pé ligeiro, roda o torno, e o artista, secundado por esse movimento inicial, cria o Universo do caos. Cilindros, pirâmides,

esferas, surgem e desaparecem, no côncavo das suas mãos; as linhas se recurvam ou se distendem, alongam-se, interrompem-se, unem-se e, num relâmpago, nascem vasos de colos esguios, candelabros, jarras e copas de esquisito feitio. Cantava no torno o esteta e, no fogo dos fornos crepitantes, cantava também a terra, a mesma terra que, antes, era poeira e rolava na pata dos animais, e agora seria cântaro para a boca fresca e lasciva da índia de ventre fecundo. Cantava o homem porque se unira à terra, e cantava a terra porque voltava das mãos do seu criador para o milagre de um monumento de perfeição.E tudo era alegria ao redor de mim, porque aquele homem era um deus." The version of this excerpt in *Itinerário de uma Viagem* merely adds a paragraph between the second and the third of this version.

43. In the original, "a fartura, a economia, o bom senso mediocre das contas em ordem, a filosofia tranquila dos livros de razão."

44. In the original, "Em frente, desdobrando-se numa tapeçaria de mica, num mar de cintilações secas, ponteadas de brilhos duros e imóveis, estende-se, por todos os quadrantes, o deserto primitivo. Nem um relevo humano mancha a página virgem da criação. Sobre a ondulação de cómoros desolados, onde as palmeiras nanicas equilibram perfis de pernaltas em repouso, despeja-se o azul carrancudo do céu. O vento morno, que percorre os areais movediços, não traz às papilas ávidas uma gota sequer de humidade. Nem um filete d'água pode resistir à sucção da terra, onde as gramíneas se retorcem à feição de cordas finas e esturricadas."

45. The illustrations are by Nikolay Abrachev, a Bulgarian immigrant who went by the Italian-sounding artistic name Nicola de Garo. According to *História Geral da Arte no Brasil* little is known of Nicola de Garo beyond notes and reviews of his show in Belém do Pará in 1924 (544, 815). In 1923 a young Gilberto Freyre wrote an enthusiastic appraisal of the artist for the *Diário de Pernambuco* and made a fatalistic prediction that such a "espírito ansioso de pensador e de místico" was doomed to failure in a tropical Recife where only the heroes have the habit of thinking (*Tempo de Aprendiz*, 317–319).

46. The *jasliciense* Montenegro did his early studies under guidance of the Brazilian painter-musician Atiliano Felix Bernardelli (1866–1905), whose family's story we told in the previous chapter. In Guadalajara Felix taught not only Roberto Montenegro but also Jorge Enciso, and Gerardo Murillo, a.k.a. Dr. Atl, all of them future *muralistas.*

47. For a brief assessment of his career and his importance to Mexican architecture, see Víctor Jiménez's monography, *Carlos Obregón Santacilia: Pionero de la Arquitectura Mexicana.*

48. The young Pellicer impressed José Vasconcelos as a student leader that was sent to Colombia and Venezuela by the Carranza administration. Vasconcelos hired Pellicer as his personal assistant and the young poet accompanied the minister in his trip to South America.

49. In the original, "la patria continental" and "poeta de la belleza."

50. In the original, "sua lírica americana" ( ... ) "a captação do homem Americano em sua totalidade moral, espiritual e étnica."

51. In the original, "Chão que mistura as poeiras do universo e onde se confundem todos os rythmos do passo humano."

52. In the original, respectively: "América, América mía!" and "uno solo sentimiento, / fundará la Democracia nueva;" "todo está en tí vivo y actual en tu cabeza y en tu corazón;" "la noticia espléndida / del progreso argentino / maravilloso mensajero de nuestros destinos;" "nuestro espíritu sera tu obra maestra / y así serás del mundo nuevo la evocadora alma."

53. In the original, respectively, "que cabe toda na bola de vidro do teu jardim" (13), "filho da obediência, da economia e do bom-senso" (13), "Alegria de inventar, de descobrir, de corer!" (14), and "o nosso espírito áspero e ingenuo fluctua sobre as cousas" (15).

54. In the original, "América, América mía! / desde el alarido del salvaje / hasta la antenna de radio-telegrafía. / Desde la selva sin sendero y el camino pastoril por la sierra, / hasta la locomotora y el hidro-avión; / desde el Cacicazgo hasta la República, / todo está en ti vivo y actual en tu cabeza y en tu corazón."

55. In the original, "Europeu, filho da economia e do bom-senso, / tu não sabes o que é ser Americano! / Ah! os tumultos do nosso sangue temperado em saltos e disparadas sobre pampas, savanas, planaltos, caatingas onde estouram boiadas, tropel de patas, torvelinho de chi-fres! ( ... )

Nessa maré de massas informes, onde as raças e as línguas se dis-solvem, / O nosso espírito áspero e ingênuo flutua sobre todas as cousas, / Sobre todas as cousas divinamente rudes, onde boia a luz selvagem do dia americano!"

56. In the original, "Fervura de Areais, / Cardos. / Cardos. / Magueyes. / Pedras que se levantam e rompem o horizonte. / Chão de cintila-ções. / Silêncios vigiados, / Homens por trás de todos os silêncios... / Campainhas de cabras. / Fogo de sarapes. / México!"

57. The first poetry collection Ronald de Carvalho wrote under the impact of the Brazilian modernists in 1922 was called *Epigramas Irônicos e Sentimentais.*

58. In the original, "Tiene la confianza creadora de un fundador de ciu-dades, el optimismo cristiano de la generación del Ateneo, los grandes vuelos de Vasconcelos, la desenvoltura de um ciudadano del mundo. Tiene ojos para ver la hermosura de lo concreto, alegría de estar vivo y humiltad para ser natural en la naturaleza, para aceptar los límites como formas gozosas ( ... ) Su obra es ante todo homenaje; fresco desgarrado, reconciliado, homenaje a la alegría" (*La Gaceta*, 5).

59. In the original these lines read, respectively: "Que águas poderão agora refletir-me?" and "É o pássaro ou o metal / que fala por tua boca, / sino de San Agustín?" and "O oleiro que desenha a talavera, / ( ... ) / ouvindo os sinos sem ver o céu / pinta com os olhos ou

com os ouvidos?" and finally "Qerétaro! foi o Greco ou Murillo que te pendurou no México?"

60. In the original, "Cualquier que sea la doctrina histórica que se profese (y no soy de los que sueñan en perpetuaciones absurdas de las tradiciones indígenas, ni siquiera fío demasiado en perpetuaciones de la española), nos une con la raza de ayer, sin hablar de sangres, la comunidad del esfuerzo por domeñar nuestra naturaleza brava y fragosa. Nos une también la comunidad, mucho más profunda, de la emoción cotidiana ante el mismo objeto natural. El choque de la sensibilidad con el mismo mundo labra, engendra un alma común" ("Visión de Anahuac" 101).

61. In the original, "¡El poeta que enviáis a París es—con todo honor y derecho—un mensajero continental!" (*Obras Completas, VIII*, 158)

62. A measure of Ronald de Carvalho's extraordinary prestige at the time of his death is that his body was allowed to leave the Itamaraty palace for the funeral, an honor that only two paradigmatic figures of Brazilian diplomatic service had had: Joaquim Tomás do Amaral, second viscount of Cabo Frio, in 1907 and José Maria Paranhos da Silva Júnior, the baron of Rio Branco, in 1912. According to Heitor Lyra the distinction was not due to accomplishments of de Carvalho's diplomatic career, but to his outstanding literary and intellectual stature (76–77).

63. The title was first given to Henrique Maximiano Coelho Neto [1864–1934] in 1928 by the magazine *O Malho* that claimed "este honroso título deverá caber a um escritor vivo que pela sua cultura, pela força creadora do seu pensamento, pela clareza da sua expressão, pelo brilho da sua phrase e pela graça e elegância do seu estilo, seja considerado o maior dos nossos prosadores" (*O malho*, no. 1315, Rio de Janeiro, November 26, 1927, 16). The name of Ronald de Carvalho was already cited as a possible winner in the 1927 election.

64. In the original, "o nacionalista integral, apologista, do Estado Forte, fazendo o elogio das attitudes reacionárias". In this preface to a new 1984 edition of Carvalho's *Pequena História da Literatura Brasileira*, Amoroso Lima, by now an important public figure in the struggle against the military dictatorship, attempted to distance himself from his friends' political stances in the first half of the 1930s, although, as we have seen in the chapter dedicated to Alfonso Reyes, this is not quite true.

65. In the original, "um exemplar de *Toda a América* na versão italiana, com prefácio de Mussolini." *Toda a América* was translated by the famous Futurist artist of fascist leanings Anton Giulio Bragaglia (1890–1960). The fascist journalist and diplomat Roberto Cantalupo, Italian ambassador to Brazil from 1933 to 1937, wrote the preface to the Italian translation of "Pequena História da Literatura Brasileira" (Arnoni Prado, 261) and a most enthusiastic appraisal of

*Toda a América* in the chapter dedicated to literature in *Brasile Euro-Americano* in 1941.

66. According to Gabriel Zaid, after the first phase to which *Piedra de Sacrificios* belongs, Pellicer would explore a more introspective lyricism with *Hora de Junio* (1937) and *Recinto* (1941). See "Prólogo," *Antología Mínima*, México: Fondo de Cultura Económica, 2001.

### 3   Alfonso Reyes: Brazil and Mexico in a Nutshell

1. The book *Homenagem a Manuel Bandeira* contains Reyes's "Acto de Presencia" (*Genio y Figura de Alfonso Reyes*, 203). Fred Ellison's article "Alfonso Reyes y Manuel Bandeira: Una Amistad Mexico-Brasileña" is a thorough account of the friendship between the two intellectuals.

2. Bandeira also refers indirectly to Reyes in "Rondó do Palace Hotel" and cites the Mexican briefly several times in his *crónicas*, particularly in "Tempo de Reis," where Reyes is featured as a patron in a small popular restaurant in Rio de Janeiro (*Poesia e Prosa*, 377–378).

3. In the original in Portuguese, "Alfonso Reyes partindo, / E tanta gente ficando…"

4. *Monterrey—Correo Literario de Alfonso Reyes* lasted from 1930 to 1937. Considered by José Emilio Pacheco as a precursor to the contemporary blog (Pacheco, 23), Reyes' one-man literary journal was an important initiative in the 1930s in terms of inter-American dialogue.

5. *História Natural das Laranjeiras* was first published in book form in 1955 in the ninth volume of Reyes's *Obras Completas*. Most of Reyes's writing done in or about Brazil is concentrated in the ninth and tenth volumes of *Obras Completas*.

6. "Ofrenda al Jardin Botánico de RíoJaneiro" (*Obras Completas IX*, 89–92) is the speech given during the ceremony of inauguration of the statue in 1935. The speech is featured on the first page of the 13th issue of *Monterrey—Correo Literario de Alfonso Reyes* together with photographs of the Cuauhtémoc in Flamengo and the cactus garden and the Xochipilli in the Jardim Botânico. This speech is dedicated to Paulo Campos Porto, director of the Jardim Botânico from 1931 to 1938, with whom Reyes cooperated on the project of a cactus garden around the Cuauhtémoc in Flamengo. Reyes compliments the Jardim Botânico for its remarkable collection of Mexican cacti and reveals that he himself brought Peyotl seeds from México to Campos Porto.

7. Fred P. Ellison's *Alfonso Reyes e o Brasil* is a thorough account of Alfonso Reyes's years in Rio de Janeiro.

8. A sign of the essay's prominence in Reyes's oeuvre is that in 1996 the Fondo de Cultura Económica published Reyes's tome for the collection "Cultura para Todos" (low-cost paperback editions of Mexican classics) and called it *México en una Nuez y Otras Nueces*.

9. Initially called *El Nacional Revolucionario*, the newspaper was created in 1929 at the national convention of the PRN (the newly founded Revolutionary party that would become the PRM in 1938 and the PRI in 1945), and would move from the revolutionary rhetoric of Cárdenas to become the government's mouthpiece in the 1940s.

10. In the original in Spanish, "hemos comenzado apenas a compararnos unos con otros y ( . . . ) de semejante comparación ha de nacer un conocimiento más exacto del proprio ser nacional."

11. In the original in Spanish, "su historia, su cultura, sus problemas económicos y sociales, sus creaciones literarias y artísticas, su pasado y su presente."

12. In the original in Spanish, "todo lo que valía la pena venía de fuera y a todo lo autóctono, fuera nativo o criollo, se le tenía por atrasado."

13. In the original in Spanish, "antiautoritarismo en la forma."

14. In the original in Spanish, "cada uno mira el mundo desde su ventana. La mía es la literatura."

15. Luis Leal once aptly described Reyes's prose as "poesía y saber unificados a través de un acercamiento basado en la reminiscencia y la evocación" [poetry and knowledge unified through an approach based on reminiscence and evocation] (Leal, 15).

16. In the original in Spanish, La síntesis histórica es el mayor desafío a la técnica literaria. La palabra única sustituye al párrafo digresivo; el matiz de certidumbre ( . . . ) establece la probidad científica; el hallazgo artístico comunica por la intuición lo que el entendimiento solo abarcaría con largos rodeos." The essay "Justo Sierra y la Historia Patria" (175–198), from which this passage comes, is particularly illustrative, since in it Reyes lays out what are for him the essential qualities of a great historical essay.

17. The *Ateneístas*—the name is particularly meaningful—were classicists who wished to rescue Greek and Roman cultures from oblivion by positivist materialism and the stale rhetoric of academicism. Vasconcelos's ambitious literacy plans for Mexico included the creation of school libraries with a collection of carefully translated classics (Homer, Aeschylus, Eurípides, Plato, and also Dante, Goethe, Cervantes, etc.), published in editions of 20,000 to 50,000 volumes.

18. In his account of the 1932 polemic with the nationalists, Guillermo Sheridan confesses without much subtlety that "A mí también me irrita la ambigüedad de Reyes, enfermo de diplomacia, y que solo en su correspondencia (ni siquiera en su diario) externase su verdadera opinion sobre 'las ruindades del nacionalismo' y sobre la forma en que se había lacerado con esas acusaciones" [I see Reyes's ambiguity as irritating as well. It is infected by diplomacy and it is only in his private letters that he expressed his true opinion about "the evils of nationalism" and about how he had gotten hurt with those accusations] (Sheridan, 52). The discrepancies in Reyes's opinions are not

contradictions but differences between statements made in public and in private. It is difficult to define which of the two is his true opinion. Sheridan, in his determination to combat nationalism, defines the contrast between the two fields in the 1930s too sharply. Reyes's "A Vuelta de Correo" (*VIII*, 427–449), for example, forewords his reply to Héctor Pérez Martínez in that polemic with a view that sees much less clearly divided opposing camps.

19. Julio Ortega affirms that "Alfonso Reyes debe haber sido el ultimo modernista: entre Rubén Darío (que era capaz de sumar Góngora a Verlaine) y Jorge Luis Borges (que era capaz de añadirle compadritos a Shakespeare)" (*Teoría Literaria*, 12–13).

20. In the original in Spanish, "el choque del jarro contra el caldero. El jarro podía ser muy fino y muy hermoso, pero era el más quebradizo."

21. In the original in Spanish, "base bruta de la historia."

22. In the original in Spanish, "no soy de los que sueñan en perpetuaciones absurdas de la tradición indígena, y ni siquiera fío demasiado en perpetuaciones de la española."

23. In the original in Spanish, respectively, "demiurgo o agente mediador encargado de gobernar la obra" and "usaba demasiado materiales y tenía la fuerza de la inexperiencia."

24. In 1933 Reyes published in *El libro y el Pueblo,* his translations of fragments of pre-colonial indigenous poetry that had been translated into French and Portuguese. See "Poesía Indígena Brasileña" en Alfonso Reyes, *Obras Completas, Volumen IX* (México: Fondo de Cultura Económica, 1959) 86–88.

25. In the original, "la historia es mucho más veloz que la geografía."

26. In the original, respectively, "robustez y lentitud de las erosions geológicas" and "vaivenes coléricos y algo improvisados con que se suceden las etapas en las demás naciones americanas."

27. In the original, "la historia es la piedra que cae en el lago dormido."

28. In the original, "esa intrusión no es necesariamente violenta."

29. In the original in Spanish, "a la majestad de la Historia no siempre conviene el que los grandes conflictos encuentren soluciones fáciles" and ""la cara del nuevo pueblo se va dibujando a cuchilladas."

30. In the original, "Algunos nos han compadecido con cierta conmiseración. Ha llegado la hora de compadecerlos a nuestro turno. ¡Ay de los que no ha osado descubrirse a sí mismos, porque aún ignoran los dolores de este alumbramiento! Pero sepan—dice la Escritura—que sólo se han de salvar los que están dispuestos a arriesgarlo todo."

31. In the original, "Y de todo ello resulta una hermosa y grande nación que nunca perdió la sonrisa ni la generosidad en medio del sufrimiento, ejemplar a un tiempo en el coraje y en la prudencia, orgullo de la raza humana, promesa de felicidad en los días aciagos que vivimos, fantástico espectáculo de humanidad y naturaleza, cuya contemplación obliga a repetir con Aquiles Tacio: '¡Ojos míos, estamos vencidos!'"

32. The full quote in Spanish reads, "miraba esto, iba a ver lo otro, corría a contemplar lo del más allá y me atraía lo que aún me quedaba por ver. Y así recorriendo todas las calles, cautivo de un anhelo insaciado ante tanto espectáculo, exclamé extenuado: '¡Ojos míos, estamos vencidos!'" In English it reads "there were sights I saw, sights I aimed to see, sights I ached to see, sights I could not bear to miss... my gaze was overpowered by what I could see before me, but dragged away by what I anticipated. As I was guiding my own tour around all these streets, love-sick with the sight of it, I said to myself wearily: 'We are beaten, my eyes'" (77).

33. In the original in Spanish, "Si aquí el coco de Alagoas / labrado en encaje, allá / la nuez de San Juan de Ulúa, / calada con el puñal."

34. The fort on the island of San Juan Úlua was ironically one of the last bastions of colonial Mexico; surrendered by the Spaniards only in 1825, it functioned as a prison from the late eighteenth until the twentieth century, featuring famous inmates such as Fray Servando Teresa de Mier and Benito Juárez (*San Juan de Ulúa—Biografía de un Presidio*, 112–126). The exquisitely carved coin banks made in San Juan Ulúa are now much-sought-after antiques. See Sandra Kraisrideja's "Carved Coconuts Highlight Mexico's History" in the *North County Times*, http://www.nctimes.com/entertainment/art-and-theater/visual/article_1ad5de79–45ad-5a3f-8412-f0a1218d0713.html.

35. In the original, "llevaba diez años de buscarse a sí propia."

36. In the original in Portuguese, "O egoismo europeu, batido de perseguições religiosas e de catastrophes economicas, tocado pela intolerância e pela fome, atravessou os mares e fundou ali, no leito das mulheres primitivas e em toda a vastidão generosa daquela terra, a Família dos Homens Cordiaes, esses que se distinguem do resto da humanidade por duas características: o espírito hospitaleiro e a tendência à credulidade. Numa palavra, o Homem Cordial."

37. In "As raízes e o labirinto da América Latina," Silviano Santiago points back to Pero Vaz de Caminha's letter to the king of Portugal, which announced the "discovery" of Brazil, as the foundational text where lies the first linguistic sign of such imaginary in relation to the colonization (84, 89–94).

38. In his attempt to negate the apologetic reading of the *cordialidade*, Sérgio Buarque de Holanda might have exaggerated its negative aspects. Pedro Meira Monteiro rightly observes that, for Buarque de Holanda, at least in *Raízes do Brasil*, "os valores liberais (...) se colocavam como uma *opção* individual, que parecia *excluir* os valores cordiais. Se nos mantivermos no plano da reflexão do historiador, dificilmente vislumbraremos, no próprio ensaio, uma saída clara para o impasse" (*A Queda do Aventureiro*, 291).

39. Cassiano Ricardo was one of the founders of the nationalistic *Verdeamarelo*, together with Menotti del Picchia and Plínio Salgado.

Without adhering to *Integralismo* (Brazilian version of Fascism), Cassiano Ricardo became an intellectual leader of nationalist right-wing *modernistas* and one of the most powerful figures in Getúlio Vargas's dictatorial Estado Novo (1937–1945). As other conservative or authoritarian figures of the Brazilian *Modernismo*, Cassiano Ricardo was neglected or mentioned briefly and out of context until Luiza Moreira published *Meninos, Poetas e Heróis*, a pioneering reading of Ricardo's main works.

40. In this long text, Cassiano Ricardo complains that in the second edition of *Raízes do Brasil* "pretendendo explicar a palavra, Sérgio alterou, descaracterizou nosso *homem cordial*" (293) and, furthermore, contests the adequacy of the term *cordialidade*—he prefers the openly apologetic *bondade*, "primeiro fundamento da nossa democracia social" (294).

41. In the original, "Creio que nunca chegaríamos a entendimento perfeito acêrca de alguns aspectos tratados e vejo que será inútil esmiuçar todos os pontos de sua réplica."

42. Another important point of view on the discussion of the Homem Cordial comes from another key *modernista*, Oswald de Andrade, in a short piece called "Um Aspecto Antropofágico da Cultura Brasileira: o Homem Cordial" (*Do Pau-Brasil à Antropofagia e às Utopias*, 139–144), presented at the first *Congresso Brasileiro de Filosofia* in 1950. In this text, Oswald, then back to the Antropofagia of the 1920s after a long period of communist militancy, claims to agree with Sérgio Buarque de Holanda's definition (there is a long quote from *Raízes do Brasil*), but offers a completely different genealogy to the Homem Cordial, closer to Ribeiro Couto. For Oswald de Andrade the *Homem Cordial* is a remnant of the culture of Brazil's precolonial indigenous matriarchal society. This *matriarcado* was, furthermore, ready for a comeback of sorts (Oswald sees traces of it in the thought of Kierkegaard, Mallarmé, Karl Jaspers, and Jean-Paul Sartre) as humanity faces fear without any help from Heaven.

43. Cassiano Ricardo's "Variações sobre o Homem Cordial" and "Carta a Cassiano Ricardo" were originally published in 1948, in the second and third issues of the magazine *Colégio—Revista de Cultura e Arte*, directed by Roland Corbisier (1914–2005), a former *integralista* who would be the founder in 1955 of the government-sponsored think-tank ISEB (Instituto Superior de Estudos Brasileiros). The model for the think-tank devised by Hélio Jaguaribe and Gilberto Amado was the Collège de France and Reyes's Colegio de México (its original name was to be Colégio do Brasil). After the 1964 coup d'état, the ISEB was closed down, its library incorporated into the Escola Superior de Guerra, and his members investigated by the military.

44. In the original, "Essa cordialidade, que Alfonso Reyes atribuía a toda a América Latina e Sérgio Buarque de Holanda considera tipicamente

brasileira, não me parece sinal de mau caráter. Ou de falta de caráter. É a marca de um caráter eminentemente humano, lírico, compreensível, racional, que faz da composição e não da oposição a lei de nossa psicologia nativa e da nossa conseqüente história política. Temos tido também as nossas lutas cruentas e guerras civis que duraram mais de decênio, como a dos Farrapos, campanhas sangrentas como a de Canudos, repressões violentas como as coloniais, para mostrar que o sangue da nossa gente também corre. Mas é a exceção que confirma a regra. Se alguma coisa devemos cultivas em nosso caráter nacional, e preservar em nossa história, como típica de nosso Humanismo brasileiro, é precisamente essa tendência inata às soluções pacíficas das nossas mais graves crises políticas. Mesmo com os tanques nas ruas... É a marca da nossa gente, da nossa História da nossa civilização. Cultivamo-la com carinho. E o 30 de março a confirmou uma vez mais." My colleague Alexandre Nodari called my attention to this quote in a different context.

45. For a brief assessment of *Jornal do Brasil*'s positions during the military dictatorship, see Beatriz Kushnir's *Cães de Guarda: Jornalistas e Censores do AI-5 à Constituição de 1988*. São Paulo: Boitempo.

46. Converted to Catholicism in the late 1920s by his mentor Jackson de Figueiredo, the modernist Amoroso Lima became the great intellectual leader of the conservative Catholic layman movement in the 1930s with remarkable influence in Getúlio Vargas's Conselho Nacional de Educação, where he fought in the name of the Church and private interests against the reformers of the Escola Nova. For an account of the debates in the council and the roles played by Amoroso Lima and the other members, see Sérgio Miceli's "O Conselho Nacional de Educação: Esboço de Análise de um Aparelho de Estado (1931–7)" in *Intelectuais à Brasileira*.

47. Anticommunism was essential to the Catholic rightwing in Brazil. In 1935, for example, in a chapter called "666" in his *Pela Ação Católica*, Amoroso Lima warns that "do outro lado do Vistula, espreitam os novos bárbaros, velam os que levantam estátuas a Judas, velam os que ergueram sobre o trono soviético aquele mesmo Animal do Apocalipse" (49).

48. In the original, "toda a revolução brasileira termina em acordo, e a pena mais rigorosa para os nossos crimes politicos nunca passou do exílio." Among other things in his essay, Cassiano Ricardo claims that "o problema das minorias raciais e culturais é quase inexistente entre nós" (39) and that "não temos problemas de desocupados, da falta de terra, da violenta diferença de classes, do ódio de raças e religiões, da excessiva diferença de cultura ou riqueza" (40).

49. It is a sign of Alfonso Reyes's diplomatic acumen that he cultivated the friendship of Amoroso Lima and Graça Aranha and also quietly supplied Cecília Meireles with material about Mexican educational

policies as she fought on the other side of the political spectrum for the Escola Nova (Soares, 258–279).

50. In the original, "sabia analisar, agudamente, o espírito latino-americano quando por exemplo afirmava que éramos a expressão típica do *homo cordialis.*"

51. The most visible traces of positivist influence are the political power of the *científicos* in Mexico and the motto *Ordem e Progresso* in the Brazilian flag. Buarque de Holanda questioned the prominence of positivism in the end of the monarchy and the establishment of the Republic. Nevertheless, the perceived influence of the tenets of positivism went well beyond those who professed to strictly follow Auguste Comte's doctrines. Positivism's ideological hegemony extended its reach in diluted or distorted form to the elite in Latin America and was taken into account by those who wished to challenge them.

52. The relative importance of the avant-garde in Brazilian culture and their trajectory since the 1920s has been a topic for discussion. As the relationship between the *Ateneo* and both the *Porfiriato* and the Mexican revolution have been distorted to make the *Ateneístas* seem in tune with the new regime, the role of the *modernistas* and their cultural clout has been exaggerated by post hoc accounts that try to enhance the connection between the *Modernismo* of the 1920s and later developments in Brazilian culture such as *Concretismo* and *Tropicalismo.* This has led to distorted views of the culture in that period with the providential erasure of the influential right-wing *modernistas* such as Amoroso Lima, Ricardo, Plínio Salgado, and Menotti del Picchia. For a brief exposition of the issue, see Randal Johnson's "Rereading Brazilian Modernism."

53. Vasconcelos was important to the *muralistas* and writers such as Carlos Pellicer, whereas Reyes helped/guided several writers, from Villaurrutia and other *contemporáneos* in the 1920s to the young Octavio Paz, in a role not unlike that of Mário de Andrade in Brazil.

54. In the original, "por la obvia imposibilidad para explicar la circunstancia trágica de 1968 por medio del mito de 'lo mexicano.'"

55. A paradigmatic example of this insufficiency is the "postdata" Octavio Paz writes, adding to his *Labyrinth of Solitude*, an anachronistic attempt to build a parallel between the brutal repression and the student massacre planned and executed by the administration of Díaz Ordaz and pre-Columbian sacrifices. See Bartra (160–161).

#### 4   When Mexican Poets Come to Rio de Janeiro

1. Roniere Menezes's *O traço, a Letra e a Bossa—Literatura e Diplomacia em Cabral, Rosa, e Vinicius* is an important study of this cultural strain in the Brazilian context.

2. Literary magazines such as *Inimigo Rumor*, *Coyote*, and *Sibila* have featured the work of young Spanish American poets and there have been several meetings with young poets such as the Festival Inter-Americano de Poesia Contemporânea in São Paulo. Poets such as the Mexican Heriberto Yépez and the Brazilian Angélica Freitas have been translated and discussed in Brazil and Mexico and anthologies such as *Radial: Poesía contemporánea de Brasil y México* (Editorial Cielo Abierto, 2012) and *Caos Portátil: Poesía Contemporânea de Brasil* (2007) attest to this contact.

3. A first version of this chapter appeared in Portuguese as "Quando os mexicanos vêm ao Rio de Janeiro," in the *Revista de Estudios Portugueses* of Salamanca University.

4. Pellicer spoke during student protests in front of the Venezuelan Embassy in Mexico. Between 1918 and 1920 Pellicer had gone to Bogota and Caracas on a fellowship from the *Federación de Estudiantes Mexicanos* with a mission to establish similar organizations in Colombia and Venezuela and start a federation.

5. In addition to his poetic works, Pellicer had a remarkable career as the organizer and founder of numerous museums, among them the Frida Kahlo House in 1964.

6. Mexico sent four airplanes and seven pilots, among them Francisco S. Espejel and Julian Nava Salinas (mispelled *Navas* in Pellicer's book), members of the first national squadron to whom Pellicer dedicates "Suite Brasilera—Poemas Aéreos." Espejel died during the air campaigns against the rebel troops of Adolfo de la Huerta between December 1923 and February 1924 and Salinas died in an accident 23 days later. The website *Mexican Aviation History* contains excellent iconographic material. Pellicer was such an aviation enthusiast that he even studied mechanical engineering for a while at the ESIME in 1923. See Gabriel Zaid's "Los años de aprendisaje de Carlos Pellicer" *Letras Libres*, Julio 2001.

7. For details on this amusing story, see Gabriel Zaid's "Siete Poemas de Pellicer" (1107).

8. José Vasconcelos appointed Best Maugard director of the drawing and handicraft department and prescribed the "Best system" to the state schools of the Federal District. In 1923, 200,000 copies of Best's book, *Manuales y Tratados: Metodo de Dibujo: Tradition, Resurgimiento, y Evolución del Arte Mexicano* (Manual of Drawing: Tradition, Renaissance, and Evolution of Mexican Art) were given free of charge and used as a textbook in state schools.

9. Emulsão Scott is a well-known brand name, once-popular among parents and feared by children who had to swallow a spoonful of the horrible-tasting medicinal potion based on cod liver oil either to supplement their diets with vitamins A and D or as a punishment for being naughty.

10. In the original, respectively, "un poco de sol desnudo;" "Estoy, solamente, / estoy, nada más." and "(...) desde del aeroplano se medita en la gloria / de unir banderas y cantar canciones." and "Abajo están las viudas y los juristas, / la Emulsión Scott y los grandes deudores." and "Abajo, en el fondo del mundo / la tinta del poema se ha empezado a borrar."

11. In the original, "el aviador antes que otra cosa es artista. (...) el acto de volar es en sí un acto de belleza. (...) Volar es el arte que encierra en sí todas las artes y economiza la tarea desagradable de exteriorizarlos." "Cuando el piloto es muy hábil para ejecutar actos de acrobacia, se tiene la impresión real de que no es el avión, sino las cosas las que se mueven." "...grandes artistas por la salvaje y magnífica espontaneidad." "El mundo es una pobre cosa / llena de gustos yanquis y consideraciones."

12. The airplane and its poetic possibilities are an ubiquitous obsession in modernism and it suffices to list but a few examples: In Brazil, Jorge de Lima's prose poem "O grande Desastre Aéreo de Ontem" (1938) and Drummond de Andrade's "Morte no Avião"; in Mexico with Luis Quintanilla's poetry collection *Avión* (1923) and Manuel Maples Arce's poem "Canción desde un Aeroplano" (1927); in Europe with Mayakovsky's poem "The Flying Proletariat," Marinetti's novel *Le Monoplan du Pape* (1912); and in the United States with George Antheil's *The Airplane Sonata* (1921).

13. Pellicer's approximation to the avant-garde was triggered by his close relationship with Juan José Tablada (1871–1945) in Bogota. Tablada had established himself in Spanish American *modernismo* when he published three remarkable books influenced by Japanese poetry, which mark a turning point in modern Mexican poetry: *Un día* (1918), *Li-Po y Otros Poemas* (1920) e *El Jarro de Flores* (1922). Together with *Feria* (1928) these books give Tablada an important place in Latin American poetry.

14. Enrique González Martinez, Vasconcelos's contemporary of the Ateneo, wrote the famous poem ("Tuércele el cuello al cisne") that urged poets to twist the neck of the symbolist swan and replace it with the austere owl of Pallas Athena. The sonnet form and the classical reference are indications of the reformist rather than revolutionary impetus of González Martinez.

15. This was a nasty allusion to the fact that three of the nine main members of the group were more or less openly homosexual. About the polemic that also involved Alfonso Reyes, see Guillermo Sheridan, *México en 1932: la Polémica Nacionalista* and about the *Contemporáneos,* see Guillermo Sheridan, *Contemporáneos Ayer.*

16. In the original, "Tu mar y tu montaña, / (...) como síntesis del Continente amado."

17. In the original, "Y la ciudad maravillosa / ( ... ) ha de ser / la curva eterna de mi gozo / que sobre el mundo he de tener."

18. He is not to be confused with his namesake, the Spanish painter Luis Quintanilla (1893–1978), friend of Hemingway and dos Passos and famous for documenting the Spanish Civil War.

19. Quintanilla's father was a friend of many of the most important Mexican intellectuals of the turn of the nineteenth to the twentieth century and Quintanilla grew up around figures such as José Juan Tablada and Guillaume Apollinaire—the great *modernista* Amado Nervo was his godfather.

20. Pascoal Ortiz Rubio, who had been the ambassador in Rio de Janeiro since 1926, got into a series of violent arguments in the press because of Brazilian critics such as the Catholic leader Jackson de Figueiredo against what they termed president Elías Plutarco Calles's anticlericism and because of Brazil's excessive support for any US external policy, which was an obstacle to Mexico's Latin American diplomatic initiatives (Palacios, 227–240).

21. Quintanilla shared the position *ad interim* together with Pablo Herrera de Huerta when Herrera de Huerta arrived in January 1929.

22. Although Quintanilla was not in Mexico at the time, he contributed poems to the *Irradiador* and *Horizonte* and was prominent in List Arzubide's 1926 anthology *El Movimiento Estridentista*. Notable also was Quintanilla's participation as director of El Teatro Mexicano del Murciélago, which, though not nominally *Estridentista* "was clearly part of the atmosphere of artistic experimentation initiated and fomented by Stridentism" (Rashkin, 101).

23. In the original in Portuguese, "você não se limitou aos hábitos da carreira. Ficou logo brasileiro aqui. E quem nos deixa amanhã é um brasileiro." I owe this reference to my colleague David Jackson.

24. Reference to Henry Ford's ambitious project of rubber extraction in the middle of the Amazon forest in his Fordlândia, a city erected in the middle of the jungle in 1928. This story has recently been retold by the historian Greg Grandin in *Fordlandia: The Rise and Fall of Henry Ford's Forgotten Jungle City*.

25. In the original in Spanish, "novia de Henry Ford. / Patria de Makunaima. / Sexo del mundo"

26. The author of the modernist epic *Macunaíma*, Mario de Andrade, exchanged letters with Quintanilla while the Mexican diplomat lived in Rio. Quintanilla followed Mário de Andrade's newspaper articles in that period and commented on *Macunaíma* in one of his five letters now in Mário de Andrade's papers in ISEB in São Paulo.

27. I owe the discovery of this beautiful poem to Rodolfo Mata and Regina Crespo, who mentioned it in "Imágenes de Brasil en la Literatura Mexicana" in *La Jornada* in 2001.

28. In the original in Spanish, "¡Que se apague unos instantes la luz / de la Bahía de Guanabara / la líquida luz del cielo / la líquida luz del mar!"

29. The first edition of *Romances del Río de Enero* (Maastrich: Halcyon, 1933) was ordered by Reyes himself; he gave a signed copy to president Getúlio Vargas. The book was included in the tenth volume of *Obras Completas* (385–402).

30. In the original, "dar las espaldas a las dichosas libertades—no son más que abandono."

31. An exception is the superb "Yerbas del Tarahumara," comparable to the best Brazilian *modernista* poetry in its renewed reading of Romantic *indigenista* literature.

32. This is particularly true because the most accessible version of the book, in Reyes's tenth volume of his *Obras Completas*, removes the quotation marks that set apart the word *devagar* [*despacio* in Spanish]. The editor must have decided on this due to Reyes's own inconsistency in this gesture of differentiation between the two languages throughout *Romances del Río de Enero*.

33. In the original in Spanish, "Río de Enero, Río de Enero / fuíste río y eres mar / lo que recibes con ímpetu / lo devuelves 'devagar.'"

34. In the original, "una como ley del péndulo, una oscilación, una bifurcación de emociones. La idea—siempre—parte y llega a término; luego vuelve atrás y se anula. Si fuere posible, destacarlo en la estrofa en la estrofa apendicular de cada romance; hacerlo en el balanceo de la frase."

35. In the original in Spanish, "Aqui se ha perdido un hombre: / dígalo quien lo encontrar. / Entre los hombres bogaba, / ya no lo distingue nadie."

36. Reyes also donated in the name of the Mexican state a garden of cacti to the Jardim Botânico as mentioned in chapter 3.

37. Both camphor and rue are traditionally used in Brazil to ward off the evil eye [*olho gordo*].

38. In the original in Spanish, "'ese hiato que divide nuestras dos culturas,' y de que fue para mí una triste manifestación el silencio absoluto que acogió en el Brasil mi librito de poemas *Romances de Río de Enero*, todo él consagrado a Río y escrito con el corazón y la cabeza. Tal vez lo reedite yo en estos dias, pues la primera edición de 300 ejemplares, hecha en Maastricht por Stols, se agotó pronto y realmente no llegó al público." This letter from Alfonso Reyes is among Ribeiro Couto's papers, currently located in the archives at the Casa de Rui Barbosa in Rio de Janeiro.

39. In a letter from Bandeira to Reyes dated March 29, 1950, Bandeira already refers a similar complaint by Reyes, probably in a previous letter. Bandeira promises to write one day about the book and quotes from his *Literatura Hispano-Americana* (1949), in which he had mentioned Reyes approvingly.

40. In the original, "os mais belos versos que já inspirou a algum poeta a paisagem de nosso Rio."

41. In 2011 the Consejo Nacional para la Cultura y las Artes (Conaculta) acquired García Terrés's outstanding personal library for the new Biblioteca de México José Vasconcelos in the Centro Histórico.

42. *Poesía en Movimiento: México, 1915–1966* was edited by Octavio Paz, Ali Chumacero, and José Emilio Pacheco and Homero Aridjis, two young poets at the time. The decision to mix young and established authors of a certain tendency, vaguely defined as a poetry that "es búsqueda, mutación, y no simple aceptación de la herencia" may have been motivated by the publication of Carlos Monsiváis's much more comprehensive *La Poesía Mexicana del Siglo XX,* also in 1966.

43. In the original in Spanish, "Al desembarcar en Río de Janeiro, además del paisaje faustuoso, me aguardaban días de más o menos enloquecido carnival, quemantes mañanas a la orilla del mar (a unos pasos de mi residencia en el llamado Jardín de Alá, tenía yo las playas de Leblon e Ipanema) y un puñado de gente afable."

44. In the preface to *Lyrical Ballads* Wordsworth defines poetry as "the spontaneous overflow of powerful feelings: it takes its origin from emotion recollected in tranquility" ("Preface to Lyrical Ballads," 151).

45. This book was published in Brazil in 2004 as *Livros Demais!* by the publisher Summus.

46. Another peculiarity of Gabriel Zaid is that he frequently revises his published poems into new versions. Zaid made several changes in several of his poems when he gathers them in the anthology *Cuestionario: Poemas 1951–1976* and includes in this book two or even three versions of the same poem.

47. Pacheco has won the following prizes: Xavier Villaurrutia (1973), José Asunción Silva (1996), José Donoso (2001), Octavio Paz (2003), Ramón López Velarde (2003), Alfonso Reyes (2003), Pablo Neruda (2004), García Lorca (2005), Reina Sofía (2009), and Cervantes (2009).

48. In the original in Spanish, "que otros llamen a esto selección natural // Para mí es el horror del mundo."

49. In the original in Spanish, "El siglo XX no cree en la felicidad ni en la victoria."

50. A paradigmatic example of this procedure is the poem "Tierra," in which Pacheco suggests a metaphorical link between the brutal repression of the protesters in 1968 and the violence in Aztec, colonial, independent, and revolutionary past in Mexico.

51. In the original in Spanish, "Como cae la lluvia sobre el mar, / al ritmo en que sin pausa se desploma, / así vamos fluyendo hacia la muerte."

52. In the original in Spanish, "Cada ciudad en la que he vivido tiene su libro. Hay un libro escrito en Washington, otro en Río de Janeiro,

uno en Londres, otro en Puerto Rico. ( ... ) Todo está presente en la poesía y de manera muy especial, los viajes, eso de andar como caracol con la casa a cuestas."

53. In the original in Spanish, "Los comerciantes venden / su enlatada alegria / y detrás de los gritos / afila los colmillos / el vampiro banquero."

54. In the original in Spanish, "Sin embargo los cuerpos, / la danza y las miradas, / la carcajada inmensa, / la fantasia de trapo, / tienen del viejo rito / vivisimos harapos."

55. This book features essays about Gregório de Mattos, Sousândrade, Raul Pompeia, Murilo Mendes, Gilberto Freyre, Lucio Cardoso, Clarice Lispector, João Almino, Rubem Fonseca, Ana Cristina César, Francisco Alvim, Armando Freitas Filho, Villa-Lobos, Aleijadinho, and Burle Marx.

56. In the original in Spanish, "no acabo de saber si Cervantes escribe en portugués, gallego, galaico-portugués, o un macarrónico de su propia invención." Zaid's review, first published in the magazine *Vuelta* in April 1983 is a classic example of the nasty `habit of hiding the painfully destructive criticism under false compliments, emphasizing Cervantes as an "oddity" in Mexican poetry and wondering on the unlike situation of a poet who finds recognition at the age of 44.

57. The medal instituted in 1963 by the Itamaraty (Brazil's diplomatic service) is given as recognition for relevant services to the nation.

58. In the original in Spanish, "sé que sólo habré vivido / en dos países que he querido ( ... ) son el mismo / en su lengua y en este mi espejismo."

59. Lyra first came to Mexico with Stan Getz's band and decided to stay. There he met his US wife, Kate (not "Katy") Lyra, when she auditioned for the TV version of his Mexican production of *Pobre Menina Rica*, a musical with lyrics by the poet Vinicius de Moraes. The show's libretto was translated by Cervantes, Álvaro Mutis and Gabriel García Márquez (Lyra, 123). Cervantes and Lyra also worked with the translation of Lyra's songs in his two Mexican albums, *Carlos Lyra* (1967) and *Saravá* (1970) (accompanied by Mexican musicians). Lyra was rehearsing a musical version of Lope de Vega's *Fuenteovejuna* at Tlatelolco with director José Luiz Ibañez when the massacre took place in 1968. He also staged "*O Dragão e a Fada,*" Lyra's musical for children. Several important Bossa Nova musicians left Brazil for Mexico in the 1960s, either for political reasons or simply because there was a good market for them in Mexico. In the liner notes of Lyra's *Saravá!* the bassist Luis Gusmão explains, "The market for work in Rio and São Paulo was horrible, as much in terms of recording sessions as in shows. To make things worse, the festivals were on the decline, with bossa substituted by the Jovem Guarda and by Tropicalismo on the new TV programs. There was the terror of AI-5, and many people wanted

to get out of Brazil for a variety of reasons. So when we discovered the interest of the entrepreneurs and businessmen and the Mexican public for our sound, there was a huge migration of artists." Among them were the master of Bossa Nova João Gilberto, who recorded a superb album also accompanied by Mexican musicians with Bossa Nova versions of classics such as "Besame Mucho" and "Farolito" (Mello 67).

60. The concept appears in Anthony G. Amsterdam and Jerome Brumer's *Minding the Law—How the Courts Rely on Storytelling, and How Their Stories Change the Ways We Understand the Law—and Ourselves.*

## 5 Érico Veríssimo's Journey into Mexico

1. The trilogy is composed of *O Continente* (1949), *O Retrato* (1951) and *O Arquipélago* (1962).

2. In the original in Portuguese, "se costumava dizer que no Brasil só dois escritores poderiam viver da pena: ele [Veríssimo] e Jorge Amado" (Pesavento 16).

3. Érico Veríssimo's long relationship with English dates from his teenage years when he studied at a boarding school of the Brazilian Episcopal [stet] in Cruzeiro do Sul. Veríssimo's father had even planned to send him to Scotland for college, but the family could not afford it. Among the occupations the young Veríssimo undertook were teaching English, and in the 1930s and 1940s translating numerous important authors such as Aldous Huxley, John Steinbeck, and Somerset Maugham for the *Editora Globo.*

4. This book, dedicated to Thornton Wilder, ends with a "Diálogo com o Leitor" [Dialogue with the Reader] in which Veríssimo expounds on the character and psychology of the American and the prospects for future relations of the United States with Brazil.

5. The problems with the *Estado Novo* begin in 1939 when the Departamento de Imprensa e Propaganda (DIP) censures Veríssimo's radio programs. In 1943 the Catholic priest Leonardo Fritzer violently attacked Veríssimo's novel *E o Resto é Silêncio* and publicly pleaded with the dictator Getúlio Vargas to burn Veríssimo's books and have the writer expelled from Brazil.

6. This highly readable small manual—at the very least an interesting sample of what was the canon in Brazil in the 1940s—is already marked by the rhetoric of modesty and bonhomie that Veríssimo uses in *México—História duma Viagem.*

7. This book repeats the basic structure of *Gato Preto em Campo de Neve,* except that now Veríssimo is with his family and actually lives in the United States. This time there are several dialogues with an imaginary character called Tobias to discuss every aspect of American culture from the perspective of a curious Brazilian reader.

8. In 1969 Érico Veríssimo published yet another travel memoir, *Israel em Abril* [Israel in April], an account of his 19-day visit as an official guest to the country in 1966.

9. The translated book, entitled simply *Mexico* does not have any of the drawings that illustrated the Brazilian editions, but features twelve photographs by Vladimir Sladon and four by Bernard G. Silberstein and Rapho Guillumette. It was translated by the eminent Linton Lomas Barrett, professor of Romance languages, editor of *Five Centuries of Spanish Literature: from El Cid through the Golden Age* (1962) and translated three novels by Veríssimo: *Tempo e o Vento* [*Time and the Wind*] in 1951, *A Noite* [*Night*] in 1956, and *O Senhor Embaixador* [*His Excellency, the Ambassador*] in 1967.

10. In the original, "oferece uma densidade estilística talvez superior à maior parte de seus romances e comparável à do texto dos dois volumes de *O Tempo e o Vento*."

11. In the original, "na esfera intellectual (...) os representantes do México eram os mais bravos *peleadores*, os mais encarniçados polemistas e os que mais dificilmente se conformavam com a derrota."

12. Paul Westheim fled Europe and arrived in Mexico in 1941 and his *Arte Antiguo de México* had been published in 1950, six years before Veríssimo's trip. Westheim's method of "captar fenómenos artísticos desde sus fundamentos espirituales y psíquicos" was a form of applied study of national character.

13. Another eminent exile from Spain who worked at Alfonso Reyes's El Colegio de México, the Galician Ramón Iglesia [1905–1948] in 1942 published *Cronistas e Historiadores de la Conquista de México—El Ciclo de Hernán Cortés* (a second edition would not come out until 1972). Iglesia compares Cortés's letters and the versions of the conquest by González Fernández de Oviedo, Pedro Mártir de Anglería, and Francisco López de Gómara. Iglesia was also responsible for an important edition of Bernal Díaz del Castillo's *Verdadera Historia de la Conquista de Nueva España* but, contrary to his own previous views, defended Gómara's version for giving Cortés his due. Iglesia died at the age of 43 while teaching as a visiting professor in Wisconsin.

14. In the original, "um escritor judeu apologista do callismo." Callismo refers to the president Plutarco Elías Calles, whom Vasconcelos hated with great passion.

15. Born in the state of Alagoas in 1910 and a member of the generation of northeastern intellectuals who shaped the thirties in Brazil, Aurélio Buarque de Holanda is famous for his *Novo Dicionário da Lingua Portuguesa*, widely used and known in Brazil simply as the "Aurélio." Of great importance were also the five volumes of the *Mar de Histórias—Antologia do Conto Mundial* Aurélio Buarque de Holanda edited together with Paulo Rónai. He was elected to the Academia Brasileira de Letras in 1961 and died in Rio de Janeiro in 1989.

16. Luis Guillermo Piazza was born in Córdoba, Argentina in 1921 and moved to Mexico in 1951, where he was secretary general of the Acción Cultural del Acuerdo OEA-UNESCO-Gobierno de México and advisor to the president of the Human Rights Commission and cultural advisor of the Unión Panamericana later called OEA. Living in Mexico since then, Piazza founded the Editorial Novaro, famous for its pioneering role in publishing comics and for the creation of the literary prize Novela México. He wrote extensively for newspapers and magazines such as the *Revista Mexicana de Literatura, Vogue, Excelsior,*" and *El Financiero* until he died in 2007. Among his many books, Piazza wrote novels (*La Siesta*, 1956, *Los Hombres y las Cosas Solo Querian Jugar*, 1963, and *La Mafia*, 1968), plays (*El Tuerto de Oro*, 1963). In 1964, Piazza wrote *El País Más Viejo del Mundo*, his own essay about Mexico's national character.

17. Clodomir Vianna Moog was born in São Leopoldo in 1906 and participated in the political campaign of the Aliança Liberal that led to the revolution of 1930. In 1932 his support of the armed revolt against Getulio Vargas's government cost him two years of detention in the north of the country. After several acclaimed novels (*Um Rio Imita o Reno* won the Graça Aranha prize in 1938) and literary essays (*Eça de Queiróz e o Século XIX, Heróis da Decadência, Uma Interpretação da Literatura Brasileira*), Vianna Moog was elected to the Academia Brasileira de Letras in 1945 at the age of thirty-nine. Vianna Moog is known nowadays mostly for his 1954 essay *Bandeirantes e Pioneiros,* comparing Brazil and the United States, where he lived from 1946 to 1950. In 1952 he moved to Mexico and lived there for more than ten years. Vianna Moog returned to Brazil in 1969 and died in Rio de Janeiro in 1987.

18. In Portuguese, "Possivelmente um monstrengo" (74).

19. In the original, "disserta sobre a grande dicotomia mexicana: indigenismo e hispanismo. E, distraído, entra na contra-mão numa rua." Surprisingly, in 1962 Moog published *Tóia*, a novel that seems to fit the description of the "monstrengo" he and Veríssimo imagined, except for being penned by a single author. Barely disguising its hybrid intent, Moog's novel, which we briefly mentioned in chapter 1, tells the story of a Brazilian diplomat who is writing an essay about Mexico. There is what could be seen as a stab at Veríssimo's book when the protagonist criticizes travel books, which "Como gênero literário, podia ser sumamente interessante ( ... ) mas não passava de uma categoria literária de segunda ordem ( ... ) acessível demais para não lhe tornar suspeito. Apressado, vanglorioso, quase sempre pedante, suficiente e charlatanesco, mais de carpintaria que de criação, tinha-se banalizado ( ... ), tanto se desmoralizara na reportagem e na sociologia do turismo ( ... ) O mal que faziam esses andadores de mundos travestidos de sociólogos! A soma de equívocos, de malentendidos e de irritações a que davam lugar!" (*Tóia* 148–149).

20. Ermilo Abreu Gómez was born in Mérida, Yucatán in 1894 and published several critical articles in the famous magazine *Contemporáneos*. Abreu Gómez edited the complete poetry of Sor Juana Inés de la Cruz—some of his scholarship was cited in chapter 1—and taught in universities such as Illinois University and Middlebury College in the United States and the UNAM in Mexico. He also wrote historical novels such as *Canek* (1940) and was made member of the Academia Mexicana in 1963. Abreu Gómez lived in the United States from 1947 to 1960, where he worked at the Pan American Union together with Érico Veríssimo. He died in Mexico City in 1971.

21. In the original, "um homem raro, dum vigor e duma lucidez extraordinários, dum entusiasmo contagiante—alegre, inquieto, franco, o melhor dos companheiros" (171).

22. In a note toward the end of this chapter Veríssimo explains that he did not take down the interviews with Vasconcelos verbatim but reproduced "com a mais absoluta fidelidade" (206) Vasconcelos's words, and the passages that were in his book were taken from *Breve Historia de México* for that purpose, with the author's consent.

23. In the original, "os historiadores norte-americanos, agentes indiretos do protestantismo que querem apagar toda a marca do espanhol na América!"

24. It suffices to list three examples of the late Vasconcelos's polemical views. In order to explain Santa Anna's defeat by Zachary Taylor, Vasconcelos says that "it suffices ( … ) to compare his strong head of Roman conqueror with the narrow forehead and the squinting eyes of Santa Anna" (181). The French imperialist adventure in Mexico is described as "the magnificent dream of making Mexico the stepping stone of a Latin resurrection in the world" (187). And the Cristera Wars, are solely caused by Calles, who "with his Turkish hatred of all things Christian, unleashed again the religious war" (184).

25. In the original in Portuguese, "[ele] era ( … ) grande orador, falava horas inteiras com um improviso vigoroso e imaginativo e sem cansar o público … Siqueiros empolgava a assistência, formava um verdadeiro campo magnético no auditório e conservava esse campo magnético com o mesmo potencial durante as horas que duravam as suas orações, nunca em nenhum momento esmorecia ( … ) ele não falava para explicar e sim para acabar uma coisa que ele havia começado plasticamente. ( … ) As suas ideias políticas só uma ou outra vez afetaram a cor e a forma dos seus argumentos—coisa rara em elementos radicais." In her newspaper columns, Tarsila do Amaral (1886–1973) mentions Siqueiros, "a very interesting speaker" (48) and his lecture in São Paulo at least three times in different contexts over a period of 15 years in 1934 (47–49), 1936 (81–83), and 1940 (419–421).

26. In the original in Portuguese, "sentido plástico do monumental;" "capaz de todas as violências e todos os cavalheirismos;" and "misto de artista do Renascimento, caudilho, agitador politico, e profeta."

27. In Portuguese, "se Rivera na sua pintura fala um *nahuatl* afrancesado, Tamayo se expressa num francês de má construção e pior pronúncia" (226).

28. In the original in Portuguese, "pelo excesso de figuras alegóricas, e principalmente pelo caráter circunstancial de muitos desses símbolos. Parece-me que os símbolos e mitos astecas ou maias oferecem menos riscos, pois não creio que o tempo possa alterar-lhes o sentido."

29. *Retrato de la Burguesía* was conceived to be executed by a team composed of three Mexican and three Spanish artists. The Spaniards, Josep Renau, Miguel Prieto, and Antonio Rodríguez Luna, were among the first of the many exiles who went to live in Mexico after Franco's victory in 1939. Siqueiros proposes that the six artists sacrifice their personal styles in favor of "stylistic or integral unity" (157) and, as a result, Prieto and Luna leave. In May 1940, the three Mexicans in the team, Siqueiros, Antonio Pujol, and Luis Arenal, participate in a failed attempt to kill Trotsky and had to go into hiding from the police. Ironically, political changes in the Union and in the Mexican government force Renau to tone down some of the original allusions in the mural, erasing flags that more clearly identified the fascist characters. Siqueiros would eventually be arrested and sent into exile in Chile.

30. In the original, "não acho que o artista *deva* fazer arte *engagé*, política, interessada; penso que ele *poderá*, se quiser, seguir esse caminho."

31. In Portuguese, "um Plymouth fabricado num país onde Siqueiros dificilmente encontraria assunto de drama nas fábricas em que cada operário possui um carro tão bom quanto este e um salário que lhe permite um nível de vida melhor que o da classe media Mexicana" (226).

32. In the Brazilian book, "enfarado da burocracia e do mundo que o cerca" (11).

33. In the Brazilian book, "que funciona como uma máquina eletrônica de selecionar fichas" (13).

34. The three years and five months when Érico Veríssimo was the director of cultural affairs at the Pan-American Union (later to be called Organization of American States, OAS) are written about in the last chapter "O Mausoléu de Mármore" (310–349) in *Solo de Clarineta*, the first volume of Veríssimo's unfinished memoirs.

35. In Portuguese, "um cartão postal colorido, lustroso, encantador, pois não, mas desprovido da terceira dimensão" (13).

36. An attentive reader may find a contradiction in the fact that Veríssimo's two previous memoirs (*Um Gato Preto em Campo de Neve* and *A Volta do Gato Preto*) were written precisely about the first of Veríssimo's two extended stays in the United States—quite an output for someone suffering from writer's block. However, Veríssimo thinks of himself first and foremost as a novelist and one could say

that these incursions into this particular genre—the travelogue—is indeed the result of a novelist's writer's block.

37. The first chapter of Veríssimo's unfinished second volume of memoirs describes how the writer, back in Brazil, doodles on a blank page and suddenly starts drawing hats he subsequently identifies as Mexican sombreros. The sketch becomes a scene of the entrance of the faithful to a Sunday Mass in Mexico and Veríssimo feels "uma vontade irresistível de escrever minhas impressões de viagem à patria de Orozco, Rivera, Siqueiros, e Juan Rulfo" (7) [an irresistible urge to write my impressions from the trip to the country of Orozco, Rivera, Siqueiros, and Juan Rulfo].

38. In Portuguese, "o relógio é um elemento decorativo e o tempo, assunto de poesia" (13).

39. In Portuguese, "um certo tipo especial de irritação" (13).

40. In Portuguese, "desordem latino-americana, das imagens, sons, e cheiros do nosso mundinho" (13).

41. In Portuguese, "Céus! Será que estou ficando metafísico? Positivamente, William Shakespeare, preciso urgentemente de umas férias" (13).

42. In the original, "sinto uma espécie de cordial irritação ante esta cidade insubmissa que não se deixa classificar, que repele todos os adjetivos que lhe ofereço, apresentando-se-nos ora moderna ora antiga; agora encantadora, logo depois sinistra; aqui bela e logo ali adiante feia...Afinal de contas, em que ficamos? Não ficamos. O melhor é caminhar, beber o México, absorver o México, pelos olhos, pelos poros, no ar que respiramos, nas vozes que ouvimos, nos cheiros que nos entram pelas narinas–gasolina queimada, pó de asfalto, tortilla, frituras, fragrância de flores e ervas..."

43. In Portuguese, "erguida sobre o cadaver de Tenochtitlán assassinada por Cortés e seus soldados ( .... ) "a aura de drama" ( ... ) "esse tom escuroso, ominoso" (42).

44. In Portuguese, "eu sabia que o epílogo deste livro não podia ser feliz! Estou talvez condenado a oscilar o resto da vida entre esses dois amores, sem saber exatamente o que desejo mais, se o mundo mágico ou o mundo lógico. Só me resta uma esperança de salvação. É a de que, entre a tese americana e a antítese mexicana, o Brasil possa vir a ser um dia a desejada síntese. / Y quién sabe?" (299).

45. In the original in Portuguese, "de ar melancólico e voz de oboé."

46. In the original in Portuguese, "apresentam um aspecto façanhudo e agressivo, e vivem numa atitude de franca hostilidade com relação ao ambiente."

47. In Portuguese, "Quantos anos precisarei para digerir o México? Quantas vidas devia viver para compreendê-lo? Mas um consolo me resta e basta. Não preciso mais nem um minuto para amá-lo" (298).

48. In the original in Portuguese, "uma vida só não basta para compreender o México, tocar sequer o coração do seu mistério. Não estou

escrevendo sobre esse país porque tenha desvendado o seu segredo, mas sim porque o amo e porque desejo entendê-lo, ou pelo menos senti-lo profundamente. Não creio que jamais alguém possa dizer a última palavra sobre o mexicano..."

49. In the original in Portuguese, "fosse como fosse, eu me sentia identificado com aquela terra e seu povo. Bom identificado talvez não fosse a palavra exata. O melhor seria dizer que eu não conhecia o México, mas amava-o. Não era a mesma coisa? Mas é claro que era! O amor, como a arte, é uma das mais legítimas formas de conhecimento."

## 6   João Guimarães Rosa between Life and Death in His Own Páramo

1. A different, shorter version of this chapter was published in Spanish as "El Páramo de João Guimarães Rosa" in *Juan Rulfo: Otras Miradas* (439–459).

2. In the original, "*Eu cá não perco ocasião de religião. Aproveito de todas. Bebo água de todo rio... Uma só, para mim é pouca, talvez não chegue*" (*Grande Sertão: Veredas*, 32).

3. In the original, "uma última revisão do autor" (*Estas Estórias*, IX). Keeping in mind that all of Guimarães Rosa's books, since their first editions, show the great care that the author took in the selection and organization of the texts, I believe that, since there is a great inequity in the degree of completeness among the texts presumably chosen for this book, this is sufficient proof that *Estas Estórias* was still far from being ready for publication at the time of its author's death.

4. In the original, "*peça mais trabalhada*" (*Relembramentos* 379).

5. Two key stories that come close to Guimarães Rosa's "Páramo" are "*São Marcos*" from *Sagarana* and "*Espelho*" from *Primeiras Estórias*. In addition, among Guimarães Rosa's work one can find narrator-protagonists who hide their identities as well as their motives in the author's only novel, *Grande Sertão: Veredas,* and also in one of his most important stories, "*Meu Tio o Iauareté*." We can still find narrators like that in other key texts from this work, if we think about the voices in the four prologues to *Tutaméia* as characters rather than as declarations of the actual author.

6. See the summary of data from the 2000 Population Census published on June 27, 2003 on the *Instituto Brasileiro de Geografia e Estatísca*'s website: http://www.ibge.gov.br/home/presidencia/noticias/27062003 censo.shtm

7. *Spiritism* also plays a significant role in *Grande Sertão: Veredas,* where Quelemém, friend, confidante, and advisor of the protagonist, Riobaldo, follows the doctrine "de Cardéque" (p. 32). For a brief panorama of Spiritism in Brazil, see Sandra Jacqueline Stoll's book, *Espiritismo à Brasileira*, Editora da Universidade de São Paulo, São Paulo, 2003.

8.  In that narrator/protagonist one can see an ironic quote from *South American Meditations* by Hermann Keyserling (see Note 10). Victoria Ocampo's guest of honor for a year in Argentina, Keyserling narrates his experience with altitude sickness in Bolivia, designated by the term *puna*, with involuntarily comical tones precisely because of his combination of pseudoscience, egocentrism, and hypochondria: "The most interesting thing in South America is the *puna*"—that alpine disease which occurs within the exact limits of determinate beds of ore and is evidently caused by their emanations. Thus I entered in its range with an inward disposition for it. Nevertheless, I was totally unprepared for what actually happened. To try to explain the *puna* in terms of altitude is as foolish and irreverent as to try to speculate upon various sorts of matches, in order to gain some knowledge of Hell. Within a very short time my organic equilibrium was destroyed. First the organs proper of balance failed me; then followed symptoms of cerebral inflammation; kidneys and liver were gravely affected; the salivary glands refused to work; the heart alone held out. This was more than an illness, it was a real disintegration of my organism— just as a stone disintegrates in hydrofluoric acid. [ ... ] During that illness I felt myself to be a part of the Cosmic Process as intimately as the embryo, were it endowed with consciousness, would experience itself as an element of a superindividual organic evolution. Then did I realize: I am Earth and a pure force of the Earth. I am Earth not merely understood as material: this nonego is an essential part of that which I experience myself to be. In the melting-pot of the *puna*, in the constellation of earthly elements of a power far greater than my own. And had I not quitted the scene of action, either death or mutation would have been the end" (*South American Meditations*, 8, 9). The pathetic and comical aspects of the protagonist/narrator of "Páramo" are seen here, and it wouldn't be impossible to classify his behavior also as a combination of pseudoscience, mysticism, ego-centrism, and hypochondria.

9.  In the original in Portuguese, "um homem, ainda moço, ao cabo de uma viagem a ele imposta ( ... ) se viu chegado ao degredo em cidade estrangeira."

10. In the original in Portuguese, "ali me recebi."

11. "Mountain sickness (in Spanish), or altitude sickness, with incred-ible headaches and nausea" (Martins Costa, 19). The subject of the Andes already appeared discretely in Guimarães Rosa's work in an odd piece called "*Terrae Vis*" published in the newspaper *Diário de Minas* on January 25, 1953 and included in the posthumous book that gathers some of his journalistic contributions: "Em duas ocasiões, voando sobre os Andes, a uma altura entre 4 e 5 mil metros, não deixei de interceptar a torva soturna emissão daquelas lombadas cinéreas, desertas e imponentes. Juro que não se tratava de sugestão visual, mas de uma energia invariável, penetrante e

direta, paralisadora de qualquer alegria. Por isso, não me espantou ouvir, tempos depois, esse slogan repetidíssimo: '*En la cárcel de los Andes...*' E, do que sabia, mais me certifiquei, quando vim a ler nas *Meditações Sul-Americanas* de Keyserling: "Nas alturas das cordilheiras, cujas jazidas minerais exalam ainda hoje emanações como as que antigamente metamorfosearam faunas e floras, tive consciência da minha própria mineralidade" (*Ave, Palavra* 323). One can observe two terms that will appear in "Páramo" in the above excerpt from "*Terrae Vis*": the uncommon adjective "*cinéreo*" and the slogan "*En la cárcel de los Andes...*" (In the prison of the Andes).

12. Once in Mexico Guimarães Rosa impressed Gabriel García Márquez and Álvaro Mutis with an intimate knowledge of Bogotá's urban scenery when they met in the house of Guimarães Rosa's translator Virginia Fagnani Wey. Before the two Colombian writers arrived, Guimarães Rosa had been complaining bitterly about his years in Bogota to the point of worrying his hosts, but when the two Colombians arrived Guimarães Rosa greeted them asking for news about a famous vagabond who used to roam the streets of Bogota and delighted them with several tales of the street life in the Colombian city.

13. In the original,"mentira nenhuma, porque esta aqui é uma estória inventada, e não é um caso acontecido."

14. In the original, "la literatura es una mentira que dice la verdad."

15. In the original, "velha, colonial, de vetusta época, e triste, talvez a mais triste de todas" and "nela estarei preso, longamente, sob as pedras quase irreais e as nuvens que ensaiam esculturas efêmeras."

16. In the original, "E há, sobranceiros e invisíveis, os páramos—que são elevados pontos, os nevados e ventisqueiros da cordilheira, por onde têem de passar os caminhos de transmonte, que para aquí trazem gelinvérnicos! Os páramos, de onde os ventos atravessam. Lá é um canil de ventos, zunimensos e lugubruivos. De lá o frio desce, umidíssimo, para esta gente, estas ruas, estas casas. De lá a desolação paramuna, vir-me-ia a morte. Não a morte final—equestre, ceifeira, ossosa, tão atardalhadora. Mas a outra, *aquela*."

17. In the original, "'Aquí, pelo menos a gente come, a gente espera, em todo caso. Não é como nos Llanos...' Nos primeiros tempos fora tentar a vida num lugarejo perdido nas tórridas planuras, em penível desconforto, quase de só de mandioca e bananas se alimentavam. Lá choravam. Longe, em sua pátria, era a guerra. Homens louros como ele, se destruíam, de grande, frio modo se matavam. Ali, nos Llanos, índios de escuros olhos olhavam-no, tão longamente, tão afunda-damente, tão misteriosamente—era como se o próprio sofrimento pudesse olhar-nos."

18. In the original, "Contudo, às vezes sucede que morramos, de algum modo, espécie diversa de morte, imperfeita e temporária no próprio

decurso desta vida. Morremos, morre-se, outra palavra não haverá que
defina tal estado, essa estação crucial. É um obscuro finar-se, con-
tinuando, um trespassamento que não põe termo natural à existência, mas em que a gente se sente o campo de operação profunda e
desmanchadora, de íntima transmutação precedida de certa parada,
sempre com uma destruição prévia, um dolorido esvaziamento; nós
mesmos, então, nos estranhamos."

19. In the original, "sem peso nem sexo."

20. In the original, "nem uma fimbria de nossas almas se roça."

21. For a quick analysis of this disease, see the article "Cotard's Syndrome:
Analysis of 100 Cases" by R. Luque and G.E. Barrios.

22. In *The Spirits' Book*, Kardec mentions different degrees of separation between the body and soul all the way up to their complete
separation, as part of a process that can be quite long and even painful. In addition, Kardec alludes to moments of partial separation or
isolation between the body and soul as an explanation for lethargy,
epilepsy, and sleepwalking. See *O Livro dos Espíritos*, especially the
second part, chapters 3 and 8.

23. For an interesting reading of *Dom Casmurro, Pedro Páramo, Grande
Sertão: Veredas,* and *100 Years of Solitude,* see Paul Dixon's *Reversible
Readings: Ambiguity in Four Latin American Novels.*

24. In the original, "*um mundo de odio.*"

25. In the original, "o meu espírito se soubesse a um tempo em
diversos mundos, perpassando-se igualmente em planos entre si
apartadíssimos."

26. "A channel through which more hate was brought into the world."

27. *Goetia* or *Goeteia* is the invocation of evil demons, in contrast
with *Magia,* the invocation of good demons. At the beginning of
the twentieth century, Aleister Crowley exposed the medieval gri-
moire titled *Goetia* in his book *The Book of the Goetia of Solomon
the King* complementing Samuel Mathers's translation. In his notes
regarding the *De Magorum Daemonimania* by Jean Bodin, Henry
Charles Lea indicates the ancient roots of the term when he says that:
"The ancient authorities Iamblichus, Proclus, Plotinus, Porphyry,
and Julian the Apostate, speak of *Magia* as the invocation of good
demons and *Goetia* as that of the evil ones" (*Materials Towards a
History of Witchcraft,* 557).

28. In the original, "El polvo / que nos mancha la cara / es el vestigio /
de un incesante crimen," from the poem "Tierra" (*Tarde o temprado,*
85).

29. In the original, "É terrível estar morto, como às vezes sei que
estou—de outra maneira. Com essa falta de alma. Respiro mal; o
frio me desfaz. É como na prisão de um espelho. Num espelho em
que meus olhos soçobraram. O espelho, tão cislúcido, somente. Um
espelho abaixo de zero."

30. The revelation of a fragment of Guimarães Rosa's diary that was written in Germany in which the author expresses his irritation with reading Machado de Assis's work caused quite a scandal in Brazil. Guimarães Rosa writes: "Não pretendo mais lê-lo por vários motivos: acho-o antipático de estilo, cheio de atitudes para 'embasbacar o indígena'; lança mão de artifícios baratos, querendo forçar a nota da originalidade; anda sempre no mesmo trote pernóstico, o que torna tediosa a leitura. Quanto às idéias, nada mais do que uma desoladora dissecação do egoísmo, e, o que é pior, da mais desprezível forma do egoísmo: o egoísmo dos introvertidos inteligentes" [I don't wish to read him anymore for various reasons: I find his style obnoxious, full of attitudes to 'impress the indigenous'; he uses cheap artifices, forcefully searching for a hint of originality; he always moves along at the same vain trot, which makes the reading tedious. With respect to the ideas, they are nothing more than a devastating dissection of selfishness, and, what is worse, the most despicable form of selfishness: the selfishness of the intelligent introverts.]. Neither the absolutely private nature of a brief observation nor the fact that we are dealing with a note written by a young and still unpublished author was taken into consideration in order that a false and opportunistic rivalry between the two authors could be promoted in 2008, the 100th anniversary of Machado de Assis's death and Guimarães Rosa's birth. The stupidest moment of this entire publicity stunt occurred when a ridiculous "competition" between the two authors was proposed in a survey in the culture pages of the newspaper *Folha de São Paulo* ("*Entre Deus e o Diabo*"), where, after the opinions of authors and critics, the readers were asked to vote online for which of the two was the "best." It would be much more advantageous to stop spreading literary gossip and making up false rivalries and, instead, attend to the fact that Guimarães Rosa read Machado de Assis with great literary benefit, as is demonstrated by his subtle use of irony at various levels simultaneously. Guimarães Rosa explicitly quotes Machado de Assis on at least one other occasion—besides "*O Espelho*"—in the story "*Carts na Mesa*" (*Ave, Palavra*, 308–311), in which he inverts all of the budgets from the famous story "*A Cartomante*" by Machado de Assis (*O Conto de Machado de Assis*, 205–213).

31. Some well-known *doppelgängers* are those that appear in E.T.A.Hoffman's "The Sandman," Edgar Allan Poe's "William Wilson," Robert Louis Stevenson's "The Strange Case of Dr. Jeckyll and Mr. Hyde" and, in the Latin American sphere, Jorge Luis Borges's "Borges and I" and "August 25th, 1983," as well as Freud's famous study about the subject in his essay "*Das unheimlich.*" For an interesting study about this topic, see "Theories and Practices of the Doppelgänger" by Andrew J. Webber (*The Doppelgänger: Double Visions in German Literature*, 1–55).

32. In the original, "cidade de tumbas e estátuas," and "o mais atrás, após todos. Como um cachorro."

33. In the original, "entre lápides e ciprestes, quase um ninho."

34. In the original, "um asilo em sagrado, passava-se em mim um alívio, de nirvana, um gosto de fim."

35. In the original, "Afinal de lá me vim" and "a um canto discreto, à sombra de um cipreste, e de uma lousa."

36. While discussing Guimarães Rosa's experience in Colombia after presenting a first draft of this work at the inauguration of the Machado de Assis professorship at the Universidad del Claustro de Sor Juana, Valquiria Wey mentioned to me that Guimarães Rosa had told her that one day he had followed a humble funeral cortège through the streets of Bogota (not of a young man, but rather one of a young lady), that after they had arrived, he hid in a far corner of the cemetery, that as he was leaving the cemetery, he came across one of the men who had carried the young lady's casket, that they both spoke of the dead girl and that the man had surprised him by returning to him the book that he had brought, an anthology of poetry in Castilian. Here, I am not attempting to, once again, search for connections between the author's life and his work—the oral account could actually be a mere draft of the fiction itself—but to search for a way of understanding in its complexity the points of contact between life and work in order to read the texts better.

37. In the original, "Na cabeça do Sr. Knopf." In this story Rubem Fonseca, an author who is known for his almost complete public silence, imagines a tense dialogue between a newspaper reporter and caustic actor accused of pornography and exploitation. Obviously, one cannot take Fonseca's opinions to be the same as the fictitious author of *O Anão que era Negro, Padre, Corcunda e Míope* [The Dwarf that was Black, a Catholic Priest, Hunchbacked and Myopic].

38. In the original "*mercado comum das letras latino-americanas / (onde só os brasileiros não vendem nada)*." From the poem "América Latina: Contra-Boom da Poesia" (*O anticrítico*, 159).

39. Guimarães Rosa participated as vice-president of the First Congreso Internacional de Escritores Latinoamericanos (First International Conference of Latin American Writers) in 1965 in Italy, where the Sociedad de Escritores Latinoamericanos (Society of Latin American Writers) was formed, and he also participated, again as vice-president, in the Segundo Congreso Latinoamericano de Escritores (Second Conference of Latin American Writers) in 1967 in Mexico. In Italy in 1965, Guimarães Rosa would give one of his few interviews to the German critic Günter Lorenz. In that long interview, which was published in Buenos Aires before appearing in Brazil, it is made clear that Guimarães Rosa does not see himself as a writer apart from his fellow Spanish-speaking colleagues, even discussing the polemic

between Borges and Asturias about politics and the future of Latin American literature.

40. Eric Nepomuceno, Daniel Sada, and Valquiria Wey spoke to me personally about this trip, which, in the end, was not eccentric at all, and much less "demented."

41. In the original, "La muerte no se reparte como si fuera un bien;" "entonces, ¿qué esperas para morirte? / La muerte, Susana. / Si es nada más eso ya vendrá. No te preocupes;" and "Pero si nosotros nos vamos, ¿quién se llevará a nuestros muertos? Ellos viven aquí y no podemos dejarlos solos."

## 7 Why and for What Purpose Do Latin American Fiction Writers Travel? Silviano Santiago's *Viagem ao México* and *The Roots and Labyrinths of Latin America*

1. A first draft of this text was presented as a paper in the Symposium "Más Allá de la Nación en la Literatura y la Crítica Latino Americana del Siglo XXI" at Yale in 2009, which contained part of this analysis of Silviano Santiago's relations with Mexican literature and culture.

2. In this case there is a visible increase in the number of Brazilians living abroad (either working or studying) especially in Japan, Paraguay, Portugal, and the United States.

3. The unacknowledged model for the project was *Colección Año 0*, Random House-Mondadori's initiative to invite seven young Latin American writers (Roberto Bolaño, Rodrigo Fresán, Santiago Gamboa, Rodrigo Rey Rosa, José Manuel Prieto, Gabi Martínez, Lala Isla, and Hector Abad Faciolince) to write a novel that took place in one designated city. The most successful of that series published in 2000 and 2001 were Bolaño's *Una Novelita Lumpen* and Fresán's *Mantra,* situated in Rome and Mexico City, respectively. Nevertheless, in an interview with Márcia Abos for *O Globo* on May 8, 2008, Tadeu Jungle, a filmmaker involved with *Amores Expressos* called it "um projeto inédito no Brasil e no mundo."

4. The choice ranged from established names such as Sérgio Sant'Anna, Luiz Ruffato, and Bernardo Carvalho to newcomers such as Cecília Gianetti and Antonia Pellegrino.

5. The 1991 legislation proposed by Sérgio Paulo Rouanet, then the minister of culture, allows for companies to invest part of their tax money into "cultural projects" that have been authorized by the government to procure private financing. In the twenty-first century about $800 million a year have been invested by private companies in the arts and humanities in Brazil—practically half-a-dozen Hollywood blockbusters. In view of the polemic in magazines and newspapers, Teixeira gave up the idea of asking for approval to use the law and financed it entirely with private funds.

6. Daniel Galera's *Cordilheira*, which takes place in Buenos Aires, and Luiz Ruffato's *Estive em Lisboa e Lembrei de Você,* were published in

2009. Joca Reiners Terron's *Do Fundo do Poço se Vê a Lua*, located in Cairo, was published in 2010.

7. In *Altas Literaturas*, Leyla Perrone-Moisés analyzes the literary references of writers such as Ezra Pound, T.S. Eliot, Jorge Luis Borges, Octavio Paz, Italo Calvino, Michel Butor, Haroldo de Campos, and Philippe Sollers. Her focus is the formation of Western literary canons and the criteria for the choices of these writers to discuss the thorny issue of literary value and the current conditions for literary production and reception.

8. *The Space In*-Between, a collection of Santiago's essays, has been translated into English and published by Duke University Press in 2001.

9. In the original in Portuguese, "Uma só cabeça e vários tentáculos, várias pernas-tentáculos que se assentam em terras diversas e variados mares, deles sugando o que podem oferecer e ofertando o produto à cabeça de um olho ciclópico, montada em um dorso gigantesco de onde saem braços, de onde saem mãos que selecionam caminhos pelas teclas do computador. A cabeça vive dilacerada pelos tentáculos que se distanciam em busca de novos apoios. Cada novo apoio, se não for uma caravela, é uma terra, se não for uma terra, é uma caravela. Se não for caravela ou terra, é uma tela de computador a ser preenchida.Sou espelho do que me liberta e me aprisiona. Tenho o corpo feito de montanhas, das montanhas onde reina imperiosa uma cabeça, cuja boca proclama que, depois de uma penosa caminhada, o horizonte é acessível e o respirar menos congestionado. De lá é que descubro outro horizonte, outras montanhas, outros horizontes mais vastos e amplos e menos acessíveis pelo caminhar dos pés, o girar das rodas e o zunir das hélices."

10. In the original in Portuguese, "em 1993 Artaud olha Havana pelos meus olhos latino-americanos. Em 1936 eu olho Havana pelos olhos europeus dele."

11. In the original in Portuguese, "as regras de construção desse jogo ficcional são distintas de outros jogos ficcionais; são outras e bem explícitas."

12. Santiago argues that "'Viagem pela hiperrealidade' serve para que de novo coloquemos uma questão que acompanha as relações entre o Velho e o Novo Mundo desde o aparecimento deste último para a consciência ocidental: por que e para que viaja o europeu?" [Travels in Hyperreality serves us to place once again a question that accompanies the relations between the Old and New World since the latter emerged in Western conscience: why and what for do Europeans travel?] (189).

13. In the original, "A viagem do europeu tem uma função predominantemente docente e modernizadora. O europeu viaja, então, como integrante de uma missão cultural e muitas vezes a pedido do país interessado. Traz diploma na bagagem, de preferência universitário."

14. In the original, "Contemporâneo do antropólogo mas caminhando em direção oposta (...) Cansado da esclerose galopante que invadia o palco burguês europeu, Artaud sai à cata de expressões 'teatrais' em que os fundamentos da experiência cênica não tivessem ainda sido abafados pelo processo de comercialização e profissionalização dos tempos modernos. É nesse sentido que, tal um novo Montaigne, faz voltar contra o moribundo teatro europeu (e a seu favor como força de rejuvenescimento) aquele sopro de sagrado e de violência, de mito e rito, que se foi esvaindo do palco ocidental pelo bom comportamento cênico, única e imperiosa exigência do teatro de tipo naturalista e burguês."

15. In the original, "A força espiritual das palavras tinha de ser idêntica à necessidade física da sede e da fome."

16. In the original, "Eco teria de ter a verdadeira curiosidade intelectual de Montaigne, Tocqueville, Artaud, e, em lugar de fazer viagem turística só pelo óbvio americano, peregrinasse também pela sua própria Europa com outra visão de mundo, talvez menos auto-suficiente, certamente menos ingênua e possivelmente menos autoritária. Necessariamente original e, por isso, perfeitamente indispensável."

17. In the original, "Os intelectuais do Novo Mundo (noblesse oblige!) sempre tiveram a coragem de enxergar o que existe de europeu neles. (...) Já não estaríamos começando a responder a uma outra pergunta? Por que e para que viaja o habitante do Novo Mundo?"

18. In the original, "toma nota do paradoxo de uma educação nacional cuja base cultural é tomada de empréstimo."

19. In the original, "colega seu de letras" and "Torres Bodet com gênio."

20. In the original, "basta abrirem a boca para entoar a velha cantilena. Esses latino-americanos são todos uns infelizes em desterro, encantados com as maravilhas da industrialização que não conhecem e da cultura occidental que conhecem como ninguém. Acreditam que as chaminés das fábricas vão nivelar todo o mundo das letras e deixar à mostra as formas ocultas e variadas da opressão capitalista. Mal sabem o que os espera no dia em que não forem mais cópias disformes, mais iguais ao original que tanto invejam."

21. It seems as if this figure's name refers to the ubiquitous bestseller writer and member of the Brazilian Academy of Letters, Paulo Coelho. When asked by the weekly news magazine *Veja* about Paulo Coelho's success in France in 1998 Silviano Santiago said "O público francês é tão medíocre ou pouco sofisticado quanto o grande público de qualquer outro país" and "o fenômeno Paulo Coelho confirma a existência, hoje em dia, de um gosto globalizado e de um mercado de livros globalizado." Santiago published in *Folha de São Paulo* in 2003 an article about the "phenomenon" called "Outubro Retalhado (entre Estocolmo e Frankfurt)" (*O Cosmopolitismo do Pobre*, 74–90).

22. In the original, "Mais e mais me habituo na redação desta narrativa à conversa triangulada. O triângulo nosso é escaleno. Se as palavras dele ocupam o lado maior, cabe às minhas o lado menor. Ao interlocutor cabe o que pode caber, espremido que fica pela assimetria gritante dos dois lados antagônicos do triângulo."

23. In the original, A qualquer preço querem aprisionar a invenção artística deles—/ Nossa invenção, você quer dizer. Anch'io—/—no quartel da história onde ficam aguardando que baixe dos céus o reconhecimento.

24. In the original, "Artaud pára de falar. Me pergunta, tomo nota do que diz, se na verdade penso como Aleixo. Não seria mais fácil se você inventasse essa passagem no romance?"

25. In 1997 Silviano Santiago published a paper comparing Artaud and Cardoza y Aragón titled "Os Astros Ditam o Futuro. A História Impõe o Presente. (Artaud versus Cárdenas)."

26. In the original, "ensinar a desaprender num país como o México, isso não é pouco construtivo?"

27. In the original, "el tenebroso, cuya sola estrella está muerta y cuyo laúd constelado lleva el sol negro de la melancolía."

28. In the original, "confundió por desesperación, el Nuevo Continente con un Nuevo contenido. Algo hay de ello, pero no bastaba a su exigencia absoluta. También mucho de Europa moría en nosotros."

29. In the original, "Quando o cérebro da Europa se cansa, ele gosta de sair a passeio pelas antigas civilizações que não fazem parte de sua tradição, como se, durante essas férias alvissareiras, a massa cinzenta, exposta aos eflúvios do calor dos trópicos, pudesse se desvencilhar do peso que a comprime naquele momento histórico. Antigamente, a Europa viajava para invadir; hoje, como não detém mais o poder econômico e bélico, viaja para incendiar as mentes sensíveis da juventude, para desenvolver nelas o gosto pelas abstrações enfurecidas."

30. In the original in Spanish, respectively, "la sangre India de México (que) conserva un antiguo secreto de la raza" and "caricaturas de la vida."

31. In the original, "una óptica gremial y vanidosa de escritor: el escritor y lo impreso ( … ) como centro del mundo."

32. In the original, "a década de 30 é a mais importante do século XX. Tudo está ali, em miniatura."

33. In the original, "corrompe as relações humanas e profissionais entre estrangeiros e cubanos."

34. In the original, "um invasor útil e desejado" ( … ) "um espaço deselegante e anárquico" ( … ) "dentro da reinante assepsia socialista."

35. In the original, "rito operário" ( … ) "se não foi o tipo de alfabetização em massa praticado na ilha que tornou o cubano crítico e cético quanto aos excessos da oralidade e da confidência."

36. In the original, "o corpo assassinado de Artaud vai renascer. Renascerá sem a antiga personalidade que o tinha conduzido a caminhos poucos

propícios à plena realização. Dali ele sairá liberto das amarras que o prendiam aos antigos costumes e desejos. ( ... ) São os orixás que se congratulam na festa que é deles, que é de todos.Por todo aquele momento, na paz e na dança, na música e no êxtase, nas vozes e no companheirismo, confundem-se Cuba, África e Europa. Abole-se o oceano, apaga-se o tempo da escravidão, brilham peles de um único e maravilhoso tom."

37. In the original, "não o fez para entrar num mundo novo, mas para sair de um mundo falso."

38. In the original, "*Viagem ao México* é um livro ilegível. Chamo-o de meu pequeno *Grande Sertão: Veredas*. Tinha de escrevê-lo, era o que tinha que escrever. A suma dos meus trabalhos."

39. "A viagem de Lévi-Strauss aos trópicos" is illustrative of the trajectory of most of Santiago's critical work before getting published in book form. It is presented first as one of the main conferences in the Associação Brasileira de Literatura Comparada, ABRALIC, in July 2000. Then it is published a first time in the Sunday cultural section of the newspaper *Folha de São Paulo* in September of the same year. Finally the essay is published in book form in *Ora (Direis) Puxar Conversa* in 2006.

40. The dates here are somehow misleading because Santiago works with the thoroughly reviewed and extended final versions of the two essays, respectively the *Raízes do Brasil* from 1948 and *El Laberinto de la Soledad* from 1957.

41. In the original, "la idea de que existe un sujeto único de la historia nacional."

42. In the original in Portuguese, "o México constitui, na obra de Silviano Santiago, um *dispositivo*, quase secreto, porém, muito eficiente, para abandonar os estudos literários e, simultaneamente, introduzir a máquina poética no estudo da cultura" and "as raízes e o labirinto da América Latina encontram, na literatura exausta da contemporaneidade, uma forma de esvaziar os ícones do passado."

43. In the original in Portuguese, "O clube da esquina é este clube sem portas e sem janelas, sem lado de fora, onde se misturam músicos e platéia, onde tudo é amizade, tudo é abertura, entrega e desejo de se soltar, de se libertar. Onde, no meio da rua, no meio da Estrada, se dança, se arma o espetáculo."

44. In the original in Portuguese, "Ah! Sol e chuva na sua estrada / Mas não importa não faz mal / Você ainda pensa e é melhor do que nada / Tudo que você consegue ser ou nada."

## 8 Nelson Pereira dos Santos and the Mexican Golden Age of Cinema

1. "In the 1960s, Glauber Rocha, the most famous member of the *Cinema Novo* generation, claimed Santos as the mentor for the

movement. More recently, Walter Salles, referring to Santos's humanistic approach in the depiction of people's struggles, stated that through his films Santos has taught him the concept of 'human geography' in cinema." http://sensesofcinema.com/2011/great-directors/nelson-pereira-dos-santos/

2. The film had a profound impact on the new generation that was to make the *Cinema Novo* of the 1960s. Carlos Diegues, for instance, claimed that "my decision to make films came after I saw *Rio, 40 Graus* (...) it was everything I imagined Brazilian cinema should be" (Fabris 202). For an extraordinary analysis of the first two movies by Nelson Pereira Santos and their relation to Italian cinema, see Mariarosaria Fabris's *Nelson Pereira dos Santos—Um Olhar Neo-Realista?*

3. These were Joaquim Pedro de Andrade, Miguel Borges, Carlos Diegues, Marcos Farias, and Leon Hirszman.

4. Under the pen name Léo D'Ávila, Rodrigues wrote the dialogue for *Somos Dois,* a musical comedy directed by Rodrigues's brother Milton in 1950. The first cinematic adaptation of Nelson Rodrigues's literary works was *Meu Destino é Pecar,* a melodramatic pulp fiction novel written under the pseudonym Susanna Flag, adapted in 1952 by the Uruguayan Manuel Peluffo for the Companhia Cinematográfica Maristela. Peluffo, by the way, had worked as Emilio Fernández's assistant in Mexico and Venezuela (Heffner).

5. The Centro Popular de Cultura was created by the national student's union in 1961 with the intention of bringing political engagement and class consciousness to the masses in Brazil. Important figures such as Leon Hirzman, Carlos Diegues, and Ferreira Gullar were involved in the initiative until the military coup d'état in 1964 abruptly cut short the experience.

6. See his interview with Ruy Gardnier and Daniel Caetano for the magazine *Contracampo* available at http://www.contracampo.com.br/29/entrevistanelson.htm.

7. Two paradigmatic examples are Carla Camuratti's *Carlota Joaquina,* an unlikely box-office hit featuring scenes in Spain, Portugal, and an introduction spoken in English in what was supposed to be Scotland, and Walter Salles's *Terra Estrangeira,* partially filmed in Portugal and Spain with Brazilian actors working alongside actors from Angola, Portugal, Turkey, and France.

8. Besides Pereira dos Santos, Martin Scorsese, Nagisa Ōshima, Jean-Luc Godard, Mrinal Sen, Stanley Kwan, Edgar Reitz, Stephen Frears, Sun-Woo Jang, Donald Taylor Black, Pawel Lozinski, Sergej Selyanov, Stig Björkman, George Miller, and Sam Neill were invited for the project.

9. He tells Sylvie Pierre, "D'ailleurs ç'aurait été beacoup plus difficile pour moi de n'aborder que le cinéma brésiliane, car j'y suis trop impliqué, et injuste pour les autres pays, car bien sûr il n'etait pas question de réaliser un film sur le cinema de chaque pays d'Amérique latine" (89).

10. In the original "o melodrama [...] foi o único momento em que houve uma indústria de cinema de verdade na América Latina" and "São filmes primorosos. Os diretores eram grandes artesãos" (Folha de São Paulo, May 1, 1995).

11. These are the following five song excerpts that appear in *Cinema de Lágrimas*: Carlos Orellana sings Agustín Lara's "Santa" in the film by the same name, Lola Beltrán sings and María Félix dubs Enrique Fabregat's "Al Contado" in *Camelia*, Miguel Aceves Mejía sings Gabriel Ruiz Galindo's "La Cita" in *Divorciadas*, Lina Boytler sings Manuel Esperón and Ricardo López Mendez's "Vendo Placer" in *La Mujer del Puerto*, and Libertad Lamarque sings a Liszt's "Canción de Amor" in *Madreselva*.

12. Helena Salem (1948–1999) was a critic and journalist who wrote or organized several books on Brazilian cinema, among them *Nelson Pereira dos Santos—O Sonho Possível do Cinema Brasileiro* (1987, Spanish edition in 1997), *90 Anos de Cinema—Uma Aventura Brasileira* (1988), *Luis Carlos Barreto* (1988), *Leon Hirzman, o Navegador das Estrelas* (1997), and *Cinema Brasileiro: Um Balanço dos Cinco Anos da Retomada do Cinema Nacional, 1995-1999* (1999). Salem also published *Palestinos, os Novos Judeus* (1977), *A Igreja dos Oprimidos* (1981)—turned into a documentary by Jorge Bodanski and Salem herself, *O Que é a Questão Palestina* (1982), and *Entre Árabes e Judeus* (1991) a firsthand account of the Yom Kippur War she witnessed as a journalist in 1974, and *As Tribos Mal—O Neonazismo no Brasil e no Mundo* (1995). A recent short biographical note about Salem was published by Carlos Alberto Mattos in the issue number fifty-nine of the magazine *Filme Cultura*.

13. In the original in Spanish, "conocía en detalle gran número de películas, sabía cómo localizarlas en las varias cinematecas del continente, y había desarrollado una reflexión sobre el melodrama."

14. In the original in Portuguese, "o melodrama foi estruturado, essencialmente, sobre quatro mitos da cultura judaico-cristã: *o amor, a paixão, o incesto,* e *a mulher.*"

15. Ivan Trujillo Bolio majored in biology at the Facultad de Ciencias de la Universidad Nacional Autónoma de México and in film at the Centro Universitario de Estudios Cinematográficos (CUEC), and has made several documentaries about nature: among them, *Mariposa Monarca...Adivinanzas para Siempre*, which won an Ariel award for best documentary short film in 1988. He started working at the *filmoteca* de la UNAM in 1980 and was made general director of this institution in 1989, remaining in that post until 2008. From 1999 to 2003 Trujillo also worked as president of the International Federation of Film Archives (Fédération Internationale des Archives du Film, FIAF) and in 2010 he was appointed director of the Guadalajara International Film Festival, one of the most important in Latin America.

16. After a legend that says "imperfecto, político, violento, 'com fome,'" one can see in the lower part of the poster a list of Latin American film-makers that includes several important names from the generation of the Third Cinema: Tomás Gutierrez Alea [La Habana, 1928–1996], Paul Leduc [Mexico, 1942], Santiago Álvarez [La Habana, 1919–1998], Alfredo Guevara [La Habana, 1931], Julio García Espinosa [La Habana, 1926], Pedro Chaskel [Alemania/Chile, 1932], Miguel Littin [Chile, 1942], Gerardo Vallejo [Tucumán, 1942–2007], Jorge Sanjinés [La Paz, 1936], Fernando Birri [Santa Fe, 1925], Carlos Álvarez [Asturias, 1940], Óscar Soria [La Paz, 1917–1988], Aldo Francia [Valparaíso, 1923–1996], Patrício Guzmán [Santiago, 1941], Fernando Solanas [Buenos Aires, 1936], Octavio Getino [León, 1935–2012], and Margot Benacerraf [Caracas, 1926].

17. In the original, "as categorias *highbrow* e *mass-cult* ( . . . ) elitizam e compartimentam a cultura, sendo, por isto, dos movimentos mais conservadores da história da estética contemporânea. A compartimentação da cultura implica esquemas de tal rigidez, que se situam fora do contexto real do desenvolvimento estrondoso da cultura de massas e da dinâmica social contemporânea."

18. The book received a second expanded and illustrated edition in Brazil in 1999 under the auspices of the FUNARTE, an institute linked to the Ministry of Culture.

19. Cristovam Buarque (1944) was a militant of the Catholic *ação popular* against the military regime and left Brazil in 1970 for a nine-year exile in Paris. When he returned from exile, Buarque became a professor of economics at the Universidade de Brasília (UnB) and in 1985 he was chosen its first independent president after the coup d'état in 1964. While at UnB he elaborated one of the first versions of what was to be called *Bolsa Família*. Buarque was elected governor of the Distrito Federal (Brasilia) in 1995 and chosen to be minister of education in 2003. In 2011 he was elected senator of the republic for Brasilia.

20. In the original in Portuguese, "um dos paradoxos da história da cultura brasileira é o fato de que o povo deixou de ir ao cinema, a partir do dia em que os cineastas passaram a analisar de forma realista a tragédia do povo brasileiro. A esquerda trouxe o povo para a tela e expulsou-o dos cinemas. Mas é um paradoxo com explicação. O povo foi considerado como tema, mas desconsiderado como beneficiário."

21. In the original in French, "Glauber Rocha nous représénte tous. Il représente le cinéma d'Amérique latine de la même façon que le cinéma mexicain, et le mélodrame en général, peut aussi le représenter. Et puis cette irruption de Glauber, c'est aussi la composante personelle de mon film: le souvenir d'un compagnon de cinéma, de tous les compagnons de cinéma que j'ai perdus, mais qui restent en mémoire."

22. In the original in Spanish, "teníamos cineastas preferidos en el exterior, Glauber adoraba a Eisenstein, Paulo César Sarraceni a Rossellini, Walter Lima Jr. a John Ford. Pero el ídolo, realmente, era Nelson."
23. In the original in Portuguese, "Voltar à Atlântida e ultrapassar o eclipse / Matar o ovo e ver a Vera Cruz."

## 9 Paul Leduc Reads Rubem Fonseca: The Globalization of Violence or The Violence of Globalization

1. Several elements of Leduc's film reappear in a film directed by Julie Taymor with Salma Hayek playing Kahlo in 2002. Taymor's film, however, contrasts sharply with Leduc's as it offers a simple, linear narrative that glosses over Kahlo's political positions and emphasizes the protagonist's likeability, adjusting a Mexican cultural and historical figure to the tastes and standards of contemporary Hollywood.
2. In the original in Spanish, "una modernidad que parece primitiva: es apocalíptica."
3. In the original in Portuguese, "o cinema, como o concebemos e sonhamos nestes 100 anos, acabou. O cinema que eu pratiquei e amei já não existe mais. O que me divertia era fazer filmes em equipe, onde todos comungavam, partilhavam da mesma ideia. ( ... ) Nossos filmes, produzidos fora de Hollywood, circulam em festivais e entre amigos. Não dispõem de público, não se pagam mais."
4. The film that epitomizes the mood of those years is Walter Salles's *Terra Estrangeira*, which opens with a black-and-white Brazilian flag with the words Foreign Land instead of Ordem e Progresso.
5. In the original in Portuguese, "curioso, e na verdade também um pouco deprimente" [http://www.literal.com.br/artigos/cineasta-mexicano-adapta-rubem-fonseca].
6. Cal y Arena actually boasts of having "el privilegio de ser la única editorial mexicana con los derechos para publicar al célebre autor brasileño Rubem Fonseca." See the presentation of the publisher in their own website at http://www.edicionescalyarena.com.mx/?P=historia.
7. In chronological order they are: *Grandes emociones y pensamientos imperfectos*, 1990; *Agosto*, 1993; *El salvaje de la ópera*, 1994; *El agujero en la pared*, 1997; *Historias de amor*, 1999; *La cofraría de los espadas*, 2000; *Secreciones, excreciones, y desatinos*, 2003; *Pequeñas criaturas*, 2003; *Diario de un libertino*, 2004; *Mandrake; La Biblia y el bastón*, 2006; *Ella y otras mujeres*, 2007; *La cofradía de los espadas*, 2007; *La novella murió [crónicas]*, 2008; *Bufo y Spallanzani*, 2009; *El seminarista*, 2010; *El gran arte*, 2011; and *José*, 2011.
8. Rodolfo Mata should be held up as an example of the benefits of government investment in international cooperation. After all his serious involvement with comparative studies in Latin America, he comes from a master's degree program at USP with a fellowship

sponsored by UNAM and the Brazilian government. Out of several important publications translated and/or organized by Rodolfo Mata, it is also worth mentioning Haroldo de Campos's *De la Razón Antropofágica y Otros Ensayos* (Siglo XXI, 2000), Paulo Leminski's *Aviso a los Náufragos* (Calamus, 2006), and two comprehensive collections: *Ensayistas Brasileños: Literatura, Cultura y Sociedad* (UNAM, 2005), and *Alguna Poesía Brasileña—Antología 1963–2007* (UNAM, 2009). In addition, Mata has an interesting monograph on Latin American poetry, *Las Vanguardias Literarias Latinoamericanas y la Ciencia: Tablada, Borges, Vallejo y Andrade.*

9. In the original in Portuguese, "eu ofereci a Rubem Fonseca a possibilidade de participar na produção do roteiro, mas ele preferiu não fazê-lo. Deu-me total liberdade para adaptar seus contos. Dei a eles coordenadas políticas e contextos nacionais diferentes, porque não me interessava simplesmente transcrever o texto em imagens, mas sim colocar, através delas, as minhas próprias preocupações. Penso que não há sentido em adaptar um texto literário de outra forma. Entretanto, isto não se contrapõe ao fato de que acredito ter sido fiel à sua obra e creio que ele assim o percebeu. Tampouco acho que tenha sentido partir da literatura para, de alguma forma, traí-la."

10. In the original in Spanish, "globalización de la violencia generada por la violencia de la globalización."

11. In the original in Spanish, "el resentimiento social que se ha echado a andar en el mundo, que no encuentra un cauce y que se canaliza por la violencia."

12. In "Placebo" the protagonist is given a bit more background as the CEO of a big company and his guide is a black man called Belisário, who takes him to a medium who sees patients under the influence of a Dr. Wolf.

13. Sixty-two of the 80 members of the PC do B involved in the conflict between 1972 and 1974 either died or disappeared. On March 13, 2012, the *Ministério Público Federal* charged Curió with the kidnapping, torture, and disappearance of five militants in September 1974. The effort to bring Curió to trial was blocked a few days later by a federal judge, but constituted a landmark in the search for justice against abuses of human rights.

14. In the original in Portuguese, "o mais longamente discutido escândalo lítero-jurídico do regime militar."

15. In the original in Portuguese, "em quase sua totalidade, personagens portadores de complexos, vícios e taras, com o objetivo de enfocar a face obscura da sociedade na prática da delinquência, suborno, latrocínio e homicídio, sem qualquer referência a sanção, utilizando linguagem bastante popular e onde a pornografia foi largamente empregada, com rápidas alusões desmerecedoras aos responsáveis pelos destinos do Brasil e ao trabalho censório."

16. In the original in Portuguese, "De abril de 1992 a novembro de 1994, morreram 11.600 pessoas em Sarajevo. Nesse mesmo período na cidade do Rio de Janeiro, 13 mil pessoas morreram de morte violenta, quase 2 mil pessoas a mais que numa cidade em estado de guerra declarada."

17. In the original in Portuguese, "Por todas essas razões, suspeito que o Brasil esteja diante de um fenômeno novo, ainda em busca de explicação. Compreende-se a violência em Sarajevo, em Israel, na Colômbia. A violência brasileira, cuja manifestação exemplar ocorre nas ruas do Rio, permanece uma incógnita. Não acredito que haja um aparato teórico adequado para entender o fenômeno."

18. The song, called "Curiosidade," is ironically said to be "plagiarized" from "Alfred Nobel and his dynamite" according to Aesthetic of the *Arrastão*. This term, originally used by fishermen referring to hauling back catch in a drag net, was used to name the notorious collective mugging sprees that groups of youngsters promoted on the beaches frequented by the affluent in Rio de Janeiro in the 1980s and 1990s.

19. In the original in Portuguese, "A barra tá pesada. Os homens não tão brincando, viu o que fizeram com o Bom Crioulo? Dezesseis tiros no quengo. Pegaram o Vevê e estrangularam. O Minhoca, porra! O Minhoca! crescemos juntos em Caxias, o cara era tão míope que não enxergava daqui até ali, e também era meio gago—pegaram ele e jogaram dentro do Guandu, todo arrebentado. / Pior foi com o Tripé. Tacaram fogo nele. Virou torresmo. Os homens não tão dando sopa, disse Pereba."

20. In the original in Portuguese, "Quem é que tá botando dinamite ( . . . )? / Quem é que tá botando tanto piolho ( . . . ) ? / Quem é que tá botando tanto grilo ( . . . ) ? // Quem é que arranja travesseiro ( . . . )?"

21. In the original in Portuguese, "O terceiro mundo tem uma crescente população. A grande maioria se transforma em uma espécie de 'andróide,' quase sempre analfabeto e com escassa especialização para o trabalho. ( . . . ) Esses andróides são mais baratos que o robô operário fabricado em Alemanha e Japão. Mas revelam alguns 'defeitos' inatos, como criar, pensar, dançar, sonhar; são defeitos muito 'perigosos' para o patrão primeiro mundo. Aos olhos dele, nós, quando praticamos essas coisas por aqui, somos andróides com defeito de fabricação. Pensar será sempre uma afronta. Ter ideias, compor, por exemplo, é ousar. No umbral da história, o projeto de juntar fibras vegetais e criar a arte de tecer foi uma grande ousadia. Pensar sempre será."

22. In the original in Spanish, "si no son indiferentes a los problemas de los individuos, tampoco adoptan una actitud didáctica al exponerlos ( . . . ) dispuestos a parodiar los discursos reduccionistas y maniqueos que tratan de explicar los fenómenos humanos y sociales de manera progresista."

## 10   The Delicate Crime of Beto Brant and Felipe Ehrenberg

*A shorter version of this chapter was published in Portuguese in the book *Indústria Radical* in 2012.

1. From 1978 to 1984 Brazilian films had between 29 and 36 percent of the domestic market. Since the complete stop in 1990 throughout the *Retomada*, this market share has grown to about 10 percent and stalled due to distribution problems.
2. Through the MinC [Ministry of Culture], the federal government launched *Cinema Brasil* with a grant of R$1 million (in 2001 about US$400,000) for full-length movies with a maximum total budget of R$1.8 million.
3. Paulo Miklos is one of the lead singers of Titãs, one of the most important Brazilian rock bands in the eighties, for whom Brant had directed some videoclips, among them "Será que é isso que eu necessito?" winner of the Brazilian MTV Best Videoclip in 1991 (Machado, 125). The hit man Anísio—the Trespasser of the title—was his first part, for which he won awards at festivals, such as Brasília, Cinema Brasil, and the Miami Brazilian Film Festival.
4. Sabotage (São Paulo, 1973–2003), born and raised in the poor Zona Sul of São Paulo, recorded one album (*Rap é Compromisso*) and worked also in Hector Babenco's 2002 film *Carandiru* before his untimely death at the age of thirty.
5. Aquino was born in Amparo, São Paulo in 1958. He wrote two volumes of poetry and worked as a journalist before winning the Jabuti (the most important literary award in Brazil) with the short stories of *O Amor e Outros Objetos Pontiagudos* in 2000. Aquino has written screenplays for movies and television. Besides the original scripts and adaptations for all of Brant's films, Aquino wrote for two first full-length movies directed by Heitor Dhalia, *Nina* (2004) and *O Cheiro do Ralo* (2006), and for two acclaimed TV series, *Filhos do Carnaval* and *Força Tarefa*.
6. Besides *O Invasor*, critics from the Associação de Críticos de Cinema do Rio de Janeiro chose Eduardo Coutinho's *Edifício Master*, Luiz Fernando de Carvalho's *Lavoura Arcaica*, Fernando Meirelles's *Cidade de Deus*, and Walter Salles's *Terra Estrangeira* as the five most influential films of the *Retomada*. See Diegues, Carlos et al. *Cinco Mais Cinco: os Maiores Filmes Brasileiros em Bilheteria e Crítica*. Rio de Janeiro: Legere, 2007.
7. In *A Utopia no Cinema Brasileiro* (159–177), Lúcia Nagib convincingly argues the case through a careful analysis of *The Trespasser* beyond content analysis of the plot and the strict preoccupation with national self-representation, taking an important step toward a fuller comprehension of Brant's relevance in contemporary cinema.
8. Sérgio Sant'Anna was born in Rio de Janeiro in 1941. He published his first book, the short story collection *O Sobrevivente*, in 1969,

which enabled him to take part in the International Writing Program at the University of Iowa in 1970. Sant'Anna has won the the Jabuti award twice, for best short story collection in 1982 with *O Concerto de João Gilberto no Rio de Janeiro* and for best novel in 1998 with *Um Crime Delicado.*

9. Vitaliano Brancati (1907–1954) was a Sicilian neo-realist novelist and playwright who worked in cinema, for instance on Roberto Rossellini's *Dov'è la Libertà* [Where is Freedom?] (1954) featuring the great comedian Antonio Totò de Curtis (1898–1967). After a brief infatuation with Fascism that lasted until 1934, Brancati's works are marked by an acute critical look both at social and sexual mores and obsessions, and he encountered problems with censorship even after the fall of Mussolini. His main novels are *Don Giovanni in Sicilia* (1941) and *Il Bell'Antonio* (1949), which was adapted by Pier Paolo Pasolini and directed by Mauro Bolognini in 1960. Biondi describes Brancati as "uno scrittore rigorosamente autocritico, un prodotto della cultura illuministica portata al calore della solarità mediterranea, nato come scrittore di fronte alla *débâcle* della ragione giovanile irretita e dai miti dello stato totalitario" (101) [a rigorously self-analytical writer, product of enlightenment culture cultivated under the Mediterranean radiance, who became a writer when confronted with the debacle of youthful reason seduced to surrender to the myths of a totalitarian state].

10. Arnold Bode (1900–1977) and art historian Werner Haftmann (1912–1999) started the Documenta in 1955 with a retrospective of classical Modernism defamed by the Nazis as "degenerate" art as well as younger artworks. Documenta takes place every five years since 1972. Haftmann left in 1968 and the show became almost entirely devoted to current art, being regarded as one of the worldwide most important art events. Brancatti's installation reproduces Inês's apartment with her crutches and features *A Modelo* [*The Model*] (a painting that features Inês in the same apartment), photographs of Brancatti, Inês, and Martins (including one of the critic at the exhibit where the painting was first shown), newspaper clippings about the scandal and the trial, and a crude caricature of the critic as a vampire.

11. Dino Campana (1885–1932) was born in Marradi, Florence. Since 1906 Campana was committed to several different mental-health institutions by members of his family. In 1907 he traveled to Argentina but returned to his home town the following year. He started publishing his poems in 1912–13. *Canti Orfici* was pusblished in 1914 and Campana enjoyed some acclaim in Florence, but his mental health worsened and in 1918 he was sent to the asylum of Castel Pulci, where he remained until his death.

12. In the original, "a artista pornô dele" and "é ele que se aproveita da deficiência física de Inês."

13. The quote is from Fernando Llanos, curator of a recent retrospective of Ehrenberg's work in Mexico. In the original, "Felipe Ehrenberg es un referente en la producción del arte experimental y no objetual de este país."

14. Pioneers of Conceptual art in México with "A nivel informativo" [At an Informational Level] shown at the Palacio de Bellas Artes in 1973, Felipe Ehrenberg, Carlos Finck, José Antonio Hernández, and Víctor Muñoz were the members of this art-collective group, active from 1976 to 1983. The name was humorously explained thus: "Pentagon because all of us Latin Americans have to do with it; the other one with the same name" (*La Era de la Discrepancia*, 220) and the group was noteworthy for "open political art with an emphasis on thinking but avoiding the pamphlet aesthetics" and "experimentation and collective process" (221).

15. The 2008 retrospective in the Museo de Arte Moderno in Mexico City and the contrast between Ehrenberg's stay in England as a self-exiled artist and his recent stay in Brazil as a cultural attaché in the Mexican diplomatic service is indicative of the limits of the label *maudit*. When the minister of foreign affairs Jorge Castañeda appointed Ehrenberg, the artist himself exposed the negative repercussions: "José Agustín accused me of 'selling out' and Paco Ignacio kicked me out of his house. 'How can you represent Fox over there,' he asked me angrily" (*Manchuria*, 167). It is ironic that Castañeda and Ehrenberg, figures of contestation of the status-quo *PRIista*, joined the state in a political landscape dominated by the right-wing PAN, in the tradition of alignment of Mexican intellectuals and artists through powerful government cultural institutions.

16. The challenge of recording and archiving works of an artist of this kind are obvious and Ehrenberg himself has long worked diligently not only to preserve documentation of his actions but also to transform them into, for instance, publishing material. While the taping and recording of "A Date with Fate at the Tate" was eventually bought by the Tate Gallery itself, Ehrenberg was one of the founding members of Beau Geste, the British-based independent publisher of self-edited books in the 1970s, and this interest has made him maintain a very thorough webpage with various works and published self-made e-books with his most recent output.

17. In Ehrenberg's own words, "cuando ya tenía 17, 19 años, llegó un amigo de mi maestro, José Chávez Morado, a México para pintar un mural en la primera oficina de la Aerolínea Varig" ("El arte es sólo una excusa" 6). Ehrenberg seems to combine rather inventively events from two different stays of the Brazilian painter in Mexico. Di Cavalcanti did visit Mexico in 1949–1950 (when Ehrenberg was seventeen years old) to participate in the Congreso dos Artistas pela Paz, but only returned to paint that mural in 1971, as one of a series in the foreign offices of the recently launched Brazilian airline VARIG.

18. They met in New York at a pivotal moment in their careers around 1969. Gerchman and Ehrenberg undoubtedly have a lot in common in their multidisciplinary creativity and their deep immersion in Latin American visual vernacular beyond the ironic appropriations of kitsch art. Gerchman, born in Rio de Janeiro in 1942, left the ENBA (Escola Nacional de Belas Artes) in 1962 and was in the center of the political and social turmoil of the 1960s in Brazil. He participated in *Opinião 66*, the collective multidisciplinary exhibit protesting the recently established military dictatorship and in the *Nova Objetividade Brasileira* in 1967, landmark of Tropicalismo. Gerchman and Ehrenberg voluntarily left their native countries after street demonstrations suffered violent government repression in 1968. Gerchman stayed in New York until 1972 and Ehrenberg in England until 1974, where his performance "A Date with Fate at the Tate" was part of a landmark of counter-culture, the international event *Destruction* in the Art Symposium (DIAS). The Brazilian and the Mexican exhibited their work together in 2000 in México City in *"Mano a Mano con Rubens Gerchman"* at the Espacio Neológico La Cúpula. At the time of Gerchman's death, Ehrenberg wrote a poignant account of their friendship in the magazine *Agulha*.

19. In the original, "Yo creo que mi obra nunca se insertó en este mercado complaciente. Por eso mi interés en internacionalizarme a través de mis viajes y en este sentido de mi trabajo como embajador cultural en Brasil he dejado una clara huella que mi interés en difundir la cultura mexicana y que mi trabajo, como artista y promotor del arte mexicano, se consolide como una manera de mirar más allá de nuestro vecino del norte."

20. "Y lucientes" features the voice of the Spanish painter Francisco José de Goya y Lucientes addressing his model and possible lover, the duchess of Alba. Margarita Martínez Duarte is a singer and has a duo (Nana Yoyolo) with Macuil Ponce.

21. In the original "a fascinação que tem o México com a morte como metáfora da vida."

22. Max Aub (1903–1972) was one of the many distinguished Spanish exiles in Mexico. Son of a French mother and a German father, Aub's family took Spanish citizenship during WWI. Aub was the Republican cultural attaché in Paris during the Spanish Civil War and was instrumental in exhibiting Picasso's *Guernica* at the Spanish pavilion in the 1937 Exposition Internationale des Arts et Techniques dans la Vie Moderne. Denounced by Franco as a Jew to the Vichy regime in 1940, Aub was interned in the forced labor camp in Djelfa in Algeria. In 1942 Aub escaped to Mexico, where he published his major works, among them the poems in *Diario de Djelfa* (1944) and the cycle of novels *El Laberinto Mágico* (1943–1968).

23. Torres Campalans, for example, lost his virginity after a visit to the prostitutes on Avignon Street with Picasso and had heated discussions

with his hated rival, the *madrileño* Juan Gris. With the help of Alfonso Reyes the painter manages to escape to Mexico, where he ends up living anonymously among the Indians in Chiapas. Another Spanish exile, Josep Renau (who was David Alfaro Siqueiros's partner in the mural *Mundo de la Burguesía*—see my chapter on Érico Veríssimo) even made a photomontage showing Torres Campalans at a Parisian bar next to the young Picasso.

24. The polemical exhibit was supposedly based on a catalogue prepared by the Ulster Irish critic Henry Richard Town for a show at the Tate Gallery in 1942, which never took place because Town was killed by a Nazi bomb in 1940. A similar exhibit appeared at the Bodley in New York in 1962 when the book was translated into English, and the ritual was repeated with the French translation, proof that Aub conceived of the novel and exhibit as parts of the same piece. In 2003 the Museo Reina Sofía organized a full retrospective exhibit of Max Aub's Torres Campalans's paintings, complete with pieces from his "companions/rivals" Picasso, Braque, Juan Gris, Matisse, Mondrian, Chagall, Delaunay, and Modiglinai, followed by Torres Campalans's sharp aphoristic commentaries taken from the *Cuaderno Verde*.

25. In the original, "um intelectual que mede sua percepção de vida pela sua razão." This is an excerpt from Beto Brant's interview to the cinema critic Luiz Joaquim for the newspaper *Folha de Pernambuco* on March 10, 2006.

26. In the original, "que só funciona da cabeça para cima."

27. Cláudio Assis (Caruaru, 1959) is an extraordinary director from Brant's generation, with two remarkable, uncompromising movies: *Amarelo Manga* [Mango Yellow] in 2002 and *Baixio das Bestas* [*Bog of Beasts*] in 2006.

28. In the original, "Agora, seu otário, é o seguinte: eu amo; você não ama nada. Quem é você?"

29. No original, "um exemplo vivo e eloqüente dos extremos patológicos a que pode ser conduzida uma personalidade que se destaca pela contenção de seus sentimentos por meio de uma racionalidade exacerbada, a qual, de repente, libera-se através do crime." This is a quote from a public statement from a group of actors and actresses who publicly repudiated Martins's behavior as the scandal of the rape trial raged on.

30. In the original, "um conceito que reputo dos mais interessantes: o crítico como estuprador da arte."

31. Nelson Rodrigues is Brazil's best-known playwright. His *Vestido de Noiva* [*The Wedding Dress*] is a landmark in Brazilian modern drama, first staged in 1943 at the Theatro Municipal, Rio de Janeiro's most prestigious stage. Several stage productions were made subsequently and a 2006 film adaptation was directed by Rodrigues's son, Joffre Rodrigues.

32. In the original, "culpas" and "pecados."

33. In the original, "antídoto da cruel ironia."
34. In the original in Portuguese, "o grande desconforto de quem assiste a sua vida pessoal e profissional escapar do seu controle."
35. In their own words Paroni de Castro's Brazilian company, Atelier de Manufactura Suspeita, "atua no limite da representação e da não-representação, da confissão pública, da máscara exacerbada, sem descuidar de estabelecer um diálogo fértil com formas convencionais da representação e redescobrir a função social das mesmas" [performs on the brink between acting and nonacting, on the brink of public confession, of exacerbated masks, without forgetting to establish a fruitful dialogue with the conventional form of acting and rediscover their social function]. Besides his work in Brazil with the Ateliê de Manufatura Suspeita in São Paulo, Maurício Paroni de Castro (São Paulo, 1961) teaches and directs in Scotland, Norway, and Italy, where he graduated from and later taught at the Scuola D'Arte Drammatica Piccolo Teatro, in Milan. Paroni de Castro studied with several leading European directors, including Tadeusz Kantor and Heiner Müller, and has himself directed more than thirty plays in Italy, the United Kingdom, Brazil, Portugal, and Norway, including work by Renato Gabrielli and Andrés Lima. Paroni de Castro and Beto Brant were longtime friends who worked together for the first time in *Crime Delicado*.
36. In the scene in *Crime Delicado*, Dr. Kraft comes to rescue his wife, Carlota, from a dominatrix, but is exposed as having abused his patients under hypnosis. The doctor is tied with a rope and a key found in his pocket opens Carlota's chastity belt.
37. In the original: "histeria auto-promocional do espetáculo."
38. Christine Höhrig translated and the writer Fernando Bonassi, the actor Matheus Nachtergaele, and the director Cibele Forjaz adapted George Büchner's unfinished play, complementing and adding scenes during four months of improvisations and rehearsals and turning the German soldier into a worker at a brick factory called Olaria Brasil. Every night the director Forjaz—who worked for ten years with the legendary director José Celso Martinez from the company Oficina—chose randomly among the several scenes and rehearsed those to be included in that night's performance.
39. In the original, "todo homem é um abismo."
40. In the original, "a gramática inacabada e extraordinária do autor."
41. *Leonor de Mendonça* (1846) was written by Antônio Gonçalves Dias (1823–1864), one of Brazil's best Romantic poets but never staged in the nineteenth century because of government censorship due to its scandalous content. The play was based on a Portuguese chronicle that tells the story of a duke, Dom Jaime I de Bragança, who falsely accused his wife of adultery and killed her in 1512 in the Vila Viçosa. In a remarkably lucid prologue (*Leonor de Mendonça*, 1–15), Gonçalves Dias compares his D. Jaime to Shakespeare's Othello

and says that whereas the Moor is moved by pride and also love, the duke's act is motivated by pride alone and thus he kills without sorrow.

42. In the novel Martins claims his failure was due to his obsession with Inês and thus he blames Inês for the compromised review in which he commends Maria Luísa's acting in the hope of convincing her not to spread rumors about his sexuality.

43. The screenplay is attributed to Beto Brant, Marçal Aquino, Marco Ricca, Maurício Paroni de Castro, and Luiz Francisco Carvalho Filho, but at least three other people, the cinematographer Walter Carvalho, Felipe Ehrenberg, and Lilian Taulib contributed decisively in unscripted scenes.

44. In the original, "se a mulher não fosse escrava, como é de fato, D. Jaime não mataria a sua mulher." In his introduction, Gonçalves Dias develops the argument that fatality in his play is man-made. The duke is forced to marry and Leonor de Mendonça dies because she is completely subjected to her noble husband. The theme echoes the author's life: Gonçalves Dias wanted to marry Ana Amélia Ferreira Vale but her family did not allow the union because of his mixed heritage.

45. In the original, "o acerto de contas com a realidade objetiva do bando de doidos que são aquelas figuras" a quote from Paroni de Castro's "Crime Delicado ou a Vida é Mais Que a Estética," undoubtedly the best critical assessment of Delicate Crime to date.

46. Of course claiming that life and art are one indivisible whole in Crime Delicado is a gross oversimplification. Whereas in certain scenes, such as the ones in the studio, it may be impossible to tell Inês Campana from Lilian Taulib, in the rape and in the court scenes (among others) Lilian Taulib definitely plays Inês as an actress.

47. Walter Carvalho is undoubtedly the most important cinematographer in contemporary Brazilian cinema, having worked on most key movies of the period, among them Terra Estrangeira [Foreign Land] (1996), Central do Brasil [Central Station] (1998), Notícias de uma Guerra Particular [News from a Private War] (1999), Lavoura Arcaica [To the Left of the Father] (2001), Madame Satã (2002), besides directing the documentaries Janela da Alma (2001) and Moacir, Arte Bruta (2005), and Budapest (2009), an adaptation of Chico Buarque de Holanda's novel.

48. For instance, Torres Campana (Ehrenberg) tells Inês (Taulib), "Encontramos o que queríamos, viu? Encontramos o que queríamos." [We have we found what we wanted, see? We have found what he wanted] (1:01:17). Painter and model take a short break because of numbness and muscle cramps from being in the same position for a long time and try to remember where they were. Inês (Taulib) softly exclaims, "Você disse que ia lembrar!" [You said you'd remember!] (1:00:23) and Torres Campana (Ehrenberg)

concedes, "É, eu disse. Vamos ter que inventar de novo." "That's right, that's what I said but we are going to have to improvise again] [1:00:28].

49. The experience with filming art and the artistic process in *Crime Delicado* has certainly left an enduring mark on the cinematographer Walter Carvalho, who later directed a remarkable art documentary, *Moacyr, Arte Bruta* (2005).

50. *Portunhol* (or *Portuñol*) is the name of the language that speakers of these two closely related languages often use to communicate with each other. Wilson Bueno's wildly inventive novel *Mar Paraguayo* may have been the first literary product of this pidgin language, much used especially across the borders among Brazil, Argentina, Uruguay, Paraguay, and Bolivia.

51. The behind-the-scenes documentary *Vertebrando-se*, included in the DVD of *Crime Delicado* shows the unedited interview conducted by Brant and Walter Carvalho.

52. In *Vertebrando-se*, the fifty-minute behind-the-scenes documentary of *Crime Delicado*, we catch a glimpse of how this section of the movie was made. Brant and Walter Carvalho asked questions and elicited unscripted statements from Ehrenberg.

53. Ehrenberg engaged then in a series of interesting initiatives combining social activism and artistic practice. As Emily Hicks explains, "immediately after the earthquake. Ehrenberg took some artists, friends, and his own family into Tepito in order to organize brigades to comfort survivors, who had been left without homes, electricity, and social services, and to distribute food and clothing. (...) Ehrenberg and the Tepiteños began to raise money (...) organized the Committee for the Reconstruction of Tepito, which included community representatives, well-known cultural activists, scientists, and specialists in fields from urbanism to finance. Between September 25 and October 1, his group managed to give food, medical attention, and drinkable water to nearly 5,000 people a day. On October 6, Ehrenberg organized the Festival of Life, which included music by rock groups, to celebrate, in Ehrenberg's words, "that we are alive, that Tepito didn't fold, and to be aware that we have to help ourselves." In addition, children's theater, concerts, and a library were organized. Hicks sustains that "in a sense, these activities can be considered an epic performance installation, in which an entire city functions as a gallery space" (Hicks, 95–96).

54. In the original, "É um momento tão íntimo que anula toda a possibilidade de violência. Nesse momento que exige suavidade, exige doçura, que exige (pausa) amor possivelmente não sei nesse momento existem iscas (não sei iscas como chama) eh, relâmpagos. Quando a modelo fica pelada e o artista fica pelado, a relação entre poder e vulnerabilidade acaba. Os dois são iguais de vulneráveis ou igual de poderosos."

55. In the original in Portuguese: "ser crítico é um exercício da razão diante da emotividade aliciadora, ou de uma tentativa de envolvimento estético que devemos decompor, para não dizer denunciar, na medida do possível, com elegância."
56. In the original in Spanish, "repugna ante todo la confusión de fronteras. Es un síntoma de pulcritud mental querer que las fronteras entre las cosas estén bien demarcadas. Vida es una cosa, poesía es otra."
57. In the original, "sempre viveu na terceira pessoa."
58. Well-known for his work on TV, in the cinema and in the theater, Marco Ricca played the protagonist and served as coproducer in *The Trespasser* and also coproduced *Crime Delicado*, a project he suggested to Beto Brant and whose screenplay he wrote with Brant, Aquino, Paroni de Castro, and Carvalho Filho.
59. In the original, "Olhava para o mundo com a pretensão dos que se achavam vacinados."
60. In the original in Portuguese, "o que é mais sagrado na minha vida, que é a minha relação com José Torres Campana." Ironically she is prompted to say so by the defense attorney who is eager to establish a motive and imply she accuses Martins falsely. The legal aspects of Inês's accusation against Antônio Martins, practically absent in the novel, hold a prominent place in Brant's film. In the film we see Martins and Inês speak during preliminary hearings, offering strikingly different versions to the events we have already seen on the screen. One of the major contributors to the screenplay of *Crime Delicado* is the criminal attorney Luis Francisco Carvalho Filho. Born in São Paulo in 1957, Luis Francisco Carvalho Filho has also worked in various roles at the newspaper *Folha de São Paulo*. Working at a renowned firm specialized in defending people imprisoned and tortured by the military dictatorship between 1964 and 1985, Carvalho Pinto was the chair of the Comissão de Mortos e Desaparecidos Políticos from the Justice Department in 1995. He has published *O Que é Pena de Morte* (1995), *A Prisão* (2002), and also a short story collection, *Nada mais foi dito nem perguntado* (2001), adapted to the stage by the theater company Folias under the direction of Ailton Graça, Atílio Beline Vaz, Bruno Perillo, Carlos Francisco, Dagoberto Feliz, and Gabriel Carmona in 2004. There are striking similarities in style and dynamics between the court scenes in the film and several stories by Carvalho Filho, such as "Injúria" (31–35).
61. Sérgio Sant'Anna's *Um Crime Delicado* is part of a very rich Brazilian narrative tradition started by Machado de Assis. *Dom Casmurro* (1899) features a first-person narrator driven by resentment and a paranoid obsession with his wife and somehow trying to prove his motives for having ostracized her and their son. In this form of narration the truth appears in spite of the narrator's manipulative intentions

and the reader's challenge is to strike the right balance between mistrusting and trusting these relatively unreliable narrators.

62. In an interview with Luis Joaquim at the *Folha de Pernambuco*, Brant is prompted to comment on one possible interpretation of the crime alluded to in the title and replies, "what pleases me in this case is the movie's capacity to enter into a dialogue with the audience's subjectivity. ( ... ) Every movie we have made has an ending with various possible interpretations that incite debate and I think *Delicate Crime* is the most subjective of them. You can follow the film through many different paths, or not." In the original in Portuguese: "O que me satisfaz aqui é a capacidade que o filme tem de dialogar com a subjetividade do público. ( ... ) Todo filme que fazemos, deixamos um final com alguma possibilidade de interpretação que abra uma discussão e acho que 'Crime Delicado' é o mais subjetivo de todos. Você pode navegar nele por várias maneiras, ou não."

63. In the original, "As características mais impactantes de *Crime Delicado* são sua concisão e seu laconismo. Cada imagem que aparece no filme serve menos para nos mostrar alguma coisa do que para fazer surgir algumas interrogações. Interrogações do ponto de vista narrativo ( ... ), mas, principal e decisivamente, o filme provoca o tempo todo interrogações morais: até onde se está dentro do limite e qual a linha de transgressão?"

64. In the original, "seqüências de acasos iluminados." Interview with Silvana Arantes for *Folha de São Paulo* on December 13, 2004.

65. In the original in Portuguese, "vai mais atrás do afeto e não da violência."

66. The pavilion at the Ibirapuera Park is iconic as the site of the traditional São Paulo Art Biennial since its fourth edition in 1957 and a suitable place for the film's version of the installation at Documenta described by Antônio Martins at the end of Sant'Anna's novel.

67. In the original, "uma gramática ao sofrimento da ausência."

68. In the original, "Não se é feliz sem ter uma gramática para contar a própria felicidade e se vai ao inferno quando o próprio sofrimento não pode ser contado."

## 11   Undercurrents, Still Flowing

1. In the original, "El mercado es una arena donde se desenvuelve el individuo en función de su ideología, sus intereses, sus valores. El mercado no tiene la culpa. Muchos en México todavía hablan del mercado del arte como si fuera el diablo: es como culpar al mar de que te ahogaste. El mercado en realidad es otro espacio del arte, como el museo, la calle o la sala de la casa; otro espacio donde el arte circula públicamente. El mercado tiene un impacto en la vida pública, y así hay que entenderlo, como a las instituciones en general. Las subastas, la especulación, ésa es la parte más vistosa, el show del mercado;

pero es mucho más que eso. Hay sobre todo un aspecto del mercado que no ha sido analizado por los teóricos del arte: la manera en que producimos una obra de arte. Y esto es crucial en mi trabajo. Cuánto dinero gastas, qué material utilizas, cómo lo trabajas: desde ahí, hay una actitud particular. Parte de mis exploraciones como artista tienen que ver con esto: la conciencia del sistema económico de producción del objeto artístico, que va a influir no solamente en el resultado estético (si es de oro o de cartón, si es grande o pequeño, si es frágil o resistente, si es impermeable o no lo es…), sino que además va a imponer unas reglas de distribución y de consumo en el mercado cultural y financiero de la obra. La actitud política, económica e ideológica de un artista comienza en el momento en que decide cómo va a ejecutar una obra. Y esto tiene consecuencias incluso en el destino de la pieza, dónde va a terminar: en un museo, en una casa, en una institución pública o en un basurero."

2. Olivier Debroise, critic, curator, and writer involved with important institutions such as the Museo de San Carlos, Museo Nacional del Arte, and UNAM's Dirección General de Artes Visuales was particularly aggressive in "Orozco es Inocente" [Orozco is Innocent], a biting review of Orozco's retrospective for the newspaper *Reforma* on October 2, 2000. He already made a brief appearance in this book as the curator of *Era de la discrepancia: Arte y cultural visual en México, 1968–1997*, a book in which Felipe Ehrenberg features prominently.

3. Cuauhtémoc Medina (Mexico City, Mexico) is an art critic, curator, and historian with a PhD in History and Art Theory from the University of Essex, and a BA in History from the Universidad Nacional Autónoma de Mexico, Mexico City. Since 1992 he has been a full-time researcher at the Instituto de Investigaciones Estéticas, Universidad Nacional Autónoma de Mexico, and has taught at the Center for Curatorial Studies, Bard College, Annandale-on-Hudson. Previously, he was the first curator of Latin American Art Collections at the Tate Gallery, London (2002–2008); director of the Seventh International Symposium on Contemporary Art Theory, Mexico City (2009); and is one of the founders of Teratoma, a group of curators, critics, and anthropologists based in Mexico City. He curated *The Age of Discrepancies, Art and Visual Culture in Mexico 1968–1997* in collaboration with Olivier Debroise, Pilar García, and Alvaro Vázquez— the exhibit featured prominently the work of Felipe Ehrenberg. The article about Orozco's exhibit appeared in his biweekly art criticism column "Ojo Breve" in the *Reforma* newspaper, Mexico City.

4. In the original, "Orozco apareció ante críticos y curadores de los centros como una carta de salvación. Se convirtió en el artista del tercer mundo cuya renuencia, abstracción y cercanía con la tradición posminimal y conceptual, podía asimilarse mejor a la cultura metropolitana. Se le idolatro como el latinoamericano cuya cercanía con

la metodología de Cage y el espíritu de Borges podía disipar el "mal gusto" barroquizante y estruendoso del americano latino. Si algo beneficio a Orozco en esa operación es lo mismo que lo pierde frecuentemente a lo largo de sus objetos y fotografías: una inclinación por un buen gusto institucional mas bien recatado, que sugiere un estado de gracia melancólica, y seduce al ojo con momentos fugaces de pasividad."

5. In the original, "una obra que hay que leer en su sitio cultural específico y que a partir de su individualidad logra inventar una identidad nueva en una realidad que se estimula y se transforma constantemente."

6. Born in São Paulo, Sérgio Cohn has edited the journal *Azougue* since 1994. In 2001 he created a publishing house, Azougue Editorial, one of the most dynamic independent publishers in Brazil with notable books, with interviews, and the most comprehensive anthology of Brazilian poetry to date, *Poesia.br* with ten volumes encompassing everything from precolonial to contemporary poetry. Sérgio Cohn has published three poetry volumes: *Lábio dos Afogados* (Nankin, 1999), *Horizonte de Eventos* (Azougue, 2002), and *O Sonhador Insone* (Azougue, 2006).

7. Angélica Freitas was born in Pelotas, Rio Grande do Sul. Besides *Guadalupe* she has published two acclaimed books of poetry, *Rilke Shake* (Cosac & Naify, 2007) and *Um Utero é do Tamanho de um Punho* (Cosac & Naify, 2012). Freitas also edits with Ricardo Domeneck and Marília Garcia the journal *Modo de Usar & Co.*

8. *Caos Portátil* included poems by Elisa Andrade Buzzo, Bruna Beber, Rod Britto, Sergio Cohn, Bruno Dorigatti, Camila do Valle, Angélica Freitas, Izabela Guerra Leal, Augusto de Guimaraens Cavalcanti, André Monteiro, Elza de Sá Nogueira, Ana Rusche, and Virna Texeira. *Sin Red ni Salvavidas*, a Latin American anthology included poems by the Brazilians Sérgio Cohn, Angélica Freitas, Camila do Valle, and Bruna Beber.

9. In the original, "pude criar um México pessoal, meio pesquisado, meio inventado e atravessado por coisas que vi ao longo do tempo. E tive a sorte de ter amigos mexicanos, que à distância pacientemente me responderam perguntas, enviaram fotos, filmes, links."

10. In the original, "pesquisa de referências serve para você aprender os detalhes, o tipo de coisa que você não sabe ou não lembra, mas o ideal é você desenhar a página depois, longe delas. Para que seu quadro seja um todo orgânico. A imagem armazenada na sua memória vai sofrer transformações em contato com outras imagens mentais e idealmente você vai conseguir criar sua versão daquilo."

11. The root of the god's name "Popolancome" is a pun on the Brazilian way of saying "you may put on Lancôme."

12. In the original, "miedo, un miedo sutil, extraño, mezcla de fascinación, sorpresa e incredulidad me invadió por completo cuando

entré en contacto con la escritura de Clarice Lispector. ( ... ) ¿Por qué
el temor ante una escritora que además escribe en un idioma que no
me pertenece?"

13. In the original in Spanish, "el rostro del embrujo literario."

14. Other notable members of the Abramo family are Athos Abramo's
son, the journalist and socialist militant Perseu Abramo (1929–
1996), and Claudio Abramo's son Cláudio Weber Abramo, founder
and president of the anticorruption ONG Transparência Brasil.

15. *Rememória* also contains an interesting interview with Lélia Abramo
(63–82).

16. In the original, "en la escritura de *Fiat Lux* se confirma una buena
noticia: la apertura de la poesía mexicana a otros cauces, luego de
años de empantanamiento."

17. In the original, "uno de los mejores poemarios publicados por
jóvenes en los últimos años, cuya sustancia radica en ser una poesía
sumamente depurada, en la que la autora toca las cosas más concre-
tas sin ser prosaica, enlazando referencias clásicas y facturas poéticas
muy nuevas, que muestra erudición en muchos temas y despliega con
soltura una enorme variedad de recursos expresivos."

18. In the original, respectively, "*pobre modo*," "*falta esencial*," and "casi
pasillo."

19. In the original, respectively, "el hambre de su abuela," "ese fantoche
de mal gusto," and "una riqueza enorme y mal distribuida / de crus-
táceos en el mundo, y de libros y de tiempo / para leerlos."

20. In the original, "en la frontera minúscula que media / entre la orden
y el hecho de cumplirla."

21. In the original, "breve y es ficticia" and "por el acato o el desacato."

### Conclusion

1. In the original in Spanish, "Que Vargas Llosa haya escrito su esplén-
dido libro sin conocer problemenle la obra maestra de Guimarães
Rosa (Brasil está más desconectado con el resto de América Latina
que con Europa o con los Estados Unidos) muestra que hay profundas corrientes invisibles que vinculan el estilo épico de las novelas
de caballería y el narrativo de algunos escritores latinoamericanos de
hoy. El mundo feudal de la selva peruana y el del desierto minero de
alguna manera hacen juego con el mundo feudal de aquellas novelas
andariegas de la Europa de fines de la edad media."

2. In the original, "durante muito tempo houve um processo simplista
de localizar a origem de influências. Uma estória no Brasil e outra
semelhante n'África? Origem Africana. Será que Portugal não expli-
caria a situação de ambos os motivos, tendo-os levado para África
e Brasil? Não são ouvidas na África do Norte e do Sul estórias que
estão no "Calila e Dinma"? Teria o africano-negro, no século VI,
influído nas Índias, onde o médico Barzuié o foi buscar? O encontro

de estórias, sabidamente velhas n'África, na Europa central e de leste, na Lapônia, na Finlândia, na Lituânia, ou na extrema Oceania, perturbou o método. Os próprios mapas etnográficos só podem evidenciar o diagrama de percurso e não o ponto indiscutido da velocidade inicial."

3. In the original, "una lógica del juego, que se sobreimpone a las expresiones particulares e individuales así como a las circunstancias precisas."

4. In the original, "cemento ideológico y, sobre todo, cultural del sistema."

5. In the original, "un poderoso disolvente de las contradicciones sociales" and "las mil caras de la lucha de clases."

6. In the original, "é engraçado: há culturas cuja a influência é perigosa, e outras não. Por exemplo, eu acho a cultura espanhola muito perigosa para nós, porque desvirtua os caracteres mais sutilmente íntimos da língua nacional. Toda a influência cultural enche uma língua de estrangeirismo, não há dúvida. Mas é curioso como o galicismo, um anglicismo, um germanismo não deturpam a sensibilidade psicológica da nossa sintáxe. Talvez por virem de linguagens distantes demais da nacional, mas o italianismo e sobretudo o espanholismo, por isso mesmo que muito mais sutís, menos 'visíveis', têm o dom terrível de deturpar as essências íntimas da nossa lingua."

7. Montaigne proceeds to complain about the tendency of "your better bred sort of men" to gloss over what they discover and "cannot forbear a little to alter the story; they never represent things to you simply as they are, but rather as they appeared to them, or as they would have them appear to you, and to gain the reputation of men of judgment, and the better to induce your faith, are willing to help out the business with something more than is really true, of their own invention" (93).

8. In the original: "aquele que não cessa de encontrar novos meios para exprimir-se, novas linguagens, novos valores e ideias, de tal modo que, quanto mais parece ser outra coisa, tanto mais é a repetição de si mesmo." Chauí's book was part of the wave of publications that commemorated the 500th anniversary of the arrival of the Portuguese to the Atlantic coast.

9. In the original in Portuguese, "algo tido como perene (quase eterno) que traveja e sustenta o curso temporal e lhe dá sentido" and "pretende situar-se além do tempo, fora da história, num presente que não cessa nunca sob a multiplicidade de formas e aspectos que pode tomar."

# Bibliography

*Bell'Antonio.* Screenplay by Vitaliano Brancati, Pier Paolo Pasolini, Gino Vicentini. Dir. Mauro Bolognini. Alfredo Bini/Cino del Duca, 1960.

*Crime Delicado.* Screenplay by Maçal Aquino, Beto Brant, Luiz Francisco Carvalho Pinto, Maurício Paroni de Castro, Marco Ricca. Dir. Beto Brant. Drama Filmes, 2006.

*Dov'è la libertà... ?.* Screenplay by Vitaliano Brancati, Ennio Flaiano, Antonio Pietrangeli, Roberto Rossellini, Vincenzo Talarico. Dir. Rossellini, Roberto. Golden Film/Ponti-De Laurentis Cinematografica, 1954.

"*Entre Deus e o Diabo.*" *Folha de São Paulo* on June 22, 2008.

"Francisco S. Espejel and Julian Nava Salinas." *Mexican Aviation History.* Web. May 13, 2013. http://www.mexicanaviationhistory.com/articulos/articulo.php?id=18

"Exhiben mexicanos sus filmes en España." *El Universal.* October 26, 2006. *Eluniversal.* Web. May 10, 2013. http://www.eluniversal.com.mx/notas/383778.html

"Orígenes del ballet en Chile—Centro DAE." *Centro de documentación de las artes escénicas—Teatro Municipal de Santiago.* N.p., n.d. Web. March 31, 2013. http://www.centrodae.cl/wp_cdae/?p=2192

"Presente de las artes: literatura." *La Tempestad.* February 3, 2013. Web. May 17, 2013. http://latempestad.mx/presente-de-las-artes-literatura

"Roberto Montenegro (1887–1968)." *Artexpertsinc.* Web. May 12, 2013. http://www.artexpertswebsite.com/pages/artists/montenegro_roberto.php

*Vertebrando-se*: *Crime Delicado visto por dentro.* Screenplay by Maçal Aquino, Beto Brant, Luiz Francisco Carvalho Pinto, Maurício Paroni de Castro, Marco Ricca. Dir. Beto Brant. Drama Filmes, 2006.

"William Henry Hurlbert Dead." *The New York Times.* September 7, 1895. Web. June 10, 2012. http://spiderbites.nytimes.com/free_1895/articles_1895_09_00002.html

Abramo, Lélia. *Vida e Arte.* São Paulo: Editora Fundação Perseu Abramo /Editora Unicamp, 1997.

Abramo, Paula. *Fiat Lux.* Mexico: Editorial Tierra Adentro, 2012.

Achebe, Chinua. *Hopes and Impediments: Selected Essays, 1965–1987.* London: Heinemann, 1988.

Aguilar, Gonzalo. *Other Worlds: New Argentine Film*. New York: Palgrave Macmillan, 2008.

Aguilar Camin, Hector. *Saldos de la revolución*. Mexico: Ediciones Oceano, 1984.

Alatorre, Antonio et al. *Libro jubilar de Alfonso Reyes*. Mexico: Unam, 1956.

Alejo Santiago, Jesús. "Gana Paula Abramo el primer Premio Joaquín Xirau Icaza." *Milenio*. March 21, 2013. Web. May 17, 2013. http://www.milenio.com/cdb/doc/noticias2011/9b8a0b2c9f384793e2c3ed810f22 0397

Amaral, Tarsila do. *Crônicas e outros escritos de Tarsila do Amaral*. Brandini, Laura Taddei (org.). Campinas: Editora da UNICAMP, 2008.

Amsterdam, Anthony G. and Bruner, Jerome. *Minding the Law—How the Courts Rely on Storytelling, and How Their Stories Change the Ways We Understand the Law and Ourselves*. Cambridge: Harvard University Press, 2000.

Anderson, Benedict. *Imagined Communities—Reflections on the Origin and Spread of Nationalism*. London, New York: Verso, 1991.

Andrade, Mário de, Bandeira, Manuel, and Moraes, Marco Antônio de (ed.). *Correspondência Mário de Andrade e Manuel Bandeira*. São Paulo: Edusp, 2000.

Antelo, Raúl. "Rua México." *Revista Z Cultural* III.2 (2007). Revista Virtual do Programa Avançado de Cultura Contemporânea – PACC/UFRJ. December 20, 2013.

Arnoni Prado, Antonio. *Itinerário de uma falsa vanguarda—Os dissidentes, a Semana de 22 e o Integralismo*. São Paulo: Editora 34, 2010.

Aub, Max. *Diario de Djelfa*. Valencia: Poesia Edicions de la Guerra & Café Malvarrosa, 1998.

Aub, Max.. *Jusep Torres Campalans*. Mexico: Tezontle, 1958.

Aub, Max. Museo Nacional Centro de Arte Reina Sofía. *Jusep Torres Campalans—Ingenio de la vanguardia*. Madrid: Sociedad Estatal España Nuevo Milenio, 2003.

Augusto, Sérgio. "Crimes sem castigo." *Estado de São Paulo*. December 17, 2011. Web. *Estadao* May 7, 2013. http://www.estadao.com.br/noticias/arteelazer,crimes-sem-castigo,811888,0.htm

Azevedo, Ricardo de & Maués, Flamarion. *Rememória—Entrevistas sobre o Brasil do século XX*. São Paulo: Editora Fundação Perseu Abramo, 1997.

Bandeira, Manuel. *Homenagem a Manuel Bandeira*. Rio de Janeiro : Officinas Typographicas do "Jornal do Commercio," 1936.

Bandeira, Manuel. *Literatura Hispano-Americana*. Rio de Janeiro: Editora Fundo de Cultura, 1960.

Bandeira, Manuel. *Literatura Hispano-Americana*. Rio de Janeiro: Irmãos Pongetti, 1949.

Bandeira, Manuel. *Panorama de la poesía brasileña: acompañado de una breve antología*. México: Fondo de Cultura Económica, 1951.

Bandeira, Manuel. and Drummond de Andrade, Carlos. *Rio de Janeiro em prosa e verso*. Rio de Janeiro: José Olympio, 1965.

Bandeira, Manuel. "Rondó do Palace Hotel." Lanciani, Giulia (coord.) *Libertinagem—Estrela da manhã*. Madrid; Paris; México; Buenos Aires; São Paulo; Lima; Guatemala; San José; Santiago de Chile: ALLCA XX, 1998. 85.

Bandeira, Manuel. "Rondó dos Cavalinhos." *Estrela da manhã*. Lanciani, Giulia (coord.) *Libertinagem—Estrela da manhã*. Madrid; Paris; México; Buenos Aires; São Paulo; Lima; Guatemala; San José; Santiago de Chile: ALLCA XX, 1998. 83.

Bandeira, Manuel. "Tempo de reis." *Poesia e prosa*. 2v. Rio de Janeiro: Aguilar, 1958. 377–378.

Barros, Salvador. "Enzo Faletto (1935–2003), el pensador." *El Siglo de Durango*. November 26, 2003. Web. May 12, 2013. http://www.elsiglodedurango.com.mx/noticia/18364.enzo-faletto-1935–2003-el-pensador.html

Bartra, Roger. *La jaula de la melancolía—Identidad y metamorfosis del mexicano*. Mexico, Barcelona, Buenos Aires: Grijalbo, 1987.

Bartra, Roger. "La crisis del nacionalismo en México." *Revista Mexicana de Sociología*, 51:3 (1989): 191–220.

Brasiliense de Almeida e Melo, Américo. *Os programas dos partidos e o Segundo império*. São Paulo: Typographia de Jorge Seckler, 1878.

Bernardi, Odyr. "Diario de Guadalupe." *Odyr Bernardi*. October 20, 2012. Web. May 11, 2013. http://odyr.wordpress.com/2012/08/20/diario-de-guadalupe-iii-inventando-o-mexico

Biondi, Marino. *Escrittori e identità italiana*. Firenze: Edizioni Polistampa, 2004.

Blasis, Carlo. *The Code of Terpsichore—The Art of Dancing, Comprising Its Theory and Practice and a History of Its Rise and Progress from the Earliest Times: Intended as well for the Instruction of Amateurs as the Use of Professional Persons*. London: Edward Bull, Holles Street, 1830.

Blasis, Carlo. *Traité élémentaire, théorique et pratique de l'art de la danse*. Milan: Forni Editore, 1820.

Boaventura, Maria Eugenia (org.). *22 por 22—A semana de arte moderna vista pelos seus contemporâneos*. São Paulo: EDUSP, 2000.

Bonfim, Manoel. *América Latina—Males de Origem*. Rio de Janeiro: Garnier, 1903.

Borges, Márcio & Borges, Lô. "Tudo que você podia ser." *Clube da Esquina*. CD. EMI-Odeon. 1973.

Bosi, Alfredo. *História concisa da literatura brasileira*. São Paulo: Cultrix, 1994.

Botelho, André. "Circulação de idéias e construção nacional: Ronald de Carvalho no Itamaraty." *Estudos Históricos*, Rio de Janeiro, no 35, Janeiro-junho de 2005, 69–97.

Botelho, André. *O Brasil e os dias: estado-nação, modernismo e rotina intelectual*. Bauru: EDUSC, 2005.

Brading, David A. "Prólogo—Alfonso Reyes y América." *América*. México: FCE, 2005. 7–27.

Brancati, Vitaliano. *Don Giovanni in Sicília*. Milano: Bompiani, 1941.

Brancati, Vitaliano. *Il bell'Antonio*. Milano: Bompiani, 1950.

Brooks, David. "Cobrador, espejo doble 'de la violencia y la globalización.'" *La Jornada*. November 30, 2007. Web. *Jornada* May 10, 2013. http://www.jornada.unam.mx/2007/11/30/index.php?section=espectaculos&article=a12n1esp

Buchloh, Benjamin, Lambert-Beatty, Carrie, and Sullivan, Megan. "To Make an Inner Time—A Conversation with Gabriel Orozco." *October* 130 Fall 2009: 177–196.

Bushnell, David et al. "History of Latin America." *Encyclopaedia Britannica*. London: Encyclopaedia Britannica Educational Corp. 2013. *Encyclopaedia Britannica*. Web. June 1, 2013. http://www.britannica.com/EBchecked/topic/331694/history-of-Latin-America

Buzzo, Elisa Andrade and Castillo, Rodrigo. *Radial: Poesía contemporánea de Brasil y México*. Editorial Cielo Abierto, 2012.

Câmara Cascudo, Luis da. *Literatura oral no Brasil*. Rio de Janeiro: José Olympio, 1978.

Campana, Dino. Bonaffini, Luigi (trans.) *Canti orfici e Altre poesie*. New York: Peter Lang, 1991.

Campos, Augusto de. *O Anticrítico*. São Paulo: Companhia das Letras, 1986.

Cantalupo, Roberto. *Brasile Euro-Americano*. Rome: Insituto per gli studi di politica internazionale, 1941.

Cárdenas Pacheco, Rocío. "Ehrenberg." *Vida Universitária—Suplemento Flama no197*. December 1, 2007. Nuevo León: UANL, 2007. http://vidauniversitaria.uanl.mx/flama/numero-197/789-ehrenberg.html

Cardoso, Fernando Henrique and Faletto, Enzo. *Dependencia y desarollo en América Latina*. Lima: Instituto de Estudios Peruanos, 1967.

Cardoso, Fernando Henrique and Faletto, Enzo. *Dependency and Development in Latin America*. Berkeley: University of California Press, 1979.

Cardoza y Aragón, Luis. "Prólogo." Artaud, Antonin. *México*. Mexico: UNAM, 1962.

Carrión, Jorge. *Mito y magia del mexicano*. Mexico: Porrua y Obregón, 1952.

Carvalho, Flávio de. *Revista Anual do Salão de Maio*. São Paulo: RASM, 1939.

Carvalho, Ronald de. *Caderno de Imagens da Europa*. São Paulo: Companhia Editora Nacional, 1935.

Carvalho, Ronald de. *Estudos Brasileiros, 1a Série*. Rio de Janeiro: Briguiet, 1930.

Carvalho, Ronald de. *Epigramas irónicos e sentimentais*. Rio de Janeiro: Annuario do Brasil, 1922.

Carvalho, Ronald de. *Imagens do México*. Rio de Janeiro: Annuario do Brasil, 1929.

Carvalho, Ronald de. *Itinerário de uma viagem—Antilhas, Estados Unidos, México*. São Paulo: Editora Nacional, 1935.

Carvalho, Ronald de. *Luz Gloriosa*. Paris: Casa Cré, 1913.

Carvalho, Ronald de. "México, país de belleza." *América Brasileira*. II:22 (1923) 15–16.

Carvalho, Ronald de. and Montalvôr, Luiz de (eds.). *Orpheu No 1 – Edição Facsimilada*. Lisboa: Contexto, 1989.

Carvalho, Ronald de. Payró, Jaime E. (trans.) *Pequeña historia de la literatura brasileña*. Buenos Aires: Ministerio de Defensa, 1943.

Carvalho, Ronald de.. Rubbia, Ferruccio (trans.). *Piccola storia della Letteratura brasiliana*. Firenze: Valecchi, 1936.

Carvalho, Ronald de.. *Poemas e Sonetos*. Rio de Janeiro: Leite Ribeiro & Maurillo, 1919.

Carvalho, Ronald de.. *Toda a América*. Rio de Janeiro: Pimenta de Mello e Cia, 1926.

Carvalho Pinto, Luiz Fernando. *Nada mais foi dito nem perguntado*. São Paulo: Editora 34, 2001.

Cavendish, Richard. *The Black Arts—A Concise History of Witchcraft, Demonology, Astrology, Alchemy, and Other Mystical Practices Throughout the Ages*. New York: Penguin, 1983.

Celso, Affonso. *Lupe*. Rio de Janeiro: Magalhães e Compania Editores, 1894.

Celso, Affonso. *Porque me ufano do meu paíz [Right or Wrong, My Country]*. Rio de Janeiro: Laemmert & Co., 1901.

Celso, Affonso. "Reminiscências mexicanas." *Revista da Academia Brasileira de Letras*, XIV: 27–28 (1923) 171–175.

Cerón Rocío. "Tránsito y Geografías. Encuentro de Poesía Brasil-México." *Ediciones el Billar de Lucrecia*. June 7, 2008. Web. May 13, 2013. http://elbillardelucrecia.blogspot.com/2008_06_01_archive.html

Cerón, Rocío and Castillo, Rodrigo (eds.). *Sin red ni salvavidas—Poesía contemporánea de la América Latina*. Mexico: Secretaría de Cultura de Colima-Conaculta, 2009.

Cervantes, Francisco. *Travesías brasileño-lusitanas*. México: J. Pablos Editor/UNAM, 1989.

Cervantes, Francisco. *Ustedes recordarán*. Mexico: Selector, 1997.

Chauí, Marilena. *Brasil—Mito Fundador e Sociedade Autoritária*. São Paulo: Fundação Perseu Abramo, 2000.

Cruz, Antônio Donizeti da. "Identidade e alteridade em *Toda a América* de Ronald de Carvalho: a vinculação do local e do global." *Espéculo—Revista de estudios literarios*. Universidad Complutense de Madrid. 2008. http://www.ucm.es/info/especulo/numero38/rcarvalh.html

Cruz, Sor Juana Inés de la. *Carta Atenagórica y Respuesta a sor Filotea*. Barcelona: Red Ediciones, 2011.

D'Amico, Silvio (dir.) *Enciclopedia dello spettacolo*. Roma: Casa Editrice le Maschere, 1954.

Daunt, Ricardo."A passagem de Ronald de Carvalho por Portugal." *Sibila*, April 5, 2009.

Debroise, Olivier (ed.). *La era de la discrepancia: arte y cultura visual en México, 1968–1997*. México: Turner, 2006.

Debroise, Olivier. "Orozco es inocente." *Reforma* 2 (2000): 4.

Dixon, Paul. *Reversible Readings: Ambiguity in Four Latin American Novels*. Tuscaloosa: University of Alabama Press, 1985.

Dunn, Christopher. "Tom Zé and the Performance of Citizenship in Brazil." *Popular Music*. 28:2 (2009): 217–237.

Eagleton, Terry. *Figures of Dissent*. London, New York: Verso, 2003.

Ehrenberg, Felipe. *Manchuria: visión periférica*. Mexico: Editorial Diamantina, 2007.

Ehrenberg, Felipe. "Rubens Gerchman en mi memoria, Rubens de mis recuerdos." *Agulha*. February 3, 2008. Web. October 4, 2010. http://www.triplov.com/Agulha-Revista-de-Cultura/2008/Rubens-Gerchman.html

Ellison, Fred P. *Alfonso Reyes e o Brasil*. Rio de Janeiro: Topbooks, 2002.

Ellison, Fred P. "Alfonso Reyes y Manuel Bandeira: Una amistad mexico-brasileña." *Hispania*, Vol. 70, No 3. (Sep., 1987), 487–493.

Fabre, Luis Felipe. *La edad de oro—Antología de poesía mexicana actual*. Mexico: UNAM, 2012.

Fabris, Mariarosaria. *Nelson Pereira dos Santos—Um olhar neo-realista?* São Paulo: Edusp, 1994.

Fanon, Frantz. *The Wretched of the Earth*. New York: Grove Press, 1968.

Feres Jr, João. *A história do conceito de Latin America nos Estados Unidos*. Bauru: Edusc/Anpocs, 2004.

Fonseca, Rubem. *Feliz ano novo*. Rio de Janeiro: Editora Arte Nova, 1975.

Fonseca, Rubem. "Large Intestine." *Oxford Anthology of the Brazilian Short Story*. London: Oxford University Press, 2006, 460–467.

Fonseca, Rubem. *O cobrador*. Rio de Janeiro: Editora Nova Fronteira, 1979.

Fonseca, Rubem. *O Buraco na parede*. São Paulo: Companhia das Letras, 1994.

Fonseca, Rubem. *Historias de amor*. São Paulo: Companhia das Letras, 1997.

Freyre, Gilberto. *Casa Grande & Senzala*. Rio de Janeiro: Record, 1992.

Frye Burnham, Linda, and Durland, Steve (eds.) *The Citizen Artist: 20 Years of Art in the Public Arena—An Anthology from High Performance Magazine 1978–1998*. New York: Critical Press, 1998, 93–102.

Gabeira, Fernando. *O que é isso, companheiro?*. São Paulo: Companhia das Letras, 1996.

García Canclini, Néstor. *Latinoamericanos buscando lugar en esto siglo*. Buenos Aires: Paidós, 2002.

García Cruz, Beatriz et al. *Premio de Literatura Latinoamericana y del Caribe Juan Rulfo—Rubem Fonseca: 2003*. Guadalajara : Editorial Universitaria, 2003.

García Terrés, Jaime. *Obras I—Las manchas del sol—Poesía 1963–1994*. México: Fondo de Cultura Económica/El Colegio Nacional, 1995.

García Terrés, Jaime. *Obras II—El teatro de los acontecimientos*. México: El Colegio Nacional/Fondo de Cultura Económica, 1997.

García Tsao, Leonardo. *Cinema of Tears*. *Variety* 1995 June 26.

Gardnier, Ruy and Caetano, Daniel. "Entrevista com Nelson Pereira dos Santos." *Contracampo*. n.d. available at /http://www.contracampo.com.br/29/entrevistanelson.htm.

Gesualdo, Vicente. *Historia de la musica en la Argentina (1852–1900)—Tomo II*. Buenos Aires: Editorial Beta, 1961.

Gómez Arias, Alejandro. *De viva voz*. Mexico: Instituto de Investigaciones Sociales, Universidad Nacional Autónoma de México, 1992.

González Matute, Laura. "Felix Bernardelli (1862–1908)—Un artista moderno en el museo de San Carlos." Revista Digital—Cenidiap 11, Julio-Diciembre, 2008. http://discursovisual.cenart.gob.mx/dvweb11/agora/agolaura.htm

González Matute, Laura. "Félix Bernardelli: un artista moderno en Guadalajara." *Félix Bernardelli y su taller*. Mexico: INBA, 1996.

Goytisolo, Juan. *España y sus* ejidos. Madrid: HMR, 2003.

Grandin, Greg. *Fordlandia: The Rise and Fall of Henry Ford's Forgotten Jungle City*. New York: Picador, 2010.

Guerra, Lilian. *The Myth of José Martí—Conflicting Nationalisms in Early Twentieth Century Cuba*. Chapel Hill: The University of North Carolina Press, 2005.

Guimarães Rosa, João. *Antes das Primeiras Estórias*. Rio de Janeiro: Nova Fronteira, 2011.

Guimarães Rosa, João. *Ave, palavra*. Rio de Janeiro: Nova Fronteira, 2001.

Guimarães Rosa, João. *Estas estórias*. Rio de Janeiro: José Olympio, 1976.

Guimarães Rosa, João. *Grande Sertão: Veredas*. Nova Fronteira, Rio de Janeiro, 2001.

Guimarães Rosa, João. *Sagarana*, José Olympio, Rio de Janeiro, 1972.

Guimarães Rosa, Vilma. *Relembramentos: João Guimarães Rosa, Meu Pai*, Nova Fronteira, Rio de Janeiro, 1999.

Gutiérrez Vega, Hugo. *Andar en Brasil*. Querétaro: Universidad Autónoma de Querétaro, 1987.

Gutiérrez Vega, Hugo. *Bazar de asombros – Vols 1 & 2*. Mexico: Editorial Aldus, 2000–2002.

Gutiérrez Vega, Hugo, interview by Arturo García Hernández, "*Antología con dudas*, mi testamento literario: Hugo Gutiérrez Vega," *La Jornada*. October 27, 2007. *La Jornada*. Web. July 5, 2009. http://www.jornada.unam.mx/2007/10/28/index.php?section=cultura&article=a03n1cu

l. Hauser, Arnold. *Social History of Art, Vol. 3: Rococo, Classicism, and Romanticism*. New York: Routledge, 1999.

Gutiérrez Vega, Hugo. *Social History of Art, Vol. 4: Naturalism, Impressionism, The Film Age*. New York: Routledge, 1999.

Hicks, Emily. "The Artist as Citizen: Guillermo Gómez-Peña, Felipe Ehrenberg, David Avalos and Judy Baca" in

Holanda, Sérgio Buarque de. *Raízes do Brasil*. São Paulo: Companhia das Letras, 1999.

Horseman, Reginald. *Race and Manifest Destiny—The Origins of American Racial Anglo-Saxonism*. Cambridge: Harvard University Press, 1981.

Iglesia, Ramon. *Cronistas e Historiadores de la Conquista de México—El ciclo de Hernán Cortés*. México: El colegio de México/FCE, 1942.

Ivo, Lêdo. "Refeição Azteca." *O Estado de São Paulo*, São Paulo, November 23, 1957. *Suplemento Literário*, n.57.

Jiménez, Victor. *Carlos Obregón Santacilia : pionero de la arquitectura mexicana*. Mexico: INBA, 2001.

Joaquim, Luiz. "Quando a pedra vira vidraça." *Folha de Pernambuco. Fundação Joaquim Nabuco*. March 6, 2006. Web. March 6, 2010. http://www.fundaj.gov.br/notitia/servlet/newstorm.ns.presentation.Navig ationServlet?publicationCode=16&pageCode=720&textCode=6510&d ate=currentDate

Johnson, Randal. "Rereading Brazilian Modernism," Texas Papers on Latin América, No. 89–04. Austin: Institute of Latin American Studies, University of Texas at Austin, 1989. http://lanic.utexas.edu/project/ etext/llilas/tpla/8904.pdf

Kardec, Alan. *O Livro dos Espíritos*. Rio de Janeiro: Federação Espírita Brasileira, 1957.

Kraisrideja, Sandra. "Carved coconuts highlight Mexico's history." *North County Times*, 3 de agosto, 2005. http://www.nctimes.com/enter- tainment/art-and-theater/visual/article_1ad5de79–45ad-5a3f-8412- f0a1218d0713.html.

Kushnir, Beatriz. *Cães de Guarda: jornalistas e censores do AI-5 à constituição de 1988*. São Paulo: Boitempo, 2004.

Kwon, Miwon. "The fullness of Empty Containers." *Frieze* 24, September- October 1995. 54–57.

Leal, Luis. "Presentación" in Reyes, Alfonso. *Visión de Anáhuac*. México: UNAM, 2004.

Levine, Suzanne Jill. *Manuel Puig and the Spider Woman—His Life and His Fiction*. Madison: University of Wisconsin Press, 2000.

Lima, Alceu Amoroso. "Homem de proa." *Companheiros de viagem*. Rio de Janeiro: José Olympio, 1971, 145–149.

Lima, Alceu Amoroso. *Cultura Inter-Americana*. Rio de Janeiro: Agir, 1962.

Lima, Alceu Amoroso. "30 de março." *Revolução, reação ou reforma?* Rio de Janeiro: Tempo Brasileiro, 1964, 221–222.

Llanos, Fernando. "Manchuria." Online video. *YouTube*. YouTube, November 14, 2007. Web. May 12, 2013. http://www.youtube.com/ watch?v=56sbUsDc01I

Lozano, Luís-Martín. "Del taller a la academia: Félix Bernardelli, maestro de una generación de pintotres jaliscienses." *Félix Bernardelli y su taller*. Mexico: INBA, 1996.

Lubow, Arthur. "After Frida." *New York Times Magazine*. March 23, 2008. Web. May 12, 2013. http://www.nytimes.com/2008/03/23/ magazine/23ramirez-t.html?pagewanted=all

Luque, R. and Barrios, G. E. "Cotard's Syndrome: Analysis of 100 Cases." *Acta Psychiatrica Scandinavica*. 91:3. March 1995, 185–188.

Lyra, Carlos. *Eu & a Bossa: uma história da Bossa Nova*. Rio de Janeiro: Casa da Palavra, 2008.

Lyra, Carlos. *Saravá!* RCA/BMG CD #74321891392 (2001).[CD Reissue]
Lyra, Heitor. *Minha vida diplomática (Coisas vistas e ouvidas)—1916–1925.* Lisboa; Porto: Centro do Livro Brasileiro, 1972.
Machado, Arlindo. *Made in Brasil: trés décadas do video brasileiro.* São Paulo: Iluminuras; Itaú, 2007.
Machado de Assis, Joaquim Maria. *Chrysalidas: poesias.* Rio de Janeiro: Livraria de B. L. Garnier, 1864.
Machado de Assis, Joaquim Maria. *Correspondência de Machado de Assis—Tomo I—1860–1869.* Rio de Janeiro: ABL, 2008.
Machado de Assis, Joaquim Maria. Sonia Breyer (org.). *O Conto de Machado de Assis: Antologia,* Rio de Janeiro: Civilização Brasileira, 1980
Machado de Assis, Joaquim Maria. *Phalenas.* Rio de Janeiro: Garnier, 1870.
Martínez, José Luis. *El ensayo mexicano moderno I.* Mexico: Fondo de Cultura Económica, 2001.
Martínez López, Enrique. "Sor Juana Inés de la Cruz en Portugal: un desconocido homenaje y versos inéditos." *Prolija Memoria.* 1(2) (2005): 139–175.
Marx, Karl. *Capital Volume 1—A Critique of Political Economy.* New York: Dover, 2011.
Mata, Rodolfo & Crespo, Regina. "Imágenes de Brasil en la literatura mexicana." *La Jornada Semanal* 352:2 (2001): 2. http://www.jornada.unam.mx/2001/12/02/sem-brasil.html
Mattos, Carlos Alberto. "Helena Salem: entre o cinema e a política." *Filme Cultura* 59 (2013): 69–72.
Matute, Laura González. "Félix Bernardelli (1862–1908). Un artista moderno en el Museo Nacional de San Carlos." *Discurso Visual—Revista Digital.* 11 (2008). Web. May 13, 2013. http://discursovisual.cenart.gob.mx/dvweb11/agora/agolaura.htm#
Matz, Jesse. *Literary Impressionism and Literary Aesthetics.* Cambridge: Cambridge University Press, 2001.
Medina, Cuauhtémoc. "El Ojo Breve / El caso Orozco." *Reforma* 25 Oct (2000): 2.
Mello, Zuza Homem de. *João Gilberto.* São Paulo: Publifollha, 2001.
Menezes. Roniere. *O traço, a Letra e a Bossa—Literatura e diplomacia em Cabral, Rosa e Vinicius.* Belo Horizonte: Editora UFMG, 2011.
Micelli, Sérgio. "O Conselho Nacional de Educação: Esboço de Análise de um Aparelho de Estado (1931–7)" in *Intelectuais à Brasileira.* São Paulo: Companhia das Letras, 2001, 293–341.
Milanca Guzman, Mario. "La música en el periódico chileno 'El Ferrocarril' (1855–1865)." *Revistamusicalchilena* 54:193(2000)17–44. Web. March 31, 2013. http://www.scielo.cl/scielo.php?script=sci_arttext&pid=S0716–27902000019300002&lng=es&nrm=iso>. ISSN 0716–2790. doi: 10.4067/S0716–27902000019300002
Minera, María. "Conversación con Gabriel Orozco." *Letras Libres.* December 2006. Web. May 17, 2013. http://www.letraslibres.com/revista/artes-y-medios/conversacion-con-gabriel-orozco

Monteiro, Pedro Meira. *A queda do aventureiro: aventura, cordialidade e os novos tempos em Raízes do Brasil*. Campinas: Editora da UNICAMP, 1999.

Monteiro Lobato, José Bento. *Na antevéspera: reacções mentaes de um ingenuo*. São Paulo: Companhia Editora Nacional, 1933.

Monsiváis, Carlos. "Notas sobre la cultura mexicana en el siglo XX." *História general de México*. México: El Colégio de México, 2000.

Monsiváis, Carlos. "Prólogo." *México—Alfonso Reyes*. México: FCE, 2005. 32–42.

Moog, Clodomir Vianna. *Tóia*. Rio de Janeiro: Editora Civilização Brasileira, 1962.

Moreira, Luiza. *Meninos, poetas e heróis: aspectos de Cassiano Ricardo do modernismo ao Estado Novo*. São Paulo: EDUSP, 2001.

Moreira, Paulo. "El Páramo de João Guimarães Rosa." *Juan Rulfo: otras miradas*. Mexico: Fundación Juan Rulfo, Casa Juan Pablos, Instituto Michoacano de Ciencias de la Educación, Secretaría de Cultura del Estado de Michoacán, Secretaría de Educación del Estado de Michoacán, México, 2010. 439–459.

Moreira, Paulo. *Modernismo Localista nas Américas: os contos de Faulkner, Guimarães Rosa e Rulfo*. Belo Horizonte: Editora UFMG, 2012.

Moreira, Paulo. "Quando os mexicanos vêm ao Rio" in Estudios Portugueses—Revista de Filología Portuguesa 4:7 (2008): 167–185.

Moreyra, Álvaro. *As amargas, não... (Lembranças)*. Rio de Janeiro: Editora Lux, 1955.

Nagib, Lúcia. *A utopia no cinema brasileiro*. São Paulo: Cosac & Naify, 2006.

Navarrete, Sylvia. "Gabriel Orozco ante la crítica." Reforma 12 (2000): 5.

Neves, Carlos Augusto R. Santos. "O Brasil e o futuro: linhas para uma presença do Brasil na vida internacional." *Política Externa*, v. 1, n°4, março, 1993, p. 18–31.

Newcomb, Robert Patrick. *Nossa and Nuestra America: Inter-American Dialogues*. West Lafayette: Purdue University Press, 2011.

Nodari, Alexandre. *45 anos do Golpe: terrorismo e cordialidade*. Consenso, só no paredão, 19 de maio de 2009. http://www.culturaebarbarie.org/blog/2009/05/45-anos-do-golpe-terrorismo-e.html

Northrop, F. S. C. *The Meeting of East and West*. New York: The Macmillan Company, 1946.

Novo, Salvador. *Continente vacío*. Madrid: Espasa Calpe S.A., 1935.

Octavio, Rodrigo. "Na terra da virgem India (Sensações do México)". *Revista da Academia Brasileira de Letras*. Nos 27–28, Julho-Dezembro (1923): 145–170.

Octavio, Rodrigo. *Minhas memórias dos outros—Nova Série*. Rio de Janeiro: Livraria José Olympio Editora, 1935.

Octavio, Rodrigo. *Minhas memórias dos outros—Última série*. Rio de Janeiro: Livraria José Olympio Editora, 1936.

Oroz, Silvia. *Melodrama—Cinema de Lágrimas*. Rio de Janeiro: Rio Fundo Editora, 1992.

Oroz, Silvia. *Melodrama—Cinema de Lágrimas*. Rio de Janeiro: FUNARTE, 1999.

Orozco, Gabriel. *Gabriel Orozco*. Los Angeles: The Museum of Contemporary Art, Los Angeles, 2000.

Ortega, Julio. "Prólogo." *Teoría literaria – Alfonso Reyes*. México: FCE, 2007. 7–13.

Ortega, Julio. "Rubem Fonseca y Juan Rulfo: caminos cruzados." *Premio de literatura latinoaemricana y del Caribe Juan Rulfo—Rubem Fonseca 2003*. Mexico: Editorial Pandora, 2003.

Ortega y Gasset. José. *Deshumanización del arte y otros ensayos estéticos*. Madrid: Revista de Occidente, 1964.

Pacheco, José Emilio. *Ciudad de la memoria*: poemas 1986–1989. México: Ediciones Era, 1989.

Pacheco, José Emilio. *Irás y no volverás*. México: Fondo de Cultura Económica, 1973.

Pacheco, José Emilio. "*Monterrey* de Alfonso Reyes." *Edición facsimilar de los quince fascículos de Monterrey—Correo Literário de Alfonso Reyes*. Monterrey: Fondo Editorial de Nuevo León, 2008. 23–31.

Pacheco, José Emilio. *Tarde o temprano [Poemas 1958–2000]*. Mexico: Fondo de Cultura Económica, 2004.

Pacheco, José Emilio. "Reloj de Arena: Borges de noche," *Letras Libres*. April 2001, 26–28.

Palacios, Guillermo. *Intimidades, conflitos e reconciliações: México e Brasil, 1822–1993*. São Paulo: EDUSP, 2008.

Pappacena. Flavia (Ed.). *Arthur Saint-León—La sténocoreographie*.Roma: Lim Editrice, 2006.

Paranaguá, Paulo Antonio (org.). *Mexican Cinema*. London: BFI, 1995.

Paroni de Castro, Maurício. "Crime Delicado ou a Vida é mais que a Estética." *Cronópios*. January 28, 2006. Web. May 11, 2013. http://www.cronopios.com.br/site/colunistas.asp?id=962#texto

Paula, Maria de Fátima C. "USP e UFRJ: A influência das concepções alemã e francesa em suas fundações." *Tempo Social*, São Paulo, 14(2): 147–161, 2002.

Paz, Octavio. *El laberinto de la soledad* México: FCE, 1959.

Paz, Octavio. *Generaciones y semblanzas—Escritores y letras de México*. México: Fondo de Cultura Económica, 1987.

Paz, Octavio et al. *Poesía en movimiento: México 1915–1966*. Siglo XXI Editores, 1966.

Paz, Ravel and Durão, Fábio. *Indústria Radical*. São Paulo: Nankin, 2012.

Pellicer, Carlos. "Dos textos inéditos." *Revista de la Universidad de México*. Volumen XXXV, números 2–3, octubre/noviembre de 1980. 18–22.

Pellicer, Carlos. *Material Poético, 1918–1961*. México: UNAM, 1962.

Pellicer, Carlos. *Piedra de sacrificios—Poema Iberoamericano*. Mexico: Editorial Nayarit, 1924.

Peregrino Júnior, João. *Ronald de Carvalho—Poesia e Prosa*. Rio de Janeiro: Agir, 1960.

Pesavento, Sandra *et al.* *Érico Veríssimo: o romance da história.* São Paulo: Nova Alexandria, 2001.

Piazza, Maria de Fátima Fontes. "Tal Brasil, Qual América? América Brasileira e a cultura Ibero Americana". *Diálogos Latinoamericanos,* noviembre 2007, número 12, Universidad de Aarhus, 42–67.

Pick, Zuzana. *Constructing the Image of the Mexican Revolution—Cinema and the Archive.* Austin: University of Texas, 2010.

Pierre, Sylvie. "Cinéma de larmes de Nelson Pereira dos Santos." *Cahiers du cinema* 492 (1995): 86–91.

Poniatowska, Elena. *La noche del Tlatelolco: testimonios de historia oral.* México: Ediciones Era, 1971.

Prado, Eduardo. *A ilusão americana.* São Paulo: Escola Typographica Salesiana, 1902.

Prado, Paulo. *Retrato do Brasil – Ensaio sobre a tristeza brasileira.* Rio de Janeiro: José Olympio, 1962.

Prado Jr., Caio. *Formação do Brasil Contemporáneo.* São Paulo: Livraria Martins Editora, 1942.

Poot Herrera, Sara. "Sor Juana: Nuevos hallazgos, viejas relaciones." Anales de Literatura Española. N. 13 (1999): 63–83.

Quintana, José Manuel. *Poesías de D. Manuel José Quintana.* Madrid: Imprenta Nacional, 1813.

Quintanilla, Luis. *A Latin American Speaks.* New York: The Macmillan Company, 1943.

Quintanilla, Luis. *Obra poética.* Mexico: Editorial Domés, 1986.

Quitero-Rivera, Marea. *A Cor e Som da nação. A idéia da mestiçagem na crítica musical do Caribe espanhol e Brasil (1928–1947).* São Paulo: FAPESP, 1998, 45.

Ramírez, Mati Carmen. *Inverted Utopias—Avant-Garde Art in Latin America.* New Haven, London and Houston: Yale University Press and Museum of Fine Arts, 2004.

Ramos, Julio. *Divergent Modernities: Culture and Politics in Nineteenth-Century Latin America.* Durham: Duke University Press, 2001.

Ramos, Samuel. *Perfil del hombre y la cultura de México.* México: UNAM, 1963.

Rashkin, Elissa. *Stridentist Movement in Mexico: The Avant-Garde and Cultural Change in the 1920s.* London: Lexington Books, 2009.

Reyes, Alfonso. "A vuela de correo." *Obras Completas VIII.* México: Fondo de Cultura Económica, 1958.

Reyes, Alfonso. "A Ronald de Carvalho." Obras Completas VIII." Mexico: Fondo de Cultura Económica, 1958. 157–159.

Reyes, Alfonso. *Obras Completas de Alfonso Reyes—IX: Norte y Sur; Los trabajos y los dias; Historia natural das Laranjeiras.* México: Fondo de Cultura Económica, 1959.

Reyes, Alfonso. *Obras Completas de Alfonso Reyes – X: Constancia poética.* México: Fondo de Cultura Econômica, 1959.

Reyes, Alfonso. *Romances del Río de Enero.* Maastrich: Halcyon, 1933.

Reyes, Alfonso. *Edición facsimilar de los quince fascículos de Monterrey— Correo Literário de Alfonso Reyes.* Monterrey: Fondo Editorial de Nuevo León, 2008.

Reyes, Alfonso. "Justo Sierra y la historia patria." *México—Alfonso Reyes.* México: FCE, 2005. 175–198.

Reyes, Alfonso. "México en una nuez" in *Obras Completas IX.* México: Fondo de Cultura Económica, 1959.

Reyes, Alfonso. *Misión Diplomática—Tomo II.* México: Fondo de Cultura Económica, 2001.

Reyes, Alfonso. "Poesía Indígena Brasileña" in *Obras Completas Volumen IX.* México: Fondo de Cultura Económica, 1959. 86–88.

Reyes, Alfonso. "Romances del Río de Enero" in *Obras Completas Volumen X.* México: Fondo de Cultura Económica, 1960.

Reyes, Alfonso. "Visión de Anahuác" in *Prosa y Poesía.* James Willis Robb (ed.). Madrid: Cátedra, 1975, 69–127.

Reyes, Alfonso. "Visión de Anáhuac." In *México.* México: FCE, 2005. 69–102.

Reyes, Alfonso. Onís, Harriet de (trans.). "Vision of Anáhuac." *The Position of America and Other Essays by Alfonso Reyes.* New York: Knopf, 1950.

Reyes, Alicia. *Genio y figura de Alfonso Reyes.* México: Fondo de Cultura Económica, 1997.

Ribeiro, Darcy. *O Povo Brasileiro.* São Paulo: Companhia das Letras, 2006.

Ribeiro Couto, Rui. "El Hombre Cordial, producto americano." *Monterrey,* No. 8. (Mar., 1932), p. 3.

Ricardo, Cassiano. *O homem cordial e outros pequenos estudos brasileiros.* Rio de Janeiro: Ministério da Cultura/Instituto Nacional do Livro, 1959.

Ríos, Brenda. *Del amor y otras cosas que se gastan por el uso. Ironía y silencio en la narrativa de Clarice Lispector.* Mexico: Fondo Editorial Tierra Adentro, 2005.

Rodó, José Enrique. *Ariel.* Mexico: Editorial Porrúa, 2005.

Rodríguez Monegal, Emir. "Anacronismos: Mário de Andrade y Guimarães Rosa en el contexto de la novela hispanoamericana." *Revista Iberoamericana.* 43:98–99 (1977) : 109–115.

Rodríguez Monegal, Emir. "En busca de Guimarães Rosa" in *Mundo Nuevo,* n. 20febrero de 1968. 4–16.

Rojas Mix, Miguel. *Los cién nombres de América; eso que descubrió Colón.* San José: Editorial de la Universidad de Costa Rica, 1997.

Romero, Sílvio. *A America Latina—Análise do livrod e igual do Dr. M. Bomfim.* Porto: Lello & Irmão, 1906.

Ronquillo, Victor. *El Nacional.* July 26, 1986. *Paulleduc.* Web. May 10, 2013.

Rosário, Miguel do. "Cineasta mexicano adapta Rubem Fonseca." *Portal Literal.* May 16, 2007. *Literal.* Web. May 10, 2013.

Rulfo, Juan. *El Llano en Llamas.* México: Editorial RM-Fundación Juan Rulfo, 2005.

Rulfo, Juan.. "Juan Rulfo: la literatura es una mentira que dice la verdad. Una conversación con Ernesto González Bermejo," *Universidad de México,* XXXIV, September 1, 1979.

Rulfo, Juan.. *Pedro Páramo.* México: Editorial RM-Fundación Juan Rulfo, 2005.

Rulfo, Juan.. "Prólogo." *Memorias Póstumas de Blas Cubas,* translation by Antonio Alatorre. Mexico: Secretary of Public Education-Universidad Nacional Autónoma de México, 1982. 1–4.

Sadlier, Darlene J. (org.). *Latin American Melodrama—Passion, Pathos, and Entertainment.* Urbana and Chicago: University of Illinois Press, 2009.

Sadlier, Darlene J. *Nelson Pereira dos Santos.* Urbana and Chicago: University of Illinois Press, 2003.

Said, Edward W. *Orientalism.* New York: Vintage, 1979.

Salem, Helena. *Nelson Pereira dos Santos—El sueño possible del cine brasileño.* Madrid: Cátedra, 1997.

Salles, João Moreira. "Sarajevo e Rio: duas guerras distintas." *Jornal do Brasil.* September 23, 2001.

Santamarina, Guillermo. "El arte es solo una excusa—Conversación entre Guillermo Santamaria y Felipe Ehrenberg." In *Armas y Letras—revista de literatura, arte y cultura de la Universidad Autónoma de Nuevo León.* Monterrey, June, 2008, Nos 62/63. 94–99.

Santiago, Silviano. *As raízes e o labirinto da América Latina.* Rio de Janeiro: Rocco, 2006.

Santiago, Silviano. "A viagem de Lévi-Strauss aos trópicos." *Folha de São Paulo* September 10, 2000: M 4.

Santiago, Silviano. "Entrevista com Silviano Santiago." *Estudos Históricos* 30 (2002): 147–173.

Santiago, Silviano. "Las botas y el anillo de Zapata." *Minas Gerais— Suplemento Literário.* VIII.345 (1973): 1–2.

Santiago, Silviano. *Nas malhas da letra.* Rio de Janeiro: Rocco, 2002.

Santiago, Silviano. *Ora (Direis) puxar conversa!* Belo Horizonte: Editora UFMG, 2006.

Santiago, Silviano. "Os Astros Ditam o Futuro. A História Impõe o Presente. (Artaud versus Cárdenas)." *Estudos Históricos,* Rio de Janeiro, n.19, 1997.

Santiago, Silviano. *The Space In-Between: Essays on Latin American Culture.* Durham: Duke University Press, 2002.

Santiago, Silviano. *Viagem ao México.* Rio de Janeiro: Rocco, 1995.

Santiago Cruz, Francisco. *San Juan de Ulúa—Biografía de un presidio.* Mexico: Editorial Jus, 1966.

Santos, Theotonio dos. "The Structure of Dependence." *The American Economic Review—Papers and Proceedings of the Eighty-second Annual Meeting of the American Economic Association* 60: 2 (1970), 231–223.

Sarmiento, Domingo Faustino. *Facundo—Civilization and Barbarism.* Berkeley: University of California Press, 2003.

Schneider, Luis Mario. "Prólogo." Artaud, Antonin. *Viaje al país de los Tarahumaras: Textos de Antonin Artaud.* México: Secretaría de Educación Publica, Dirección General de Divulgación, 1975.

Schwartz, Jorge. "Abaixo Tordesilhas!" *Estudos Avançados* 7(17) (1993): 185–200.

Schwarz, Roberto. *Misplaced Ideas—Essays on Brazilian Culture.* London: Verso, 1992.

Schwartzman, Simon et al. *Tempos de Capanema.* Rio de Janeiro/São Paulo: Paz e Terra/ Editora da Universidade de São Paulo, 1984.

Sheridan, Guillermo. *México en 1932: la polémica nacionalista.* México: Fondo de Cultura Económica, 1999.

Sheridan, Guillermo. *Contemporáneos Ayer.* México: Fondo de Cultura Económica, 1985.

Soares, Gabriela Pellegrino. *Semear Horizontes: Uma história da formação de leitores na Argentina e no Brasil, 1915–1954.* Belo Horizonte: UFMG, 2007.

Souza, Eneida Maria de. "O discurso crítico brasileiro." *Crítica Cult.* Belo Horizonte: UFMG, 2007. 45–62.

Sucena, Eduardo. *A dança teatral no Brasil.* Rio de Janeiro: FUNART, 1988.

Smith, Maya Ramos. *Teatro musical y danza en le México de la belle époque (1867–1910).* Mexico: UAM, 1995.

Tacitus, Cornelius. Anthony R. Birley (trans.) *Agricola and Germany.* Oxford/New York: Oxford University Press, 1999.

Tapscott, Stephen (Ed.). *Twentieth-Century Latin American Poetry—A Bilingual Anthology.* Austin:University of Texas Press, 2000.

Távora, Juárez. *Petróleo para o Brasil.* Rio de Janeiro: José Olympio, 1955.

Tatius, Achilles. *Leucipe and Clitophon.* Tim Whitmarsh (trans.) London: Oxford University Press, 2003.

Tello Garrido, Romeo. "Prólogo." *Los mejores relatos de Rubem Fonseca.* Mexico: Alfaguara, 1998. 4–16.

Temkin, Ann, Orozco, Gabriel, and Fer, Briony. *Gabriel Orozco.* New York: MoMA, 2009.

Tenorio, Mauricio."A Tropical Cuauhtemoc—Celebrating the Cosmic Race at the Guanabara Bay." *Anales del Instituto de Investigaciones Estéticas,* 1994, vol. XVI, núm. 65, 93–137.

Vaillant, George C. *The Aztecs of Mexico—Origin, Rise and Fall of the Aztec Nation.* Harmondsworth: Penguin Books, 1950.

Valle, Camila do and Pavón, Cecilia (Eds.). *Caos portátil—Poesía Contemporánea del Brasil.* Mexico: Ediciones El billar de Lucrecia, 2007.

Vargas Llosa, Mario. "Thugs Who Know their Greek." *New York Times*: A.7. September 7, 1986. *ProQuest.* Web. May 10, 2013.

Vargas Llosa, Mario. "Un hombre de letras". *El País,* Sunday, February 20, 2005. 11, 17.

Varella, Luiz Fagundes. *Cantos do ermo e da cidade*. Rio de Janeiro: Garnier, 1880.

Varella, Luiz Fagundes. *Poemas de Fagundes Varela*. São Paulo: Cultrix, 1982.

Vasconcelos, José. *Breve Historia de México*. México: Ediciones Botas, 1938.

Vasconcelos, José. *La Raza Cósmica—Misión de la raza iberoamericana—notas de viajes a la América del Sur*. Paris: Agencia Mundial de Librería, 1925.

Vasconcelos, José. *Ulises criollo*. Madrid; Barcelona; La Habana; Lisboa; París; México; Buenos Aires; São Paulo; Lima; Guatemala; San José: ALLCA XX, 2000.

Ventura, Roberto. *Estilo Tropical—História cultural e polêmicas literárias no Brasil*. São Paulo: Companhia das Letras, 1991.

Venturi, Robert. *Complexity and Contradiction in Architecture*. New York: MoMA, 2011.

Verani, Hugo J. *La hoguera y el viento—José Emilio Pacheco ante la crítica*. México: Unam/Era, 1993.

Veríssimo, Érico. *A volta do gato preto*. Rio de Janeiro; São Paulo; Porto Alegre: Editora Globo, 1961.

Veríssimo, Érico. *His Excellency, the Ambassador*. New York: Macmillan, 1967.

Veríssimo, Érico. *México—História duma viagem*. Porto Alegre: Editora Globo, 1957.

Veríssimo, Érico. *Night*. New York, Macmillan, 1956.

Veríssimo, Érico. *Noite*. Rio de Janeiro : Editôra Globo, 1958.

Veríssimo, Érico. *O senhor embaixador*. Porto Alegre: Editora Globo, 1965.

Veríssimo, Érico. *O tempo e o vento*. Porto Alegre: Editora Globo, 1950.

Veríssimo, Érico. *Time and the Wind*. New York, Macmillan, 1951.

Veríssimo, José. *Estudos de Literatura Brasileira—Segunda Serie*. Rio de Janeiro: Garnier, 1901.

Vieira, Antônio. *Sermões Escolhidos—vol. II*. São Paulo: Edameris, 1965.

Villa, José Moreno. *Cornucopia de México y Nueva Cornucopia mexicana*. Mexico: FCE, 1985.

Wordsworth, William. "Preface to Lyrical Ballads." The Norton Anthology of English Literature. Ed. M. H. Abrams. Vol. 2. New York: W. W. Norton & Company, 1993. 753–765.

Yañez, María de los Angeles and Morales Lara, Pilar. "Voces cruzadas—Cartas de y para Agustín Yáñez." *Literatura mexicana*. Vol VIII, Núm. 2, Unam—Centro de Estudios Literarios, 1997. 793–808.

Zaid, Gabriel. "Homenaje a la alegría." *La gaceta del Fondo de Cultura Económico*. No 374. México: February 2002. 4–5.

Zaid, Gabriel. "Prólogo," *Antología Mínima*, México: Fondo de Cultura Económica, 2001. 7–12.

Zaid, Gabriel. *Cuestionario: Poemas 1951–1976*. México: Fondo de Cultura Económica, 1976.

Zaid, Gabriel. *Demasiados libros.* Barcelona: Anagrama, 1996.

Zaid, Gabriel. *"La chica de Ipanema"* Vuelta 112, México, Marzo de 1986.

Zaid, Gabriel. *Livros Demais!* São Paulo: Editora Summus, 2004.

Zaid, Gabriel. "Los años de aprendizaje de Carlos Pellicer" Letras Libres, Julio 2001.

Zaid, Gabriel. "Siete poemas de Pellicer." *Revista Iberoamericana.* Vol. LV, Núm. 148–149, Julio-Diciembre 1989, 1099–1118.

Zanini, Walter et al. *História Geral da Arte no Brasil.* São Paulo: IMS, 1983.

Zé, Tom. "Defeito 2: Curiosidade." *Defeito de fabricação.*" CD. *Luaka Bop Inc.* 1998.

Zweig, Stefan. *Brasil, um país do futuro.* Porto Alegre: LP&M, 2006.

# Index

Printed in the United States of America